JILLIAN HART
Sweet Blessings

&

Blessed Vows

Love Inspired

Recycling programs for this product may not exist in your area.

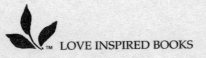

LOVE INSPIRED BOOKS

ISBN-13: 978-0-373-65155-9

SWEET BLESSINGS AND BLESSED VOWS
Copyright © 2012 by Harlequin Books S.A.

The publisher acknowledges the copyright holder of the individual works as follows:

SWEET BLESSINGS
Copyright © 2005 by Jill Strickler

BLESSED VOWS
Copyright © 2005 by Jill Strickler

www.LoveInspiredBooks.com

Printed in U.S.A.

CONTENTS

Books by Jillian Hart

Love Inspired

*Sweet Blessings
*Blessed Vows
*A Soldier for Christmas
*Precious Blessings
*Every Kind of Heaven
*Everyday Blessings
*A McKaslin Homecoming
 A Holiday to Remember
*Her Wedding Wish
*Her Perfect Man
 Homefront Holiday
*A Soldier for Keeps
*Blind-Date Bride
†The Soldier's Holiday Vow
†The Rancher's Promise
 Klondike Hero
†His Holiday Bride
†His Country Girl
†Wyoming Sweethearts
 Mail-Order Christmas Brides
  "Her Christmas Family"
†Hometown Hearts
*Montana Homecoming
*Montana Cowboy

Love Inspired Historical

*Homespun Bride
*High Country Bride
 In a Mother's Arms
  "Finally a Family"
**Gingham Bride
**Patchwork Bride
**Calico Bride
**Snowflake Bride

*The McKaslin Clan
†The Granger Family Ranch
**Buttons & Bobbins

JILLIAN HART

grew up on her family's homestead, where she helped
raise cattle, rode horses and scribbled stories in her spare
time. After earning her English degree from Whitman
College, she worked in travel and advertising before
selling her first novel. When Jillian isn't working on her
next story, she can be found puttering in her rose garden,
curled up with a good book or spending quiet evenings
at home with her family.

SWEET BLESSINGS

Every good and perfect gift is from above, coming down from the Father of the heavenly lights, who does not change like shifting shadows.
—*James* 1:17

Chapter One

The jingle of the bell above the door announced a late customer to the diner.

Amy McKaslin glanced at the clock above the cash register that said it was eight minutes to ten, which was closing time, and sized up the man standing like a shadow just inside the glass doorway.

He wasn't someone local or anyone she recognized. He was tall with a build to match. He wore nothing more than a flannel shirt unbuttoned and untucked over a T-shirt and wash-worn jeans. He had that frazzled, numb look of a man who'd been traveling hard and long without enough rest or food.

Road exhaustion. She'd seen it lots of times. He wasn't the first driver who'd taken this exit off the interstate. It happened all the time. With any luck, he'd be a quick in-and-out, looking for nothing more than a shot of caffeine and a bite before he got back on the road.

That was a much better prospect than last night, when a half dozen high-school kids had piled into a booth. Amy enjoyed the teenage crowd, but it had been nearly midnight before she could lock up and head home. Not good when her son was waiting for her, and she was paying a babysitter by the hour.

Tonight, Westin would be waiting, too, and on a school night when little boys should be fast asleep. He was an anxious one, always worrying, and she prayed the lone stranger had somewhere he had to go, too. Someone who was waiting for him. She turned the sign in the window to closed before any teenage clique decided to wander in.

Forcing a smile after being on her feet since 6:00 a.m., she grabbed a laminated menu. "Table or booth?"

The loner shrugged, looking past her as if he didn't see her at all. His eyes had that unfocused look drivers got when they'd been staring down pavement and white lines for too long, and the purple smudges beneath spoke of his exhaustion.

Yep, me too, buddy. She led him past the row of tables, washed and prepped for morning, to the booths in the corner, where the night windows reflected the brightly lit dining area back at her. Already she was thinking of home. Of her little boy's after-supper call.

"Come home, Mommy," he'd said in that quiet way he had. "I told Kelly not to read me any more of my story. You were gonna tonight, remember?"

She remembered. Nothing was more serious than the promises she made to her little boy. Almost there, she thought, as she watched the clock's hands creep another minute closer to ten. Aware of the man behind her making less noise than a shadow, she slid the menu onto the corner booth.

She whipped out her pad. "What can I get you to drink?"

Haggard. That was one word to describe him. The overhead light glared harshly on his sun-browned skin and whisker-stubbled jaw as he folded his over-six-foot frame behind the table. "Coffee."

"Leaded or decaf?"

"I want the real thing. Don't bother to make fresh. If you got something that's been sitting awhile, I'd rather have it." He pushed the menu back at her. "A burger, too. With bacon if it's not too much trouble."

"Sure thing." As she scribbled up the ticket, already walking away, something drew her to look one more time.

He had gone to staring sightlessly out the window, appearing tired and haunted. The black night reflected back the illusion of the well-lit café and his hollow face. The man wasn't able to see through the windows to the world outside. It was within that he was looking.

Her heart twisted in recognition. There was something about him that was familiar. Not the look of him, since she'd never met him before, but it was that faraway glint in his eyes. One that she recognized by feel.

She, too, knew what it was like to feel haunted by the past. Life made a mark on everyone. She didn't know how she saw this in this stranger, but she was certain she wasn't wrong. The regrets and despair of the past yanked within her, like a summer trout caught on a fishing hook. As she grabbed the carafe from the burner, where it had been sitting since the end of the supper rush, she risked another glance at the man.

He sat motionless with his elbows braced on the table's edge and his face resting in his hands.

Hopelessness. Yeah, she knew how that felt, too. Pain rose up in her chest, pointed like an arrow's tip, and she didn't know if it was the stranger she felt sympathy for or the girl she used to be. Maybe both.

She slid the cup and saucer onto the table. "I hope this is strong enough. If not, I'll be happy to make a fresh pot that will hold up a spoon. You just ask."

"Thank you, ma'am." He didn't make eye contact as he reached for the sugar dispenser on the small lazy Susan in the middle of the table.

Whatever troubled him on this cool late-spring night, she hoped at least a cup of coffee and a meal would strengthen him.

Something sad might have happened to him to make him a traveler tonight, she speculated. Maybe some family tragedy that had torn him from his normal life and had him driving on lonely roads through the nighttime. She knew that pain, too, and closed her mind against it. Some pain never healed. Some losses ran deep as the soul.

She put in the order, catching sight of her sister. "This is the last one. I already turned the sign over."

Rachel glanced at the ticket and pivoted on her heels to remove one last beef patty from the cooler. "If you want to take the floors, I'll total out the till. Have those other guys left yet?"

"No." Amy had almost refused them service when they came in, a little too bright-eyed and loud. They'd quieted down once they started eating. "They were just finishing up when I walked by."

"Good. I don't like them. I know they've been in before, but not this late."

Amy knew what her sister didn't say. *Not when we're alone with them.* Yeah, that had occurred to her, too. Big-city crime didn't happen in their little Montana town, but that didn't mean a woman ought to let down her guard.

She could see the two rough-looking men through the kitchen door with their heads bent as they both studied the totaled check.

"Don't worry," she reassured her sister. "We aren't exactly alone with them."

"Good." Rachel slapped the meat on the grill. "We may get out of here before eleven, if we're lucky. Say, how's Westin holding up?"

Westin. Amy's stomach clenched thinking of all her little one had gone through. "He had a rough day, and now we're just waiting for the test results. They can do a lot for asthma nowadays. It won't be like what Ben went through."

They both fell silent for a moment, remembering how ill their brother had been when he was Westin's age. They'd had to keep oxygen in the house just in case of a severe attack. They'd almost lost him a few times, calling the ambulance while his lips turned blue and he struggled for breath that was impossible for him to draw in.

Amy's stomach clamped into a hard, worried ball. It wouldn't be like that for Westin. She would make sure of it. How, she didn't know, but she certainly had the strength to will it. That, with prayers, had to make a difference, right?

"I slipped a little gift for him into your coat pocket. Don't get mad at me. I couldn't resist."

"You got him that video game, didn't you? You're spoiling him, you know. It was supposed to wait until his report card."

"Yeah, yeah, but you know me." Sweetheart that she was, with a heart-shaped face and all gentleness, Rachel shrugged helplessly, as if she had no choice but to spoil her nephew.

Since it was impossible to be even a little mad at Rachel, Amy just rolled her eyes. "I'm sure he'll be thrilled."

"Oh, excellent!" Pleased, Rachel set the hamburger buns on to toast.

Yep, it was hard to do anything but be deeply grateful for her big sister. Amy gave thanks, as she always did. They'd lost their parents long ago, when they were all still kids. It had only made her hold tight to the loved ones in her life now. Her sisters, her brother and her son. So tight, there was no way she'd let them go.

It looked as if the two men, who'd initially been upset there was no alcohol served in the diner, were getting ready to leave. Although Amy couldn't smell alcohol on them, she suspected they'd imbibed sometime earlier in the evening. Not that she approved, but there was no outward reason to refuse service. In a small town, turning away customers tended to be bad for business.

Still, they'd done nothing more than laugh a little too loudly while they'd waited for their burgers. Now, with any luck, they'd pay and be on their way. She'd breathe easier once the door was safely shut behind them. They had that rowdy look to them. Men like that…no, it was best not to remember.

Her life was different now. *She* was different.

There was a ruckus from table five. "Hey, waitress! What pie do you got?"

Oh no, and here she'd been wishing them out the door. Amy had to dig deep to remain patient and courteous. She didn't like the way they were looking at her. As if she were a slice of pie with whipped cream on top. "We have a few slices of apple left."

"Nah. I was hopin' for something sweeter." The one on the left—with a gold cap on one front tooth—gave her a wink.

As if. "I'll be your cashier if you're ready."

"It's too bad about that pie. You must be just about done here. Maybe you'd like to come out with us?"

"No, I have to get home to my little boy." She waited.

One gave her an oh-I'm-not-interested-now look.

The other didn't so much as blink. "Then maybe you need a night out worse than I thought."

"Sorry. Will this be cash or charge?" Hint, hint. *Let's go, boys. Out of my diner.* She waited, trying to be courteous but firm.

"It'll take us a minute." The one who was not so interested in her reached into his back pocket for his wallet.

Good. Rachel's call bell jangled, signaling the last customer's burger was ready. She left the men to their arithmetic, glad for an excuse to put as much distance between them as possible.

She caught a movement in the window's reflection. The loner was in the act of lifting his coffee cup. Had he been watching her?

"Hey, waitress." They were talking to her again.

She dreaded turning around, but these weren't the first tough customers she'd dealt with. "Yes?"

"Are you sure you don't have a bottle or two hid in back? I know you said you don't got beer to sell. But me and my buddy here sure could use a couple a beers."

"Sorry, we don't have a liquor license."

"What kind of place don't serve beer?"

"A family restaurant." Amy kept her smile in place as she withdrew the order pad from her apron pocket.

The bigger of the two swore.

She flinched. Okay, she didn't want any trouble. She wanted them gone, the faster the better. She pivoted on her heel, hoping this was the end of it. *C'mon, just leave your money and go.*

In the window's reflection, she again noticed the lone stranger. Sitting hunch-shouldered as if uninterested, but his gaze was alert. He didn't move, although she could feel how his every muscle was tensed like a wolf watching his prey. Waiting to spring.

It strengthened her. She knew it was the Lord at work in her life, as He always was. For every bad customer, there was always another who was not.

Thankfully, there was no trouble. The offending parties left a pile of greenbacks and pounded to the door, chewing on toothpicks and making as much noise as possible as they went. The bell chimed when the door shut.

Trouble averted. Relieved, she hurried over to turn the dead bolt. *Thank you, Father.*

Her reflection stared back at her in the glass. She

saw a woman of average height and weight, with her hair pulled back in a tight ponytail. Her face was shadowed by too many hollows. The circles beneath her eyes looked like gouges from too many nights without sleep.

Maybe tonight she'd sleep better. A girl had to hope. She had so much to do before she could get home and into her warm bed. There was this one more customer, and then clean-up, and she could be home by eleven, eleven-thirty, depending. Westin would be listening for her. The hard knot in her stomach relaxed a smidgen, just thinking of her little boy. Yeah, she couldn't wait to get home to him. To see his sweet face.

Rachel peered at her over the hand-off counter, where a plate piled high with a deluxe bacon burger and fries waited beneath a warming light. "Our last customer looked road-weary, so I made the burger with an extra patty."

"I thought you might." Amy didn't bother to change the total on the ticket she left on the table with the meal. "Can I get you anything else?"

The lone wolf was staring out the window again. He shook his head.

He seemed so far away. His black hair was cut short, but not too short. Just enough for the cowlick at the crown of his head to stick up. It made him seem vulnerable somehow, this big beefy man with linebacker's shoulders and a presence that could scare off a mountain lion.

Curiosity was going to get the better of her, so before she could get caught staring at him, she left a full ketchup bottle next to the meal ticket and went to collect the money the other men had left.

"I don't believe this. I should have known." She recounted the stack of ones.

"What?" Rachel appeared in the doorway, dishcloth in hand. "Didn't they pay?"

"For only half of the total. I should have watched them closer. I just didn't want to be any nearer to them than I had to be." It wasn't the end of the world. It was only five dollars. "Men like that just make me so mad."

A flash of movement caught her attention. The loner stood with the scrape of his chair. Without a word he took off down the aisle.

She looked at him with surprise.

"Should I give Cameron a call at home?" came the woman's voice from the kitchen doorway. "He can handle it for us."

The waitress dropped the bills back on the table. "It's not worth it. Men like that—"

She didn't finish the statement, but Heath Murdock could read it in her stance. She wrapped her slender arms around her narrow waist as if in comfort and he had to wonder if a man like the two lowlifes that were out in the parking lot had hurt her somewhere down the line. Not just a little, but a lot. And because he knew how that felt, he headed for the door.

The world was a tough place and sometimes it was enough to break a man's soul. There was a lot he couldn't fix that was wrong in this world and in his own life, but this…he could do this. The dead bolt clicked when he turned it and he went outside into the gust of wind that brought new rain with it.

He felt the woman watching him. He didn't know if she approved, or if she was instead one of those ladies who disapproved of any show of strength. But it didn't stop him. He knew what was right. And walking out on a check was stealing, plain and simple. Not to mention the disrespect they'd paid to the perfectly decent waitress who'd done nothing more than remain polite.

A small diner in a small town didn't probably make much in sales. Heath knew he had justice on his side as he stalked across the parking lot. A pickup roared to life. Lights blazed in the blackness, searing his eyes.

Trouble. He could feel it on the knife's edge of the wind. Through the blinding glare of the high beams, he made out a newer-model truck with big dirt-gripping tires. A row of fog lights mounted on the cab were bright enough to spotlight a path to the moon.

The engine roared, as the vehicle vibrated like a predator preparing to attack. Heath didn't have much of a chance of stopping them now. Not when they were already in the cab and behind the wheel. When the engine gunned again, their crude words spat like gunfire into the air. The truck lurched forward with an ear-splitting squeal of tires.

Heading straight for him.

Heath didn't move. A small voice inside him whispered, "This is it. Let it happen. Stand still and it will all be over."

It was tempting, that voice, inviting as it tugged at the shards of his heart still beating. All he had to do was not move, that was all.

He held his breath, letting it happen, feeling time slow the same way a movie did when the slow-motion button was hit on the remote. His senses sharpened. The rain tapped against his face with a keen punch and slid along his skin. So wet and cold.

The wind blew through him as if he were already gone. His chest swelled as he breathed in one last time. He smelled the distinct sweetness of wet hay from some farmer's field and the petroleum exhaust from the truck. The headlights speeding toward him bore holes into his retinas.

Just don't move. It was what he wanted with all his being. He felt the swish of the next moment, although it hadn't happen yet. The truck gaining speed, the squealing tires and the stillness within him as he wished for an end to his pain.

But even the wish was wrong. He knew it. His spirit bruised with the sin of it. At the last moment he sidestepped, the same moment the pickup veered right and careened off into the rain. Time shot forward, the rain fell with a vengeance and his lungs burned with the cold. He listened to the subwoofers thumping as the truck vanished.

Lightning split the sky. The sudden brightness seared his eyes and cleaved through his lost soul, and then he was plunged into darkness again.

Alive. He was still alive.

Wind drove icy rain against him like a boat at sea and wet him to the skin. Water sluiced down his face as he stood, shivering from the cold and a pain so deep it had broken him. Being alive was no victory. He felt that death would have been kinder. But not by his own choice and, once again, hopelessness drowned him.

"Are you all right?" Her concern came sharp and startling as the thunder overhead.

Heath turned toward her, like a blind man pivoting toward the sound that could save him. But nothing could. Lost and alone, he was aware of what he must look like to her. His clothes were soaked through. His hair clung to his scalp and forehead. Rain dripped off the tip of his nose and the cleft in his chin.

There, in the cheerful glow of the diner's windowed front, the two women stood framed in the light. Two women, one a half inch or so taller than the other, with blond hair pulled back from nearly identical faces. They had to be related. The classic features of girl-next-door good looks ought to be a reassuring sight.

Except both women were watching him with horror-filled eyes. He must look like a nut.

With the darkness tugging him and the brutal rain beating him back, he ducked his head and plowed into the storm. He splashed through puddles and the water seeped through the hole in his left boot. As he went, his big toe became wetter and his sock began to wick water across to his other toes.

"Goodness, you gave us a scare!" The waitress was holding the door for him. Concern made her seem to glow as the light haloed her.

He blinked, and the effect was gone. Maybe it was from his fatigue or the fact that adrenaline had kicked in and was tremulous in his veins. He still had the will to live, after all.

Thunder crashed like giant cymbals overhead, and it felt as if he broke with it. As he trudged up the steps and into the heat of the diner, bitterness filled him. There was shelter from this storm, but not from the one that had ripped apart his life.

No, there was no rest and no sanctuary from the past. Not tonight.

The waitress moved aside as he shouldered by, and he felt her intake of breath. The concern was still there, for she wore it like the apron over her jeans and blouse. As sincere as it was, he had no use for concern or sympathy. Those paltry emotions were easy to put on and take off and the words, "I'm sorry for your loss" came back to him.

Words meant to comfort him, when for a fact they were for the speaker's benefit. To make the speaker feel safe from the brutal uncertainty this life sometimes had to offer.

He'd learned it the hard way. Life played tricks with a person. Get too much, become too happy and bam! It could all disappear in the space between one second and the next.

It was a lesson he would never forget and he doubted the pretty waitress with her big blue-violet eyes and lustrous ponytail of gold would ever understand. What tragedy could happen here in this small little burgh miles from frantic big cities and desperation?

None, that's what. His boots squished and squeaked against the tile floor as he ambled down the aisle. The faint scent of perfume stayed with him, something subtle and sweet that made him think of dewy violets at dawn's first light and of hope. *That's* what that fragrance smelled like, and he wanted nothing to do with hope.

He didn't look back as he lumbered the length of the diner to the booth where his burger waited. He reached into his back pocket and hauled out his wallet. Dropped a ten on the table. "I've changed my mind. I want this to go."

"Sure thing."

She'd said that phrase before and just like that. Politely cheery words held up like a shield as she efficiently went about her work. Amy, her little gold nametag said. Amy. She didn't look like an Amy. Amys were cute and sweet and bubbly, and this one was somber. Polite and nice, but somber. She liked to keep people at a distance. He knew enough about shields to recognize one when he saw it. He had too many of his own.

She returned with a container and he took it from her. He didn't like to be waited on. He tipped his plate and the burger and fries tumbled into the box.

Ever efficient, the waitress reached into her crisp apron pocket and laid a handful of ketchup packets on the table. That annoyed him. He couldn't say why. Maybe because he felt her gaze. Her heavy, questioning gaze as if she were trying to take his measure. Trying to figure him out.

He'd given up long ago.

"There's no charge." Her voice followed him like a light in a bleak place. "For what you tried to do."

"I pay my own way."

Whatever kind of man he looked like, he had standards. He had pride. He had no use for handouts. He wasn't looking for a soup kitchen and a quick revival meeting to patch up the holes in his soul.

He doubted even God could do that. So he faced the storm. What was a little wind and rain? Nothing.

He was so numb inside that he didn't feel the icy

rain streaking in rivulets along the back of his neck. He didn't feel the water squish into his boot as he crossed the unlit parking lot and became part of the chill and the night.

Chapter Two

"What's with you?" Rachel asked as she tied off a bulging black garbage sack. "You're attacking that floor as if it's your own personal enemy."

Amy put a little more shoulder power into the mop. The yellow sponged head compressed into a flat line, oozing soap bubbles as she wrenched the handle back and forth. "I'm trying to get the floor clean."

"Yeah, but we don't want the tile to come off with the dirt."

She had a point, Amy realized as she gave up on the faintest of black streaks—she'd need to buff those out. Otherwise the floor sparkled. She dunked the mop into the bucket, surrendering, and rubbed at the small of her aching back. "Is this day over yet?"

"Go home. I can finish up."

"No, I told you I'd stay and I will. We leave together."

"What about Westin? He's waiting up for you. I don't have anyone at home for me. You go on."

"No. We share the work. And that's low, using my son to get me to do what you want." Amy loved her sister, who meant well. Who always gave too much. "You know I'm thinking of him."

Was it wrong that she was thinking of someone else, too?

Yes. Determined to sweep the lone stranger from her mind, she lugged mop and bucket to the industrial sink and, with a heave, emptied the dirty, soapy water. There. The bucket was clean and so was her… well, her list of distractions. Westin came first. Always first. She had no business thinking about some man whose name she didn't know.

Men always led to trouble. Sure, there were a few good ones in the world, but they were as rare as hen's teeth, as her grandmother used to say. And you couldn't always tell the mettle of a man, no matter how wonderful he seemed, until it was too late.

That was the truth. There were so many things she wished she could go back in time and change. She'd right every mistake and every problem that had blown up into a bigger problem.

But there was one thing she would never regret, and that was deciding to keep her son. It hadn't been easy for either of them, but they were a team, and somehow they'd get through this. With the good Lord's help. And, of course, her family's.

Rachel wrestled a second garbage bag out of the industrial-sized bin and tied it off. "If you want to trade shifts tomorrow, let me know. Or, if you need me to sit with him so you don't have to pay a babysitter, I'm available. You know how I love to spend time with my nephew."

"Thanks, I'll let you know. This means I'm doing the early-morning shift tomorrow?"

"Paige gets back in two days. We just have to survive until then."

Amy dumped a dollop of soap into the bucket and ran fresh hot water. "Survive? I think we're doing really good on our own."

"Except for the short-handed part."

Paige was their older sister, who ran everything perfectly and was out of town. And while chaperoning the youth-group trip to the Grand Canyon was great, no one had known ahead of time that the cook was going to up and quit out of the blue and leave them shuffling to fill his position and cover most of Paige's duties.

Rachel, her soft heart showing, straightened from garbage detail. "You've been working way more shifts than I have. I know, you don't mind. You can use the extra tip money. Speaking of which, please take me up on my offer to babysit. I know you think it'll be imposing, but I really want to help. I'm supposed to spend tomorrow doing the books, so it's done for Paige's inspection when she gets back. I can just take

everything over to your place. Maybe alternate post-
ing to the ledgers with playing a few games, video
and otherwise."

There was no way Amy could say no to her sister's big doe eyes. And Rachel knew it. Not to mention it would help with the babysitter's bill. But that
wasn't the driving reason she agreed. "I'm sure Westin would love to spend his day with his Aunt Rachel.
He's been wanting to play Candyland with you."

"Oh, that's my very favorite game. Probably because I've always had a sweet tooth." Rachel cheerfully grabbed the bulging garbage bags, one in each
hand. She was gone with a slap of the door.

Thunder cannoned overhead, echoing in the empty
dining room. Amy rocked back on her heels. Wow,
that was a good one. As she turned off the faucet
and hefted the bucket from the sink, her heart went
out to her son miles away. Had he heard it, too? He
didn't like storms.

I'll be home as soon as I can, baby. Just one patch
of floor left. Moving fast, she leaned the mop against
the wall and hustled down the aisle, flipping the
chairs onto tabletops as she went.

She stopped at the last booth. It was where *he'd* sat.
The stranger. The image of him remained as brightly
as if he'd been on a movie screen, how he'd stood with
feet braced and shoulders wide in the rain. How he'd
faced down the oncoming blaze of headlights and
refused to move. He was either really brave or he

had a death wish, and she'd nearly fainted with horror watching as the truck had careened toward him. Certain he was about to be hit, she'd started running toward the door until, at the last moment, he'd stepped out of harm's way.

Then, as if he'd done nothing of consequence, he growled at her, refused her thanks and left the diner with his meal in hand. He just stalked out the door, eager to be on his way, solitary and remote.

Wasn't that just like a man?

Oh, well, he was gone. She wished him luck. She didn't know what else to do. She would add him to her prayer list tonight. He'd made her feel things she'd worked hard to keep buried. Feelings and memories she'd banished after her son was born and she'd come home a different woman from the girl who'd left for big-city excitement with a chip on her shoulder and something to prove—only to find out that home wasn't as bad as she'd thought.

The back door blew open and slammed against the wall. Rachel came in with the wind and rain. "Whew. It nearly blew me away out there and it's getting worse. Let's hightail it out of here while we can."

"I'm almost done." Determined to finish, Amy upended the final chair. Something dark tumbled to the floor.

She knelt to retrieve it. Mercy's A's was scrawled in worn gold-and-white letters on the black fabric of a man's baseball hat. The bill had curved into a sagging humped shape as if from years of wear. Her loner had sat at this table, but had he been wearing a hat? She didn't remember one.

It had been a busy day and a busier evening rush. Anyone could have left that cap anytime during the supper hours, but there was something about it that made her think of him. Maybe it was the color; her loner had been wearing black.

Her loner—that's how she was thinking of him, as if she knew him. Maybe it was that she recognized a part of herself in the man. Maybe because she understood it wasn't only courage but something stronger that had made him stand motionless staring down death.

Yeah, she recognized the feel of despair that clung to him. She knew a like soul when she saw it.

She stowed the cap in the lost-and-found box, tucked it beneath the cash register and got back to work. Rachel was clattering around in the back office—it was little more than a closet, which it had been years and years ago when their parents had run the place.

But after their death, Paige had taken over and decided the front counter was no place to work on the books. So she'd checked out a how-to guide from the library and put them all to work. Amy had chosen the soft yellow paint because it was her favorite color. Of course, she was nine years old at the time. Now the color only reminded her of times best left forgotten.

So she was happy to finish the mopping while Rachel muttered about over-rings in the cramped little office.

Amy glanced at the clock—ten thirty-eight—before rapping on the door, which was open. All she saw was Rachel's back as she hunched over the plywood desk built into the back wall. That didn't look comfortable. "I'm done out here. Is there anything I can do to help?"

"Nope. This tape is a mess. I need to talk to whichever of the twins did this today." Frustrated, Rachel slid back in the folding metal chair and rubbed her forehead with both hands. "Those two are giving me a serious headache."

Their teenaged cousins were not the most faultless of employees, but they were eager and worked hard. "They just have a lot to learn."

"I know." Rachel's sigh spoke more of her own tiredness than of her upset at the girls, who had both turned seventeen last month. "I'm just going to throw all this in a bag and take it home. I'll make the deposit tomorrow."

"Sounds good to me—"

The lights blinked off and stayed off. Pitch black echoed around them.

Amy didn't move. "It looks like we lost power. Do you think it's off for good?"

It stayed dark. That seemed like answer enough. Amy was trying to remember where the flashlights were when Rachel's chair creaked and it was followed by the rasp of a drawer opening. A round beacon of light broke through the inky blackness. Leave it to Rachel. Amy breathed easier. At least they'd be able to close up without feeling their way in the dark.

Lightning flashed, and immediately thunder crashed like breaking steel overhead. Closer. The front was coming fast and moving toward home. She thought of her little boy. Westin was safe with the babysitter, but he'd be worried. She couldn't call to reassure him. It wasn't safe with the lightning crackling overhead and besides, if the power was out, then the phone lines were probably down, too.

She grabbed her purse from the shelf and her jacket hanging next to it, working in the near dark, for Rachel was hogging the flashlight to zip the cash receipts and the day's take into her little leather briefcase. Once that was done, Amy hurried ahead and rechecked the front door—locked, just as it was supposed to be—and followed the sound of Rachel tapping through the kitchen toward the back door.

Outside seemed just as dark. An inky blackness was broken only when lightning strobed overhead and speared into the fields just out of town. It was definitely heading south. All she wanted to do was to get home before a tree or a power line blocked the road out of town.

She manhandled the door closed and turned the key in the dead bolt. The wind whipped and lashed at her, strong enough to send her stumbling through the puddles. In the space between lightning bolts, she could feel the electric charge on her skin. It came crisp and metallic in the air.

Rain came in a rage and it bounced like golf balls over the battered blacktop lot and over them. She hadn't gone two yards and she was drenched to the skin. Following the faint glow of Rachel's flashlight, she let the wind hurl her toward two humps of shadows that became two parked cars as they stumbled closer. The windshields gleamed, reflecting the finger of fire sizzling overhead. Lightning snapped into a power pole a block or two away. The thunder boomed so hard, Amy's eardrums hurt with the shock.

Maybe that's why she didn't see another shadow until headlights flashed to life. She recognized the row of piercing fog lights blazing atop a pickup's cab. Oh, heavens. It was the two men who'd hassled her in the restaurant.

It happened so fast. The truck screeched to a halt inches from Rachel, who'd been in the lead. The passenger door thrust open and suddenly there he was, the dark form of a stocky man, muscled arms held out with his hands closed into fists. Everything about him screamed danger. He stalked toward Rachel like a coyote ready to strike.

Amy didn't remember making the choice to fight instead of run. She was simply there, between the man and her sister. Protective anger made her feel ten feet tall. "Get out of here. Now."

"Hey, that's no way to talk. I just wanted to give you girls a chance to make back your five bucks. Maybe even earn a tip." The strong scent of hard liquor wafted from him.

She wasn't afraid; she was mad. "That's a horrible thing to say. Shame on you. You get back in your truck and leave us alone, or I'll—"

"Yeah, what are you gonna do, pretty lady?" he mocked, and then the smirk faded from his shadowed face.

For out of the black curtain of rain emerged another man. One who stood alone.

Maybe it was the glaze of light snaking across the sky behind him. Or the way his dark hair lashed in the wind, but he looked like a warrior legend come to life. There was no mistaking the sheer masculine steel of the man as his presence seemed to silence the thunder.

He didn't utter a word. He didn't need to. The look of him—iron-strong and defensive—made the troublemaker shrink back as if he'd been struck. The ruffian cast one hard look at Amy—she saw the glint of malice before he leaped into the cab and slammed the door. The truck shot through the downpour, roaring out of sight.

Amy realized she was trembling from the inside out, now that the threat was gone. She swiped the rain from her eyes. She didn't know why some people behaved the way they did. As long as Rachel was safe.

They were both safe. She remembered to send a note of thanks heavenward.

And her loner—her protector—waited, his back to them, his feet braced wide, his fists on his hips looking as invincible as stone as he watched in the direction of the road, as if making sure those troublemakers weren't doubling back.

"Oh, I can't believe those men! If you can call them men." Rachel walked on wobbly legs toward her car. "I've got to sit down."

"They scared me, too." Amy opened her sister's car door and took the keys from her trembling hand. She sorted through them for the ignition key as Rachel collapsed onto the seat.

"Are you all right?"

Amy turned at the sound of his voice, rough like the thunder and as elemental as the wind.

He was simply a man, not legend or myth, but with the way he looked unbowed by the rain and lashed by the storm, he gave the presence of more.

When he spoke, it was as if the world silenced. "He didn't hurt you, did he? I came across the parking lot as fast as I could."

But from where? Amy wondered. He could have come out of the very night, for he seemed forged out of the clouds and dark. She swiped a hand across her brow, trying to get the rain out of her eyes and saw the faint glaze of lightning reflecting in the windows far down the alley. The town's only motel. That's where her loner had come from.

"You arrived just in time," she assured him, standing to block the rain for her sister. "We're all right."

"Thanks to you. Again." Rachel was still clutching the briefcase to her chest.

Amy knew what she was thinking. Rachel had their day's take tucked in her leather case. It was a lot to lose, had the men been interested in money only.

"You ladies want me to call the sheriff?" The loner kept his stance and his distance like a protective wolf standing on the edge of a forest, ready to slip back in.

"No, it looks like the phone lines are down, too. I'll stop by and see the deputy. I drive right by his place on my way home—"

Lightning flashed like stadium floodlights, eerily illuminating the parking lot and the three of them drenched with rain. Thunder exploded instantly and a tree limb on the other side of the alley crashed to the ground, smoking.

The rain increased so she had to shout to be heard. "This is dangerous. Get inside. I'll—"

She didn't get to finish her invitation for breakfast in the diner. The lightning returned and made every surface of her skin prickle. Here she was, standing up in the parking lot, and how dangerous was that? She yanked her car door open and dove into the seat, grateful for the shelter. Through the rain-streaked windshield, she could see her loner in the parking lot, a dark silhouette the storm seemed to revolve around.

Rain hammered harder, sluicing so fast down the glass she lost sight of him. When the water thinned for a second, he was gone. There was only wind and rain where he'd stood.

Good. He'd returned to his motel room, where he'd be safe. The car windows began fogging and she realized her fingers were like ice, so she started the engine and flipped the defroster on high.

In the parking spot beside her, Rachel's old sedan came to life, too, the high beams bright as she put the car in gear, creeping forward as if to make sure Amy was okay.

Amy wasn't okay, but she knew her sister wasn't going to drive off and leave her sitting here. So she buckled up and put the car in gear. She ignored the groan of the clutch because it needed to be replaced and, after creeping forward, realized she needed both the wipers and the lights on.

Rachel's car moved away and Amy followed her, steering through the downpour that came ever harder. But her gaze drifted to the rearview, where the motel ought to be. She couldn't see it; there was only darkness. Remembering the loner and the way he'd stood as if he were already not a part of this world, she wished…she didn't know what she wished. That he would find rest for whatever troubled him.

She would always be grateful he'd stepped be-

tween her and possible danger twice. Lord knew there
had been times when that wasn't always the case.

The rain pummeled so hard overhead, she couldn't
hear the melody of the Christian country station or
the beat of the wipers on high as she let the storm
blow her home.

"Mom!"

The instant Amy had stumbled through the front
door, she'd been caught by her son. His arms vised
her waist, and he held on tight, clinging for moments
longer than his usual welcome-home hug as thunder
cannoned over the roof and shook the entire trailer.

Oh, her sweet little boy, the shampoo scent of him,
fresh from his bath, and the fabric softener in his
astronaut pjs just made her melt. She feathered her
fingers through his rich brown hair the color of milk
chocolate and when he let go, he didn't look scared.
But his chin was up and his little hands balled tight.
Westin was great at hiding everything, true to his
gender.

Only she knew how storms scared him. The hitch
in his breathing told her his asthma medicine was
working. The image from earlier today of the needle
pricking along his spine tore at her. Her little one had
had a rough day, and she remembered how he'd set
his jaw tight and not made a sound. Tears had welled
in his eyes but he hadn't let them fall.

Her tough little guy.

She knelt to draw him against her. "I figured you'd be sound asleep by now and I wouldn't get to read you another chapter in your story like I promised."

"The thunder kept wakin' me up. It's loud. So I just stayed awake."

That was his excuse. Tough as nails, just like her dad had been. Every time she looked at him, she saw it, the image of her father, a hint that always made her remember the man who'd been twenty feet tall for her. Who could do anything.

There were the little things Westin did that would twist like a knife carved deep. In the innocent gestures, as he was doing now, chin up, arms crossed in front of his chest, all warrior. Tough on the outside, soft as butter on the inside. Yeah, he was just like her dad.

"Okay, tiger, it's way past your bedtime. Get to your room and under your covers. I'll be back in half a second."

His big brown eyes stared up at her. She caught the flash of fear when it sounded as if golf balls were hitting the roof with the force of a hurricane, but she nodded, letting him know without words that she was here now. He might be cowboy-tough, but he was a little boy who needed his mother. She wouldn't let anything hurt her little one.

"'Kay," he agreed, "but hurry up! We got a light all set up and everything. Bye, Kelly!" he called to the woman in the shadows of the tiny kitchen.

"G'night, don't let the bedbugs bite!" came the answer and then her cousin by marriage emerged from the dark with her coat in hand. Kelly slipped one arm into the raincoat's sleeve and then the other. "Hi, Amy. I got the dishes put away, too, just to help out. If you want me tomorrow night, just give me a call. You know I can use the extra cash."

"Sure." Amy dug through her apron pocket and counted out a small stack of ones. Tips had been sparse with the state economy the way it was and they'd been even worse tonight.

She regretted that three-quarters of her tip money was already gone, but there were other places to cut corners. Her son's care was not one of them. "Rachel wants to come over and spend time with him tomorrow, but if I have to work at night, I'll give you a call. We're still short-handed. Are you sure you don't want a job at the diner?"

"It's harder to do my school work and wait tables at the same time. I have a test Monday." Kelly settled her backpack on one shoulder. It was heavy with college texts and notebooks.

Amy had wanted to attend college, too, like so many of her friends and cousins had. Sparkling-eyed freshmen going to classes and chatting over coffee and learning exciting new things. There were a lot of reasons that had kept her from that path, mostly her own choices and the fact that a college education took money neither she nor her family had.

She admired Kelly for sticking to the hard course. It couldn't be easy working several jobs and studying, too. "Drive safe out there. The roads are slick."

"I will. Heavens!" Kelly opened the door and the racket was deafening.

Hail punched the pavement and hammered off the row of trailers lined up in neat order along the dark street. Ice gleamed black as it hid lawns and driveways and flowerbeds starting to bloom.

The wind gusted and Amy wrestled the door closed. She pulled the little curtain aside and watched through the window in the door, making sure Kelly got to her car safely and it started all right. In a town where few people ever bothered to lock anything, Amy turned the dead bolt and made sure Kelly made it safely down the lane.

It's just the storm, she told herself. That's why she felt unsettled. But she knew that wasn't the truth.

The hail echoed like continual gunshots through the single wide, and she circled the living room, dodging the couch. A thick candle, one she'd gotten for Christmas, sat in the center of the coffee table and shed enough light for her to see her way around an array of toy astronauts and space ships arranged in the middle of a battle. The windows were cold, streaked with ice and rain and locked up tight.

Amy knew it wasn't the storm that bothered her. It was those two men tonight. The harsh, brash way they'd laughed over their meal. The suggestive leers they'd shot at her. The way they'd walked out of the diner without fully paying, as if they had the right. It all burned in her stomach, the anger and the help-lessness of it. They probably thought nothing of it, just two guys out having some fun.

But it was a big deal, their lack of respect. She wasn't some questionable woman. She had standards and morals she lived by. What hurt is that times like this and men like that reminded her of the days when she'd behaved in ways she deeply regretted.

Don't think about it. It's over and done with now. She'd do best to erase the entire experience from her mind. She'd told the incident to the deputy on her way home. He lived four doors down. He was on his way out on an emergency call, but he told her he'd be by the diner in the morning if she wanted to file a report. She didn't. There was no point. Things like that were public record and she wanted to keep as far away from the ugliness of the outside world as she could. For her son, and for herself.

This trailer wasn't much, but it was hers and she'd worked hard to make the best of it. The tan shag car-peting was nothing fancy, but it was freshly vacu-umed and in good repair. She'd laid it herself, after buying it as a remnant from a flooring outlet store in Bozeman.

Last year she'd retextured the walls in the living room and applied several coats of the lightest blue paint. The couch had been in the family for what seemed like generations. She'd reupholstered it and made the throw pillows that cheerfully matched the walls. Pretty lace curtains—she'd made a good yard-sale find with those—hung on decorative rods she'd mounted and gave the cozy room a sense of softness.

This was her sanctuary, and Westin's boyhood home. She breathed in the serenity and felt more centered. She knelt to blow out the candle, and darkness washed over her. Tonight the shadows did not seem as peaceful. Hail echoed through the spaces and corners of the trailer and filled her with trepidation, as if the past could rear up and snatch away her life here.

I'm just tired, that's all. Amy rose, breathing in the faint smoke rising off the wick and peppermint-scented wax. The uneasiness remained.

"Mom!" Westin stood in the wash of light from his bedroom door, looking like a waif in pjs that were a size too big. He was holding his stuffed Snoopy by the ear.

Her heart broke. Why was she letting the unease from the past trouble her? There was no reason to look back. She'd come a long way, and she'd done it all by herself—okay, with the help of God and her sisters. Westin was waiting for her, and no way was she going to let him down.

"Are your teeth brushed?" she asked, because it was her job as a mom.

"Kelly made me."

"And what about your prayers?"

"Yep. I told ya. I'm really, really ready."

"Then get into bed, young man. Hurry up."

He ran, feet pounding as he raced out of her sight. The squeak of the box spring told her he'd jumped onto his mattress and was bouncing around, all boy energy, even this late at night.

If only she could harness it, she thought wistfully, as she bent her aching back to blow out the other candle on the little dinette set in the eating nook. Every bone in both feet seemed to groan and wince as she headed down the hall, drawn through the darkness by the light in her little boy's room.

Westin was waiting and ready, tucked beneath his covers. A candle in a stout holder—Kelly must have placed it there—shone brightly enough on the pillow to reveal the boy's midnight-blue bedspread with the planets sprinkled all over it. The rings of Saturn. The storms of Jupiter. The icy moon of... Jupiter? She couldn't keep straight which moons belonged to which planets, but she should know it by heart because it was nearly all Westin talked about.

"Kelly and I saved the chapter on black holes for you to read, Mom!" Big blue eyes sparkling, Westin hid a cough in his fist and scrunched back into the pillows. Snoopy, clenched tightly in the crook of one arm, was apparently anticipating the wealth of information on black holes, too.

"I've been looking forward to this all day." Amy settled onto the bedside and held the heavy library book open in her hands. The spine cracked, the plastic cover crinkled and she breathed in the wonderful scent of books, paper and ink. She cleared her throat and began to read.

As exciting as gravity was, and as awesome as it was to hear about some stars exploding their matter into space, while others sank into themselves, Westin's eyelids flickered. He yawned hugely and fought hard to stay awake. When she got to the part about gravity sucking light and matter into the net of a black hole, Westin's lids stayed shut. His jaw relaxed. Snoopy kept watching her, however.

She slipped a bookmark between the pages and set the book on the nightstand. She just watched her son sleep for a few minutes with her heart full. Then she rose, blew out the candle and shut his door tightly.

The hall was pitch-black. Hail still rattled against the walls. Listening to the wind groan, Amy slipped into the darkness of her room. There was a tiny reading light, run on battery power, on her headboard. She unclipped it and flicked it on. It was a faint light and not strong enough to scare away the deep shadows from the room.

The uneasiness was still inside her. It was the loner. Tonight he'd somehow breached the careful shield she kept around her. Maybe it wasn't that he'd broken through her defenses as much as she saw through his. And what she saw there reminded her of hard lessons she'd learned.

When a person lost her innocence, there was no way to get it back—even if she surrounded herself with family and friends, lived in a small rural town where she'd lived nearly all her life, where she knew everyone, where nothing bad hardly ever happened.

She could work hard, do her very best, pay her bills on time, make a home, raise a son and sometimes, like tonight, there would be something that would remind her.

Some wounds ran too deep to heal. And there lived within her a scar that cut into her soul. She was as lost as the loner had seemed to be. And as wounded.

In the dark, alone in her room, she felt revealed. In an act just short of desperation, she switched on the clock radio by her bed and forgot the lights were out. Tonight there would be no soothing twang of familiar Christian songs to lull away some of the void.

She hurried about her bedtime routine, the little habits reassuring her, making her feel as if everything was in its place. She washed her face, flossed, brushed her teeth, smoothed cream on those little lines beside her eyes and mouth. She changed into her soft flannel pajamas and knelt to say her prayers.

The storm was moving on. The hail turned to rain as she crawled under the covers, and then to silence.

But it wasn't a peaceful silence.

Chapter Three

Heath growled in frustration from beneath the pillow that he'd wedged over his head. But it wasn't working to block out first light.

It was his brand of luck. His motel room faced east—and that meant bright searing sunlight was finding its way through the gaps in the fifty-year-old curtain, and it lit up the place like a lighthouse's beacon. The light seemed to pulse and dance because the old heater that clattered like a hamster running on a squeaky wheel all night long and wouldn't turn off, was spewing hot air full-blast beneath the curtains.

Oh yeah, it was another night in a long string of countless nights without much sleep to speak of. His eyes were gritty, his mind numb and his back muscles aching from the sagging mattress. By the time he'd stepped into the shower, he was already resigned and so the fact that the water stayed cold even when he'd turned the knob to full force hot didn't bother him so much.

These days not much did. His single duffel bag was ready to go and waiting by the door. He never bothered to unpack. When he was dried off and dressed, he tossed his toothbrush and half-rolled tube of toothpaste into the bag's side pocket. He then added his unused razor. He scraped a hand over his two-day stubble—not too long to itch yet and he didn't care if he looked a little on the scruffy side.

He squinted into the mirror as he zipped up the duffel. The man who looked back at him had the weary look of a drifter. The worn-down-to-the-nub soul he'd seen in so many of the homeless men he'd treated when they had stumbled into his emergency room.

He winced. Any thoughts of his old life brought up the beginnings of a pain so black, it would drown him. Or, maybe it already had, he reasoned as he looked away from the man in the mirror and slung the battered bag over his shoulder.

The stranger staring back at him didn't resemble Dr. Heath Murdock, not in any way. He was no longer the vascular surgeon with a specialty in trauma medicine, who could handle any crisis, any unspeakable catastrophe with the calm steady confidence of a man born to save lives.

What he couldn't stand to think about were the lives he'd failed to save.

So he headed out into the morning and welcomed the crisp bite to the early-spring air. The cheerful sun burned his eyes. Blinking hard, he ambled along the cracked sidewalk, uneven from the towering maples lining the parking lot, their roots exposed like old arthritic fingers digging into the dirt.

Head down, he dropped the room key off at the front desk where a tired woman in brown polyester mumbled thanks without looking up at him. He saw a home dye job and graying roots. The deep creases in the woman's face were testimony of too many decades of hard living and heartbreak.

Yeah, he knew. He unlocked the passenger door of the old pickup. The truck used to be his granddad's. Faint memories of sunny days riding around the Iowa farm with his grandpop washed through him.

Good times. Times he could tolerate thinking about. He dropped the duffel on the passenger floor, where decades of boots had worn scuffs. Tiny bits of straw and dried grass seed remained dug deep into the grooves around the door. The distant voices of long ago echoed for one brief moment—*Grandpop, when I grow up I'm gonna be just like you!... Lord I hope so, son, 'cuz there ain't nothin' better than bein' a cowboy.*

The voices silenced as he slammed the door hard and breathed in the scented air.

There was hay and alfalfa growing next door in fields that rolled out of sight. The faint scent of irrigation made him feel like breathing in a little more deeply. When he pulled out his wallet, there were no pictures inside and no credit cards. There was nothing but a driver's license and insurance card and, tucked between the two, his social security number.

Not that the jobs he'd been working lately had required legal ID.

He checked the thin bills—forty-six bucks left. That wouldn't get him far. Looked like it was time to think about working for a while. This town with dust settling on the main drag through town—only one pickup had bothered to drive past this early in the morning—didn't look like a hopping place…and that was just about his speed these days.

Across the parking lot he recognized an older-model compact car, neat and clean and familiar. The waitress. He watched as she hopped out of the vehicle. She was wearing jeans and a red T-shirt that was baggy more than it was form-fitting. Her long blond hair was still damp from a shower and dancing on the breeze.

He watched her, unable to look away, as she took two steps toward the back door, skidded to a halt on black tennis shoes and spun. She scurried back to her car, muttering to herself as if in great frustration. She hadn't locked her car, so it took only a moment to yank it open. Then she bent down and he couldn't see her beneath the door.

He leaned his forearms on the truck bed and

watched as she bobbed up into sight. Her hair was more disheveled and she was muttering harder to herself as if she were having a very bad morning. This time she had a small tan purse in a death grip as she paced across the parking lot, looking as if she was working up a good head of steam. Yeah, he used to have mornings like that—

In a flash, it was right at the edge of his mind, the days of rushing out of the house, leaving too much behind him undone and two shadows in the doorway he couldn't let himself see even in memory. Breaking into pieces, he slammed the door on the past and locked it well. Some things a man couldn't live through.

Not that he was alive. Only his heart was beating, that was all.

He hung his head, hidden behind the pickup as he heard the waitress's rapid gait stop in midstride. He peered through his lashes, not lifting his head, to see her hesitate, looking around as if she felt him there, felt him watching her. But she didn't spot him. Was she remembering last night and feeling jumpy? Any woman would. He hadn't meant to make her uneasy, he just didn't want to talk to her. He didn't want a lot of things.

Maybe there was another place to eat in town.

He followed the alley to the front street. On the far side of the empty two-lane road, a train rumbled along the tracks hauling a long string of box containers. The bright black-and-blue paint of inner-city graffiti marked the sides of the cars, heading west, probably to the ports of Seattle or Portland.

Portland. He wondered why he even let that word into his mind.

A lone pickup, vintage fifties model, perfectly restored in a grass-green and shining chrome rolled down the street and pulled into a spot directly in front of the diner. The Open sign in the front window and the door open wide to the morning was invitation enough.

The man who climbed down from the pickup's seat without bothering to lock up as he loped up onto the sidewalk looked to be a retired farmer. There was the look of a hardworking man to him, lean, trim and efficient. Gray-white hair fringed the blue cap he wore.

He pushed through the screen door that slapped behind him and voices rose from inside the restaurant.

"That's what I like to see, coffee waiting...."

A woman's lilting laughter answered.

It was all Heath could hear before a puff of wind changed direction, taking the words away. In the glint of the sparkling front window, Heath could see into the diner. He watched the man take a booth at the front window, his coffee cup full and already waiting for him. A regular customer? He probably showed up every morning now that he no longer had a farm to tend and ordered the same breakfast.

It was early yet, but the rest of the main street—

which was what, only four blocks long?—was as dark
as could be. The only other sign of life was the flash
of a neon sign newly blazing on a quaint coffee shop
on the corner. Drive-through Open, it announced in
cheerful blue letters.

Heath's stomach rumbled as he debated what to do.

The whisper of a car approaching on the road had
him turning around. There was no mistaking the big
gray cruiser with the mounted red and blue lights
and the emblem on the doors. The local law had arrived. The passenger window whispered down as the
car pulled up alongside the curb. Behind the wheel
was a man in uniform, as fit and as steely as only a
marine could be.

Recognizing his own kind, Heath gave a salute.
"Is there a problem, sir?"

From inside the cruiser, the uniformed deputy gave
him a cursory look and, finding him satisfactory, sa-
luted him in return. "We don't get a lot of out-of-
towners this time of day. Need some help, soldier?"

"I can find my way, sir." His years in the military—there was a time Heath didn't mind remembering.

His service in the first Desert Storm had done
more than change his life. It had made him know the
true meaning of being a man. And what medicine was
all about. Individuals. People. Not five years spent
afterwards in one of the best hospitals in the coun-

try could change the integrity he'd learned in service to this country.

It was the only thing holding him together.

The deputy cracked a grin. "I was Marine Recon."

"I was the doc that patched up your kind. You Special Forces guys seem to get into trouble on a regular basis."

"I let a few of you sawbones work on me a time or two. I blame the ache in my arm on those docs. It couldn't have been the two bullets and grenade shrapnel I caught. You wouldn't happen to be the customer Amy McKaslin was tellin' me about last night? You stopped her and her sister from bein' hassled?"

"I didn't do much. I just showed up. Did she get their license plate?"

"No. You didn't happen to—"

Heath recited it from memory. "You look those boys up. The way they acted, it was no way to treat two real nice women."

"Exactly." The deputy reached for his radio. "You wouldn't object to making a statement, would ya? I don't take well to women being threatened in my town."

"They skipped out on part of their bill, too." Heath saw the lift of surprise of the officer's brow, and knew the waitress hadn't told the whole story. Probably because it was a matter of five dollars. "I'll sign whatever you need me to."

"Drop by the office after you're done eating. It's

down past the hardware and keep going. You'll see us." With another salute, the deputy drove on.

Heath felt a ghost from the past—it was his own spirit. The man he used to be: whole and full of optimism and enthusiasm. Full of heart.

There wasn't much left of that man. He didn't recognize his reflection in the diner's windows. He merely saw a man who looked more tired and aged instead of a vibrant, driven marine. He was like any man about to patronize a typical diner in a typical rural American town.

A bubbly waitress—not Amy—led him to the table in the back. It suited him. He had a view of the train still rolling by like an endless caravan. He ordered the special—whatever, he didn't care—and thanked the waitress for handing him a local paper.

In his reflection in the window he caught sight of a man he used to know, just for one moment, and then it was gone like the train, the caboose slithering away and leaving a clear view of the park across the street. He stared for a long moment at the lush green grass waving in the wind.

The waitress returned with a carafe of steaming coffee, poured his cup full and dashed off with her sneakers squeaking on the clean tile. The coffee was black, had a bitter bite, and he drank it straight. He enjoyed the punch of caffeine.

He turned to the classified ads and browsed through them. The waitress returned with a huge plate stacked high with sunny-side-up eggs, sausage links, pancakes and hash browns. Just the sight of it brought back memories of his grandma's kitchen, where the syrup was the real thing and the jam homemade.

"Do you need anything else?" the waitress asked, producing a bottle of—just as he'd predicted—real maple syrup and a canning jar of what looked like blueberry preserves.

Before he could shake his head no, she was gone, rushing off to bring coffee to the new arrivals.

Alone in the corner, he ate until he was full. He felt like the outsider he was as more people arrived, friends greeted friends and family said hello to family. Cars began to crawl down the main street, mostly obeying the speed limit.

By the time kids were walking by on their way to school, Heath was done.

He pushed the empty plate and the newspaper away. There were no temporary jobs in the local paper. Maybe there'd be something in the next town along the highway. As for the blond waitress from last night, he wasn't disappointed over not seeing her again. He'd pay, leave a tip and be on his way. But would he think of her?

Yeah. He'd think of her. He couldn't say why as he headed down the aisle, past families and friends gathering, past conversations and everyday average human connections. There was something about the woman and it made him wonder…

No wondering, man. No wishing. He dropped a small stack of bills on the counter and pushed through the door.

Once again losing sight of the man he used to be, he ambled down the sidewalk. He was already thinking of moving on, as weightless as the wind.

Amy spotted long-time customer Bob Brisbane through the small window of the hand-off counter. The warmer lights cast a golden hue as she squinted through the opening, standing on tiptoe to see if he was alone. He was late this morning joining his buddies, who met every morning like clockwork to share gossip over breakfast, coffee and the morning paper.

Over the background music from the local inspirational station and the din of the busy diner, she could pick up Jodi's cheerful good morning as she poured Bob's coffee. As the two exchanged small talk of family and last night's storm, Amy cracked three eggs and whipped them in a bowl, with just enough milk and spices.

By the time Jodi had arrived with the order ticket, Amy already had the omelet sizzling next to a generous portion of link sausage and grated potatoes.

"Is that Mr. Winkler's order you've got nearly ready?"

"Yep, just need to add the bacon—" Amy used the spatula to lift the eight blackened strips of bacon, cooked just the way kindly Mr. Winkler liked it, and added it to his order of buttermilk pancakes and two poached eggs and handed up the plate. "I think I've almost caught up. Who knew it'd be such a busy morning?"

"It's the power outage. It sounds like nearly half the county was out of electricity last night, and a lot are still out this morning." Jodi bustled away with the order.

The noise in the dining room seemed to crescendo, or maybe it was because she was trying so hard to listen for the doorbell. She'd hardly been able to sleep last night, for she was troubled not only by the weather and the stress of normal life, but also because she couldn't get the loner out of her mind.

As she added plenty of cheese, smoked sausage, onion and jalapeños to Mr. Brisbane's omelette—how anyone's stomach could handle that at 6:23 a.m., she didn't know—she thought of the loner again. Last night rewound like a movie, to the place where he'd stepped out of the storm, looking more intimidating than the lightning forking down to take out a transformer half a block away.

By standing tall, he'd stopped whatever those awful men had planned. She knew in her heart he was leaving, maybe he'd already left, but she had prayed he might stop in for breakfast before moving on. She'd been watching for him between scrambling eggs and frying bacon and browning potatoes and whipping up her family's secret pancake recipe.

Had she seen him? No, of course not. She'd been busy, that was one problem, but there was only so much of the dining room she could see from behind the grill. Maybe he wasn't coming. He certainly didn't seem eager to see her last night. And she'd had the sinking feeling when he'd seemed to disappear in the storm that she'd never see him again. He'd more than likely followed the road out of town and she had responsibilities. People who counted on her. She ought to pay attention to her work—the omelet oozing melting cheese and the sausages nearly too brown.

She whisked the meat and eggs onto a clean dish, handed it up with her left hand as she turned bacon with the other. Wherever her loner was, she prayed the good he'd done for them was returned to him tenfold.

With the edge of the spatula, she scraped the grill—she liked a tidy kitchen—and studied the last meal ticket on the wheel. It looked like Mr. Whitley had shown up, the sixth member of the retired ranchers who met every morning at the same table. She cracked three eggs neatly—Mr. Redmond's Sunrise Special was the last of the first wave of the usual Saturday-morning rush. Maybe she'd be able to take a few minutes away from the grill, grab some coffee and—

Jodi shouldered through the doors, loaded down with empties, which she unloaded with sharp clatters at the sink. "Well, I tell you, that just about breaks my heart."

"I'm betting you don't mean the pile of dishes to clean?"

"Nope. I waited on a man this morning. Striking, young guy, somewhere around our age, maybe a bit older. You know how on some folks it's hard to tell?" She washed and yanked a paper towel from the dispenser to dry her hands.

Amy's pulse thickened. It was as if her blood had turned into sand, and her heart was straining to pump it through her veins. The background sounds of the cooking food and customers in the dining room faded to silence. Why was she reacting this strongly to the mere mention of the man?

Unaware, Jodi continued on. "Well, I tell ya, I've never seen a sadder-looking man. People got all kinds of heartaches, we both know that, but it just sort of clung to him like an aftershave or something. Just so much despair."

Amy knew. She'd seen it, too.

She tossed the used paper towel. "He looked like he was down to his last dollar, but he left me a five-dollar tip."

"You mean he was here and left?" *And I didn't see him?* The spatula clattered forgotten to the counter as she went up on tiptoe to peer at the long line of booths in front of the sunny window.

Of course he wasn't there, and she rocked back on her heels. "Finish this up, will you? I'll be right back."

"Well, sure, but what—?"

Amy pushed through the doors and left without answering. She hurried down the center aisle where old-timers argued over politics and the weather, where early risers read the day's paper over coffee. A typical morning, with the scents and sounds and people she knew so well, and she couldn't explain why she felt so desperate. It was as if she'd failed to do something important, and that didn't make any sense at all.

The cap. She remembered, skidded to a stop in the doorway, let the glass door swing shut as she reversed and dropped behind the counter. The cap was still there on the top of the plastic bin and she grabbed it without thinking, pounding out the door, and making the bell jangle like a tambourine. Her shoes hit the pavement and the fresh breeze punched her face.

She ran half a block, past the diner and the drug store closed up tight. He was nowhere in sight. What was she doing running off like this? She'd left eggs on the grill. The sunshine slanted into her eyes, too bright to see up the sidewalk where it stretched the rest of the length of town. There was only one more block before buildings gave way to green pasture. He wasn't here. The hat probably wasn't his. So why was she standing here wanting something, and she didn't even know what it was.

What she should do was go back inside, rescue the

Sunrise Special from the grill, concentrate on her job
and not give the loner another thought. She didn't like
men—she didn't trust them. She got along just fine
in the world when they were customers or friends of
the family or family. She had a policy against inter-
acting with the male gender for any other reason. So,
had she lost her senses, or what?

No, she was shivering in the brisk wind because of
her conscience. Her faith taught the golden rule—to
do unto others, and she had to thank him, if she could.
Even if it was only to return his hat, *if* it was his hat.

A strange sensation skidded against her jaw and
cheek, or maybe it was the trees whispering in the
breeze. Either way, she turned toward the sensation
and there was a man's dark form, a man dressed all
in black, a shadow moving in the sun-bright alley.

It *was* him.

"Hey, wait up!" She started toward him, but the
wind snatched her words and she feared he hadn't
heard her. He kept on walking with his purposeful,
leggy stride. She saw an older-model blue pickup,
dusty and well used, parked at the motel's alley-side
lot.

There. She had her answer. She firmly believed
that the angels above wouldn't have brought him to
her diner twice if there hadn't been a reason.

Determined, she jogged after him, with the cap
clutched tight in her hand. "Hey! Mister!"

He had to have heard her this time. His brisk gait

stiffened. His shoulders tensed to steel. His long athletic legs pumped noticeably faster as he bridged the last few yards to the driver's door of his truck, unlocked the door and yanked it open. He was behaving as if he didn't want to talk with her. As if he wanted to avoid her.

She wasn't about to let a little thing like that get in her way. "Is this your cap?"

He turned, meeting her gaze through the window of the open cab door. His was a chilling look as he studied her from head to toe.

She was intensely aware of her scuffed sneakers and the knot in the right shoelace keeping it together as she jogged closer. As if resigned, he left the door open and backed away from the truck. A dark look masked his face. She held out the cap so he could read it.

He let out an exasperated sigh. "Yeah, it's mine."

"Good. Then I don't look quite so silly running after you at six-forty——" she glanced at her wristwatch "——seven in the morning."

"You don't look silly at all. Not at all. Just the opposite."

"Good. I try not to make a fool of myself before noon, at least." She held out the cap.

The sight of him in full light startled her. He'd looked solemn and mighty in the night. By day he seemed taller than she'd figured. Tall and lean—not skinny, but not bulky either.

As he approached, she swore she saw a softening of his hard mouth, as if he almost remembered how to smile. She bet he had a nice smile but that softness vanished, leaving only the stark mask of his face.

Somehow she had to get up her courage to talk to him. "I didn't get a chance to thank you last night. You disappeared into the rain before I could."

He took the hat she offered, looking at it, then at the ground. At anything but her. "Just doing what anyone would do."

"No, that's not true." Standing here went against every life lesson she'd learned, but somehow it felt as if she were doing more than returning the cap, more than thanking him. It felt personal. He couldn't know how hard it was to slip from behind the hard shell she held up to men, and he'd already been gruff to her.

But she kept going. It was the right thing to do.

"A lot of people hate to get involved. My sister had our day's earnings on her, and if there had been trouble, well, we could have lost more than that. It's heartening to know there are men like you in this world. I just wanted to thank—"

"C'mon, lady, you can't be real." He hardened before her eyes, his mouth twisting, his dark eyes flashing black. He grabbed the cap by the bill and lopped it onto his head. Gave it a yank to secure it in place. "I don't want your thanks. I don't need your thanks. Whatever it is you're thinking you can get from me, forget it."

Amy's jaw dropped. His fierceness shocked her. She reeled as if he'd slapped her, and she couldn't think, couldn't move. She could only stare after him as he about-faced and climbed into his truck.

Without a look back, he gunned the engine and drove off with a roar, leaving her in his dust.

Chapter Four

What a perfectly horrible man! She was still fuming many hours later as she trudged across the school's back field that had been divided into over a dozen peewee soccer zones. Kids were everywhere, with their parents and siblings streaming from the jammed parking lot. She'd left her reliable sedan parked beside the city street because she knew there was no way she'd find a spot close coming so late.

Half of the games were in progress. Kids played in groups of six, their primary-colored shirts and shorts bright in the noon sun. Whistles shrieked over the sounds of coaches' orders rising above the children's voices.

A dog barked as he ran from one field to the other, happily evading the grade schooler who ran after him. "Rufus! Rufus, get back here!"

It was little Allie McKaslin. Her cousin Karen's kid was the same age as her Westin. She wore the red-and-white uniform of the team the diner sponsored. With her fine blond hair flying, she managed to snatch the leash, halting the big golden retriever. Apparently, the match hadn't started yet.

"Hey, Allie!" Amy called to the little girl, circling around a game in progress, hurrying past the orange cones serving as goal posts. "Where's the rest of your team?"

"Oh, hi, Amy!" The blond little sweetheart laughed as the dog gave her a lick across her face. "It's way, way over there."

"Want to come over with me?"

"Yeah!"

Girl and dog fell in beside her, the dog swinging at the end of the leash trying to sniff everything and Allie hopping along as if she were playing hopscotch.

All that energy. Amy sure could use some of that right now. The ice chest was unbelievably heavy—hadn't she vowed last week not to bring so much stuff? She glanced at the spectators lined up a few feet beyond the foul lines. She saw familiar faces, but it took her a while to spot her family.

Once she did, it was hard to believe anyone could miss the crowd of McKaslins. Her sisters and cousins were settled into folding canvas chairs, talking, laughing and shouting encouragement at the soccer players as they warmed up. Vaguely she was aware of Allie handing the dog's leash to someone else and a chorus of greetings, but her gaze shot straight to her son.

Her little Westin looked handsome in his red shirt and matching shorts and sleek dark suntan. He'd been watching for her, as always, and gave her a quick wave. She sent one back his way, waggling her fingers and losing her grip on the corner of the cooler.

"Whew, I got that just in time." Rachel came to the rescue, rising smoothly from the nearby chair, and they lowered the chest in unison. "It weighs a ton. What did you put in there? Anything good?"

"Open it and see."

She heard the short blast of the coach's whistle, one of the high-school girls on the local team, and looked up just in time to see Westin charge the ball. He stumbled but managed to recover. He drew back his foot and sent the ball limping through the orange cones.

Amy whistled. Rachel shouted. The extended family clapped and hooted. Amy's heart melted as her little boy held up his fists in victory.

Linna, the coach, stopped it with the ball of her foot. "All right, Westin! Good job."

Amy warmed inside as Westin beamed. They'd worked so hard this past week on that kick. She was so proud of him. He looked more confident as he shot her a winning smile before joining the other children in line, waiting their turns with the ball.

"Wow, he's gotten that kick down good." Rachel snapped open the cooler. "What do you have in here—ooh, my very favorite. You shouldn't have."

"I couldn't resist." It was pleasure to watch the happiness light her sister's face as she dried off the strawberry soda can on her sweatshirt and popped the top. She owed Rachel more than she could ever repay, and whatever she could do to make her sister smile made her happy, too.

Cousin Karen came over, her six-month-old daughter on her hip. She held out a plastic container. "Thought I'd make a trade for one of those sodas."

"Not your grandma's famous cookies?"

"Two whole dozen. I was making a batch for us last night and I couldn't resist doubling it. Did you want me to take Westin after the game, or is Rachel going to?"

"Rachel said something about spoiling him this afternoon. I know, it's hard to believe." They both glanced at Rachel, who was sipping her soda, seated in her chair, baseball cap shading her face as she rooted for every kid who kicked the ball.

"Thanks, though. How's little Autumn doing?" She couldn't resist stroking the baby's rose-petal-soft cheek.

The baby girl gurgled and gave a wide grin.

Amy's heart split wide open. "Oh, she's a sweetie."

"She is, most of the time." With a wink, Karen nuzzled her beloved daughter. "Do you want to hold her?"

"You know I do." Amy handed the cookie container to Rachel, who let out a squeal of delight, and took the little girl in her arms. She stopped to watch as Allie, Karen's oldest daughter, boldly gave a mighty kick at the soccer ball...and missed.

She looked so cute that it was hard not to laugh, and the spectators did their best to hide their chuckles and sound encouraging instead. Allie got a second chance—this was the warm-up, after all—and managed to bump her toe against the ball and it hopped forward a few inches.

Amy, along with Karen and the rest of the crowd cheered as if Allie'd made the winning goal.

She felt a tug on her hair—Baby Autumn had a handful wrapped and gave a joyful gurgle. "You want all the attention, do you, darling?"

"Oh, don't hog the baby!" Rachel set her soda can in the holder in the chair's arm, brushed chocolate cookie crumbs off the front of her sweatshirt and held out her hands. "It's my turn."

Gently Amy disentangled her hair from Autumn's dimpled fist and handed over the baby. Rachel immediately started cooing.

Whistles blasted—the game was about to start. Westin's cheeks were pink with delight as he crouched into the huddle.

"Hey, where's Paige?" Another cousin—Michelle—knelt down between the chairs. "Oh, wait, I know, she's chaperoning the youth group. Isn't she supposed to be back today?"

"Not today! Don't scare us like that!" Rachel teased. "She's going to interrogate me about the books I kept while she was gone, and I'm not very good with the books. I have until tomorrow, the day of doom, when she gets ahold of the ledger."

"I brought those terrible nacho chips, they were on sale in the Shop Mart, and I got three bags for the greater good of everyone else. So please, eat them before I do." She dropped a bright red bag on Amy's lap.

"Okay, but who's going to rescue *me* from these chips?"

"I will." Rachel was all too quick to snatch the bag and yank it open, making them all laugh.

Michelle gave Amy's hair a quick inspection. "Don't you go putting off your hair appointment again. Your highlights are growing out. Don't argue, just come anyway. Well, I'd better get back to my little ones."

After Michelle hurried back to her toddlers and baby, Amy and Rachel crunched chips, sipped on cool sodas and watched as the game started. The teenage girls were trying to direct the little kids, who were doing their best, but ran the wrong way, missed the ball, kicked to the wrong team and forgot what to do when the ball came to them.

"This is so funny," Rachel said as she grabbed

her camera and began taking snapshots in quick succession.

Her sister's laughter warmed her through, and Westin's squeal of happiness as he kicked another goal uplifted her even more. The crowd cheered, and Amy soaked it up.

This was why she was so grateful every day. She had the warm Montana sun on her face and the loving acceptance of her family and friends surrounding her. Not to mention her little boy grinning from ear to ear as he ran a victory lap, forgetting to go back to the game, which went on without him.

"Oh, I've got that recorded." Cousin Kendra came over with her handheld DVD video recorder. "I'll make a copy for you. He's too cute."

A shadow moved at the corner of Amy's eye, drawing her attention to the far edge of the school yard, beyond the tall chain-link fencing to the road out of town.

She recognized the man inside the blue pickup, which was creeping along in obedience to the school zone speed limit. She was surprised he'd stayed in town this long. The loner didn't look right or left, just kept a slow steady speed down the tree-lined lane and kept on going until he was out of sight.

His sadness clung to her as if it had somehow seeped through her skin and settled in her bones. She decided Jodi, the morning-shift waitress, was right.

He was the saddest man she'd ever seen. It made it hard to stay angry with him, because he was alone.

And she was not.

The crowd around her came to life, yelling this time for little Allie, who kicked and missed a perfect goal shot. Westin came running to fend off a little boy in a blue uniform, giving her the chance to try again. Everyone leapt out of the chairs and onto their feet, shouting encouragement.

Amy was on her feet cheering, too, as the goal was made, but she couldn't see for the tears in her eyes. Tears that hurt as they fell, not from pain but from gratitude. She never questioned that God was good, look how gracious He had been to her when she had made so many mistakes.

And the loner...

Please watch over him, Father, she prayed, because she knew how bitter loneliness could make someone. And how bleak hopelessness could be.

Heath shifted into fourth gear as the town fell behind him and he accelerated on the two-lane country road. The look on Amy's face had stayed with him the entire time he'd been at the sheriff's office. Even when he and the deputy found out they'd served in the first Desert Storm within twenty miles of one another, *she* had been in the back of his thoughts, and that was saying something.

He couldn't get rid of the dark trembling feeling in

his gut, that bad feeling he got whenever he did something he regretted. And what he'd said to the blond-haired woman who'd been decent enough to return his hat, who was simply a nice person—

He couldn't get past it. He'd been mean to her when she'd done nothing to deserve it.

It wasn't like him to behave like that. He never should have acted that way. He'd just been...wrong. Sure, there were a dozen excuses as to why he'd done it, but really, he didn't want to get close to a woman again. In any way, shape or form. There were plenty of reasons, but what did it matter, in the end? Excuses didn't erase the way he'd intentionally pushed her away.

"Some of the nicest people you'll ever meet, the McKaslins," the deputy had told him after he'd filled out a report on last night's troublemakers. "When I first came to town to interview for this job, I'd stopped afterward for a bite to eat at the diner. It was after the lunch rush, and Amy was alone in the place."

"Is it her restaurant?"

"The family's. Those women work hard, I tell you, and they make some of the best meals around. Anyway, after Amy grilled up my burger and gave me a whole batch of fries, she whipped up the best shake I've had anywhere."

When Frank had gotten up to refill the coffee cups, it would have been a good time to have left. But for some reason Heath hadn't made a break for the door.

He'd sat there, torn between wanting out and wanting to stay and hear more.

The deputy was more than happy to keep talking. "Amy found out I was the new deputy and offered me the apartment upstairs, it was vacant at the time, to stay in while I looked for a place in town. That was real nice, don't you think?"

"Sure." Built-in business, Heath had thought. Those McKaslin sisters were smart. It went to figure that Frank would buy most if not all of his meals at the diner if he was living above it.

"Empty real estate is pretty scarce around here, even apartments, and so I jumped on her offer. But Amy and her sisters wouldn't take a penny of rent, no sir. They kept me fed and happy, even fed my brothers when they came to help me move in. I tell you, I've never met a nicer family. Generous. Kind. They're the kind of folks who don't think about getting more than they give. With the things I've seen in my life, it's reassuring to know there are still honest-to-God good people in this world."

Yeah, the deputy's words kept replaying in his head like a CD stuck on repeat. Words that grated against his conscience with every mile that passed.

Good people. Generous and kind. Those words hurt him in a way nothing had in a very long time. Longer than he wanted to count or to think about. For about as long as he'd turned his back on his old life.

Nothing could hurt like the pain he left behind, but the prick of his conscience just kept going on and on.

Maybe it was the soft green of the rolling country-side, where new crops grew in endless fields on either side of the narrow country road. It was idyllic, it truly was. Like something on television with a filter over the camera lens to make the greens brighter and the blues deeper, to make life more vivid and beautiful than it could ever be in reality.

Tidy driveways veered off the main road, about a quarter of a mile or more apart, where mailboxes stood bearing the family name, some in the shapes of barns or decorated to look like a duck. The graveled driveways wound through the green fields and the country homes seemed to smile, although it was only the reflection of the sunlight on the front windows.

He saw everything from trailer homes to lavish houses. It was all so neat and quaint, with horses grazing in white-fenced pastures and now and then a farmer riding a tractor along the fence line. Irrigation tossed water into the wind, and thousands of tiny rainbows glittered midair in the spray.

The beauty surrounding him made him feel keenly what he'd become inside—ugly and bitter.

Had he become so hard and callous that he could no longer recognize good when he saw it? He remembered the look on the waitress's face. The stunned shock and the sudden hurt as if he'd reached out and slapped her—not that he would ever hit a woman.

But that's how much harm his panicked words had done.

C'mon, lady, you can't be real. Whatever it is you're thinking you can get from me, forget it.

Yeah, he could hear how it would have sounded to her. He'd become so bitter, it felt as if it was all he was. Nothing but disillusionment and pain, and he was ashamed of himself. Ashamed. He wasn't a bad man. He didn't go around hurting people.

So why had he said that to her?

Because he'd stopped believing in good, in kindness, long ago. It was easier than the truth he could not bear to face. It was easier than trying to understand why God had taken so much from him. And why—

Black pain clamped so tight on his heart, he gasped. Air caught in his throat. He'd swear he was having a heart attack, but he knew better. It was a different kind of pain in his heart. A different kind of damage.

The road stretched ahead of him, rolling and ribboning up the gentle rises and falling out of sight in the slow dips. Then it rose again in the distance, like a thin black thread lying along the endless green. The road could carry him far away, past those mountains rising up thousands of feet, the rugged, bare-faced granite and white glacier caps holding up the vivid blue bowl of the sky.

Yeah, he could keep going on this road, keeping on

just the way he was. Adding this stain on his soul to go along with the emptiness in there. He could drive east and once he had those mountains behind him, he could forget this place ever existed and with it the wrong he'd done. He *could* go on.

But he didn't want to be the kind of man who did. He might have lost everything on a rainy night over two years ago. That didn't mean he had to grow into the kind of man who went around causing harm.

No, Lord knew there were enough of those kinds of people on this earth already.

Was he going to be one of them? Suddenly he saw how it worked: One mistake after another, one harm caused after another, until it was a way of life.

So he stopped in the middle of the road. With the windows down, sweet fragrant air breezed into the cab. As it bathed his face and tickled his hair, he debated. Then he checked for traffic—not that there was a vehicle in sight in either direction. And, with no one but God to witness it, he pulled a U-turn and headed back the way he came. Not so bitter a man, after all.

Not so lost.

The diner was jammed. Amy gave thanks for the warm sunny day because they could use the tables set out on the brick patio at the side of the building. Without them, they'd be turning business away. As it was, they were almost out of those tables, too.

As Jodi seated another soccer family, Amy filled

orders as fast as the grill would cook them. She was glad the twins—young though they were—had shown up early to help with some of the prep work.

"Westin is like the coolest kid ever!" Brandilyn— or was it Brianna?—grabbed the order for table three and, instead of hurrying, stopped, cracked her gum and gave a high-wattage smile. "I can't wait until I get to be a mom. Not that I'm in a hurry, 'cuz I hope I can get into college first."

It was Brandilyn because Brianna sidled up to actually take the plates from the warming lights. Amy could clearly see the name badge on her collar.

Equally as blond and cute and full of teenage charm, Brianna cracked her gum, too. "Like, college is a year away. We're supposed to be waitresses, Brand. So, like, waitress, okay?"

"Oh, right!" With a swing of her head, which sent her ponytail flopping, Brandilyn grabbed the last plate and followed her twin down the aisle.

"We were never like that when we were their age," Jodi commented as she brought in a bin of dirties and dumped them on the counter. "Right?"

"Right. We never giggled. Never used words like *cool*." Amy laughed as she unloaded small glass plates of house salad from the refrigerator and uncovered them. "Is it me, or does it seem like a century since we were that young?"

"For me, two centuries at least." Jodi hadn't had the easiest life, either, but she managed to smile.

"Those two are the cutest things. I adore 'em, except they make me feel about twelve hundred years old."

"Oh, wait until they pull you aside for their senior life class assignment." Amy trayed the plates and left Jodi to finish them as the fryer beeped. She had fries to rescue.

"I'm afraid to ask," Jodi said as she spooned out the creamy salad dressings.

"They wanted to know what school was like in the 'olden days.'"

"What?" A spoon clattered to the floor and rattled to a stop. "The olden days?"

"Sure. I'm practically thirty and, as they said, that's 'like ancient.'" Amy lovingly mimicked the twins' intonation as she set the basket out of the grease and turned to add slices of cheese to half of the frying meat patties. "You gotta love those two."

"Or something!" Jodi was laughing—or maybe crying. Several years older, Jodi was well into her midthirties and, Amy suspected, unappreciative of being called ancient. "I've got a few crow's feet, but goodness! The olden days. Did they really say that?"

"Honest and truly. I wish I could say they meant to be insulting, but they said it as cheerful as could be. Just wait." Amy reached with the tongs to rescue the buns from the browning rack—but missed. Her fingers froze in midair, woefully short of the metal tongs.

The screen door behind her squeaked. Turning, she saw a tall, broad-shouldered man fill the doorway.

Her loner was back, and he didn't look happy. "Can I come in?"

"We're busy."

"I need to talk to you."

"I'm busy."

Heath knew that look and what it meant when it was on a woman's face. He was in the doghouse, no doubt about that. His hand was raised in a loose fist to knock on the metal door frame, but since he'd already been spotted, he lowered his hand. He tried to gather up his pride and his troubled conscience.

The other waitress took one look at him, grabbed her tray of salads and disappeared through the swinging doors, leaving him alone with Amy McKaslin, who turned her back on him to whisk two burgers from the grill with a neat jab of the big metal spatula. She deposited them on well-dressed bottom buns, added bacon to one and sauce and pineapple rings to the other and, finishing with the top bun, loaded them onto plates.

He knew the look of hard, honest work. His conscience smote him even harder as, with her back to him, she kept on working. Her golden-blond ponytail bounced in rhythm with her movements, the curling end brushing at the collar of her T-shirt. It was a vulnerable thing, seeing the soft creamy skin and the visible bumps of her vertebrae. She was small-boned and fragile, and yet she worked with a strong capability that said she was made of steel, too.

He'd hurt her more than he'd realized, and he felt sick about it. He could see that in the rigid way she kept her back to him as she worked. Flipping strips of bacon, stirring sautéing onions, changing gloves to drop fresh oversized buns onto the rack to warm.

"Maybe you could spare a minute?"

She didn't so much as flinch. "I don't really have a minute to spare."

"I can see you're in the middle of a lunch crowd."

She arched her brow, her face a set mask as she rushed by to lift a bin of sliced tomatoes from the industrial refrigerator. Okay, she wasn't going to make this easy for him, he understood it. He respected her for it, too. She was a nice person, but she wasn't a pushover. He liked women with a bit of grit to them.

So he tried again. "I just wanted to apologize. I'll only take, say, thirty seconds of your time."

"Believe me, if you want to apologize properly, it's going to take a lot more than thirty seconds." She kept her back to him, swapping gloves again, dressing toasted buns with relish and mayonnaise, adding lettuce and tomato.

She didn't seem quite as angry. Maybe that was a good sign. He gave his cap's bill a tug as he thought. He wasn't sure what to say other than that he'd behaved like a donkey's behind. Without reason. "Can

I come in? Or are you going to make me stand here and grovel for forgiveness from ten feet away?"

"Are you going to grovel?"

He thought he heard a smiling sound in her voice, but he couldn't be sure. "How would you like it? On my knees? Prostrate on the floor? Maybe wearing sack cloth and covered with boils?"

"Boils? I'd like to see you suffer, but there are health codes to uphold. I guess I'll have to settle for prostrate on the floor. Would you like a towel? The tile's clean but it's the old-fashioned kind and it's cold to lie on."

"Well, if you want me to suffer..." He didn't finish the sentence, and he liked that she turned from her work, a hint of a smile tugging at the curving corners of her soft mouth.

"I do want you to suffer," she confessed, but the questioning tilt of her deep-blue eyes said differently.

She was studying him, as if measuring his intentions, not in a harsh way but in a way that made him feel as if he had a chance of measuring up. But why should he care about that? All he needed to do was ease his conscience, apologize and move on.

He had places to go. A job to find. A past to keep forever buried.

"Come in. It's not locked." She went back to work, flipping the burgers, dumping a huge pile of freshly cut potatoes into the French-fry basket, lifting another out of the golden oil full of crisp, hand-battered onion rings.

He turned the screen-door handle and the hinges rasped as he stepped inside. Could use some grease, he thought, looking around. The white tile floor was probably original, most likely put in sometime in the sixties. The kitchen was small and simple, but clean. Chrome shined. The countertops were a perfect white. The appliances up to date.

He didn't know what made him open his mouth or where the words came from. He surprised himself when he heard his voice say, "Want some help?"

She dropped her spatula. Spun on her heel. Surveyed him up and down with her intelligent eyes. "Do you have a food handler's card?"

"Got one a while back. It's still current."

"Okay, then. You can seat folks. Gather up the empties. Bus. Can you do that?" It wasn't a question the way she said it; it was more of a challenge. As if she wanted to see if he could measure up to her standards.

He hadn't had a challenge in a long while. Not that he was worried—he liked to work hard. She pointed at the sink and he washed up, letting the hot water scald his skin. He didn't know what whim he was following, but whatever it was, it had to be a good one. His conscience wasn't bugging him. His stomach was calm. He felt as if he was finally doing something right as he grabbed an empty dishpan and shouldered through the swinging doors.

Out of the corner of his peripheral vision, he saw Amy watching him in surprise before the doors swung closed, stealing her from his sight. He didn't know why, but he felt a sense of rightness click into place like a key in a lock, and it was as if a door opened. In his old life, he would have chalked it up to Providence, but he'd long since stopped looking—or wanting—God's hand in his life.

But now he just saw it as a fortunate occurrence. That's all, not Providence. He spotted a family leaving one of the booths. The father took the wiggling toddler from his wife, who looked kind but a little harried, as she encouraged her older two sons—both wearing different colored soccer uniforms—to stop goofing around on their way down the aisle.

Heath looked away and froze his feelings so he felt nothing at all. He was just a man staring out the window, working in a diner, more interested in the few cars crawling by looking for parking. The family passed by on their way to the cash register up front.

Only then did he plop the bin on the seat and start clearing.

Chapter Five

Amy flipped the double patties on the garnished bottom bun, added hot sauce, jalapeños and hot peppers, and heaped fries on the last plate on the last order of the Saturday lunch rush. Through the hand-off window she could see the last of the families were waiting for Jodi to ring up their meals.

Amy turned to begin clean-up and then halted in midstep. What was she thinking? She *wasn't* thinking, that was the problem. Her thoughts had been scattered like dust in the wind and she couldn't seem to get them focused. Not since the loner had returned. He was a good worker—she had to give him that. Through the swinging doors she could just see the top of his head as he wiped down the outside tables.

She still didn't know if she had completely forgiven him for being so rude to her, and that was wrong. It was her faith to forgive. He'd offered her a sincere apology and she had accepted it. But deep down his harsh demeanor grated. See, it was good never to trust men. Whether they meant to or not, they caused pain.

She'd had enough pain in her life and certainly wasn't about to look for more. So, why did she keep wondering about him? Why had he come back? Why was he helping out? Where was he going, that he had time to spare instead of rushing off to wherever it was that he'd been heading?

The swinging doors burst open—it was one of the twins. Tall and willowy and coltlike in the way of teenagers, and radiating pure energy.

Brianna, a touch theatrical, gave a deep meaningful sigh. "I'm, like, totally starving. I'd give anything for, like, a totally loaded chiliburger. Oh, and can I have lots and lots of fries? I burned off, like, an awesome amount of calories."

Maybe the twins were terrible behind the cash register, but they were fun. Amy bit her lip to keep from laughing and got to work. Knowing Brandilyn would be waltzing in any second with the exact same request, she set two buns on to toast while she dished out two scoops of the chili stocked in the fridge, put them in a bowl and placed it in the microwave to warm.

Brianna, in the middle of counting up tip money, stopped to add, "Ooh, and, like, cheese, too." Then she looked down at the big stack of ones, rolled her eyes, huffed out another sigh and started counting all over again.

She loved the twins, but really, she was glad she'd never have to be a teenager again. She wouldn't go back for anything. Sometimes it was painful to look at the girls and remember when she'd been that age—and far too rebellious. She'd been the top student in her class all through high school, but she'd never made it through her senior year.

And the years after that…no, she wasn't interested in looking back at that time. It was better to act as if she'd been able to erase it from her memory, like words from a blackboard, so that it was as clean as if it had never been.

"Here's your cut." Brianna slapped a stack of ones on the counter. "Oh, and isn't Heath totally awesome? Are you, like, gonna hire him for keeps?"

Heath? So that was his name. She resisted the urge to peer through the doors—she could hear the faint clink and clank of dishes as he bussed. She deliberately kept her voice low and even. "He offered to pitch in and help us out for this shift. I don't know what his plans are."

"You should make him take the cook job. Well, only if he can cook, you know? 'Cause, like—"

Brandilyn burst through the doors, ready to finish her twin's sentence. "He'd be cool to have around.

He's this awesome mysterious kind of guy. Like from movies and stuff. You know he's a good guy, but he's so totally distant and almost scary."

"But nice," Brianna added. "Definitely nice."

"Yeah." They nodded together, both blond heads and ponytails bouncing. "Don't you think he's nice?"

Amy flipped the meat patties, shaking her head. There they were again, trying to find her a husband. And, to use their words—as if!

She did her best to hide a smile, because she didn't want to encourage them. "I'm just interested in hiring a cook. You girls go get your sodas. Your burgers are ready."

"Cool!" they said, spun on their heels and blew through the kitchen, leaving her alone.

As she dressed the buns and built the sandwiches, she let her mind wander over the possibilities. Heath. The name suited him and she liked it.

"So, are you going to tell me about the job?"

Startled, her hand flew to her throat. Trembling, she tried to catch her breath. He stood there, legs apart and braced, dressed in black jeans and T-shirt, his dark gaze fixed on her. He reminded her of a lone wolf, lean and sizable and fierce-looking. She didn't feel in danger around him, but she didn't feel exactly safe either.

"You scared me. I didn't hear you there."

"Sorry."

He didn't look sorry. And yet she thought she heard a sense of humor warming that one word.

He looked less imposing as the hint of a grin curved the far corner of his mouth. "Next time I'll stomp my feet and bang hard on the door so you can hear me coming."

"Great idea. Maybe you could rattle some pots."

"I'll try."

The grin spread across his hard-shaped lips until it softened his chiseled features.

It was infectious, and she couldn't help smiling in return. That was dangerous, no doubt about it. She'd learned the hard way men can't be trusted. Of course, there were a few shining exceptions in the world like Pastor Bill and Uncle Pete and her brother, but this dark loner with his guarded stance and his discontent definitely looked like trouble.

He looked like the kind of man who, no matter how good, was always moving on. The kind who left devastation in his wake.

"I don't think you're right for the position." She hated being so terse, but it was the truth. Judging by the way he kept staring at the door, he was already as good as gone. "There's no way I want to train someone who's got to be somewhere else by the end of the week. Sorry."

"Who said I had someplace else to be?"

"Well, you were driving through town, remember? I assume you had a destination in mind."

"I've got nothing important ahead of me."

It was the way he said it—as if it was no big deal, a take it or leave it kind of a way. Amy wasn't fooled. In the silence that stretched between them, as she set the two plates oozing with big juicy sandwiches and mountains of fries under the warmer, she felt the seconds lengthen and stretch.

And she saw the edges of his shoes, scuffed and worn and patched with duct tape and shoe polish over the tape to disguise it. He'd done a good job, but she recognized the same technique she used on her shoes when times were lean.

I've never seen a sadder-looking man. People got all kinds of heartaches, we both know that, but it just sort of clung to him like an aftershave or something. Just so much sadness. Jodi's words came back to her as bold as a touch from heaven above, and Amy shivered down deep, not from the cold but from the simple truth that he was in need.

She knew exactly how that felt. "That chiliburger smells good. Would you like to have one with me? And don't get all worked up when I tell you it's free. You work a shift, you get a free meal. It isn't charity, it's our policy."

He had the grace to blush a little. "I was a jerk,

and I'm sorry for it. The truth is, I don't like charity. I can make my own way through life."

"Sure, but we all need a little help from time to time. Even us strong stoic types."

Her words rubbed him wrong, and if her tone had been less friendly and less matter-of-fact, it would have set him off again. He still had his pride—he'd about lost everything else.

But Amy was already slapping beef patties on the grill, and the truth was, he'd worked in enough restaurants to know a free meal with a work shift was policy in a lot of places. It had nothing to do with her thinking he needed charity.

Besides, he had no right getting mad at her. She ran a good business. She treated her waitstaff well—he'd have to be blind not to see it. And she looked exhausted. While she came across as energetic and competent, he could see the telltale signs of the tiredness she was covering up. The slight droop of her shoulders. The pale tint to her face. The dark smudges that bruised the delicate skin beneath her eyes.

He respected anyone who worked so hard. Maybe it was simple good luck that he'd come back. A job? Here? He thought it over as he looked around for something needing done—the garbage bin was full—and he tied off the sack, hefted it out of the plastic container and blew through the screen door.

Stay here? Why not? The warm sunshine seemed

to embrace him and the gentle breeze felt like a caress against his forehead. The familiar urban smell of sun-warmed blacktop was softened by the scent of ripening grasses from the fields visible at the end of the long block, where town ended and the country began. The scent of fresh lilacs reminded him of his grandmother's house as he hefted the sack into the Dumpster.

Feeling lighter somehow, he gazed up at the small second story, which was visible from the back of the building. He hadn't noticed it before. A row of windows sparkled and glinted in the light, and he spotted a row of stairs rising along the far side of the building. The deputy had mentioned an apartment. Was anyone living there now? There was no sign that someone was.

"Hey, quite an afternoon, ain't it?" The grizzled clerk from the hotel crossed the alley. Nearly bald, what little hair he had was white as snow, and he walked with a stoop and a limp. He was a lean man, nearly skin and bones, but he had spryness to his step. "You workin' for the girls?"

"Thinking about it."

"You couldn't find nicer people. It's heartening how those girls have worked to make a go of this. They could use some help after that cook they hired just ran off. Got a notion to see North Dakota and left them shorthanded. You a good cook?"

"I'm passable."

"Good. Okay, then. See ya around."

Heath chuckled, watching the man limping down the alley to where the sidewalk led around the corner of the building.

"If you pass Joe's muster, I guess you've got yourself a job."

It was Amy, nothing more than a shadow behind the mesh of the screen door. She was hard to see as she reached for the door, and then the squeaking hinges gave way to the flare of sunlight. Her hair gleamed like polished gold, her red T-shirt glowed like a ruby and her white flowered apron ruffled in the breeze. She smiled, holding the door open for him.

If that wasn't a sign he ought to stay, then he didn't know what was. He was down on his luck, had been for a long while, but that didn't mean he was without luck. It was amazing how fate stepped in at the last moment with a job or something to help him get by. He used to chalk it up to the Lord, when he'd been naive, when he'd believed there was good in the world and someone wise and compassionate in charge of the universe.

He knew better now, but he did long for those simpler times. Simpler because he'd had faith, because the world had been friendlier and less cold when he'd truly believed. Life since had been complicated and everything seemed a little nicer here, in this small town where people smiled as they went about their business.

Yeah, this might be a real nice place to stay for a while.

He caught the edge of the screen door. Her smile fading, she turned away from him and moved farther into the kitchen. Moving easily, she handed him a platter. She'd given him an enormous helping, but he decided not to complain or take it the wrong way.

He'd work the rest of the day, that would make things a little more even. "I can see you need help around here. Your cook took off on you, right? And now you think I might do the same."

"I need help, don't get me wrong. I'd love to hire someone to deal with the grill—cooking isn't my favorite thing, not that I'm complaining. It's just…how long would you be interested in staying?"

"So, you meant what you said. You'll hire me?"

"Something like that. You didn't answer my question." She pushed through the doors and led the way.

"Oh, hire him, Amy!" One of the teenage waitresses called across the dining room, where she sat near the front door with her identical sister.

"Yeah, you've been working here totally too long every day. That's not good for you. You need time for exercise and rest and stuff."

Amy slid her plate on the edge of a small table. A table for two, and Heath had the distinct impression that she didn't want him eating with her or cooking in her kitchen.

"Sit down, get comfortable, help yourself to a soda." She gestured to the empty tables, leaving it clear. She hadn't forgotten how he'd treated her. And he didn't blame her, because forgiving was one thing, but she clearly was a woman who didn't trust easily.

I'm the same way, he thought with relief. He chose a booth near the window, so he could look out while he ate. His stomach growled, and his mouth watered. The scent of the burger alone was incredible. Amy had made him a big sandwich. It took both hands to hold it and it was all he could do to take a bite. Cheese dripped, chili oozed and the beef tasted good—fresh, not like it had been overprocessed and frozen and shipped across a continent. He'd bet the supplier was local. She probably bought straight from the local butcher.

It was the tastiest food he'd had in a long time.

He turned his attention out the window, where a lazy Saturday afternoon shone like a dream. He had the feeling the town hadn't changed much in fifty years. A few cars ambled past. A pair of boys raced by on their bikes. Beyond the park and railroad tracks he spotted black-and-white cows grazing in a field, and the sharp blast of a horn said the train would be coming through at any moment.

He'd been a boy the last time he'd sat and really

watched a train, and he felt the thrill of anticipation as the horn tooted, announcing its imminent arrival. The earth would rumble, or at the very least it would seem that way if he were close enough, as the huge black engine charged into sight. Heath counted three engines hitched together, capably drawing the long snake of the freight cars behind. His grandfather had loved trains. He'd given Heath a real Lionel railroad set—a collector's item now, but who knew what had become of it?

If Granddad were here, he'd have liked this place. He would have said no town could be half bad if it had a train going through it. His grandfather had always longed to travel, and maybe that was what trains always meant to him, but he'd been a farmer with his feet rooted firmly in Texas soil.

This cozy rural town reminded Heath of his summer trips to stay with his grandparents. Not the terrain—there was no mistaking Montana with her mountains and lush rolling valleys for the dry brown flat expanse of central Iowa. But this place, too, was a one-street town, where folks went just a little bit slower, were kinder, and knew their neighbors. In that way, it felt familiar—not like home, no, never that, but a good place to stay for a while.

The phone rang somewhere up near the cash register. Down the aisle, Amy hopped up, chewing on a long French fry, and jogged to catch it. She told the twins to relax as she skirted the counter, reached down and popped up with a handheld receiver. She brightened like creek water when sunlight hits it and turned her back, her voice a warm melody.

He ate everything on his plate—he was hungrier than he'd thought. He polished off a tall glass of frothy root beer and considered. The waitresses had given him a fair cut of the tips. He had cash enough, added with what he'd had in his wallet, to see him through the rest of the week or so, if he was careful. He wasn't in a bad position, not bad at all.

There was no reason to accept Amy's job offer. This place, while it reminded him of better times in his life, had too many families. Too many friendly people. He'd leave, it was the best decision.

Still, it was with regret that he pushed out of the chair and took his plate back to the kitchen. He would have liked working here.

Amy shouldered through the doors and took his plate from him before he could add it to the stack Jodi, the other waitress, was rinsing.

"Hey, where are you going?" Amy looked friendly enough, he decided, but there was a hard set to her face. She slipped a key into his palm.

He stared at it, confused. "A key? What for?"

"To the room upstairs. I thought—I mean Rachel and I thought—that you might want to stay there. You did want the job, right?"

Amy watched, heart racing, trepidation rushing through her bloodstream. Heath studied the plain, ordinary key, as if she'd offered him a handful of radioactive waste.

Maybe he thought this was charity, too, since he was touchy on the subject. "The apartment can be part of your pay, if you want it. It isn't much, but it's clean and furnished. Why don't you go take a look at it and decide it you want to stay there, even just for the night instead of in another motel room."

"You seem pretty sure of this. You were worried about me running off and leaving you shorthanded."

"It's still a concern of mine, but Rachel has faith in you. She said she liked the cut of your character, helping us out the way you did last night, and stepping in today when others wouldn't have. Besides, she also pointed out that we're shorthanded now, that's the problem. We'll solve it by hiring you. Do we have a deal?"

He looked around, took his time before he answered. "I know I made a donkey's behind of myself when we first met, and I'm sorry for the way I acted. I won't do it again. If you can put the way I treated you behind us, then I'd like to work here."

Should she be surprised that he'd apologized again? She didn't have a lot of experience with an honest apology from a man—well, those from her brother didn't count, and brothers were brothers. She knew she could trust him. But what about Heath—could she trust him?

She studied him, trying to see more than what he appeared to be. With the slant of the sun through the door, burnishing his powerful frame with vivid light, he was startling. He was a big man—not bulky with thick muscles, but not lean either. There was a latent power that seemed to burn in him, leashed and waiting.

His hair wasn't black, as it had appeared last night in the dark, but a rich bitter-chocolate-brown. His high forehead and strong cheekbones were not harsh, but intelligent and well-defined. Although he was handsome, his features were set in an unmistakable expression that said, "Keep away." He was a private man and a self-sufficient one.

"I can put it behind us." Amy understood, too, having pride. "Go check out the room. Let one of us know if you need anything, all right?"

He was already shaking his head, already pushing through the door. "I don't need anything. When did you want me to start?"

"How about you come in around four? Rachel's in the kitchen tonight, and she'll walk you through the prep and train on the grill. Is that all right?"

"Yep." His mouth compressed into a tight thin line. Serious, sincere, he met her gaze. The impact of their eyes meeting felt like a jolt of lightning to her soul.

"I don't want you to worry about me," he assured her. "I work hard. I do my best. I don't want to cause anyone any harm or grief. I just want to be left alone."

His words weren't harsh, but they were definite. Don't get too friendly, he was saying.

Well, good, because that was her motto, too. She was close to her family and her friends, but that was it. At least this was something she and the loner agreed on—distance. Maybe he knew, too, it was the only way to keep safe.

"Rachel will be waiting for you at four," she said in agreement.

As if he understood, he gave her a curt nod and disappeared from her sight.

Heath didn't set his hopes high as he fit the key into the decades-old knob. From the outside, he wasn't expecting the place to be much at all. He turned the key until the lock released. No dead bolt, he noticed. Then again, there probably wasn't much crime in a town like this.

The door swung open, giving in to gravity when Heath released the knob and it shuddered to a stop against the wall. He saw only dim shadows, the outline of lemony light ebbing around the pull-down blinds at the windows and noticed the mildew and dust odor of a room long unused.

He decided to leave the door open. Maybe some

fresh air would improve the place. It was a good thing he'd known not to expect too much. There'd been a time in his life when he'd gotten so much, he came to take it for granted. His old self, the man he used to be, would have been disappointed for sure over this room where the floorboards beneath his feet groaned and creaked.

He yanked the first blind and it slipped out of his fingers, rolling up with a bang. Bright afternoon light filtered through the screened wood-framed window. Since he wanted fresh air, he tried to open it, but it was stuck. The old paint had gotten damp and tacky. He used a little muscle and the wooden frame began to give. Sunshine seemed to welcome him as he let the fragrant fresh breezes slide past him and into the apartment.

His jaw dropped. Now that he had some light to see better, he couldn't believe his eyes. The front room was bigger than he'd expected. There were the shadows of bricks at the inside wall and the hollow of a fireplace. In front of that sat a living-room set. Two couches and a chair had to be second-hand, because the style was several decades old, but the furniture was clean and the tan upholstery looked like new. He sat on the nearest couch to test it out, and a little cloud of dust rose from the impact of his weight. But what was a little dust?

The cushions were comfortable. There was a small

coffee table if he wanted to put up his feet, and, wait… was that a TV remote? He leaned forward and reached out. Yeah, it was. So, were was the TV?

He hit the power button and in front of him, propped on the end table between the couches was a color thirteen-inch screen. An old Western movie flashed the bright pictures of a cattle round-up. The volume was on low, so it was more of a humming drone in the silence.

It wasn't half-bad, he decided as he scoped out the rest of the room. There were two doors in the end wall, the bedroom and bathroom, he figured. And, behind him on the inside wall near the front door was a dark archway that led into what was probably the kitchen. Amy was right, it was clean and comfortable.

Yeah, he could live here. It was a far better place than anywhere he'd stayed in the recent past, which he thought of as his second life. The old life was gone— he was never going back. He couldn't.

His chest began to seize with pain and he carefully wiped even the mention of his past from his mind. It was some time before his chest relaxed and he could breathe normally again—before the silence surrounding him held no traces of memory.

Outside he heard the rasp of tires on the alley's pocked blacktop and the purr of an engine coming closer. A car door snapped shut, echoing. He listened to the tap of a woman's shoes as she hurried to the back kitchen door, directly beneath his open window. The rasp of the screen-door hinges was preceded by a woman calling out.

"Amy! Amy!" It sounded like the other sister's voice, Rachel, the quieter one. "Help, quick! Emergency!"

Adrenaline shot into his veins—it was a call to action. Like a soldier jumping for his weapon, he was on his feet and had his hand on the doorknob. His attention focused so intently that the outside stimulus fell away. He was ready to roll. The sister needed help.

The screen door slammed shut, and her voice went on. "I can't get this ledger thingy to balance and Paige is gonna flip out when she sees it."

A ledger thingy? What was a ledger thingy?

His feet stopped moving, and his hand seized the rail. He realized he was already halfway down the stairs, heart pounding, ready to offer assistance however it should be needed, and there wasn't a real emergency. No one was in danger. No one needed medical attention.

Amy's voice, soft as lark song, answered, confirming the problem. "Paige is so good at bookkeeping she can't see why everyone doesn't understand it."

"It's like the whole double-posting thing. Why post it twice? I say, add up the numbers from the cash register, subtract it from the checks from the checkbook.

But no, there have to be ledgers and accounts payable and amortization schedules."

"Here's a strawberry soda. Sit down, drink it, relax. What time did Linna say the team party would be over?"

"Four."

"Good. We have some time before I have to go. Between the two of us, we ought to be able to figure this out before Paige gets back and blows a circuit."

The sisters sounded less dire as they talked, and now they were laughing easily. He wiped his face with his free hand. He'd walked right into that one, hadn't he? Just like that, he was the old Heath Murdock again. He couldn't stop the past, even in a place like this, hundreds of miles away from home.

He breathed deep, trying to calm down. He took in the surroundings, as if that reminded the deep places in his gray matter that he was in Montana, not Oregon. It was different here. Dry, with a faint haze of dust in the air. And there was the heat of sunshine baking the earth and wildflowers and, farther away, the growing crops. He was no longer walking the old path. He was no longer a doctor ready to offer aid. He couldn't help anyone.

Not anymore.

The sisters were laughing, and Amy was saying, "Why did you put this here? I can't believe you did that."

Rachel chuckled, as if she found her own mistakes the funniest thing. "Yeah, it's wrong, I know, but all I can say is that it sounded like a good thing at the time."

"You are a horrible bookkeeper, Rachel Elizabeth McKaslin."

"I know. It's not news, so when Paige flips out when she sees what I've done with her books, we'll have to both tell her that I told her so. She just wouldn't listen."

"Rachel, you do realize we couldn't pay someone to do this bad a job on purpose."

"Yeah, yeah."

It was a good-natured conversation. Heath didn't mean to listen in, but his feet seemed to have become cemented to the stair beneath his boots. The sisters went on talking, laughing and joking as if they were the best of friends. The deputy's words came back to him. *I've never met a nicer family.... They're the kind of folks who don't think about getting more than they give.* That would sure be a change in his life, he thought, glad that he was going to stay.

He eased down onto the step and let the filtered sunlight from the reaching branches of the trees next door flicker over him. The rustle of leaves, the distant drone of a tractor, the hum of a passing bumblebee, the warm murmur of voices from inside the restaurant...these sounds soothed at the knot of tension he always carried with him.

He felt better than he had in a long, long while. He took a deep breath, letting the clean country air fill him up. A movement through the leaves caught his attention—it was a kindly-looking elderly lady in the next house down the alley a ways. He watched her amble down her porch in a baggy blouse and jeans. The brightly colored garden gloves on her hands and the wide-brimmed hat shading her face told of her intentions.

It was timeless, the picture she made as she knelt at her flowerbeds and bent to work. Maybe weeding, he decided, as she produced one of those metal claws from behind a bush and attacked the ground. A smoke-gray cat sauntered from the shaded porch and curled around the lady, who took off a glove to scratch beneath the feline's chin.

Heath could almost hear the contented purr. Or maybe it was the memory of how his grandmother used to tend her vegetable garden on hands and knees, humming one of her favorite tunes—she was always humming. And he was reminded of how she'd stop to indulge one pet or the other as well as her grandson, whose baseballs often went astray in her flowerbeds.

Those were good memories, and he ached from remembering in a different way. He'd been happy as a boy visiting them. And sitting here remembering made the agony within him ease. Not that he'd ever be happy. No, never that.

The sisters were laughing again, their voices closer, coming from the kitchen by the sound of it. There was some clanging and a bang of cupboards, and then a triumphant, "I found it!"

He wondered what they'd been looking for as the voices faded away to a distant murmur. They must have gone into the dining area.

Quiet filled him. It wasn't happiness, but it was something positive. It felt right that he was here, working for people who were honest and worked hard. And, judging from those roughnecks who'd caused trouble in the lonely diner at night, maybe he could do some good here at the same time. Keep a protective eye on the sisters while he built up his cash funds. It felt right to have the chance to do some good.

It had been a long time since he'd made a difference anywhere.

Chapter Six

"Listen up, bird, you don't want to make a nest on my nice table. Really." The woman's kind words matched the gentle morning.

From his place at the open window at the small table in the kitchen, Heath couldn't see who was talking to birds this early in the morning but he recognized Amy's voice.

He shoved back his chair, neatly missing the refrigerator, and with cup of instant coffee in hand let his curiosity lead him downstairs and around the corner of the building. Maybe she could use some help.

The rumbling rhythm of the train rolling down the steel tracks hid the sound of his footsteps as he rounded a tall hedge of blooming lilacs to the gate through the latticed fence around the outside eating area. Small climbing roses, their buds closed tight, clung to the tall crisscrossed wall, and beyond the green leaves and canes, he could see Amy's profile as she cleaned up the beginning of a bird's nest on one of the patio tables.

The robin hopped from the corner edge of the wall to the top of a chair back. The red-breasted bird looked determined to build her nest. She carried a sturdy tuft of a twig in her beak. The creature did not move, even though Amy was only on the other side of the small metal table.

"I'm sorry, this is my table. You can't build a nest here. Besides, it's not far enough off the ground. There's a cat just across the alley." Amy gathered up the last of the twigs the bird had nestled between the rod of the umbrella and the folded tablecloth yet to be spread out. "This isn't a safe place for your babies anyway."

The robin cocked her head and chirped before lifting her wings as if ready to fight.

He really ought to step in and help Amy out, but this was a wild bird. Surely it would take off at any minute.

But it didn't. Amy deposited the twigs in a small bag she'd produced from her pile of cushions and tablecloths in disarray on another tabletop.

"I'm really sorry," she explained as she sprayed down the table and wiped it clean. "You have to find somewhere else to make your home."

The bird didn't move.

"Please, shoo." She waved her hand at the robin,

who still refused to fly off. "The health department won't like it if you live here. Go. Shoo."

The robin chirped angrily before deciding to retreat to the fence.

"Good. Thank you."

Amy disappeared inside the restaurant, absorbed in her work, moving quick and fast. Her hair was wet from showering and pulled back at her nape. She didn't see him standing on the other side of the gate.

He didn't want to startle her, so he was glad the latch squeaked and the hinges rasped as if they hadn't been opened in years. It was enough noise that she popped her head out the door, spotted him and smiled.

"Good morning. You don't know how happy I am to see you. This is by far our busiest time of the week. Sunday brunch." She was friendly but all business as she led the way to the coffeepot and reached down two cups. "Don't tell me you're drinking that instant stuff someone left in the cupboard about five years ago?"

"It tastes all right."

"No it doesn't." With a smile, she took his cup and gave him a fresh one.

He breathed in the good-quality coffee. "Thanks."

"Rachel said you did great last night and that you've worked a few grills before, from the looks of it. She was very impressed."

"I worked at a truck stop in Dillon for a time. A few other places before that."

That explained it. Amy dumped creamer into her cup, gave thanks and drank deep. The rich taste soothed her. She'd been up late last night, going over the books as she'd promised her sister. Rachel was starting to be much better at bookkeeping than she would admit, but Amy knew she wasn't the most confident person. She'd double-checked her sister's work, just so Rachel would rest easy. Everything was right, squared away and ready for Paige's inspection later this afternoon.

"Do you think you're up to manning the grill? It'll take two to keep up, once church lets out."

"I'm up to it."

"Great." With coffee in hand, she rushed back to the side door, calculating how much she could get done in the time she had left. There were the tables to wipe, the cloths to spread out and anchor down, the new cushions to put in every chair, and she wanted a good sweeping before—

Wings fluttered in the air in front of her face. It was the robin. The bird had apparently taken her advice, the tabletop would not make the best place to raise her family, and now she was starting a nest in the spokes of one of the umbrellas.

"Not again." Amy skidded to a halt as the bird lighted on a chair back and glared right back at her.

"This is why I can't grow flowers or a vegetable garden. I can't chase anything off. Not the deer that walk right up to my home and eat my lilacs and carrot tops. Not even a bird who should know this is a bad place to build a nest." She looked at her watch. There was no way she had time to wage a battle of any kind. "Could I ask you—?"

"Sure." He moved past her, waving his free hand. "You have to find a better place, sorry."

The robin took one look at him and fluttered off, perhaps for good.

"Thank you. I'm running behind this morning." She had a nice smile, a sincere one, and he was glad he'd been able to help.

It felt good and solid in his chest. "Want me to set up here? I can do it."

"That would be great. I've got to run and pop the cinnamon rolls into the fridge. Oh, that reminds me. Do you attend church?"

It was a question simply spoken without judgment or expectation. But Heath felt a thud in the center of his chest, and it was as if everything inside him were falling. He gripped the chair for support as he tried to say without malice, "No. I don't attend."

"Okay. I would have offered you a ride, but if you'd rather stay, Jodi should be in any time. Oh—" Amy cocked her head, listening. The tiny gold crosses at her earlobes winked in the sun. "Oh, here she is. I'll tell her you'll be here to help. I know she'll appreciate it."

In the next heartbeat, she was gone, going about her morning work as if it was just another Sunday

morning, another day in her week. Leaving him alone
to try to calm the rush of memories he could not stomach. Memories he did not want.

Up in the trees beyond the privacy wall and the tall
lilac bushes, the robin chirped. The train rumbling by
brought with it the last of the cars and its cabooses.
He waited until the train's noise grew softer, until it
was gone. He waited until the sounds of the morning,
of the leaves and the birds and the clatter of dishes
inside the diner crowded out the shadows.

Quietly, purposefully, he wiped down the tables,
snapped the freshly laundered tablecloths into place
and figured out the strange decorative clips that held
the cloths down in the wind. He heard Amy's car
start in the lot behind the restaurant and the tires
rasp on the pavement as she drove away. He caught
sight of her as she pulled onto the main road in front
of the diner.

She waved, friendly but with that polished manner
of hers that kept her shield firmly in place. Cool and
firm and polite. If he hadn't seen her with the wild
bird, he never would have guessed she was such a
sweetheart. So soft and good of spirit that wild birds
did not fear her.

He knew, too, that he and Amy were more alike
than different, and that was oddly surprising. A
small-town waitress and a big-city doctor. Maybe
that's why he felt as if he wanted to stay on. Because
he saw a kindred spirit in Amy McKaslin. She, too,

kept nearly everyone at a distance, kept safe. Did she, he wondered, recognize the same in him, too?

He wondered what pain she hid so carefully. She looked lovely, the kind of woman who'd probably had a golden life growing up in this cozy small town. Adored by her family, she probably had been a cheerleader and class valedictorian.

But that didn't make a person immune to tragedy. To pain. He knew from first-hand experience that no one had the perfect life, no matter how it seemed. There was no telling what scars were hidden deep inside a person.

Somewhere nearby church bells tolled, rich and resonant.

Feeling ties from the past, ones he could not face, he retreated inside. He shut the door behind him so he could no longer hear the bells.

While he treasured the silence, he felt no peace.

"...and then Mrs. Winkler said God made all the stars in the heavens." Westin paused to cough into his fist, straining against his car booster seat.

Amy glanced anxiously into the rearview mirror, but he looked fine. His color was good. His next breath came clear. Maybe the new medicine the specialist had prescribed was doing its job. *Please, Lord.* She wanted a normal childhood for her little boy. With all of her heart.

To her delight, Westin shook his head as he often

did, and ran his fingers through his hair. The fine strands stood straight up from static electricity. He was beyond cute.

And he knew it, too. He gave a charming grin and kept on with his story. "I asked about the galaxies, too, and Mrs. Winkler said that the stars in the heavens means the galaxies, too, but she's wrong. I told her that galaxies are not stars. And that the galaxies are speeding away." He held up his hands as if he were holding a globe and pulled them apart. "She must not got any cable. Or she'd know that."

"Not everyone watches the science shows."

He looked crestfallen. "Me and George better pray for her so she can have cable." He grabbed his ragged Snoopy dog, which had been his favorite stuffed toy for most of his life.

"That's a good idea, baby."

"Yeah, I know." While squeezing George around his middle, Westin bowed his head. His lips moved in an earnest prayer.

She couldn't help keeping one eye on the mirror. Her little boy was her everything. She felt as if she shone from the inside out from simply watching him.

Since the morning was pleasant and sunny, she had her windows down. She had escaped a few minutes early from the overflowing church parking lot, and was already on her way along the tree-lined residential streets to work.

As she drove, Pastor Bill's sermon weighed on her;

while she usually felt renewed and refreshed after Sunday service, she didn't today. Today she felt unsettled. She would have preferred a sermon that hadn't made her think of the man she'd hired. But the message and text had struck her hard, giving her a gnawing feeling that she could have handled things much better with Heath.

"Mom!" Westin squirmed, drawing her attention, all bridled energy. She marveled at how the seat belt managed to hold him still as he lunged against it and stretched his arm as far as possible so the stuffed dog popped up next to her head rest. "George wants strawberry waffles with the white stuff."

"Whipped cream. Not syrup? I thought George liked syrup."

"He changed his mind, but he wants lots of sausage."

"With syrup or ketchup?"

"Both!"

It was good to see her little one in good spirits—it was more than she could say for herself.

The Lord does not look at the things man looks at. Man looks at the outward appearance, but the Lord looks at the heart. That was the text Pastor Bill had spoken on in his compassionate and compelling way. The verse from 1 Samuel wasn't something she'd read in a while—with Paige gone, she'd been too busy to make the last two weeks of her Bible study group, and with Westin's asthma peaking since Christmas, her attendance had been spotty. Maybe that's why today's passage had taken hold of her, as if her spirit was hungry.

Man looks at the outward appearance. Is that what she was guilty of? Making, if not judgments about Heath, then certainly assessments. He was down on his luck; it sure looked that way. He wore clean but far from new clothes. His truck was at least twenty years old.

But he'd left Jodi a good tip, and Rachel had said he'd worked hard when she'd called early in the morning to go over the week's work schedule she'd made.

"I don't know what Heath told you," Rachel had reported. "But he has a talent of understatement and a gift of modesty. I was prepared to work two jobs, training him and cooking, which, as you know, is demanding on our busiest night of the week. But he just took over. Ten minutes into the dinner rush, he was handling the grill like a pro."

"You're kidding." Amy had nearly dropped the phone as she rummaged through her dresser drawers looking for socks to match her tan trousers. Amy had assumed Heath was like so many others who passed through looking for work. Some were not to be trusted, but others, they had their reasons for wandering.

That's what she'd assumed about Heath. But she could only see his outward appearance. The Lord could look into everyone's heart, sure, but how could she? She knew from lessons learned that a man can show one face convincingly, but his motives and his agendas and his true nature can stay well hidden.

She zipped down the alley and into the back lot, recognizing the few cars parked there. Rachel hadn't beaten her here, but Cousin Kelly had, and the clatter and bang behind the screen door told her Jodi was busy already.

"Grab your backpack, please," she told her son as soon as she'd cut the engine and tucked the keys into her pants pocket.

"George is coming, too."

"Then hold him tight." Amy bent, jamming one knee on the back seat so she could help Westin. He squirmed and struggled and yanked on the buckle and bopped from the seat the instant he was free.

Amy backed up, waiting as he bounded from the car holding his stuffed dog around its middle and holding onto his backpack's strap with the other. She shut the door, remembered to grab her purse and followed him in.

Her boy bounded ahead of her, his backpack bouncing in rhythm to his gait and poor George, loose-limbed from years of being dragged around, jiggled like a rag doll. He yanked open the screen door with great zeal and the old hinges squealed in protest.

Westin skidded to a halt in midstride. "Hey! You're not supposed to be in here. Mom, he's a stranger."

Amy removed her sunglasses. Heath had his back to the grill, staring at Westin as if he'd never seen a child before. He probably hadn't realized she had a son. Maybe he hadn't noticed the pictures of Westin tacked in the little office, along with Paige's teenage boy's photos. "Heath, this is my son, Westin. Westin, what do you say?"

"I'm pleased to meet you, sir." Westin snapped to attention like a little soldier. He held out his dog. "And so is George. Did you know the star that's closest to the earth is called Alpha Centauri and it's four light years away?"

Instead of answering, Heath stared.

He was probably unaware of the exciting facts about space, so Amy ruffled Westin's head. "Go and find Kelly. She's waiting for you."

"Okay, Mom." He paused to cough quickly in his fist and kept on talking. "But light years aren't like real years. They're, like, way bigger. Light travels so fast it's like this. Zoom." He held his hand level and, imitating a rocket, his hand shot upward. "That's fast."

"Uh, yeah." Heath looked bewildered.

She couldn't blame him. He'd probably spent little or no time around children. "Go. Quick. I've got to get to work."

"Okay, but I got this book in here," he tapped on his backpack, "and it's about our space and stuff. Did you know—"

"Go," Amy interrupted. "You'd better hurry. I bet George is hungry."

"Oh, yeah! George always wants sausages." Westin took off for the double doors, giving them a mighty shove so they smacked against the wall and swung back and forth hard.

She caught glimpses of him dashing over to Kelly at a booth, where her college books lay open before her. Her face lit up with greeting and she gave George and Westin kisses on their cheeks. With her son being cared for, now she could turn her thoughts to work.

But Heath had returned to the grill, stirring scrambled eggs with the spatula as if it took every bit of his concentration. His back was an insurmountable barrier between them.

Maybe he didn't like children. Or maybe the issue was with her. Lord help her, she could not forget what he'd said to her so cruelly. *Whatever it is you're thinking you can get from me, forget it.* He was a good-looking man. Perhaps he was used to women thinking they'd be the ones to land him. To put a ring on his finger and chain him down in one place.

She didn't know. Before her old bitterness could surge up, she tasted it sour in the back of her throat. She didn't want to be bitter, but it wasn't easy. She'd tried so long and hard to forgive herself for her shameful mistakes, and Lord knew she did her best to forgive the man who'd hurt her so thoroughly. But remnants remained, flaring up like those geyser fire-storms in the sun.

The Lord looks at the heart. Pastor Bill's under-standing voice filled her head as she washed her hands in the sink. She couldn't see into anyone's heart, not really, but there were probably clues. She watched out of the corner of her eye as she tore off a length of paper towel to dry with. Heath worked sure and efficiently, making omelets now, squinting to read Jodi's scrawl on a ticket before fetching a new package of sausage links from the fridge.

"Looks like you have everything under control." She had to approach him because her apron was hang-ing on a hook next to the refrigerator. "Let me know when you need a hand. It always takes two at the grill on brunches."

"Okay." He lifted one wide shoulder in a shrug, not exactly careless, but the message was clear: stay back.

She could respect that. In fact, she preferred it. A polite and efficient working relationship worked for her. She reached around to tie a bow at the small of her back as he passed by her. The faint aroma of soap and spicy aftershave made something stir inside her. A yearning for the life with a husband she'd always dreamt of. The comforting hugs, the sizzling kisses, the shared closeness.

It was odd she'd feel any longing for that old, spent dream. She had too many years under her belt to be-lieve romantic love existed. Maybe that's what women wanted to believe. Maybe it's what they needed to believe.

Every once in awhile, it probably did happen. She'd see it now and then, the genuine tie of deep affection that bound husbands and wives together. It was like the glow of dust in the night sky Westin had shown her, the spiral arm of their Milky Way. A soft luminous miracle. True love ought to shine like that.

But miracles were rare. She'd learned for sure that the fall was not worth the risk. She'd already had one miracle in her life, she thought, as she pushed through the doors and checked on the number of empty tables. As Rachel rushed in the front door to help seat families, Amy spotted Westin, hunched over a book on the table, showing Kelly something very important on the page.

She had her one miracle in life. It was enough.

On her way to check on the status of the buffet, she stopped to say hello to her cousins—Kendra was nice enough to have already copied off the video of Westin's game. Her uncle Pete and aunt Alice always had a kind word to say to her. There were friends from school with families of their own now, with their greetings. She received many compliments on the food.

She fetched fresh fruit trays from the fridge, warmed cinnamon rolls to set out, helped with the coffee refills while Rachel, late and breathless, took over hostess duties. She checked on Westin and

George—their order of strawberry waffles and sausages had been a big hit.

The diner hummed with the scrape of flatware and the ring of stoneware and the cheerful rise and fall of conversations. Kids clamored around the dessert table, excited by the choices while their parents talked and leisurely went for seconds from the buffet. Neighbors and friends would stop to talk in the aisles, and through the order-up window Amy could see Heath, cap on, his attention focused on his work. She never saw him look up at the crowd, only to read order tickets or Rachel's scrawl on what was running low at the buffet.

"Oh, the crepes were divine." Kelly pulled her aside. "I see you have a new cook. He's great."

"That's what everybody's been saying." She felt arms wrap around her waist and hold on.

It was her son with his big grin and sparkling eyes who gave her a tight squeeze and then hopped away. "George and I have to go, Mom!"

"You two be good for Kelly." The sight of her little boy walking out of her sight tugged at her, as it always did. Already she missed him.

Pastor Bill and his wife were the last of the after-church crowd to arrive, as usual, looking composed and happy and friendly. It was impossible not to want to give them a hug, which Amy did, and offered them their choice of available tables. They wanted outside beneath the umbrellas, for the afternoon was a beautiful one.

This is why she was so grateful to live in this small rural town in the middle of farming country. It was far from the bustle of larger, urban centers that as a teenage girl she'd thought were exciting. But she'd been wrong.

Roots. Family. Community. There was no place like home. No place.

And what about Heath? The talented cook fate—or, more correctly, God—had sent their way. He worked so well, he needed no help on the busiest of times and he kept to himself, alone, lost in shadows.

Jodi was wrong. There was more than a great sorrow about him, wrapping him up like a blanket. It was so sharp and agonizing, Amy could feel it radiating off him like heat from an August sidewalk.

Through the order-up window and across the length of the diner, their gazes met. Locked. A jolt of blackness shocked her so deep in her heart it forced the air from her lungs.

Unable to blink and unable to look away, she gasped for breath. Shocked, she realized it was his heart she saw before he turned his back, breaking the connection.

He did not look her way again.

Chapter Seven

Heath couldn't get the image out of his mind. The image of Amy McKaslin with her son. He hadn't guessed that she was a mom. Nope, he couldn't reconcile it. Maybe because he didn't want to.

All through the afternoon and into the evening he worked. The diner closed at eight, early on Sunday nights. There had been no place open on the six-block length of the main street, except the dark-tinted neon lights in the far alley at the edge of town—the tavern.

He knew how it would be inside that dim, small building. The air would be soured with smoke where men sucked down alcohol to hide from their troubles. There'd be darts and a pool table—nothing worth going in for. He'd seen it all before and he wasn't interested.

He'd learned the hard way. There wasn't anything strong enough to obliterate his problems or anesthetize his pain, so he climbed the stairs to his apartment and sat in the tepid current of the window air conditioner and watched a movie of the week on the TV. He played with the rabbit ears until he had a pretty good picture and not much static.

That night he tossed and turned as dark images haunted him. He woke as wet as if he'd been drowning in the Atlantic waters, sweat sluicing down his face and stinging in his eyes.

The television mumbled in the background—he must have fallen asleep on the couch. The place was hot and the walls seemed to be closing in on him. He did the only thing he could and launched straight to the door, yanked it open and dropped to the steps. Gulped in the cool night air.

A train gave a long low note of warning as it rumbled through town. The rhythmic hum of engines and the grinding on the steel tracks hid the calm night. It was like the noise of a city, traffic and a background hum that never silenced.

For an instant Heath's mind hooked him back into the past: the whine of trucks downshifting on the interstate had accompanied him as he'd bounded out of the emergency-room doors, rain pouring down his face, slick beneath his shoes, glossing the blacktop of the Portland hospital's emergency zone. Images assaulted him: ambulances' strobes, the hustle of the team, the bright crimson splash of blood on the sheet-covered gurney—

Thunder exploded like a gunshot, startling him out

of the past. He let the cold and wind wash over him. Breathed in the metallic scent of thunder and waited for the lightning to flare.

There it was, a jagged finger thrust from the sky to the distant fields. One, two, three, four...

I gotta get out of here. Thunder crashed like metal through the iridescent clouds. Heath swiped the wetness from his face, not sure if it was only rain. How had he made such a big mistake? He never would have taken the job if he'd known about the boy. That's what he got for acting on impulse. For thinking he could stay awhile. What was it about those big blue eyes of Amy's that made him feel as if he'd be all right?

He was alone. He was always going to be alone. There would never be anyone to understand, anyone to turn to and no chance to change the past and make things right. He'd give his life, his soul, everything and anything if only he could go back in time to that crucial moment on another night of rain and thunder. Change one little second. One tiny decision. If only...

There were no "if only"s. The past was done with. He'd been over it a hundred billion times. Looking back wouldn't bring him closer to what he deserved.

Leave. That's what he'd do. He hated to run out on Amy, when she'd been worried he was the type of man who would do just that. He let the wind and rain blow him through the front door and it took less than two minutes to jam the few possessions he'd removed from the worn duffel bag back into it. With a final zip, he was done. He settled the strap on his shoulder and turned off the window unit and the TV, feeling lower than low. It was a cheap shot, taking off without so much as a note.

What would he say to the McKaslins? Leave them a note that he'd made a mistake and to keep his paycheck. Brunch and the Sunday supper crowd had brought in enough tips to give him adequate traveling cash.

As the cold rain and violent night enveloped him, he dug his truck keys from his pocket. Rain streaked down his face and got into his eyes. With his free hand he wiped at his face and almost missed the sound of glass breaking.

At first he thought it came from the alley, maybe from the direction of the old woman's house, but he heard it again. He swore the crashing sound of shattering glass came right behind him. But that didn't make any sense. Who'd be out in this storm? Lightning shot like a flare from west to east and reflected in a bright flash on a vehicle's windshield.

Then darkness reclaimed the night. Rain pelted with wild abandon from a hateful sky beating Heath back as he tossed his duffel to the ground at the bottom of the stairs and ran around the front. Wet branches hung low with the weight of the rain and sodden leaves slapped his face and head. He didn't stop. Thunder drowned out the sound of a loud cowboylike holler somewhere near the front door.

Heath knew who those men were before he skidded around the corner in a patch of loose gravel, so he wasn't a bit surprised when he saw the two low-lifes he'd chased off before. They stood side by side without a coat or heavy shirt against the mean storm, laughing with their hands full of big rocks.

"This here is for the deputy comin' by my place." The taller one pitched a heavy rock through the window.

Heath cringed at the tinkling sound of shattering glass. Rain spilled through the jagged, gaping hole in the window. Fury hurling him forward, he tore into the open like a wild man. Heath's vision turned red as he tackled both men and rolled them out on the road.

"Hey, man!" one of the troublemakers held up his hands, surrendering. Blood stained his hair where he'd hit the curb.

"This ain't your business!" The other twisted onto his feet, shook off the rain and raised both fists. "You want to fight, we'll fight—"

The strong scent of cheap whisky and cheaper vodka tainted the wind. All Heath could think was that it was guys like this. They were responsible. Drinking and careless, their judgement impaired. Savage wrath choked him. How did these people do it? How could it be entertaining to hurt someone? How could there be any satisfaction in destroying someone's life? He wanted vengeance. He wanted justice. He wanted his life back.

And men like these. They were responsible—

Headlights sheened on the black river of road and the splashing sound of tires hydroplaning on a skid snapped him back to himself. He felt tall and terrible and broken. Endlessly broken.

Vaguely he was aware of the cruiser door opening, black rain falling like bullets, the thugs shouting and taking off. Their footsteps pounded across the road where water ran like a river and another cruiser squealed to a stop nearby, headlights blaring as another officer joined the hunt. Heath was only a half step behind, his military training kicking in, but in the few seconds it took to cross the road, he saw the two drunks on the ground, facedown in the mud on the other side of the railroad tracks.

"Not the brightest guys," Frank explained later, after the two had been cuffed and hauled away in the sheriff's car. "Down at the tavern they talked about what they were gonna do here. One of the waitresses heard the whole thing and called me the minute those two were out the door. Good thing, too. Look at this."

Frank shook his head in disgust at the damage. "It's not too late yet. I'll give John a call and see if he'll open up the hardware store."

Heath's guts twisted looking at the damage. Two sections had been broken out of the large front windows, glass reflecting darkly with the rain and the night. There was only one thing to do. "I'm fairly good with a hammer. I figure I can get this boarded up before—"

Headlights pierced the black storm, coming as if out of nowhere. Heath knew it was Amy even before the dome light flashed on to reveal her face pinched and pale. She'd drawn her hair back in a quick ponytail and a shank of hair lay twisted and at an angle over her cowlick. The storm deluged her in the ten seconds it took for her to race through the light beams to the sidewalk.

"Careful." He held out his arm to stop her. "Glass."

"Oh, yeah." She hadn't looked down. Dazed, she froze, staring at the wreckage with rainwater sluicing down her face, wetting her hair so that even the shank trying to stand up became slicked to her head. Her coat clung to her willowy frame and she looked younger, much too young to be a mother of a grade-school boy. She looked so vulnerable it made Heath's rage flare again.

"They'll pay for this," he ground out, his hands finding the curves of her shoulders. "Every penny. I'll make sure of it."

"It's not just the glass. Oh, look, it's just so much damage."

Her reaction came so quietly, without hysteria or upset or anger. Beneath his hands, the rounded curve of her shoulders quivered—with fear or repressed anger or just from the cold he couldn't tell. She was fragile, feminine and small—and as he towered behind her to block her from the brunt of the icy rain, his chest jolted from the inside out. It was as if the locked door had been wrenched open a scant inch and feeling poured through him.

"Paige is going to split a seam when she sees this. She just got back tonight—" She sounded lost, as if she didn't have the first clue where to start. "What about breakfast? We won't be able to open."

"We'll get it boarded up. Frank—" Heath glanced around, but the deputy was nowhere to be seen. His car idled along the curb where he'd left it. Maybe he was making the phone call to the hardware-store owner. "I'm here anyway. I might as well take care of it."

"No, this isn't your problem. That's good of you, but, oh, I don't think we're insured for something like this. We only have basic liability."

Solid. He hadn't felt like this since the old days. Steady and calm and ready to handle what came. He saw the ghost of the man he used to know inside him as lightning flashed. In the brief illumination, he saw his reflection in the shattered window. Cracked and distorted, black in places, that was him. There was no way to repair damage like that. It wasn't like a window a worker could remove from its frame and fit in a new one as good as new.

No, the human spirit wasn't like that.

As swift as the lightning came, it vanished, the brilliant white light receding into the darkness. But the hole—the void inside him—remained. Which did he choose? The void or the light? The road rolled out behind him, gleaming darkly with streaming water, gurgling like a current toward the edge of town and beyond.

I want that path. He craved oblivion like an addiction. Desperately he'd take anything to stop the feelings flowing through him like the floodwater, fast and ruthless. His duffel bag was within reach, sitting in a puddle, and it would be nothing at all to grab it up and go. No, he'd fix her windows first, then go. He'd be safe, he'd never have to remember—

She sniffed, wiped at her eyes with the tip of her finger and let out a shaky breath. He didn't know why, but he could feel the wave of her shock rolling through him like an ocean tide. Rolling higher until he was full of it. He did not want to be the one to comfort her. He didn't want to be the man she turned to, because her need and her touch would make him real again, would make him alive again. All he wanted was the night and the darkness.

He deserved nothing more.

"There's no sense in you standing in the rain." He took one long look at his drenched duffel bag, knowing this would take him where he didn't want to go. But he couldn't walk away. "C'mon, let's get you inside."

She fumbled in her pocket. "Oh, they're in my car. The keys."

Crestfallen. That's how she looked, staring in disbelief. "Nobody's hurt. That's the important thing. It's just glass. It can be fixed. I don't know why I'm so shook up."

"You and your sisters don't deserve this, that's why." He hated leaving her, but it gave him time to let the cold settle across his face. Breathing deep, he let the night batter him and knock its way inside until he felt icy calm.

He killed the engine and took the keys, flicked off the headlights and shut the door. The street was flooded, and his splashing steps gave him something to think about other than the woman standing alone and the road whispering to take him away.

"What are you?" She studied him with fathomless eyes, shadowed and unreadable as he unlocked the front door, the bottom half shattered.

"What am I? Most people ask who." He gave the rock on the carpet a shove with his foot and swept the big shards of glass out of a path with the side of his boot. With care, so he wouldn't get cut. The big chunks scraped out of the way,

"Careful," he told her as she inched by him, her shoulder warm and wet against his chest.

"Oh, look at this. What is wrong with people?" The first flush of a healthy fury spread across her cheeks. "I can't thank you enough for being here. You probably stopped this from being a whole lot worse."

"I don't know about that." Guilt kept him from

saying the truth. The rain hammering the roof echoed and amplified the sound in the empty restaurant. "Right place at the right time, I guess."

"You have a knack f-for it," she said as her teeth chattered.

He cradled her small hands between his. "You're ice. Sit. I'll get you something hot."

"Oh, n-no, you don't have to wait on me. I can—"

"You didn't even wear a warm jacket." He released her hands and peeled off the thin coat, more like a windbreaker than anything. No wonder she was borderline hypothermic. "Sit."

"But I—"

"Don't argue." The words came out harsher than he'd intended. Her eyes rounded and she dropped into the nearest booth.

He shouldn't be taking his feelings out on her. This wasn't her fault. He still wanted to leave. Maybe it was better if he did. He could talk to her some, tell her enough so she'd understand. Yeah, it sounded like a plan, but it didn't set right in his stomach as he flipped on the light and went in search of the right ingredients.

"If a wild-eyed woman comes bursting through the door, don't call Frank. It's my sister Paige. She's used to being in charge. I'm warning you before she shows up so you're prepared."

The pot clanked on the burner. "Why do I need to be prepared?"

"Because you look at me, Rachel and Jodi funny."

"What do you mean by funny?"

"Like you're wondering how fast you can make it to the door."

"You mean, in case of a fire?"

Amy swiped the wet bangs plastered to her face. He was going to joke, was he? She couldn't believe it. "Are you denying it?"

"Yep." Clangs came from deep inside the shadowed kitchen. He'd turned on only the small light over the sink, and the rip of the refrigerator door opening had her wondering what he was fixing.

"Hot tea is fine. Maybe I should—"

"Stay." His command was firm.

If she wasn't still so shaky, she'd give him a piece of her mind. Amy Marie McKaslin did not take orders from any man.

Not ever again.

The diner phone rang. Her sisters knew she was here. She'd promised to call right away and report in, but she had yet to do it. She knew Paige would be rushing here, driving as fast as the storm would allow. So that left Rachel at home with Westin wondering what had happened. Talking to her sister sure sounded like a good idea. She'd feel a lot better just to hear Rachel's voice.

But Heath beat her to the phone, turning his strong back toward her and cradling the receiver against his ear. His deep baritone rumbled low and the storm blowing inside made it impossible to hear his words.

What she needed to do was to get up and start cleaning up. The damage was ugly, but it could be made right so they could open tomorrow. That wasn't what had hit her so hard.

It was the shock of seeing the destruction. It was as if the past had come back around. Seeing the black reflective shards on the carpet made her remember, when she didn't want to ever think about that time in her life again.

Heath ambled toward her, as shadowed as the night surrounding him, and stood just shy of the fall of light through the door. He made a fine picture standing there like something out of a movie. Wet dark hair was plastered to his scalp, his face was damp, his jacket clung to his linebacker's shoulders and his worn black jeans were snug against his long lean legs.

He swiped his fingers through his hair. "That was the deputy. The store owner told him where the spare key was hidden and said to help ourselves."

"That would be John through and through. He's one of the good guys."

"The way you say that makes it sound like we're far and few."

"I didn't know you were one of the good guys." Her throat ached and she looked away. She'd meant to tease, but it had backfired on her. She'd long ago given up trying to figure out which were the genuine men and which were the ones in sheep's clothing. She hardly knew Heath...did she even know his last name? Rachel had given him paperwork to fill out, not that Amy had had time to look.

He said nothing more. His waterlogged boots squished as he left. Amy rubbed her face, but that didn't help the pain building behind her forehead or the fact she had a long night ahead of her. What she ought to do is start cleaning up the glass. Get it out of the way so she could board up the windows.

It felt better to have a plan and it gave her something else to think about besides the man in the kitchen rescuing a cup from the microwave. She could see him at work at the counter—stirring something into the steaming cup, reaching up to search through the cupboard, standing at attention like a soldier as he contemplated his choices.

"I love any kind of tea," she told him, pushing off the booth's bench seat and finding out her legs were steady again. She hadn't taken two steps when Heath shouldered through the doors with one of the huge latte mugs in hand.

"Where do you think you're going? Sit down and drink this. No, it's not tea."

He meant business, she could see that. His gaze pinned hers with a no-nonsense look. His jaw drew tight. He looked about as easy to push over as a heavyweight boxing champion. "It's hot chocolate?"

"With everything on it but a cherry, because I couldn't find any in the pantry."

"I can't believe you did this." She hardly looked at the rich cocoa heaped with whipped cream and dribbled with chocolate. "I thought you were nuking some tea water."

"No, this is better." He fumbled, self-conscious, as he slid the brimming cup before her.

"I'll say. Thank you."

"It's what my mom always made me when I was down and out." And my wife, he didn't add. There was a lot he didn't add. "I told Frank I'd come over and help him. We'll get a couple of pieces of plywood in place, and that'll keep out the rain and any skunks or creatures looking to get out of the rain."

"I'm perfectly capable of helping, too. This is my family's diner. I ought to—"

"No. The hot chocolate will warm you up. You've got a heavy load to carry, being a single mom. And I—" His chest hitched and he didn't want to care. He didn't. So he said nothing more and backed away toward the door, feeling the night and the endless road calling to him.

A tall, brown-haired woman with Amy's big blue eyes and nearly the same delicate structure to her face climbed out of the storm, crunching across glass on heavy, tooled riding boots. "What is wrong with people? I leave for a week and this place falls apart. Who are you?"

"The cook." He slipped past her, figuring this had to be the oldest sister everyone had talked about.

Paige McKaslin gave him one measuring glance, seemed to find him below par and dismissed him with an efficient shake of her head. "Amy? What's going on here? I know our insurance isn't going to cover this."

Heath left the sisters alone and took refuge in the endless night. The rain was calming, but the storm had tossed broken tree branches into the road. The big round headlight of the oncoming train seemed to hover eerily in the dark gleaming night.

He rescued his duffel; everything inside had to be sopping wet. He hefted the strap and water gushed out from the bottom of the bag. He tossed it under the eaves at the apartment door and a motion caught his attention in the shadowed window.

Amy moved away, her arms wrapped around her middle.

He understood without knowing why that she'd seen the bag. She knew that he'd packed and would leave her high and dry without a cook, just as she'd feared he would. Her disappointment rolled like fog misting up from a river. It shamed him, but there were worse things.

She didn't wake at night, locked in a nightmare without end and hearing the cries of her child dying, the way he did.

He prayed to God she never would.

Chapter Eight

Amy sat in her car, shivering in the chilly dampness. Paige's black SUV blended with the dark world, the taillights floating pinpoints of light as smokelike fog rose from the sodden earth like thousands of souls to heaven.

Amy had felt much better after Heath's cup of cocoa. The rich velvety brew had melted the shock from her system and warmed her up enough for her synapses to start firing again. She'd helped Heath and Frank hold and nail the sheets of plywood, while Paige swept up the glass, and, with a wet vac, dried up most of the rain damage.

Except for the two booths nearest the door, every table was fine. They'd be open for breakfast bright and early at 6:00 a.m. as usual, which, according to her battered sports watch, was two hours and five minutes away. She could snatch a little sleep—it wouldn't be much, but some was better than none.

It sounded like a good idea, but the dark windows above the diner kept drawing her attention.

She remembered how hard Heath had worked alongside Frank, competently driving nails with a hammer as if he'd been a carpenter somewhere along the line. She could picture it, him in a hard hat, a T-shirt and jeans, thick heavy boots and a carpenter's belt at his hips. His face, neck and arms were sun-browned, as if he'd worked outside in his last job.

So, what was he doing working as a cook? He'd make so much more as a union tradesman. And why was his bag packed and dropped, as if he'd been on his way out for good without so much as a goodbye, just as she'd pegged him for.

Yeah, she could pick 'em. The only type of man she seemed to attract was the kind that left. Commit-ment-shy, free-and-easy, or simply wanting an entan-glement-free life. That's why she'd given up hoping she'd ever find a good man to marry. She had a son, she had a mortgage payment and she had responsi-bilities to her sisters that went beyond part ownership of the restaurant.

Responsibility was a concept few men grasped— maybe it was just the effect of testosterone on the brain. Whatever it was, she'd found out it was easier and safer to keep every single one of them at a rea-sonable distance. Tonight had been illuminating for very good reasons—every time she began to weaken God had a way of reminding her.

Deeply grateful, she shivered in the cool blow of the defroster, waiting for the engine to warm up. If she closed her eyes, she could still see it. The smashed window crisscrossed with fractures like a giant spider's web. The dresser's mounted mirror in the little bedroom she'd rented in an older neighborhood in Seattle's university district. The tiny window in the front door. The windshield of her car. Glass shards cutting her bare feet as she hurried to sweep them up. From her favorite little juice glasses with the daisies on them. From a beer bottle thrown against the kitchen wall.

It was important to remember. Never to forget. She already had what she needed. Her son. Her family. There was no need to look for more. She had enough. More than she thought she deserved, and that made her grateful.

As for Heath—the image remained of his shadow moving across the darker background of the storm, rescuing his duffel bag from the wet ground and taking it back upstairs. Had he changed his mind about leaving? Or was he merely getting his pack out of the rain?

It was probably the latter. Men left. It's what they did. He'd taken one look at her son and leaped to the wrong conclusion, thinking that she was on the hunt for a husband. Isn't that what a working single mom wanted? A man to foot the bills so she wouldn't have to?

If she had a nickel for every time someone advised her to start dating so she didn't have to work so hard, she'd be able to buy her own four-star restaurant on the Seattle waterfront, like she'd always dreamed of.

The last thing she wanted or needed was another man to tell her what was wrong with her, to take over her life and destroy it and run off with every last cent she owned. Whether Heath was that sort of man or not, it didn't make one bit of difference. She wasn't interested.

But maybe he didn't understand that. The way he'd avoided looking at her after he returned from the hardware store with Frank had said it all. The more she thought about it, the angrier she got. She'd do better to take a deep breath, chill out and forget it. Let him leave. She'd get up in... She glanced at the clock, okay, less than two hours' time and man the grill. It was no big deal.

Then why was she so angry?

Because it was easier to feel anger than to face the truth, to pull up the memory of Heath standing at the grill after Westin had talked to him. She'd somehow seen inside him at that moment, to where his heart was as dark as the center of a black hole, a place that allowed no light, nothing but an endlessly collapsing void. What could cause that kind of pain?

She saw the flicker of a movement at the window. It had to be him. She imagined him gazing, not at her but in the opposite direction. Looking east where the road led. Did he regret staying long enough to help her and her sisters out—again?

A lot of men wouldn't have bothered to get involved at all. But he had. He'd chosen to stay when he could have walked away. Was he up there alone in the utter darkness without the benefit of a single light on, wishing he'd made another choice? Making plans to leave with the dawn?

She didn't know why, but if he left that way, she would have regrets. There would always be the feeling that she'd left something undone.

For all his good deeds to her, she'd done nothing in return. Everything within her felt at war. She didn't want to get close to any man—and yet there was something in Heath that tugged at her as if a line ran from his soul to hers. Why else could she feel his pain? See the infinite void within his heart?

She ought to go home, and yet she knew if she did Heath would be gone by morning and she would never know—what, she wasn't sure. She knew she already cared about Heath too much. More than was safe. More than was sensible for a woman with her luck. And yet, she would never rest easy if he were gone come sunrise. *Show me what to do, Lord. Please, I need your guidance.*

Then again, maybe He'd given her enough already. She was exhausted and thinking in circles. She had a son to get home to.

"Car trouble?"

Amy recognized Heath's voice even as adrenaline jetted into her bloodstream and her hand was curling around the strap of her purse to use it as a weapon. He'd scared ten years off her life.

She shoved open the door. "Would you stop doing that?"

"Want to hit the hood lock for me, and I'll take a look." He flicked on a flashlight, the small beam reflected with eye-stinging brightness in the thick fog. "What's the problem?"

"In order for the car to go, the driver has to put it into gear."

"You mean you've been sitting here on purpose? It's almost four in the morning and it's starting to freeze. The roads are already dangerous enough."

"I never thanked you for the hot chocolate."

"That can't be why you're sitting out here alone in the dark. Even in a town like this, it can't be entirely safe." The mist turned into translucent flakes as the water froze in midair, shrouding him with a strange dark light. It made Amy remember how he'd seemed in the kitchen after Westin had left.

"Maybe I'd better drive you," he offered.

"I'm not afraid of a little ice on the road. Goodness, I learned to drive in the winter."

That polite shield again. Heath took in Amy's picture-perfect smile—not too wide, not too bright but just enough. There was nothing appreciably different about her, she was still wearing her thin jacket,

and at least it had dried hanging above the heat duct
in the restaurant. Her hair was still yanked unevenly
back in a quick ponytail that was beginning to sag.
Her flannel pajamas were very eye-catching.

"Isn't that Saturn?"

"As you may have noticed, my little boy is into
astronomy. He got me these for Christmas this year.
Wasn't that thoughtful? They are the softest jammies
I've ever had."

They sure looked soft, quality combed flannel bottoms fell to the tops of her sneakers, and he
was shocked that he noticed the way her slim ankle
showed, just a bit. She was wearing knitted cable
socks that would have made anyone else's ankles look
less than slender and shapely.

Not that he ought to be noticing Amy's ankles—
or any woman's.

He rubbed his left hand, where the ring hadn't
been ever since he'd tossed it off the bridge after
leaving the hospital. When he'd almost gone in the
water with the ring.

Lord knew he hadn't had the courage then. He'd
been naive enough still to believe that there would
be hope somewhere, someday. Hope for what, he
couldn't have said. Maybe it seemed impossible that
something so sudden and horrific could be real.

He'd been in too much shock to realize that trau-
matic things happened all the time. Bad things happening to other people is what had made him, if not

well off, then doing better than most. A new car, a nice house, a boat for Sunday afternoons on the lake.

But time had shown him one thing. His losses were real, death was final and his grief and guilt were never going to end. Every day since, he'd regretted not jumping off the bridge when he'd had the chance.

Although he wasn't much of a churchgoer, not anymore, he was still a believer. And his faith taught that it was against God's law for a man to take his own life…in the end, as much as he'd wanted it, Heath had not been able to choose his own death.

Not that he had chosen to live either. He'd stopped being alive in every way that mattered long ago. What he wanted was oblivion—to keep from remembering, from feeling, to hide from the guilt that rose up like a tsunami. How could he have oblivion if everywhere he went, children made him remember? It wasn't Amy's fault that she was lucky enough to be a mom, that her little boy was alive and well, that he'd picked out pajamas for his mom with a planet design and he was as cute a little boy as Heath had ever seen.

And looking at Amy's son led Heath down the only obvious path. If Christian had lived, what would he have been interested in? Planes? Or trucks? Football or baseball? Would he color with those big chunky crayons made for little kids or would he prefer to finger paint? Would his big brown eyes have sparkled with joy over pancakes and sausages? Would he carry around a stuffed toy everywhere he went?

The tsunami overtook him, obliterating him. Heath took the hit and tried not to let it show. He didn't trust his voice, so he didn't say anything. It was better just to let it pass. It always did...eventually.

"Look at you." There was sympathy in her dulcet voice and her grip settled around his wrist, but it felt distant as if she were touching him through yards of Jell-O.

"What are you doing up at this hour to notice that I'm freezing to death in my car?"

He didn't answer. The air he breathed in scorched the linings of his nose and sinuses and stung deep in his chest. Maybe he could be like the fog, freeze up and just let the pain slide right off his soul.

"You did so much for us tonight." She left the engine idling as she stood and, shivering, searched him as if trying to figure out what was going on inside his skull.

It was private, not her business. He watched the ice particles in the air fall like the tiniest specks of snow and cling to her hair and eyelashes and melt against the softest creamiest skin he'd ever seen on a woman. Her soul shone in her eyes, and as she studied him, he felt as if the deepest part of him had been revealed. Without words. Without communication of any kind.

Sadness shadowed her eyes. "Let me take you upstairs."

"What about your boy?"

"He's asleep in his bed, and he'll be fine for a few

hours more. After Rachel came over to look through the books with Paige, we got to talking. Suddenly it was midnight and so she made up a bed on the air mattress. She does it all the time, which worked out fine tonight, since the tavern called to let me know they'd called the cops and it was providential she was there to stay with Westin."

"That's pretty amazing. Frank told me he'd been called by someone hearing threats." Heath felt as cold as the outside air. "Not a lot of folks would get involved like that."

"We're a small community. I send the tavern a lot of business, you know, tourists looking for cocktails or a cold beer after a hot day in the car. We don't have a liquor license, so I send customers over. They do the same. It works out. I guess it's a small-town thing. Now, will you go upstairs before we both freeze? Or will I have to carry you up?"

"You've got to be kidding. I bet you've got a steel core, Amy McKaslin, but there's no way you can carry me up the stairs. I'll drive you home."

"I don't need a chauffeur."

"Humor me. I won't get a wink of sleep unless I know you're home safe."

"I'll call—wait, you don't have a phone." Amy shook her head, scattering the tiny wisps of golden silk that had escaped her disheveled ponytail. She looked like a waif in her too-big coat and her flannel pants. "I'll be all right."

"You never know that for sure. You can take all the precautions you want, but sometimes it doesn't matter. So, do me this favor, okay?"

"Driving me home isn't a favor."

She didn't understand. He didn't need any "should-have"s that resulted in more tragedy. He prodded her around the hood of the frosty sedan. The blacktop and then the concrete sidewalk beneath his feet were slick. "Is this my imagination, or is it snowing?"

"It's snowing."

"It's May."

"Welcome to Montana."

At least Amy's nearness gave him something else to think about. She smelled faintly of hot chocolate and shampoo and of the spring snow caught in her hair. A small blanket of faint freckles lay across her nose and cheeks, but that wasn't what made her cute. What drew him and held him was the quiet lock of her gaze on his. Although she said nothing, he sensed it. She'd seen the duffel bag, of course. She knew what he intended to do. She ought to be angry, but she wasn't.

"You have to wrench on it or it won't open." Her hand bumped his as she grabbed onto the door handle. "Just yank—there it goes. It sticks."

"I see."

Her car was pretty old. They'd stopped making this model, oh, about ten years ago, he figured, not that he was a car expert. But she kept it clean and in good repair. As he held the door while she settled into the bucket seat, he noticed it was clean and repaired with duct tape, which wasn't so noticeable on the gray upholstery.

She wasn't raking in the bucks at the family diner. He didn't need to see her car to know that. The restaurant did a healthy business, but this was a small town. It sounded as if it supported three sisters and their families, and it couldn't be easy.

He thought of the life he'd left. The suburban acreage in Lake Oswego, a nice tree-filled suburb of Portland. He'd even had a stretch of lakefront beach. It was a view his wife had loved. It was why he'd bought her the house. Thinking of home made his knees go watery as he crunched through the ice and snow to the driver's side. The house was gone. Everything was gone. Even if he wanted to, there was no going back.

She waited until they were safely across the railroad tracks and a few blocks from her trailer park. "Are you going to tell me why you're so eager to go?"

"You aim straight, don't you?"

"I don't see any point in pretending I didn't see the bag. You were going to slip out, weren't you, when you came across those horrible men."

"That's pretty much what happened." He kept his gaze on the road. It was tricky, he had to go slow because the fog absorbed the light and reflected it back, so the town streets were nearly invisible. Plus, he wasn't familiar with this stretch of highway.

He didn't offer more of an explanation. He figured she deserved to rant and rave or silently fume...or just accept it—whatever she needed to do. He was wrong. There was no denying it.

Amy McKaslin had a real life. What would she know about his? She had sisters and a business and a son, maybe more kids. He didn't know. She didn't wear a wedding ring, so he figured she was divorced. His guess was that she struggled to make ends meet, like any family.

He really didn't want to know anything else about her. He was already part of the fog, rolling with the rising wind. Already anticipating the dawn and the snowy drive through the state. Where he landed next was anyone's guess.

He'd leave it up to fate, or God, if He was still noticing.

"You'll need to turn right up here." Amy broke the silence and leaned forward against the restraint of the shoulder harness to help look along the road's shoulder. "There's the sign. Right here."

He caught a flash of a small sign, the kind apartments and house developments use. Oak Place, it said in snow-mantled letters on a spotty green background. He followed the narrower lane along a windrow of shrubs and turned, as Amy indicated, by a line of small mailboxes mounted on a two-by-four.

He saw the first trailer house. It was neat and maintained, but a good thirty years old. Then a second, newer one. And more, all quaintly lined up along the road, windows dark except for the occasional flood-light blinking on as the car drove by.

"Mine's the one with the rose arbor. Just pull in under the awning."

He did, noticing the single-wide was modest, and its front yard was white with snow. Another vehicle, which he remembered was Rachel's, had nosed in beneath a makeshift carport, and the whole passenger's side was covered with ice and snow.

"Home sweet home." Amy reached for her purse from the floor behind his seat. "Did you want to come in? I'll make you hot chocolate this time."

"No, I just wanted to see you were safe."

"So you could leave?"

"Something like that."

Amy wished she could be angry with him, but it wasn't that easy. How could she be angry with someone that wonderful? He spoke so well and knew how to make hollandaise sauce without checking a recipe and stood tall when danger called. Not the usual wanderer looking for a job. And that left the question, why? She instinctively knew it was a question that would only make him turn away.

Some things were better left in the past where they belonged. She thought of the foolish girl she used to be. Everyone deserved at least one free pass, one "do over." Maybe that's the way it was for Heath.

"If you want to come in for a second, I'll write you a paycheck."

"It wouldn't be right. I'm running off and leaving you shorthanded again."

"You work, we pay. It's that simple."

"Nothing is ever that simple."

"This time it is." Amy wished she didn't like Heath so much. That's what this was—she couldn't lie to herself anymore. And why bother? He was leaving. "Come in for a few minutes and warm up, before you head back."

"I'd appreciate that. It's a long walk."

"And cold." All the way up the slick steps, she wondered what she was going to say to Paige. Her older sister had been upset they'd hired a man with no references; they hadn't even asked him to fill out an application, just the paperwork required by the state and federal government.

Amy fit her key in the lock and wiggled it until it gave way enough to turn—it was tricky in the freezing weather. The bolt clicked and she opened up, grateful for the warm air fanning her face as she entered. Peace. It wrapped around her every time she came home. The pile of toys neat in the corner by the couch. The pictures of family—of her sisters, of Paige's son and dozens of Westin from the moment he was born on up.

She noticed Heath closed the door behind him, looking neither right nor left as he followed her into the kitchen. While he set the keys on the corner of the counter, she filled two cups with tap water and set them in the middle of the mounted microwave. It hummed as she extracted items from the cupboards. Aware of Heath watching her the whole while, his presence shrank the small space until it seemed there were only the two of them and the walls pressing in.

For some reason, he must have felt it, too, because he didn't look comfortable. Maybe because he was a big man and the alley kitchen was narrow. He hardly fit in the walkway between the counter and the corner of the stove. Edgy, he didn't seem to know where to look, glancing quickly from the toys to the pictures to Westin's artwork tacked on the fridge.

Maybe it was the trailer—a lot of folks looked down on them, as if they were only for poor people. But she wasn't poor. Not when she had so many blessings.

Maybe it was because she was still in her pajamas and they were more strangers than friends. She reached for the business checkbook and a pen. "Did you want to take a seat?"

"Sure."

He didn't look any more comfortable in the small chair at the little dinette set that had once been her mother's. The set was a bright Valentine's-Day-pink with metal sides and legs. It was a very feminine-looking table—and if that wasn't bad enough, all six-plus feet of him barely fitted in the small chair that was as pink as the little table.

The microwave dinged. She removed the steaming mugs and ripped open two packets of cocoa mix. "I know, it's not sophisticated but this kind does have the little mini marshmallows."

His jaw clamped and a muscle jumped along his jaw.

Okay, maybe he didn't like marshmallows. "I can scoop them out if you want."

"No, it's all right."

It didn't look all right, but she didn't say anything more. She stirred the mix until it dissolved and spooned the tiny marshmallows from his cup.

"You think I'm looking for a husband, don't you? That's why you're bugging out of here as fast as you can go. No, it's okay. I'm not mad." She slipped the mug in front of him.

It had flowers on it and said in rainbow-colored writing, The Best Mom Ever! with, I Thank God for You printed beneath it.

Heath stared at it as if the cup were the single most horrible thing he'd ever seen.

"It was the only one without a chip in it. I have a six-year-old boy and no dishwasher. Being hand-washed around here is hazardous for mugs."

The color drained from his face.

Maybe it wasn't the femininity of the cup that was bothering him. If she'd been thinking, she would have remembered there was also the Bible passage on the mug. He wasn't a churchgoer. She knew how it felt to feel pressured about one's faith or lack of it. Through her own experience, it seemed God came to those who needed Him most when they needed Him.

Heath surely looked as if he were a man hurting. She switched the cups and reached for a spoon to transfer the frothy marshmallows. "Maybe you wouldn't mind this one as much. It's just got a little chip."

"No, don't bother." He nudged the damaged mug back. The tendons stood out like ropes in his neck.

"Look, I can't do this." He pushed away from the table. "Keep the money. I appreciate the job, I do. I just—" he glanced around, the light draining from his eyes as he headed to the door "—can't."

She hadn't even had the chance to finish the check. Where was he going? And on foot? She grabbed the keys, for she meant for him to drive back to town. He could leave her car at the diner and she'd catch a ride to work with Rachel. It was too cold for him to walk all the way to the diner. She hated to think of him cold and alone and miserable.

What would make him bolt out of here as if he'd been set on fire?

Then she looked behind her at the wall. Westin's framed baby pictures decorated the space between the fridge and the wall. Adorable pictures of her son when he was first sitting up and learning to walk.

In those pictures, it was hard to miss his downy soft platinum hair, sparkling blue eyes and the way he was all boy. Westin at that age had a spirit as sweet as spun sugar....

Looking at those pictures, she realized exactly why Heath's heart was as lost as one of the black holes Westin was always reading about. Tears wet her cheek before she realized they were falling.

Please, Father, she prayed, *help him.*

There was no answer in the endless silence.

Chapter Nine

She found him in the snow, just standing there as if he'd gotten only that far before the pain took over. Tiny perfect crystal flakes had gathered in his dark hair and graced the breadth of his shoulders. He was such a big strong man and yet how could any one person be mighty enough to withstand the immense grief he'd known?

Sympathy moved through her as she laid a hand on his wide back. She wasn't surprised at all that he felt like steel. But she wasn't prepared for the virulent explosion of emotion, like a supernova's shock waves, that radiated from him and into her. She felt as if she could feel his soul.

Oh, Heath. She'd never known such agony; not the loss of her parents when she was young, not the desperate life in a cruel city. Nothing she'd been through compared to the pain she felt rolling through her.

It was an all-encompassing pain. And how could

it be anything else? A child was infinitely precious. How well she remembered the thrill and the intense burst of love she'd felt the first time she'd held her son in her arms. She tried to imagine Heath with his son. The pride he would have felt. And more, so much more. He would have harbored every hope of happiness for his son. A joyful, carefree childhood and the chance through education or training to achieve his dreams.

She knew, too, Heath would have dreamed of spending the years to come with his boy. Of lazy summer afternoons fishing along the shady banks of a quiet river. Of loud roaring crowds and hot dogs and a perfect view of home base. Of college graduation and the pride a father took in his son growing into a fine man.

The ashes of those dreams remained, imprinted forever into Heath's soul. But otherwise, they were gone like ashes scattered in a bitter wind.

She leaned her forehead against the unyielding plane of his shoulder blade. She was barely aware of the bitter cold, accumulating snow and dissipating fog curling around them, shrouding them from the neighbors, from the street, from the world.

There were just the two of them and Heath didn't move. Except for the rise and fall of his chest and the thump of his heartbeat, he could have been cast in stone. In some ways, Amy realized, he was.

She hadn't held a man in a long time, but she simply did it without knowing why. She wrapped her arms around his waist, feeling the thick muscled feel of him, and held on. Overcome, she pressed her cheek against his back and did the only thing she could. She let him know that he wasn't alone.

And so they remained until the sun warmed the cold black mountains to the east. The first streaks of gold haloed the tiniest of snowflakes that fell like a promise over the crisp white earth. Dawn came as wide streaks of light broke free from behind the mountains.

Heath slipped from her arms, without a word of explanation or apology. She pressed the keys to her car in his hand along with the thick fold of bills—her tip money from yesterday, since his paycheck was still half-written on her kitchen table.

He didn't say a word as he pushed the keys and money back into her palm. Pure pain twisted his face as he walked into the glare of the sunrise and disappeared from her sight.

The most beautiful mornings seemed to always follow the cruel storms.

The cheerful sun had Amy blinking against the brightness as lemony rays shot through the slats of the diner's white window blinds. She poured two cups of coffee from the first batch of brew of the day. The front door was still locked—they had four minutes to go until opening time, and she needed it.

Stifling a jaw-splitting yawn, she brought both cups of coffee to the far booth near the kitchen, where Jodi was lacing up her tennis shoes. She was bleary-eyed from working a late shift at her second job. Single moms had to do what they could to make ends meet, even if it was working late at night.

The dawn seemed unaware of their indifference. Sunshine beamed between the slats in the opened blinds and warmed the morning. Amy tried to keep her thoughts on the day ahead—Westin had a doctor's appointment this afternoon and she needed to go grocery shopping. She had to call Kelly because, with Heath gone, she was likely going to have to work a shift tonight and would need a baby-sitter.

"I suppose Paige'll be here soon on a rampage." Jodi winked as she gave the sugar canister a nudge and it slid to Amy. "She's been gone for two weeks. She'll have all kinds of energy saved up for us. I'm looking forward to it."

"Sure, because you're not related to her." Amy loved her oldest sister. Everybody did. Paige was just...used to being in charge and that had been fine when Amy was ten but now that she was twenty-five, it was a different story.

Plus, when Paige found out Heath was gone, Amy was going to get another lecture on the proper method of interviewing employees to safeguard against this kind of thing. Poor Paige, she did everything she could to protect herself, to keep bad things from happening. She tried so hard, but, as far as Amy saw, there wasn't much to be done about preventing some things.

Just like with Heath. Amy dumped plenty of sugar into her coffee and stirred, watching the dark liquid, remembering how Heath had made her hot chocolate last night. Odd, she couldn't remember the last time a man had made her anything at all—maybe if she could remember her father, but she couldn't. The everyday minutia of that happy life had blurred with time. She couldn't draw his face in her memory anymore. And as for Westin's father, well, he was more the kind who demanded to be waited on.

Remembering how lost Heath had seemed, shrouded by fog, blanketed by snow, she hoped that wherever he was, he'd found peace. Surely God took special care of lost souls, saved or not. She'd always found great comfort that in spite of the dark, lonely time in Seattle when she'd turned her back on her faith, God was watching out for her regardless.

Not that she would have recognized it at the time, but she was wiser now. She had faith that Heath wasn't alone—not truly.

Across the empty main street a freight train rumbled along the tracks, the boxcars hiding the green park and meadows as they rolled endlessly on. Amy sipped her coffee, savoring the peace, and tried again not to think about Heath. Tried not to wonder where he was. Had he found a motel to catch a few hours' sleep before driving on?

Finally, the caboose capped the end of the long procession and, as the train disappeared from sight, the town fell silent and motionless. Not even the white-faced Herefords in the field behind the tracks moved. Nor did the thickets of buttercups and dandelions. If she squinted, she could see the brand-new roofs of homes in the subdivision beyond that. All was still there, too.

Peace. Amy absorbed it as she sipped her coffee.

"There's Mr. Brisbane's truck." Jodi swigged back the last of her coffee. "Time to get to work."

Amy took her cup with her, leaving Jodi to flip around the open sign and unlock the front door. It was a few minutes before six, but for the morning group, it didn't matter. They were more family than customers anyway.

Amy just wished she wasn't so beat. Exhaustion weighed her down, and she felt as though she was moving in slow motion as she pushed through the swinging doors into the kitchen. She was on the grill for the breakfast shift, so her thoughts were already turning to putting on extra bacon for Mr. Winkler and maple sausage for Mr. Brisbane. She was thinking ahead to their orders—she needed to open a new can of jalapeños—so when she saw the hulking man at the grill, she didn't recognize him. Adrenaline shot into her blood. *Oh, no, more trouble...*

No, it was Heath. He was at the grill. He was starting to cook.

What was he doing here? She hadn't spotted his pickup in the back lot when she'd arrived. She hadn't heard him come in, but it really was him. He didn't look up as he slapped thick strips of bacon onto the grill. The sizzle and snap filled the long stretch of silence as her thoughts switched tracks and she realized that he was real and no dream.

"'Mornin'." Abrupt, cold as glacial ice, he kept his back firmly turned. He finished with the bacon and began setting links of sausage on the grill.

He'd been busy while she'd been in the dining room drinking coffee. Bread stood in the industrial-sized toaster ready to be put down. The pancake batter was mixed, and he'd already put a pan of muffins in the oven. Incredible.

"Good morning." Amy opened the fridge and pulled out a big batch of cinnamon rolls, iced and fresh and ready to be heated. "I wasn't expecting you."

Heath remained silent and stiff. A stone statue couldn't have been less interactive.

He stared through the order-up counter into the dining room while he worked, as if he were very interested in Jodi's conversation with Bob Brisbane about the snow that had come and gone, and the damage to the front windows.

The kitchen seemed silent in contrast. Way too silent. Questions rushed to the tip of her tongue, but she didn't ask them. She didn't know why Heath had returned, but she sensed if she asked him about it, then he'd be gone for good. So she reset the oven, careful not to get too close while she rescued the perfectly baked muffins.

"Sorry I'm late."

He didn't sound sorry, he sounded empty. "It was just a few minutes. Don't worry about it."

"It won't happen again."

"Okay."

He was treating her as if their earlier emotional intimacy had never happened. She could still feel the deepest of sorrow clinging to him. And if he needed distance to cope, she could give him that. It wasn't as if there could be more anyway. She wasn't looking for love—that was absolutely out of the question. Maybe they would wind up as friends, and a girl could never have too many of those blessings.

Heath looked like someone who could use a friend, too. "Did you get any sleep?"

"I didn't, but that's not unusual." She loaded the industrial-sized toaster as the door jangled, announcing another customer. "You?"

He shook his head instead of answering and turned his back. His message was clear. The conversation, such as it was, was over.

The deputy shouldered through the threshold, uniformed, his hat in hand. He caught her gaze, nodded once as if he wanted to speak with her when she got the chance, and took a table near the back.

Since Heath looked purposefully busy, keeping his back rigid, his head turned, it wasn't hard to figure out there was no point trying to help out in the kitchen. He could handle it, and he clearly wasn't comfortable around her, so she let him be. On her way past the coffee station, she snatched the carafe and the back of her neck tingled. She knew Heath was watching her, although when she looked up, his attention was on his work.

It was likely to be a busy morning, she thought as she squinted at the sun-bright windows. Several pickups and cars were starting to fill the parking slots outside. Jodi was busy with the regulars, so Amy grabbed a folded newspaper and headed straight for Frank's table.

She didn't ask if he wanted coffee, he always wanted coffee, so she simply turned over the cup in its saucer and filled it with the steaming brew. "I don't know if I thanked you enough for all you did last night."

"It's my job, you know that. I was glad I was able to help out."

"It wasn't your job to stay after those men were arrested. Or to carry plywood and nail it up, and nothing you say is going to convince me otherwise." She handed him a menu. "Will those guys be out on bail anytime soon?"

"The bail bondsman wouldn't cover them, so they're staying until their hearing on Monday morning. Maybe a stint in lock-up will give them time to do a little thinking, and they'll straighten up."

"I hope so, for everyone's sake." At least she didn't have to worry about any more retribution, at least for now. She trusted the local law enforcement to keep an eye on the situation. Just think, if both the deputy and the sheriff hadn't been so willing to hop out of bed in the middle of the night, how much more damage would those two drunks have done?

Amy shuddered at the thought. "Do you need some time, or do you know what you want?"

"I already have a hankering for your eggs Benedict." He scanned the listings. "You wouldn't be able to make that a combination meal for me, would you?"

"For you, anything." She took back the menu, scribbling on the ticket as she went and underlining, Generous Portions, because she owed Frank, too.

"Order in." She clipped the ticket to the wheel, but Heath ignored her as he sprinkled cheese into the open face of a cooking omelet.

It was pretty clear this was how it was going to be between them. As the morning passed in a flurry of activity, Heath didn't look at her once. He spoke to her only when absolutely necessary for the job.

While she was disappointed, if that's what he needed, then fine. Thinking about what he'd lost, she gave deep thanks for her son. The best gift she'd ever been given. She couldn't let her mind roll forward to imagine losing Westin—no, she couldn't *think* about it. She just couldn't.

But for what Heath had suffered, he had her respect. She didn't question him. She didn't try to talk to him more than necessary. Paige came in, all aflurry, bent on calling every last glass man in the phone book to get the best price. She was a good businesswoman, but Amy's heart was no longer in the loss of a window or the thoughtless retribution of two sorry men who'd been fired from the mill, as Frank had told her on his way out the door.

She might have a ten-year-old car and a job that wasn't fancy, exciting or impressive, but she could provide for her son. She lived modestly and she didn't have a high-school diploma. Some people might not think she had a lot, but they would be wrong. She had everything. Everything that mattered.

Although the morning was busy, she made sure she found time to give Paige a hug, call her son before Rachel took him to school, and thank God for the blessings in her life.

Rachel poked her head around the corner and into the small space where Amy was popping aspirin for her headache. "Is the coast clear?"

"It's clear. Paige went to the bank." Amy tipped back her head and swallowed. The aspirin stuck in her throat, and the acrid bitter taste filled her mouth. She washed it down with her lukewarm soda—it wasn't much help. "It's almost time for me to go pick Westin up from school. I've almost got these orders done."

"The ones I was supposed to do?" Rachel brightened like the first star on a clear summer's night. "Oh, Amy. I love you, I love you, I love you. Oh, you know how I hate doing paperwork."

"That's what you get for promising to buy out Paige's share of the restaurant next year."

"I know." Rachel glanced heavenward. "I'm going to need some help with God on that one, but I'll get the hang of crunching numbers. Really, I will."

"Or you'll get me to do it." With a wink, Amy pushed away from the desk, taking her soda with her. "I'm gladly relinquishing the paperwork to you. I'll keep my cell on if you have a question. I think I did everything right, but you never know."

"Oh, I owe ya! Thanks." Rachel lowered her voice. "Is Heath still working out as well?"

"He handled the breakfast and lunch crowd like a pro. We couldn't have found anyone better."

"Oh, I'm so glad. He's heaven-sent, I have a feeling about it." Rachel backed out of the way, since the built-in desk was at the back of the closet-office and there wasn't a lot of room to turn around in the narrow space. "Oh, and you're out of sugar. I added it to the bottom of your grocery list, though."

"You're a sweetie. Thanks." Amy grabbed her purse and caught sight of Heath putting the last of the dishes in the dishwasher. He snapped his head back to his work, as if he'd been listening, or at least watching for her.

A muscle tensed along his jaw before he turned completely away.

Amy looked at the long lean line of his iron-hard shoulders and remembered how cold his back had felt against her cheek. She left without a word, without even saying goodbye, figuring he wanted it that way. Rachel had to be right—Heath was a blessing, and she prayed hard, hoping he could stay on. But if he couldn't take being around children, and a lot of children came to the diner, then she'd understand.

The screen-door hinges squeaked, but it was a pleasant sound as she stepped out into the beautiful day. The fragrance of the lilacs carried on the wind, and she breathed deep. The warm fresh air invigorated her, at least a little. It was hard to believe last night had been so bleak, but a few puddles remained as a reminder and she stepped around them.

It was a spring day like so many that had come before. Like so many that would follow today. But the moment seemed brighter, accented by the chirp of birds and the meow of a cat enjoying the shelter beneath her car. As she knelt to shoo it gently away, apple blossoms fluttered along the warm rays of the sun.

As tired as she was, she felt as if she'd picked up a second wind. The thought of spending the afternoon with her son picked up her spirits. She tossed her purse on the sun-warmed seat, rolled down her window and dug her keys out of her hip pocket.

"Amy?"

Heath stood in the shade of the building, blending very neatly with the shadows in the dark jeans and T-shirt he wore. His hands were jammed into his pockets, his arms muscular and his frame lean. He looked ready for a fight.

Had he come to explain himself? Or to give his two-weeks' notice? Either way, she saw a man struggling. A man alone.

She glanced at her wristwatch. "I have a few minutes before school lets out. What do you need?"

"To apologize." He ambled forward, tentatively, into the scorching kiss of the afternoon sun.

"For what?"

Somewhere down the street a dog barked. She waited as he came closer. Exhaustion had dug harsh lines into his noble face. He walked slowly, and it was as if all the life inside him had gone out. "For walking away from you like that. It was rude."

"I think I understand."

His head rolled forward and he gasped for breath, as if she'd struck him. But it was from the truth of his past, the fresh mention of what he'd lost.

If she were in his shoes, she could never speak of such a loss. And while she had so many questions, there were so many things she didn't know about him and what had happened to him. How old had his son been? Had his marriage crumbled beneath the strain of a child's death? What greater loss or hardship could there be in a marriage? She didn't ask because he was in enough pain, so she waited, wondering what he would volunteer.

"I had my duffel packed. You know that. I had made up my mind to leave. But this morning when I was walking back here, the snow started to melt. It was a strange thing, to see snow on the ground and flowers blooming up through it."

"If you've been in Montana as long as I have, it's not so strange. Wait until it's the middle of July. It's weird to cancel a Fourth of July picnic because of a blizzard."

Her attempt at humor at least eased the depth of the lines dug around his severe mouth. "I got to thinking. You and your sisters are having some trouble, and I helped out some."

"Yes, and we'll always be grateful to you."

"I haven't made a difference to anyone in a long while." He stared hard at a small puddle on the black-top between them.

She waited while the minutes ticked by and a dog started barking down the street and Heath struggled to find the right words. The dog barked on and on until someone called out, "Would you shut up!" and he did.

Then there was only the hush of the wind between them.

He took a ragged breath, betraying all that it cost him to explain. "I'm grateful to feel useful again. I've been wandering for so long—ever since the funeral. Once they were gone, I roamed from one town to the next because I had...nothing."

Once they were gone. Amy's heart dropped, realizing he'd lost not only his son.

"I can't make any promises, but I need to stay for now."

She read the bleak truth in him. "Of course. Rachel and I both think you're a godsend. I know you're not a believer—"

"I am, I'm just...lost."

"No, you're never lost."

His throat worked. He stared up at the trees where cheerful leaves whispered and danced. The dog down the street started barking again.

"There is one more thing. A favor you can do for me." He withdrew his right hand from his jeans pocket and there, on his palm, was a nine-volt battery. "You have a son. Put this in your smoke detector. Do it the minute you walk through the door. Don't put it off."

The battery was warm from his body heat. She stared at it, wondering how he knew that she'd taken the old one out last week because it had been beeping at 2:46 a.m. There hadn't been a new one left in the junk drawer to put in its place.

Oh. Realization washed over her with a new horror. He was already walking away, part of the shadows and hard to see through her tears.

Chapter Ten

Memories had followed him to sleep, rearing up in his nightmares until he woke for the fourth time in a cold sweat, shouting his son's name. The rasping heave of his breathing sounded loud in the small bedroom where the curtains billowed at the open window, letting in the ghostly silvered light of a half moon.

With the echoes of his son's name dissipating like smoke, Heath flung off the sheet and raked his hand through his wet hair. The pure golden light of first dawn blasted against the undersides of the pull-down blinds that were wobbling in place over the open window. The sunshine bled through the billowing sheers and onto the foot of his bed.

At least the night was over, he could be glad for that, even if he was awake at 4:55 a.m. He lay there for a while, listening to the cheerful birds and a train's low keening whistle and the rumbling as it chugged along. The dog that had been barking yesterday let out a few yelps and fell silent.

He gave the old blind a good yank and it only rolled halfway up. It annoyed him, but when he sat back on the edge of the bed, he could see the peaceful river valley. It shone so green and beautiful, a perfect carpet at the feet of the great mountains ringing the low lush valley. The breeze felt cool on his face, and it was almost as if he could forget.

It was a world apart here. He could pretend that Portland didn't exist. The way the enormous mountains marched like giants in all directions, it seemed as if nothing else could possibly be on the other side of their amazing rugged peaks. He wanted to believe that the quiet harmony of this place was a world apart from the more desperate one he'd been running from. He was so weary.

So infinitely weary.

As for Amy McKaslin, she knew the unspeakable truth. The look on her face after he'd given her the battery, when realization hit, said it all. He'd watched her realize the horrible truth he could not say. She should have hated him, but no, not Amy. She was a mom—it was his guess that little Westin was her very world. She'd understood.

But no one could truly comprehend the grief and guilt until they'd walked this path.

He wished no other parent ever had to.

He'd tried to work for a while, tried to put all his

sorrow and rage and desperation to good use. He'd worked long hard hours in the ER and he'd made a difference, but there was still death and loss, illness and injury. People still died.

The last straw had been working alongside the pediatric specialist for an hour trying to save a seven-month-old girl. The infant had been symptom-free after a car accident, for she'd been safely buckled in her infant car seat and had then presented that afternoon with shocky symptoms. Heath heard the baby's cry, realized something was wrong, had chewed out the admittance nurse and ordered the young mother and her baby into the nearest available trauma room.

He put in a call to the peds surgeon, but it was too late. Massive internal bleeding. He'd done everything, even prayed to a God he knew good and well didn't protect innocent children.

He'd broken down afterward. No procedure had been spared, and they had all worked so hard for the little red-haired girl and her silently crying mother. Even the mother comforted him, he'd taken it so hard.

He'd sat in the corner and the grief he'd been holding back flooded him like a tidal wave crashing to shore and there had been no recovering. It had been six weeks since the fire. Five and a half weeks since the funeral. All because he'd been too busy, too tired, too forgetful to buy a three-dollar battery.

He'd never be all right again—never. There would be no peace, no forgiveness, no anything. He didn't want there to be. He didn't deserve it. He'd failed the two people who mattered more to him than anything. He didn't deserve the right to anything.

But now, after all these months, he was soul-weary. Tired of wandering. He was a man who liked roots, who missed the bonds of family and friends and colleagues and patients. He deserved the harsh sting of loneliness. Not that he'd ever settle down or try to live a normal life, but it sure felt nice to think about resting here for a while. He could help out the McKaslin sisters, salute the deputy when they crossed paths, breathe in the serenity of this place and just exist without a past, without a future.

After he shaved and showered, he popped a cup of water into the microwave for instant coffee, then heard a car pull to a stop in the back lot. Curious, he ambled around to the living room, where the old blinds snapped up with an echoing twang and down below was a spotless forest-green SUV.

It wasn't more lowlifes looking for trouble, just the oldest sister. The serious one. With dark glasses shading her eyes, her brown hair tight in a ponytail, she walked soundlessly across the parking lot. She carried a bunch of ledgers in one arm. Remembering Amy and Rachel's discussion about keeping the books for Paige almost made him smile.

Yeah, they looked like a real nice family. It wasn't a bad thing, helping them out.

It was early, but he stirred up the coffee and

slurped it down as he maneuvered the steps. Paige had left the back door wide open, guarded only by the unlocked screen.

He didn't want to startle her, so he knocked before he opened up. "Hello?"

"Oh, hi. Heath, isn't it?" Paige had the look of a woman who had too much to do in too little time. She was taller than Amy and Rachel, and not as vibrant. There was a quiet steel in her he immediately respected. She ran a good restaurant and, as far as he could tell, she managed the extended family, too. "Come on in, although you're early. I just put some coffee on...oh, that isn't that old stale instant stuff? It's got to be years and years old."

"You don't rent the apartment often?"

"No, it got to be too much to deal with. One kind of trouble after another, and to tell you the truth, I have as much of that as I can handle right now." She smiled to soften her words and gave a self-conscious shrug. "You might as well sit down and enjoy some coffee. I've got some baked goods still out in my Jeep."

"I can get 'em for you if you want."

"Wow, that would be great." Relief and appreciation lit her eyes that looked so tired. "I didn't lock it."

Working here might require more involvement on a personal level than he was used to, but he liked feeling useful. He almost recognized the man he used to be.

The morning light felt gentle, and already the air

was beginning to warm. He lifted the back hatch of the SUV and was instantly assaulted by the wave of cinnamon and sweetness and doughnut goodness. The delicious aroma distracted him, so he didn't notice her until it was almost too late.

Amy McKaslin in a pair of navy shorts and a matching T-shirt, her hair drawn back, speed-walking along the alley. She looked for a moment as though she regretted that she'd been spotted. As if resigned, she diverted from the alley and cut between the lilacs to the parking lot. She was breathing heavily and sweat glistened on her brow.

"You caught me. I'm trying to keep to a workout program, but it's impossible with my schedule. I haven't walked for about three weeks and I'm ready to keel over."

"I could save you with a cinnamon roll."

"No, then I'd have to walk even more."

Heath hadn't thought he would be glad to see her, but he was. She'd breached the distance he kept everyone at, and he wasn't bothered by it. He wasn't sure if that was a good sign or a bad one. "Are you working this morning?"

"Nope. I gotta get back to my little boy. It's almost time for him to get up. I've got Mrs. Nash, she's next door, keeping an eye on him for me. Ooh, huckleberry coffeecake. That's absolutely incredible. You should sneak a piece before the customers start arriving, because it goes fast. I've gotta get going. Bye!"

She was hurrying away from him, he could see it. What had happened stood between them. He wanted to ask her if she'd taken his advice and changed the battery in her smoke detector, but he couldn't say the words. If he asked, then it would be too close to talking about what happened, and he just couldn't say the words.

So he watched her hurry off, her long tanned legs stretching and bunching, her muscles rippling, her ponytail flickering back in her wake. Swept by sunlight, she disappeared around the shadows from the tall maples at the block's end. The same dog started barking until someone yelled at it to stop.

It was five-thirty; a train rolled through clanging and clattering and tooting so loudly he swore the earth beneath his feet rumbled. There was a comforting rhythm to a day starting out here, at the diner. He set the baked goods on the counter, put a big square of huckleberry coffeecake on a plate, grabbed a fork and headed for the coffee station.

Paige had already poured her cup, so he did his own and took the closest booth by the windows. He set down his food and saw the teenager on a motorcycle coming to an idling stop at the curb out front. He tossed a half dozen rolled newspapers onto the front mat and drove off with the rough rumbling sound of a small motorcycle in need of a muffler.

Heath hopped outside, noticing the handle on the door could use some tightening. Then he gathered up the papers, set all but one on the top of the counter by the till and unwound the rubber band from the last roll. The crisp newsprint splashed across the front page was about the upcoming Founder's Day jubilee.

Sipping his coffee, he began reading the local news. As he read, he recognized several of the names in the articles or in the letters to the editor section. It was odd to live in a place and feel a part of it again.

The deputy dropped by a few minutes early, and Jodi came rushing in behind him, out of breath. Mr. Brisbane rolled to a stop at the curb in his grass-green classic pickup.

It was time to go to work.

Heath knew the exact moment when she walked in the diner. It was as if a warm summer's dawn had touched the dark places in his soul.

He finished dressing the sandwiches for table four and didn't even need to turn around. He could feel the radiance of her, becoming more brilliant as she moved closer. The screen door slapping shut, her sneakers squeaking on the freshly cleaned tile and the thump of her purse landing on the corner shelf were all clues.

Clues he didn't need. His heart turned toward her the way a flower does toward the light, and he knew, would have known even if he had been rendered deaf and blind, that she was coming to stand beside him.

"Hey, I'm ready to go. A few minutes late—"

Paige scowled from the other side of the order-up window. "A few minutes? I'm docking your pay."

"Ha! I was trying to make those calls from home while I finished up some laundry. You know, the calls to the glass-replacement people?"

"Sorry. I'm still docking you." A ghost of a smile was the only hint that Paige was teasing.

Amy, however, was not as deadpan. "Okay, then I'll just go back home and let you take over for Heath."

Heath's head was spinning; he was trying to make sense of the growing brightness within him. The luster he felt came from her, from Amy, there was no doubt about it. She made some comment to her sister, something that he couldn't follow, his brain couldn't seem to focus on that. But he was aware of her moving away, gliding like a pianist's scale—one note flowed into the next, trilling away like music and rolling back again.

The women were talking, familiar and companionable with one another. Families were like that. He'd been close to his sister, teasing her gently just to see her smile. Family ties, they were a fine thing.

And while he'd missed the late-night long-distance calls and the quick emails sent when his parents or his sister had had time enough, it wasn't the loneliness that made him keenly aware of Amy standing beside him, making him tingle like electrical feeders siphoning up from the ground in a lightning storm.

No, this wasn't about the long stretch of loneliness or the need for a soft place to rest, just for a moment. This stirring within him was powerful enough to rock his soul.

He couldn't force his gaze away from her. Exhaustion marked her. She didn't look as if she'd caught up on much missed sleep last night. The bruises beneath her eyes were a dark purple. He remembered her comment from yesterday, how getting little sleep was not out of the ordinary for her.

As she wet and soaped her hands in the sink, he wondered what kept her awake at night. The past? Her responsibilities?

"My car is making this horrible noise and you know there goes another six hundred dollars." Amy rinsed, grabbed a paper towel and dried, still talking to her oldest sister, still unaware that he was watching her and pretending not to.

Car trouble? He had noticed the clutch felt a little soft when he'd driven it, but there was no noise. He didn't need to see the worry on Amy's face or how modestly she lived to know a car repair bill would be a hardship.

"Didn't you just get the last thing paid off?"

"Yeah, the transmission." Amy wadded up the paper towel and tossed it into the trash.

He heaped fries on the plates, laid down the orange sections for garnish and slipped the last orders of his shift on the hand-off window. Paige, always efficient, circled around to serve the sandwiches.

"I guess it's your turn to go home." Amy busily tied on her flowered apron and began hauling out bowls, measuring cups and spoons. "Before you go, can I make you something to eat?"

He saw the big round blue of her eyes watching him, innocently unaware that he *felt*. "No, I'd better get out of here."

She had no idea how true that was. It was as if he'd stepped on a land mine and he knew if he so much as breathed wrong, the charge would go off.

"Okay. Are you working the late shift tonight?"

"No. I told Paige I'd best be here late, so none of the women are here alone. Considering what happened. But she said she'd be fine."

"That's decent of you."

That's me, he wanted to say, *decent to the core.* But it wasn't true. If he were decent, then he wouldn't allow any feelings for her into his heart. He had no right, not to anything. Not to a future or happiness or the chance to love again. He'd failed to keep his loved ones safe.

He'd failed them.

Amy knew, and she didn't treat him with hate or accusation. When he'd handed her the battery yesterday, her face had crumpled with sadness. She was a compassionate woman, she gave people the benefit of the doubt. Wild birds weren't scared of her, and she was like spring come to his frozen tundra heart.

"What kind of noise is your car making?" He couldn't believe he'd said it.

Neither could she because she looked up from pouring teriyaki marinade into a big bowl and she studied at him with wonder. "Well, why am I surprised? Let me guess. You've been a mechanic, too."

"Not a journeyman or anything, but I worked at one of those quick lube places. I did brakes, tune-ups and radiators."

"What do you know about carburetors?"

"They can be expensive to replace."

"Great. That's just what I know about them, too." Amy capped the bulky industrial-sized bottle of marinade and gazed across the distance between them, a few feet, and yet it felt as wide as the Pacific Ocean.

She unwrapped fresh chicken filets and slipped them into the bowl, covered them well with the marinade, clipped on the top and left them in the refrigerator beside a bowl with the exact same thing in it. It was good to keep her hands busy so she wouldn't be tempted to take Heath up on his generous offer.

She did the same with the perfect stack of petite filet mignon the butcher had delivered fresh and wrapped. She tenderized the meat, aerated it, sprinkled the family's secret steak flavoring and covered the dish. After fitting it into the crammed fridge, she turned around and there was Heath, reaching for the notebook to sign out.

"Excuse me." She moved a step back.

He didn't.

"Come by here for dinner tonight, okay?" she asked, talking to fill the silence falling between them. To cover the sound of the rushing in her ears and the fast tinny beat of her heart. "Come in the back, let them know what you want. That's the rule for our employees."

When he didn't answer, her brows creased. As if frustrated with him, she shook her head, scattering stray gold wisps of her hair that fell into her eyes. She shut the refrigerator door and blew the bangs out of the way.

Try to act normal, he coached himself. Act like nothing is happening.

Except it was.

He wanted to smooth the wayward strands away from her face. He wanted to trail his fingertips across the soft curve of her cheek to know if her creamy skin was as soft as it looked. He wanted to brush tiny kisses along the barely noticeable freckles sprinkled across her nose and cheeks.

It was an impulse, this deep yearning to take care of her and to care for her. It scared him. Suddenly the walls felt as if they were inching in and he was caged. Out—he wanted outside. Trying to keep a lid on his panic, he moved casually but as quickly as he could, and spotted the full garbage can by the back door.

It was the perfect excuse to leave. He tied off the sack, grabbed his baseball cap and tore outside into the building heat of the midday sun. The bright round disc was nearly straight overhead and his shadow was small as he marched over it, walking fast and far, wanting peace. And if he couldn't have those, than he'd settle for being numb again. His heart hurt like an arm or leg long unused, crying out to protest the stretch and bend of weakened muscle.

Heath swore the chambers of his heart were expanding, ready to explode like a bomb. He tossed the heavy bag into the big green Dumpster and dragged in deep, cutting breaths. The hot breeze and the wide-open space of the back parking lot made some of that edgy panicky feeling fade.

The thing was, he didn't want to care. Caring came hand in hand with vulnerability. Vulnerability brought inevitable loss. He was better off alone because caring about people only led to hurt. There was no other way about it.

"Heath?"

Amy stood on the threshold, the dim kitchen behind her, and the bright wash of spring before. She was as vivid as the day—her golden hair, creamy skin, soft pink T-shirt, ruffled calico apron. She shaded her eyes with one slender hand. "Are you okay?"

"Yeah, sure." It was a lie, they both knew it.

Answering her honestly would only lead to talking, and talking to confessing and that's what he'd done. Look at what trusting someone led to. She'd come to ask how he was because she cared. She remained standing in the hot sun, waiting for him to come closer.

No. This was as far as his involvement went. He tugged the bill of his cap low, as if to keep the sun out of his eyes, but it was so that she couldn't see in.

Without a word, he pivoted on his heel and followed the wind as far away from her as he could get.

Chapter Eleven

"I think we're going to stay slow," Paige said as she unpacked canned goods from the earlier, midmorning delivery. "The noon hour is past, and we didn't have much of a rush. Why don't you pack that sandwich to go, if you'd rather. I'll stay and handle all this. I know you put in way too many hours while I was gone."

Amy wrapped the sandwich good and tight and slipped it into a plastic bag. She sealed the zipper lock and looked around for a suitable size to-go bag. She chose the smaller size and snapped it open beside the meal she'd made for herself.

"Rachel and I tried, but there's no filling your shoes."

"Yeah, yeah. Compliments will get you everywhere. Oh, I saved a few brownies for you to take home. I know they're Westin's favorites."

"That will make my little boy smile."

"Just trying to keep my nephew happy." Paige took

time to smile before she hauled the heavy box into the storage closet. "Go home. Enjoy some time off."

"I will. I've got books to return and a house to clean." If she hurried, she'd be done in time to pick up Westin from school. "Oh, I found out the time for his graduation on Friday. It's two o'clock in the gym."

"I'll be there with the video recorder. Oh, I bet I can get Jodi to stay a little longer to cover me." Paige abandoned her restocking to dart over to the little office. "I'll write it on the calendar so I don't forget to ask her."

She had no sooner started to scribble than the phone rang. "I'll get it. Go. Get out of here while you can!"

Amy filled two containers of pasta salad, wrapped up the last of the brownies and decided on two cans of iced tea. Since her sister was still on the phone, Amy grabbed up the stuffed to-go bags, one in each arm and darted out into the brilliant May sunshine.

She heard the window air conditioner rattling at full speed, so she dared to climb the stairs and knock on the door. No answer. She knew he was in there. The air conditioner was loud, so she gave him the benefit of the doubt and knocked louder.

Nothing.

Okay, that was a clue. He was home. He clearly wasn't going to answer the door. Yep, maybe that was her answer. He'd seemed upset, really upset. First distant, then friendly enough and then angry, at least she *thought* he was angry. After she'd gone and talked on and on about her car troubles.

All he had ever done since practically the moment he walked into the diner for a meal was to help her and her sisters. He'd defended them, he'd worked for them, he'd scared off vandals and he must be feeling as if the requests never stopped.

At least, she thought that was the issue. She'd never been good at figuring men out. Who knew what they wanted or needed and why they acted the way they did. It was probably because she couldn't really remember her dad. She had certain memories, sure, but she couldn't recall the experience of having him in her life. Only the absence that came with his passing.

No, she was terrible when it came to figuring out men. She'd failed miserably with Westin's father, but then, she'd been nineteen, so very young. She'd kept a wide berth from men since. She served coffee and meals and made polite conversation with men every day in the diner, but that was different.

But Heath…no, she didn't know what to do with him.

Looking back, Amy remembered that John had called from the hardware store about halfway through the lunch rush. While she'd busily fried up barbecue burger specials and rolled up house club wraps and filled big bowls with taco and chef salads, she'd listened to Paige down the narrow hallway at the desk. Apparently John had found replacement windows at cost, and he'd said Heath had volunteered to install them.

Heath. She couldn't get away from thinking about him. Not even though she tried. Paige had gone on about what a great find Heath Murdock was between serving orders and waiting tables. Amy had shaken her head, tossing a teriyaki chicken filet on the grill.

She knew so little about him. Where he'd grown up, all the things he must have done for a living, how long he had been drifting. What were his favorite foods? Where had he learned to make hot chocolate like that?

What she knew for sure, as she stood now on the hot outdoor staircase, was that his heart was lost. His hopes decimated. His future only ashes from the past. She knew exactly how hard it was to look back with regrets—huge, devastating regrets. She'd been an impulsive teenager who thought she knew everything. She'd ran headfirst into the realities of life. But she wasn't alone. She'd had a family to return to, a job, a home and the chance to start over.

It wasn't pity she felt for him. It was recognition. There was a time when she'd felt as if her life was nothing more than cold ashes slipping through her fingers. A dark cloud settled on her soul simply remembering that desolation. She knew what it felt like to have no hope. To have been knocked so thoroughly to the ground it seemed impossible to climb back up onto your knees and stand.

No one she trusted understood the bleak depression that had nearly choked her when she'd returned, broken and humiliated. Sure, her family had known hardship, and they certainly weren't living a carefree and luxurious life, but not even Rachel and Paige could know what it felt like to look ahead and see nothing but a dark endless void where a future was supposed to be.

Amy sighed, wondering if she should knock one more time. Heath still hadn't opened his apartment door. Was he in there, hoping she'd go away? Was he sorry she'd figured out what had happened to him?

If anyone had known what had really happened to her in Seattle, she didn't think she could stand it. That person wouldn't look at her the same way again, not without remembering.

Maybe it was like that for Heath. He didn't want to remember.

The Lord must be walking with him every second of the day. How else could Heath have kept on living? He probably wouldn't admit to it and he probably couldn't see it, but no one could survive immense sorrow without grace.

Amy set the bag lunch she'd packed for him on the top step, knocked again and headed down. Hugging her own lunch close, she thought of her blessings. Every single one of them sweetened her life like lilacs on the breeze. Tears burned in her eyes for the man upstairs. God had brought him into their diner for a reason. He had kept him here for that reason.

Is there something I should be doing, Father? Or am I to let him be? Surely Heath needed respite from his drifting. Maybe that's why he was here. To strengthen before moving on. She didn't know, but she would do that all she could.

She was almost to the bottom of the stairs when the old, weatherbeaten door scraped against the frame as it opened.

"Amy?"

He looked as if she'd woken him from a nap, and instantly she felt contrite. His hair was disheveled, a dark mop of tousled locks that made her fingers tingle. She'd never had the longing to run her fingertips through a man's hair before. With him towering over her in a wrinkled T-shirt and a crease mark from a pillow against his jawline, he looked adorable. All six-feet-plus of him, so rugged and tough, and she warmed deep inside. A new part of her soul felt as if it had winked on, like the first star in a calm summer sky.

She shook the image out of her head. There were so many extremely good reasons why she needed to rein in her growing affection for the man. But not her regard. He'd done so much good in so short a time. "I know you didn't get lunch at the diner, so I fixed a sandwich for you. I guessed and made roast beef with swiss and spicy mustard."

"Perfect." He raked his hand through his hair, making every strand stick straight up.

Even more attractive, but not in a cute way. In a way that made her wish—even when she knew better. "I tossed in a few other goodies too, chips and salad and dessert. If you're not hungry now, it'll keep in the fridge for later."

"That was pretty thoughtful of you. Say, is there a bookstore around here?"

"Not unless you're in the mood to drive to Bozeman. The Shop Mart has a book section."

"A pretty small section. I already checked it out."

"That reminds me. There's the county library on the other side of the tracks. Near the grade school."

"It's been my experience libraries only let out books to permanent town citizens. I had a library card in Portland. I read all the time. But not since I left." He shrugged one granite shoulder. "I'll survive. Thanks for the lunch."

"My pleasure."

He'd lived in Portland. Oregon? Or Maine? It was all she could think while time suspended and the twick-twick-twick of the neighbor's sprinkler faded to silence. The brilliant greens of the trees and the stunning blue of the sky and the purple of lilac cones bled their colors until the world around her was gray and Heath was all she could see.

She gasped as a strange sensation moved through

her. It was as if he'd cast a fishing line, a hook had sunk deep into her heart and he'd begun to reel her in.

"I have an idea," she found herself saying. "I'll tell the librarian to add you to my account. That way you can check out books. I'd offer to do it for you, but I'm sure I can get Mrs. Pendleton to bend the rules."

"Wow, that'd be great of you."

"We've trusted you to cook for our customers, I think you're reliable enough for a library card. Besides, now I get to do something for you. Something that matters."

She glowed like her own light source, Heath realized. Maybe she didn't know it, he'd rarely seen the like. All brightness and kindness and all that was wholesome in this world. Everything that he'd stopped believing in, had pushed away from and denied.

He couldn't speak. His hand found the railing and his grip closed around the worn smooth wood. She'd known what he'd done and look at her, trusting him enough to be responsible with library books. When the truth was, the truth she couldn't see and he couldn't speak of, was that he'd been irresponsible with the greatest of God's blessings. Shame filled him like cooling lead and he could feel it move through him, hardening his spirit and his heart.

"Oh, I'm going there now," Amy called as naturally as if she were speaking to one of her sisters. "Did you want a ride?"

He managed one shake of his head. That was all.

"Okay. Make sure you ask for Mrs. Pendleton, then."

He kept staring at her.

Okay, time to go. She took one step and it felt as if the hook in her heart dug deeper.

She laid a hand on her chest and didn't know what to think. She left him standing above, so still it didn't look as if he breathed. As she dug her keys out of her jeans pocket, she wondered why it felt as if she were leaving a vital part of herself behind.

She was fine. Just the same as always. Nothing had changed in her, right? She started the engine, cringed at the horrible knocking clanging sound and put the car in gear.

All the way across the railroad tracks and the few blocks to the new brick library on a tree-lined corner, she felt the tug of that hook. Felt a powerful bond she did not want.

It was a bond she did not need.

Her car was in the shady parking lot of the modest, single-story library across from the elementary school. The streets were quiet, the students presumably tucked away inside the building, learning great things.

Forcing his attention toward Amy McKaslin's car, he didn't have to think about the empty playground, which would probably soon be full of kids running and shouting and laughing, just glad to be free. It was strange, he'd cut himself off for so long, he'd forgotten that people lived in tidy little homes that lined tree-shaded streets. Moms would come to pick up their little ones, or to meet them at the bus stop. Kids would come running with artwork and demerit notes, eager for a snack before dashing outside to play.

He almost kept going, because the library building was compact and it would be hard not to bump into Amy, since she was in there. He wasn't ready to see her. The truth was, he wanted to see her. Even if it was a bad decision. Even if there was a powerful, unexplained bond between them. So he chose a parking spot close to the exit, hopped out and locked up.

As he strolled toward the double glass entrance doors, a woman somewhere in her forties passing him gave him a nod. It felt odd, because for so long he'd been as good as invisible.

The interior of the library was cool and crisp and smelled of paper, binding glue, leather and dust. Good scents. He caught a gray-haired robust woman giving him the once-over from behind the gleaming counter of the front desk. Chances were good that she was Mrs. Pendleton, who hadn't been as easy to win over, he guessed, as Amy had counted on.

It took him only a second to orient himself. He found the mystery suspense section. The library was small, but they had a good selection. This is what he'd been missing, and better memories rolled through his mind. Memories of taking a rainy Saturday going from one bookstore to another, drinking espresso and browsing through the bays. Finding just the right story to read next.

He pulled out a favorite author's older book and read the dust jacket.

It was as if an angel touched him on the shoulder, stirring him from the book and leading him to her. Amy. He knew, as she glanced up from thumbing through a card-catalogue drawer, that some things happen for a reason.

Not that he was willing to admit his life was governed by more than fate. But it sure felt that way, and the shifting of his soul was as if a part of him leaned toward the light, toward life. Her.

Her hair was down, that's what was different about her. When she worked, it was always tied stringently back. Golden streaks rippled like water in her darker blond hair, buoyant and rich and so lustrous. Those golden locks framed her soft oval face, emphasizing the delicate cut of her high cheekbones and the fine curve of her chin. Soft rosy cheeks and a rosebud mouth, she appeared so fresh and wholesome, she was beautiful all the way through. He knew that because he could feel her spirit, which was all spring light. His heart thumped as if it was doing more than pumping his blood.

He was coming back to life. Amy was doing this to him.

What should have been painful was not. His chest warmed as if he'd downed a big mug of steaming hot chocolate, melting through him until he was no longer cold.

Across the way, she hadn't noticed him. Her slim fingers walked along the old catalogue cards. A wrinkle dug between her eyes as she concentrated. It was a cute thing, the way she bit her bottom lip and folded back a shock of hair that tumbled into her eyes.

She moved her lips, as if repeating a Dewey decimal call number, trying to memorize it. Then she shoved the tiny drawer shut and took off in the opposite direction, walking quick and sure, on a mission.

His soul ached when she disappeared into the stacks.

Brought back to reality, he realized he was standing in the middle of the aisle with a book held open in his hands. Shutting it, he clasped it by his side and followed her.

There was no denying what he felt. No denying that what felt like an elastic cord stretched between her spirit and his. He'd felt this before, but not this strong. Not so incredibly intense.

She reappeared, carrying a thin book, and that's when she saw him. Recognition brightened her features and her smile moved through him like spring wind through new leaves. Shaken, he gripped the solid wooden side of the book bay, but it didn't save him. He was falling, not physically, but in another way. His heart was tumbling, his senses spinning, his soul quieting until there was only her.

"Hey, I'm glad you showed up," she whispered, coming closer, the pad of her sneakers rasping loudly in comparison to the absolute stillness in the library. As if uncomfortable, she glanced around, folded a lock of hair behind her ears, and didn't meet his gaze. "Mrs. Pendleton is making up a card for you, on my account. Make sure you remember to get it."

"Are you on your way out?"

"Yep. I'm going to sit in the shade and read until school lets out. My errands have taken about six times longer than I thought they would."

"You have somewhere to go?"

"Home to clean my house. Now that Paige is back, I can get to the things I got behind on."

"I noticed your house was a complete mess. Terrible." It had been perfect, comfortable, tidy and homey. With just the right amount of chaos, like the toys on the floor, to make a person want to sit down on that deep-cushioned couch and stay forever.

Maybe it wasn't the comfortable living room that made him feel that way. Maybe it was Amy.

"I see you've found a book. Excellent. I guess I'll see you tomorrow morning. I'm working the breakfast shift. It's Jodi's day off." She took a step back, maybe needing distance, maybe wondering why he was staring at her without saying a word.

He knew why she was edging away, talking about

work and acting as though nothing had changed between them.

Everything had.

"I'm done looking. I'll head out with you."

"Oh, sure thing."

He couldn't tell if it was surprise or fear that had
her retreating.

As they walked together to the front counter, a
calm sense of rightness breezed through him. It was
as if that calmness took root and spread. It was odd,
this link he felt with Amy. They moved in synchrony.
He'd bet they were breathing with the same rhythm.
Their hearts pumped at the same pace.

He had no business doing this, walking beside her
as if he'd be there for the rest of forever. Waiting while
she added the book to a small stack on the counter
and glided it across the sparkling clean countertop
to the librarian. He watched her bend to dig through
her purse.

She produced the small laminated card and
snapped it on top of the books. "Mrs. Pendleton, this
is the man I was telling you about. Heath Murdock."

"Hello, ma'am."

The middle-aged woman peered over the tops of
her glasses to give him a surly once-over and frowned
as if he fell short of her standards. "I've got the card
made up. Let me get it." Tight-lipped, she turned to
sort through a small stack of paperwork.

Amy's nearness danced along his awareness, filling his senses. The apple-sweet scent of her hair and skin. The curve of her jawline as she lifted a graceful arm to check her watch. The rhythm of her light breathing, timed with his. She was color in his world of darkness and shadow. He wanted her more than he had the words to say.

Or the right.

Chapter Twelve

The librarian returned, took his book with tight-lipped suspicion and scanned the book and card. He watched, not at all surprised that the system was still the stamped date on the pocket card instead of the efficient computerized system he'd known in Portland.

Listening to the thud of the stamp, the snap of the book closing and the hush of the dust jacket sliding across the counter took him back to his boyhood days of checking books out of the country library. Good memories.

"It's due back in two weeks." Mrs. Pendleton gave him a look that said she'd hunt him down if he dared to be late or mistreat her book.

Yeah, the librarian when he'd been a boy was just as protective of her books. Not blaming her at all, and knowing she needed reassurance since he was a stranger, he managed his most doctorlike tone. "Yes, ma'am. I won't be late."

Her brow shot up, as if in surprise, as if he just might meet her approval. Then she dealt with Amy's stack of books. Two hardbacks on astronomy and an inspirational paperback.

"For your boy?" He nodded toward the science volumes.

"We had to special order them, you know, the interlibrary loan thing. He's had to wait forever—well, according to *him*—so this will be a great surprise for him."

"Has he always liked astronomy?"

"*Moon* was his first word."

Mrs. Pendleton finished with her work and presented Amy with the stack of books. "It was good seeing you again, Amy. You tell Westin I've ordered a brand-new book on quasars, like he was asking me about last month. It'll be a few weeks yet before it comes in, and I've got to catalogue it, but I'll save it for him. He'll be the first one to read it."

"Oh, thank you!" Amy tucked her library card away in her purse, grabbed the books—all perfectly ordinary things.

She was not ordinary. Not to him. Looking at her made his eyes burn, like someone who'd lived too long in the dark. Walking beside her made him ache from the intensity of being next to her.

He held the heavy glass door for her. With a quick, "thanks!" she waltzed past him, leaving him dizzy. He followed her out into the afternoon where leaves whispered and birds chirped. Perfect clouds sailed across a sky that was as blue as a dream.

Amy checked her watch again. "I'm going to wait here until school gets out. No sense in going home only to turn right back around."

"Doesn't he take the school bus?"

"We live too close, and he's only in kindergarten." She tucked that strand of hair behind her ear again. "I suppose you're heading back to the apartment?"

"Hadn't really figured on what I'd do next. Maybe I'll just sit here with you for a while. It's been years since I've had the time and the inclination to sit in the shade and read a good book."

"There are some benches over there, beneath the maples. That's where I was going to wait. I can see the front doors of the school from there."

"Sounds good."

Amy chose the wooden bench that gave her the best view across the street and sank against the hard wooden back. It felt good to sit, she'd been on her feet all day, even if she hadn't put in a full shift at the diner. She'd worked the last three weeks almost straight through, sometimes a fourteen-hour shift. So she didn't feel a bit guilty thinking of all the things she still had left to do.

She let the sweet wind sweep over her and tangle her hair. Let the warmth of the afternoon soak through her. "It just feels good to relax for a minute."

"I don't suppose single moms get a lot of relaxation time."

"No." She laughed at the idea of lounging around in her robe and slippers. "Everything would fall down around my ears if I did that."

He took the end of the same bench and set his book next to him on the long length of boards between them. He stretched out his legs, drawing the denim fabric tight around his muscular legs. "It must be a lot to shoulder alone. A child, a home and a business."

"I don't mind. Besides, I'm not alone. I've got my sisters, and boy, do I owe them. There hasn't been a day that has gone by since Westin was born that Paige or Rachel weren't doing something to help out. Paige doesn't have a lot of spare time since she has a teenage boy and handles most of the business end of the diner. Yet she still finds time for me."

"She seems the type."

"Ben, that's our brother, he's half a world away in the Middle East. He's in the air force. And as busy as he is being an airman, he sends a monthly package of stuff for Westin, just to help out. I can't tell you how blessed I am."

Of course, she realized, it might not seem that way to him. She lived humbly, stretched every penny to make ends meet and sometimes she couldn't. Her car wasn't new, her house wasn't fancy, and her clothes were department-store discount.

But across the street in the third classroom down,

where bright cutout flowers decorated the big windows, her son sat in the second row, fourth desk over. He was safe and happy and loved, with an extended family who cherished him.

Heath cleared his throat, his gaze following hers. "You seem pretty lucky to me."

His infinite sadness filled her. Tears burned in her eyes. "I learned long ago, the hard way, that I already had everything that mattered."

"The hard way?"

Oh, she didn't want to tell him. Nobody knew, although she suspected Paige had an idea, and Amy didn't want the clear respect in his gaze to dim or fade away. He'd see her differently. But she felt compelled, as if it was inevitable that she would tell him her secrets, the way he'd done his best to tell her his.

She took a shaky breath to fortify herself. To take time to find the right words. "I wasn't always the squeaky-clean Christian you probably think I am. It's not that I never lost my faith, I just took it for granted. Like living here in this small town where everybody knows everything about you because they remember when you were born and watched you grow up. I know you come from a big city, so this place must seem lackluster to you."

"No, I wouldn't say that. It must be tough, on one hand, because I'm guessing Westin's father is around here somewhere. Is he not involved?"

"Oh, no. When things got…complicated, Westin's

father told me that he didn't want any entanglements tying him down—and if I thought he was going to be committed to anyone or anything, then I was wrong. He packed my bags and put me outside in the middle of a Seattle rainstorm. In November. Without the money from the paycheck I'd just cashed."

He remained silent, but she knew this story of hers wasn't what he'd expected it to be.

"I was just eighteen and I thought I knew it all. I left this place I thought was small and boring and dumb. I didn't even wait to graduate from high school, I wanted out of here so badly. Paige did her best, but—"

"Paige?"

She sensed his unspoken question. Why not your parents? "Dad died when I was seven in a hunting accident. Mom died two years later from lung cancer. She was a heavy smoker. So, Paige was sixteen and the state said she could keep us. She left school to run the diner. She got her GED but it was hard for her, handling so much responsibility, and I didn't make it any easier."

"I have a hard time picturing you as a rebellious teenager or living in a big city."

"The Lord looked over me or else I never would have made it. There were times when I was broke. I'd saved up my tip money from the diner for two years, and I had twelve hundred bucks in the bank. I thought it was a fortune. It went like water downhill. My car died halfway across the state, in a mountain pass, and the tow bill alone took a quarter of my cash."

"Not good."

"No. By the time I'd found a room to rent in a house in Seattle and paid first, last and the deposit, I was broke. But, like I said, I wasn't alone. A great job came my way. I started out bussing for a really nice waterfront restaurant. It was beautiful along the water. Seattle is so green, and the water is brilliant on sunny days and a soothing gray on rainy ones."

She closed her eyes, trying not to remember. Wishing more than anything she could go back and change her decisions. "Westin's father was the bartender at the restaurant. He was charming and about five years older, oh, I thought he was so smart and suave. Distinguished. I'd never had a drop of alcohol before I met him. I'd never done a lot of things. I was young and naive and I thought it was sophisticated to drink and go to parties, and when he asked me to live with him, I thought he loved me."

"You were in love with him." It wasn't a question but a statement, as if he understood.

Ashamed, that's all she felt now, but yes, she'd been so deeply in love. "I was just some innocent romantic girl who wanted to be loved when all he wanted was a maid and someone in his bed. Someone to borrow money from. I knew it was wrong, but I justified it. I wanted so badly for someone to love me, to really love me. And I just...compromised everything

I believed in. Six months later I was pregnant, penniless and fired from my job for fraternizing. The restaurant, come to find out, had a strict policy against their employees dating."

"Was Westin born here?"

"No. I found a job in a diner, not in the good part of town, but the finer restaurants where the tips were good didn't want a pregnant teenage waitress, for some reason." She shrugged, trying to hide her pain.

There was no way she could hide anything from him. Heath breached the distance between them by laying a hand against her nape. The instant his skin contacted hers, a jolt of emotion so strong and pure rolled through him, from her heart and into his. A wave so dark with regret and hopelessness that his soul beat with recognition. She'd run from home looking for love and she'd found pain and betrayal.

In her heart she believed she was unlovable. That if she loved like that again, so wholly and true, it would never be returned.

He could picture how hard she worked, hounded and broken, spending long hours on her feet and her back screaming with pain as the months passed. He knew without asking she worked until she went into labor. And was back at work shortly thereafter. Exhausted, afraid, alone. Scared.

She saw that he understood all that she didn't tell him. It was odd, how they could speak without words. How he could know.

She sighed, a painful sound. "I came home two weeks later. I'd called Paige to ask if she could wire me the bus fare. She took me and Westin in and never said a word. She never scolded. She never made one mention of all the times she'd told me this could happen. She just…loved me. Like a big sister should."

Heath didn't say anything, so she kept talking. "That's why I'm here. I look around at the town I thought was so lame and boring, and I see people I've known since I was little. Friends and relatives and neighbors who say hi to one another and who pitch in if there's trouble.

"Did you know Mr. Brisbane and his morning group started a donation jar to help with the cost of the windows? It's not the benefit of the money, it's the thought behind it. I want to raise my son in this community of good people, well, mostly good people. I know how lucky I am."

She studied the elementary school again, growing quiet.

Yeah, Heath thought. In his opinion she *was* pretty lucky. "You put the battery in your smoke detector, like I asked?"

"As soon as I walked through the door."

"Good."

Was it his imagination, or was she leaning into his touch? She seemed to be, her skin warm and smooth, pressing toward him. He dared to come a few inches closer. Then it was as if nothing separated them, not distance or pain from the past. Not the fact that he had no future and that she didn't believe a man would love her enough to stay.

He only knew that he wanted to try. And he couldn't. "As you probably guessed, my wife and son died in a house fire. When our house caught fire, it was because of a short in the wiring. I had a late-night call—I used to work in an emergency room."

"Like a doctor?"

"Yeah. I was a doctor." He shut off the memories forcing their way up, memories that would break him all over again. He couldn't let them run wild, he could only take out one and leave all the rest buried.

Not easy, but he tried to find words for the past he'd never told another living soul. "There was a bad accident, a drunk driver took out a car full of high-school kids coming back from a football game. They were good kids, driving responsibly according to witnesses, no alcohol. The driver did everything he could to avoid the pickup coming at him, but there wasn't much he could have done."

"Did they all die?"

"No. Two kids died on impact, but three others were so critical the medevac didn't think one of them would make it alive to the landing pad.

"I worked nonstop in the OR. A whole team of us, I was working on just one kid. I got a letter from her mother, the day I walked off the job. Her name was Kari, I don't know why I remember that after all this time, but she'd been accepted to one of the Ivy League colleges on full scholarship. She had so much promise. I didn't know that when I was working on her, I just saw someone who needed me. I didn't think she'd make it.

"I tell you, I'd never been so exhausted, but we got her stable enough, closed, and got her into recovery. She did time in ICU, but she recovered. Instead of going home, I went in to assist another surgeon. It didn't make any difference, we lost the young man, and I was heading home, just coming out the ER entrance to go to my car when the ambulance pulled up. And my son—" His voice broke.

"My son." He couldn't say any more and put his face in his hands. "He was on the gurney and I—"

He shook his head. There was nothing more to say.

What could a person do to ease so much suffering? Amy felt helpless. This big powerful man so mighty and strong felt so fragile. Not weak, no, never that. But he'd been broken.

She laid her hand on the vulnerable nape of his neck, where his sun-browned skin was hot. Comfort. It was all she could offer him.

It was a while before he straightened, all the color drained from his face. He took her hand from the back of his neck and she thought, here it comes, he was going to push her away. It was what she expected.

But then he lifted her knuckles to his lips and kissed each finger. Warm and sweet and reverent.

"Christian was eighteen months, three weeks and five days old. The coroner said my son never suffered. The door to his room was left open, so my wife could listen for him in case he needed her, and the smoke took him. But she...she tried to get through the flames to the baby."

He shook his head as if he didn't want to remember, as if it were impossible for him to say the words. With care, he kissed her hand one more time and, as if with regret, laid her hand on the bench, away from him...and stood.

He walked away, the invincible line of his shoulders defeated. Across the street, the traffic monitors wearing their bright orange vests came out with their cones and flags. Amy doubted that he even noticed, although he was facing them as they spread out at the intersections, setting up the safety cones and chatting as they worked. Alone, he stood feet apart and braced, arms behind him, his head bowed.

Amy knew there were no words that could comfort him. There was no comfort for such a loss. She could say she was sorry, but what good were those words? She wished she could hold him until his pain stopped. Find a way to heal the broken places in his soul.

Across the street, a bell jangled shrilly, announcing the schoolday's end. Within a few seconds the doors flew open, busses were puffing into place, and children's shouts of freedom filled the air. Kids with lunch pails, kids with art projects, kids streaming to

the busses and others arrowing toward the intersections. The monitors stood at attention, ready to direct the inflow of cars hurrying to jockey for position
along the front of the school.

Life, it was everywhere he looked. Heath squeezed
his eyes shut, but the brilliant colors and images remained like a snapshot in his head. The shrill screams,
the gleeful laughter, the shouts as boys called out to
other boys and the giggle of girls reminded him that
life went on, without him, but it went on just the same.

"Mom!" A little boy was hopping up and down at
the corner across the street, a paper he held flapping
in the breeze.

Heath recognized Amy's son, dressed neatly in a
navy T-shirt that said Astronaut In Training in white
letters beneath a print of a space shuttle orbiting earth.
The boy was so animated, leaping in place, hair sticking straight up, and a smudge of what looked like
paint on his cheek.

The traffic monitors stepped out to hold up traffic, their bright flags snapping. Westin sort of skip-
walked across the street, separated from the pack of
kids, and dashed across the grass to his mother.

"Look what I made. And I didn't make one mistake! And I got in trouble." To his credit, the boy tried
to look contrite.

"What did you do this time?" Amy sounded stern,
but it was only an act.

Heath wasn't fooled as she knelt to draw her child

into her arms, holding him close, keeping him safe. Studying his artwork of Jupiter with the big storm and narrow tiny rings. Amy remarked over his excellent painting skills and then got him to hand over the note from his teacher.

"I talked when it was quiet time. I know." Westin rolled his eyes. "But it's very, very hard to be quiet all the time."

"On your second-to-the-last day of school? We'll talk about this when we get home, young man. Why don't you go see what books I got for you. They're on the bench, go look." With a loving pat, she steered him in the direction of the bench.

Heath heard Westin's, "All right! Excellent!" and was surprised it wasn't agony to watch the boy drop to his knees and flip open the first book. He was instantly absorbed by the color photographs from the Hubbell telescope.

Watching him, Heath felt his throat ache, trying not to look back into the past. Fighting to stay in the moment instead of being pulled backward into suffocating sorrow.

As if she knew how hard he was struggling, she came up beside him and laid her hand on his forearm. A simple gesture, but the connection reminded him that, for this moment anyhow, he wasn't alone.

This was a pretty fine moment in the right-here-and-now.

"Mr. Murdock!" It was Westin, holding open the

book with care. "Mom! You gotta see this. Look at this cool picture. It's seventeen light years away. That's really, really far."

It hurt to look. It would have hurt more not to. Heath fought the tiny flicker of fondness for Amy's son. A little boy so different than his Christian would have been, but the boy made him remember the cheerful toddler babbling away, building his simple vocabulary of "Da!" And "No!" And "Uh-oh!"

"…Will ya, Mr. Murdock?"

Heath focused, realizing Amy's son was asking him something. "Sure." Whatever it was, he didn't mind. He just needed to think about something other than Christian. "What do you need?"

"Ice cream, but Mom's bringin' it."

"Sorry." Amy shrugged. "Don't worry about bringing anything. Just come as you are. With the upset over the vandalism, we didn't get to the welcome-home dinner we planned for Paige. And then we've got Westin's upcoming graduation to celebrate."

"I'm gonna be a first-grader!"

Amy saw the hesitation pass across Heath's face. It was strange how she could read his emotions. She knew he was uncertain about what he'd agreed to. She knew so many things that lived in his tattered heart. Those were the things that mattered. One day, he'd be gone, he was not a man to come to love or lean on.

But she loved him all the same. For the way he smiled, as if he wasn't breaking apart or remembering another little boy, while he hunkered down on the bench. "A first-grader, huh? That's pretty fine."

"Yeah. I know." Simply, Westin held out the book and turned the picture. "Cool. Did you wanna see?"

Heath's eyes looked so bleak. Then he smiled, just a little, but it was like the full moon rising on a bleak night.

It changed everything.

Chapter Thirteen

Amy lit a second citronella candle, shook out the match and set it into the cooling barbecue coals. Supper had been simple grilled burgers over hot coals in the barbecue pit at her development's riverside park. Not fancy, but then, she figured Heath hadn't been living with luxuries since he'd walked away from his job as a surgeon.

After everyone had stuffed themselves with more dessert than was wise, it was hard not to drift off for a quick nap. The sun hazed through the cottonwoods and glinted on the swift river, moving faster for the snowmelt still occurring in the mountains.

The only one who seemed as if he wasn't content was Heath, finishing off a second slice of lemon pudding cake. Paige's teenaged son, the one with the endless appetite, was working on his fourth piece of cake.

"See what you get to look forward to." Tender, Paige ruffled her son's hair on her way from the table.

"Feeding a bottomless pit. I think the government ought to give two deductions for teenaged boys, since they eat enough for at least three people. Maybe even four."

"It makes sense to me," Rachel commented from the folding camping chair where she was watching over Westin and one of the neighbor girls who were wading along the river's tamer edge. "I'll start a petition. I'm sure there are a lot of people who'd sign it."

"Mom, is there any more cake left?" Alex set down his fork, his plate clean of even the tiniest crumb. "I'm still hungry."

"See what I mean?" Paige dumped the empties in the nearby garbage can and carried the cake plate over to him. "You might as well just eat all of it. Unless anyone else wants a piece. Speak up now or forever hold your peace."

She waggled the plate in Heath's direction, but he shook his head. He'd spent the entire meal being polite, speaking rarely and watching them just as he was doing now, his face set, his arms folded over his chest, so invincible and stoic it was hard to read his emotions. The shadows in his eyes remained.

Every time he noticed Westin, did he remember all that he'd lost? It troubled her deeply, how silent Heath was. She longed to comfort him. To lay her hand on his cheek and feel the pain of his heart move through hers. If only she could let him know he had a friend.

She held the last can up to him, dripping from the melting ice in the cooler. "More soda?"

"Nope. I'm good."

"There's one of Rachel's oatmeal cookies left."

"No thanks." He turned so he couldn't see the sun-warmed river where Westin waded, busily searching for rocks. He focused his interest on the last bites of cake on his plate, when really it was her he was trying to avoid seeing.

He'd tried to stay numb, tried to keep enough distance, but she pulled at him like temptation, making him want what was forbidden. What he could never let himself have again.

"Westin! Not so deep." She called out while she returned the can to the cooler and began stacking in the jars of mayonnaise, mustard and ketchup. "You know to stay where it's shallow."

"I know, but it's not high over here!" He shouted, hardly audible over the rushing gurgles of the river and the faster rumble of the white rapids farther downstream. The hem of his denim shorts had dipped into the water, growing darker and tugging down around his knees. "I gotta look for moon rocks."

"Look for moon rocks closer to the beach." She snapped a lid on the plastic container of macaroni salad. "I mean it, young man. Do it now, or get out."

"Okay, okay!" Westin took one more step. "One more moon rock. Please, Mom? Ple-e-ease?"

"No, you're out too far." Riverbeds were in constant change, and what had been safe only a few days ago might not be today. Amy didn't like how close her little guy was to the swift current that made no noise as it rushed endlessly downstream. "Come in a few—"

"Mommm—!" Westin's shout was cut as he plunged downward as if someone had grabbed his ankles and wrenched.

Amy watched in horror as he disappeared completely from her sight. He didn't pop back up again. The plastic lid slid from her fingertips and rolled out of sight. She couldn't believe what she'd just seen— he was gone. Completely gone.

"No!" She was running, twisting and turning her ankles as she hit the big river rocks along the outer bank. Three minutes. That's all she could remember from her safety days when she took swimming lessons. That's all the time she had to get into the river, find him and get him breathing again.

Panic made it seem as if she flew across the sandy shore and there was no pain as she hit a small boulder with the inside of her foot and dropped to her knees on ragged rocks. She surged upward, seeing only the spot where Westin had disappeared. The quick menacing waters rippled and rushed, as if he'd never been.

She heard splashing sounds and suddenly there was Heath, running and then jumping as the water swallowed his feet and calves. Knee-deep he lunged, swimming like an expert, swift strokes that took him in seconds to where Westin had gone down.

Rocks impeded her as she hurried, lunging into the deep water, which ran across her skin like cold ice. With a power of its own, the river grabbed her and drew her away from where Heath took a great gulp of air, dove head first, his long muscled legs kicking water everywhere. And then he, too, was gone from her sight.

Please, God, please. Give me back my Westin. Oh, God, please. She wasn't the best swimmer and the current had her, she was spinning along like a big piece of driftwood past the point where Heath had dived. Heath surfaced in front of her, his big solid body a barrier that kept her from being carried away on the current.

Water sluiced off him. His skin was as cold as hers as he pulled her the few feet out of the strongest part of the current. "My cell phone's on the table. Someone call 911."

Heath took another great gulp of air, his black hair slicked to his scalp, his features sharp, his concentration focused. In a flash she could see the doctor in him, how he'd fought for his patients on the operating-room table. This is how he fought for Westin now.

As hard as she would fight. She dove again, seeing nothing but silt-tinted water and jagged rocks on the riverbed. She heard more splashing as Paige and Rachel joined the search. Shouting his name over and over as water closed over Amy's head and became silence.

How many seconds had gone by? She let the current take her as she desperately scanned from left to right. He had to be here. Her lungs burned and she came up, panting and coughing.

She could see Heath's dark form rising up to the surface, bursting through like a whale, spewing water. Empty-handed. No Westin.

Amy dove back into the water. She was going to find him. She was going to haul him up by his collar, lecture him on the dangers of getting into the deep current and he'd be grounded. For about six million years. He'd be grounded so good, he wouldn't be able to leave for college until he was forty-six years old. Like a mad woman, she let the water take her, keeping her eyes open as she tried to study the rock bed through the shifting green waters for the bright white T-shirt her little boy had been wearing.

"Amy!" A steeled hand gripped her upper arm, hauling her up. Her lungs exploded and she gratefully dragged in air.

Heath. He looked like a different man, harsh jaw set, eyes narrowed. He looked warrior-fierce. Marine tough. "He would have gone with the current. You get the others to start combing downstream. I'm going to go into the deeper part of the river. We don't have much time. Do you understand?"

She nodded, barely responding. Wild-eyed, she

searched the silent water. "He's here. He's got to be right here."

"He isn't. The current has taken him." Heath couldn't tell her it was hopeless. He knew. A parent never gave up. A parent never stopped loving. A child was the sweetest gift of them all, the greatest blessing that God could give two people in love, and He'd been at work, saving other people's children when his had needed Him.

He gave Amy, so fragile and valiant, a gentle shove into the calmer shallows where the others were combing the hip-deep waters. For a body. He couldn't tell that to Amy, as he filled his lungs with air and submerged.

Heath let the current take him, knocking him along the rocky bottom. Boulders bashed into him and he scraped over them fighting to see through the silt stirring up from the bottom. Westin couldn't have broken away from the powerful sweep of water.

It would have taken him from where the shallow shelf suddenly ended toward the middle, faster part of the river. It was like a jet stream, moving faster than the water surrounding it, and it would have taken him—

Darkness rose quickly ahead of him and the brutal force of the current slammed him against a submerged tree. Pain exploded in his left shoulder, he felt his fourth and fifth ribs crack and knew what the sharp arrow of pain was even before he felt the blood and the rest of the air in his left lung sluicing out of him. He had to get out of the water or he'd drown. He had a punctured lung.

Help me, Father. He prayed with all his might, to the bottom of his soul. He hadn't been able to save his son, who'd been dead on arrival, but he had to do this. His life was forfeit anyway. But Westin. *Please, let me do this one thing. This one right to put against the wrongs of my past. Please, do not let me fail.*

That's when he saw the flash of white. He clawed his way through the spear-sharp limbs, broken and bare, and prayed for one last ounce of strength.

"Over here!" Paige was waving the ambulance to the edge of the parking lot. Amy surfaced, hopes falling. The vehicle bounced over the curb and ambled across the grass, dodging picnic tables and barbecue pits and hauled up near the edge of the bank. Medics hopped out, and headed toward the river. Behind them a fire truck charged down the street.

No Westin. Time was running out. Treading water, losing hope, Amy started to pray one more time—

And then she saw Heath breaking the surface, Westin wrapped across his chest, and there was blood staining the river and streaming across Westin's torn shirt. Agony tore from her throat as she took out after them.

Heath was coughing. It was his blood. Trickling across his bottom lip. His face was gray, and his gaze locked on hers and she saw deep inside him, his soul that was no longer breaking. He began to sink, and she was there, holding him up as the first EMT reached them.

"Hold 'em steady!" the young man ordered and started mouth-to-mouth on Westin.

His lips were still pink, his little face nicked and gashed. The medic breathed life into him and after three breaths, he moaned, moved and threw up the water he'd swallowed. Somehow they were at the shore; she realized her sisters were pulling them in. And they weren't alone.

Dozens of people had come out of their homes with blankets and pillows and first-aid kits, many more were in the water. They'd started a human-chain search. The cheers that lifted above the wind and the sirens and the fear brought tears to her eyes and gratitude to her soul.

The EMTs took Westin and he was awake, searching for her in the crowd. "Mama," he said, the same way when he'd been much littler and sick or frightened.

"It's okay, baby," she said as someone wrapped her in a blanket and a fireman tried to take her vitals. "I'm fine. I have to see him."

She pushed her way through the big bulky men with medical gear and stood at Westin's feet, where he could see her while he was given oxygen and a heart monitor was set up.

"What about Heath?" she asked Paige, who'd come over to wrap her in a sisterly hug.

Rachel came with the news. They were calling in the medevac. "They're not sure he'll make it to the hospital, but they're gonna try to save him. And how I hope God is with him, for the difference he's made for us today."

"We're ready to go, ma'am," one of the EMTs told her.

Westin looked so tiny and helpless, his eyes searching hers for comfort. She'd been given back her son, and for that she would be thankful until her last day. But her thoughts were with Heath who lay motionless, as if already gone, surrounded by a dozen firemen and a score of strangers.

She had time for a quick prayer, hoping it was in God's plan to save him, before she was whisked away, holding Westin's hand. And if not, then God's will would be done, but it saddened her. No, it went deeper than sorrow. Deeper than grief.

Please, Lord, don't let it end this way.

As they raced into the sunset, toward the hospital in Bozeman, she gave thanks for the sweet blessings in her life. And she knew beyond all doubt that she would be forever grateful to the loner who'd drifted into their lives.

Chapter Fourteen

Three days later.

"Are you sure there's no one to come get you?" asked a concerned gray-haired lady wearing a volunteer's badge and exuding authority. "I don't think they let someone on pain medication just go home alone. I need to call someone about this."

"I didn't take my pain meds. And I'm not driving." He planned on calling a cab, but he didn't see the need to tell her that. He was alive, not that he was exactly happy about it.

When he'd felt his strength leaving him in the river, with Westin on his chest, he'd been glad he'd held out long enough to get the boy to his mom. Then he'd been relieved because it was over, finally, this struggle to live when he'd died long ago. The life drained out of him and he'd welcomed it. He'd yearned to see the bright light where he hoped his loved ones were waiting.

But he'd lost consciousness. When he'd come to in recovery, he knew God had failed him again. Failed him. Heath was alive. He'd come close to death, as he had so many times in the last few years. Every time God had snatched him back, had forced him into exile here, where Heath could not live, could not feel, could not love.

What kind of God was that?

Heath was done with God, done with faith, done believing there was any rhyme or reason or benevolent Father looking over His children.

He just wanted to get his stuff, get in his truck and leave. He didn't want to talk to anybody, he didn't want to see anybody, and since he'd asked and been told that Westin was just fine, there was nothing left to do.

No, that wasn't true. He had to say goodbye to Amy. And then he'd leave.

"When's Heath getting outta the hospital?" Mr. Brisbane asked as Amy freshened his coffee.

"As far as anyone could find out, maybe today, probably tomorrow." Amy tried not to let her disappointment show. Heath had made it through surgery and, while in recovery, had left orders that he didn't want to talk to anyone. Not even her.

The only reason she knew anything at all was that

one of her favorite customers, who'd been her mom's good friend all those years ago, volunteered at the hospital in Bozeman and rooted out the information for her. Otherwise, Heath had not only written her off, but had also refused every gift, flower, balloon and phone call she'd tried to send, as well as gifts everyone she knew of had tried to send.

Paige was cooking this morning, her hair tied back, her face tight in concentration as she worked. Too tight. Amy knew full good and well that her sister was listening through the hand-off window. Paige, while she was grateful that Heath had saved Westin, was highly insulted by his self-imposed isolation.

"It just don't sound right," Mr. Winkler commented as Amy turned the pot to his cup. "I say something's wrong with that young man. It ain't good manners to go refusing folks who just want to say thanks."

"Ain't that the truth," Mr. Redmond added, holding out his cup for the next refill.

What they didn't know about Heath Murdock. Amy finished her rounds with the coffeepot and was saved by the order-up bell. She gladly fetched the order of ranchero chicken omelet, the daily special, piled high with hash browns and sausage links.

Frank seemed glad to see her. "That sure looks good. Say, you might want to let Paige know the Hayman brothers have agreed to pay for the damage they caused. You let her know there'll be a lawyer calling her later today."

"She'll be glad to hear it." The plywood still covered the first two windowpanes, but John had promised the glass, which had to be special-ordered, wouldn't take more than a few weeks to come in. "How about you? You aren't in uniform. Must be your day off."

"Yep. Thought I'd go fishing."

Things seemed back to normal. Westin had graduated, and she was so proud of him. He was a big first-grader. Her baby was growing up. It made her glad and sad at the same time.

Someone called her name. Her cousins had gathered for breakfast in the back corner booth, and Karen was waving her over. She had a few minutes, so she stopped to chat. Karen's baby was smiling so sweetly, and Kendra was without her little girls today, for they were home with Grandma. Kirby, also sans her little ones, and Michelle, with her little Brittany snoozing in her car carrier tucked neatly into the corner, sat opposite them.

They were talking about T-ball practice, which was to start on Monday, and Karen offered to be the first car-pool driver, offering to ferry Westin, too.

A big extended family was a wonderful thing. She sneaked them free cinnamon rolls and lattes, and as the bell on the front door jangled to announce a new customer, she grabbed a trio of menus to seat the elderly Montgomery sisters. Through the window, as she was leading them to their preferred patio seating near the rose trellis, she caught sight of a yellow taxi—all the way from Bozeman—slowing down at the front curb.

Heath. She knew it was him even before she saw the silhouette through the windows in the backseat. She recognized the mighty line of that neck, the chiseled profile and the dark shock of hair. As she waited for the Montgomery sisters to slide into their favorite booth, she tried to look through the open doorway, but the wall blocked her view.

Although she could not see him she knew he'd climbed from the cab and was circling the building. Still, after all they'd been through, even after he'd cut off contact with her, her soul moved in cadence with his.

The Montgomery sisters were finally settled and she laid out their menus and left, realizing only as she was already halfway down the aisle that she hadn't filled their coffee cups...and she had the coffeepot in her hand. She plopped it on the counter, rounded the corner and headed straight out the back door.

"Amy, don't be foolish—" Paige started to say.

She slammed the door on her way out, to cut her off. Foolish? No, she wasn't going to make a fool of herself. Paige didn't need to worry. She marched up the stairs and beat on the aluminum screen door frame, staring through the mesh to the darkness within.

He couldn't have gone far. He'd probably beaten

her up here by a matter of seconds. "Heath! Don't you hide in there."

"I'm moving kind of slow." There he was, ambling into sight from the back of the apartment.

Dear heavens, did he look bad! He was drained of color and thin, as if he'd lost weight. Several days' growth stubbled his jaw. He moved carefully, in obvious pain. Her anger ebbed like a tide washing out to sea as she saw how deliberately he kept his injured side still. The slow steps he took. The way he winced, as if in great pain he wouldn't admit to, when he opened the screen door and gave it a push.

She came in, but not any farther than just inside the threshold.

He'd brought his bag out. That's why he'd taken longer to let her in. He had the big battered duffel nearly full, the steel teeth of the zipper gaping like a great white shark's jaws. He added wrinkled clothes that must have been sitting in the dryer for a few days. He tossed in a toothbrush and a half-rolled-up tube of toothpaste.

"You came up here for a reason." He didn't sound angry but he didn't sound anything close to being glad to see her. "I heard Westin's doing good."

"They kept him overnight for observation but let him go early so he could finish his last day of school."

"Good for him." He turned his back, all steel and distance. He left no doubt as he zipped the bag closed. "This is goodbye."

"I know." She'd known this moment would come. It had been inevitable. How could anyone heal from wounds that went so deep? From losses that could never be made right? "I'm glad I got to know you, Heath Murdock."

"Likewise." He winced as he lifted the pack onto his good shoulder, took a couple of small steps forward, and wished. Man, did he wish. "I don't think I'll ever forget you, Amy McKaslin."

"I'll think of you every time I look at my son. He's alive because of you. There is nothing on this earth that I can do to match what you've given me."

"You've already done it." It was a hard thing to explain and he knew he'd fail at it, so he didn't even try. "Walk me out to my truck?"

"Okay." She held the screen door open for him and led the way down the narrow stairs with the same grace she'd always shown.

He'd been rude to her, refusing to see her in the hospital, and look at her, the woman who couldn't chase away a robin was the same one who offered him understanding that was unexpected and impossible.

"Maybe I should carry your bag, since you injured yourself pretty good rescuing my son."

"I'll carry it, thanks."

They walked the rest of the way to his truck in silence. The pleasant summer morning seemed the same as any other. Sprinklers ticking and clicking, mist spraying and the dog barking down the alley.

Heath waited until he'd stowed his bag before he turned to her. "Everything inside me is yelling at me to get going. I've got to. Do you understand? It's not about you."

"I know. You've been honest all along, and I appreciate that. You're a fine man and it's been my privilege to know you."

Words escaped him, and he could only stare as the wind played with the fine wisps of gold escaping from her ponytail. She looked so beautiful, from the inside out, it made him awaken. The ice within him was cracking apart and the tundra of his spirit could not stand the change. He wanted to return to the blessed icy winter and hibernate forever.

But the heat of the day warmed him through. The flickering leaves, the shade from the trees and the scents of rose gardens and mown lawns and mist from the sprinklers made him long for blessings he could never have. Not ever again.

Still, the world teased him. There were the customers' cheerful voices rising and falling from the opened windows. The drone of a private plane soared overhead, and from somewhere far down the alley came the irritated cry of a toddler in one of the little homes as a young mother's voice crooned, "Did you fall down? Come here my sweet boy."

Life, it was everywhere. He couldn't escape it. He was breaking apart from the inside out all over again. He knew it was wrong but he took the step into thin

air, knowing full well he was already falling to an
inevitable doom. In truth he could not stand here pretending he could walk away from Amy and not feel
a thing.

Because he couldn't. His heart was cracking into
smaller pieces, surprising him that there was enough
of it left to do so. He'd give anything to be able to
stay and step into Amy's life like a man who hadn't
failed everyone he held dear.

"I'm not going to try to talk you into staying. I
know this is what you have to do."

"It is. I don't belong here with you." *Although I
wish I did.* He fought the urge to pull her into his
arms. To hold her, protect her and cherish her for all
the days of his life.

If only he could deserve her. To have a life with
her and her son.

She gestured toward the diner. "At least go get your
paycheck. Paige is stuck behind the grill, and I know
she wants to say goodbye."

He followed her, taking in the airy way she moved
in her faded denim Levi's. He memorized the golden
ripple of her hair in the wind and the sweet apple scent
of her skin and the way her mouth looked even softer
whenever she met his gaze. Memories were all he was
going to have of her.

Until he stepped through the front door and saw
the usual morning crowd. The retired ranchers and
the commuters in their power suits, young mothers

and the women whose children were grown. Families and single people in for a quick bite. Friends and neighbors and people who mattered to him.

Frank was the first to stand. Then the morning retirees. Heath watched, disbelieving, as person after person stood and began to applaud until the little diner was ringing with the sound.

Paige came out from behind the grill to thank him for Westin, for what he'd done for her family and pressed the paycheck envelope in his hand. He'd done what any one of them would have tried to do, and many had brazened into the river. He hadn't been alone in that water. He saw now he hadn't been alone when he'd pulled Westin to the surface.

Maybe, even, before that, when he'd lost all hope. When the waters had been too murky to find his way.

"Come back real soon, now, you hear?" Bob Brisbane clasped him on the shoulder.

"That's right, we don't want you traveling too far." It was Clyde Winkler. "The diner hasn't had such a good cook in a long while."

"He's a doctor," Mr. Redmond corrected him. "He's not really a cook."

Everyone in the diner came to shake his hand, to wish him well, to express surprise and dismay that he wasn't staying.

Amy had disappeared by the time he was done. Paige was back behind the grill. New customers began to stream in, and so he took his leave. As he was walking away and starting his truck, he wondered what he was going to do now.

Faith was a funny thing. He'd thought he'd lost it forever, but it wasn't true. God hadn't left him, God hadn't given up on him. Heath didn't know why things worked the way they did. He only knew that he was standing at a fork in the road. That everything he'd lost—family, friends and a home—had been waiting for him here, in this small Montana town, all along.

He turned the ignition and put the truck in gear, taking his time and looking around. Amy was nowhere in sight, but he could feel her as if she were half of his soul. He didn't want to leave. She'd given him no reason to stay—if he could have.

It was with regret he put the pickup in gear and headed for the interstate.

Amy sat in the warm still air of the apartment because she couldn't face anyone and there was nowhere else to go, unless she wanted to leave the diner for some privacy. Plus, it gave her a perfect view of Heath as he drove away.

She watched his truck amble along the main street through town, slow in obedience to the posted speed limit. The vehicle grew smaller until the angle of the buildings hid him from her sight. Forever. That was all she would ever see of Heath Murdock, capable cook and, for lack of a better word, soul mate.

She ran her fingertips across the library book he'd left clearly in the middle of the coffee table. Sorrow drained all the light from her spirit, and she felt as heavy as lead. The punch of pain in her chest wasn't her heart shattering. It couldn't be. She wouldn't let it be.

She didn't want the warm syrupy rich flow of affection to fill her up, but it did. She knew that loving Heath Murdock was the second biggest mistake of her life. Why was it the bitter truth that as responsible and hardworking and good a man that Heath was, he couldn't promise her anything more than Westin's father had? For different reasons, sure, but it was a pattern with her. One she'd been smart enough to escape this time.

This time she'd kept her dignity. This time she'd spotted danger before she lost her heart.

But it was no consolation as sadness overwhelmed her and tears started to fall.

Chapter Fifteen

Good old Oregon rain. It fell in a misty drizzle that was so fine, it seemed to hang in the air. Heath had forgotten what a vibrant green Portland could be in early summer. The cemetery seemed to shine with greenness. The deep velvet-green of the grass, the dark forest-green of the cedar and fir trees. The brighter newer greens of the aspens and maples.

Three years today. Heath traced his finger along the date etched in the marble. His wife and son shared a grave. He knew that's what she would have wanted. His dear wife and son. He wished he could go back in time and find time for the small things, to check the batteries in the smoke alarm so he could be now where he belonged, with his family. That's what he'd wanted, all this time he'd been grieving. He wished he'd perished with them.

He didn't know why he was here to lay white roses

on one grave and tie floating balloons to the other marker. But somehow it was part of God's plan. He was no longer bitter or despondent. Because he had something he thought he'd lost with his grief.

Good memories. Of a happy marriage. How they'd anticipated Christian's birth, how happy they'd been the day he'd come home. How one little boy who had brought so much chaos had also brought love and joy.

His cell phone jingled, and he reached into his coat pocket and checked the caller ID. Good, he'd been expecting this call. Heath answered, heard the good news and stood in the rain. He just breathed in the fragrant grass and trees, heard the sound of car tires on wet pavement on the busy road at the side of the cemetery.

He'd spent a few weeks handling things that should have been taken care of long ago. But he was done. He'd put his affairs in order and he was free.

Free to go home.

The pad of a footstep had him turning around. His mother had flown up from Kansas, and she stood beneath the wide brim of an umbrella, her eyes gleaming with emotions only he could understand.

"Have you forgiven yourself, finally?" she asked, loving. Always loving.

He nodded. Somehow things had changed. And he knew why. God had led him to Amy. God had given him a second chance.

Maybe. He was ready to find out. He took his mom by the hand and escorted her through the rain and grass.

"Westin?"

The house was unusually quiet. Amy dropped the armload of staticky, dryer-fresh clothes on the couch cushion. The hum of the pedestal fan in the living room breezing cool wind across her face was the same, but there was something different in the air. She couldn't place it until she stepped into the kitchen.

It was the scent of roses. She could only think of one person who would bring her roses—Heath. There, on the pink Formica table lay a dozen pink roses, per-fect petals cupped tight, as if they were getting ready to open. Her favorite kind, too, and there was no way he could know it. She caressed the silken buds and turned toward the sound of her son's voice outside, blowing in with the wind.

"Wow, I hit it! I really did!"

Was he out there with Westin? Then she heard Heath's rumbling baritone, warm with a chuckle. "You sure did. That was some hit. Do you think the neighbor lady will let us go into her yard to get your ball?"

Heath. Her heart wrenched seeing him for real standing in her yard, illuminated by the bold bright sunlight. He was unaware she was at the window, and his back was to her as he approached the chain-link fence. He looked fine in his usual jeans and T-shirt and with a baseball cap shading his eyes.

"Westin, is this your baseball?" Mrs. Nash's jagged voice, made shaky by the first stages of Parkinson's, was more beautiful for her kindness.

Amy could see her sidling up to the fence, holding a small white ball in the palm of her hand. The wind shifted, carrying away the strands of the conversation, but she was spellbound watching as Heath took the ball, smiled at Mrs. Nash, and then turned with the ball in hand, held the way a pitcher did, ready to throw.

"I'm ready! I'm ready!" Westin ran backward and held up something bulky in his hand—a new baseball mitt.

Heath sent the baseball sailing in a slow arc across the front of the lawn. Westin, instinctively keeping his eye on the ball, wove back and forth and then stepped back, holding the stiff glove up and the ball plopped right in.

"All right!" Westin turned toward the window, and then grinned when he spotted her behind the screen. "Did you see, Mom? Did you see?"

"I saw. That was excellent, baby."

"I know!" Pleased with himself, he reminded her so much of her brother, a natural athlete and naturally confident.

What was Heath doing here? He probably had no

idea what he was doing to her. What she'd been trying to deny ever since he'd walked into her life that stormy night. The gentle scent of tea roses filled her kitchen and brought tears to her eyes, because she didn't know how she was going to hold on to her heart now that he'd come back.

"Mom! Mom!" Westin pounded up to the door and used both hands to shade his eyes so he could see her through the mesh screen. He was out of breath, wheezing a little, but his face was rosy from playing and, she hoped, happiness. "Me and Mr. Murdock are so thirsty, we're gonna dry up like this. Whoosh!" He flickered his fingers, as if what he was saying was perfectly clear.

"Well, I certainly don't want you and Mr. Murdock to go whoosh."

"Like dried-up dirt!" As if he were choking, Westin made a fake gagging sound, because he was in such a good mood and he knew it would make her laugh.

Careful to keep her eyes averted, she retreated to the fridge and pulled out two cans of black cherry soda and a pitcher of sun tea. "Can you take a glass of ice tea out for Mr. Murdock?"

"It's Heath." There he was, on the step behind Westin, shading his eyes, too, with both hands. Oh, he looked good. With the sun burnishing him, he looked younger, bolder. Brighter. "I'm a great fan of black cherry cola."

"Mom! Me and Mr. Murdock, we're alike! We both like baseball and we both drink cherry pop! And look! Look what he got me. It's a real baseball glove, for T-ball! And I can catch real good with it! You saw, right?"

"I saw."

Heath stood in the background, hands fisted at his hips, so invincible and stoic it was hard to read his emotions. She needed to be realistic. He'd probably come back just to say hello, like so many of the customers in the diner had asked him to. That was all. It would be smart to hold back her heart.

But she feared it was too late. "Westin, did you say thank-you for the glove?"

"Yeah! Ooh, thanks for the pop!" He loped away, feet pounding, confident that she'd come to watch.

She pushed the screen door open. Heath hadn't moved; he was standing on the cement walkway that cut through the middle of her lawn. Petunias brushed his shoes in bright, splashing colors and it was strange to have him here, in the middle of her yard, when she'd tried so hard to banish him from her thoughts. From her dreams.

She gripped the iron railing and she didn't remember the stairs or her feet padding on the concrete. Only that she came to a stop in front of him. He towered over her, blocking the sun and, standing in his shadow, she could no longer deny the truth in her heart. He was the one. The one who would be her one true love. Forever.

And he wasn't hers to keep.

"Thank you for the lovely flowers."

"And you look even lovelier." He laid his hand against her face, cradling her tenderly.

She pressed into his touch as the shine of his soul moved through hers. There was no more darkness or grief. Only hope.

He'd faced his past. She could feel it. He could go back to his old life, or maybe a new one somewhere else, a dedicated surgeon and such a very good man. He deserved all the happiness he could find.

It took all her dignity to keep her voice steady and her hopes from crashing to the ground. "It's almost lunchtime. Why don't you stay for the meal, as our treasured friend of the family?"

"You're fooling yourself, if you think the reason I'm standing here is friendship. I don't want to be your friend."

Her bottom lip trembled.

Yeah, he knew what she was feeling. He felt the same. As if he was taking a step off the northern rim of the Grand Canyon and looking at the distant rocky floor beneath him. And stepping into thin air, anyway, knowing he was going to fall. But he had faith.

"I've come for you and your son." Tender love rose through him until he was so full he could hardly speak. But he'd gone through a lot to get to this point in his life, and he was going to do this right. "I know you've been hurt before, and you don't want to trust any man like that again. But, Amy, you are the blessing I thought I'd never find. If you agree to be my wife, I vow to cherish you above all others. If you marry me, I will never hurt you, never betray you, never leave you."

This couldn't be happening. Surely this was a dream. She had to be hallucinating or something, but Heath's hand against her cheek trembled, and she could feel his genuine love for her, soul-deep and everlasting.

It was the same love she had for him in her soul. "You came back here to propose to me?"

"Not empty-handed." He pulled a ring from his pocket. A rich gold band with a big center-cut stone. Brilliant and perfect and probably expensive. "Amy, will you do me the honor of becoming my wife? To honor and cherish for the rest of my life?"

"Oh, yes!" Tears burned in her eyes as she leaped up to hug him, holding him tight. So very tight. Joy lifted her up as Heath wrapped his arms around her and lifted her off the step and kissed her long and sweet.

Her soul sighed, complete.

As he slipped the ring on her finger, she could see a glimpse of their future. Of happy days just like this with the breeze whispering through the trees and the sun smiling down on them together. As a happy family.

As she followed her son up the front steps, she remembered to give thanks for this unexpected blessing. The sweetest of them all. Heath took her hand, kissed her cheek and they went into the house together.

* * * * *

Dear Reader,

Thank you for choosing *Sweet Blessings*. It was
such a joy to return to The McKaslin Clan. Cousin
Amy, the youngest of her family, is a single mom
who works hard to provide for her small son. She's
given up on believing that there are men who are
noble, strong and faithful in this world. Until Heath
Murdock wanders into her family's café for a late-
night meal. She recognizes in him a great wound.
With God's help, both Amy and Heath discover that
true love can heal even the greatest sorrow.

Wishing you the sweetest of blessings,

Jillian Hart

BLESSED VOWS

My purpose is that they may be encouraged
in heart and united in love.
—*Colossians* 2:2

Chapter One

How did she get talked into this? Rachel McKaslin asked herself as she peered into the basement's deep-box freezer. The answer was easy—because she had a teeny-weeny problem saying no. Especially when it came to saying no to any member of her family.

Which was why she was hanging nearly upside down in the freezer and freezing. Her fingertips were numb from shoving packages around. There was a roast in here somewhere. She knew it was in here. But could she find it? No. She did manage to find everything else, though: packages of hot dogs, boxes of frozen fish fillets, bags of frozen vegetables and a big sack of ice pops. The Popsicles she'd been looking for the last time she'd been searching through this freezer.

Wasn't that just her luck?

She grabbed a couple of grape Popsicles and heaved herself over the edge of the freezer. Her feet hit the ground—yes, she loved being short—and she rubbed the small of her back. A home-cooked meal, that's what her brother Ben had requested for his military buddy, who'd apparently been eating more MREs than real food for the last few years.

Okay. Frozen fish fingers probably didn't exactly qualify as the main course of an old-fashioned home-cooked meal.

It would have helped if Ben had called while she'd still been at work at the diner. She could have made up something right there to bring home. Or she could have stopped by the store and bought a roast like the one she couldn't manage to find now.

Maybe it was time to call in reinforcements. Maybe her sister Paige could send someone over from the diner with a to-go box. And after putting in a twelve-hour day on her feet, she'd be more than glad to give that a try.

It wasn't as if she could cook a roast that wasn't here. Ben would understand. But would his best friend?

She sighed. Well, with her luck, probably not.

She closed the freezer lid, flicked out the overhead light and at the base of the narrow stairs rising up out of the basement, she could hear the *briiing* of the phone.

Great, how long had it been ringing? She imagined Paige calling, worrying about why Rachel hadn't answered after the twenty-seventh ring. Paige was a worrier. Or maybe it was her sister Amy checking in from her latest househunting quest. Or Ben—if it was Ben, then she could explain about the failed roast recovery mission.

She tried to dash up the stairs, but her bunny slippers on the narrow steps slowed her down. By the time she flew up and into the kitchen and wrapped her hand around the receiver, the ringing died. The dial tone droned in her ear. And she didn't have caller ID.

Her cell phone began to chime the opening bars to "Ode to Joy." Excellent! Whoever had called was trying her other phone. Except, where was it? As the electronic music grew louder and louder, she followed the sound into the kitchen and to the round oak table where her duffel bag sat, still zipped. She dug around until she found it.

And it was still ringing. Whew. She flipped it open. "Hello?"

"Ah, is this Rachel McKaslin?" a man's gravelly voice asked, as if uncertain he had the right number.

A man's voice she didn't recognize. I think I know who this is. "Yep, that's me." She yanked open the freezer door on the fridge. "Is this Jake, by chance?"

"That would be me. Your brother told you I was comin', but did he warn you about me?" There was a smile to Jake's voice.

Without a doubt a very handsome smile, she thought as she tossed the ice pops into the freezer section of the fridge for later consumption. "Yep, he sure did. The question is, did Ben warn you about *me?*"

His warm, easy chuckle came across the line. "He did. Ben said that you are the generous and lovely soul who agreed to look after us at the last minute *and* on a Friday night. I take that to mean you cancelled a date?"

"Who, me? Date?" She bit her bottom lip to keep in the snicker.

"Well, it *is* a date night, and I understand you're a single attractive lady."

Yeah, right. Not since high school. There were a lot of great men in the world, good and decent men. She firmly believed that, but they never seemed to be interested in her. Maybe it was because she was always so busy, and that didn't leave a lot of time to date. But that didn't explain why no one ever asked her out. Most men were looking for a more worldly woman and, as she looked down at her fuzzy pink bunny slippers, she was anything but worldly.

"I thought I'd sacrifice a date night for Ben's best buddy," she said diplomatically so he wouldn't know he was wrong, wrong, wrong about her. The reason why she was about to be a bridesmaid for the umpteenth time, and not a bride. "It's the least I can do for the man who braved machine-gun fire to help haul my brother to cover a while back."

"He was shot. I couldn't just leave him there for the enemy to trip over."

"My family and I, we're all so grateful to you." Rachel couldn't imagine the kind of courage it took for someone to do their job in the military. "Because of you, our brother's home safe and sound."

"You're giving me a lot of credit. I was just doin' my job. And Ben's a pretty tough guy. I should know, since we serve together. It takes more than a bullet to stop him."

Humble, with a sense of humor. Judging by the deep rumbling baritone of his voice, Rachel figured that Jake had a drop-dead handsome face to match his charm, his smile and his voice. Which meant he was far, far out of her league.

Too bad. She sighed, not really disappointed. She had resigned herself to her unmarried status. She trusted God's plan for her life. Maybe she wouldn't always be single. Maybe He was simply making her wait for the very best man.

The thing was, she was getting extremely good at waiting.

"Rachel, can I ask you something?" There was a slight hesitation in his attractive baritone, as if something was wrong.

He's canceling. That's why he was calling at the last minute—not that she blamed him. From his perspective, he was probably imagining that being with his best buddy's over-thirty-year-old spinster sister wasn't the most fun way to spend an evening. As her slippers scuffled along the kitchen floor, she supposed he was right.

It was just as well because the roast she'd planned to rotisserie was missing in action. "I know Ben probably felt he needed someone to meet you, since you came all this way and he ran off to spend a romantic evening with his bride-to-be. But eating supper here probably wasn't your first choice. I understand if you'd like to cancel."

"Backing out isn't in my nature. The trouble is, I can't get to your house."

"Oh, you're lost."

"That's not my problem. I found my way here from the airport just fine. But getting to your house is harder than you'd think. I'm parked down the way in your driveway."

"You're here?" No way—she hadn't heard anyone come up. Then again, hadn't she just been in the basement nearly upside down in the freezer?

"How long have you been sitting out there without me knowing it?" Rachel headed straight to the sink and yanked the curtain out of the way. She squinted through the long rays of sunlight. The parking area and the gravel lane leading up to it were empty.

"I'm not exactly at the house yet. Look down the road and you'll see my problem."

A break-down? A flat tire, what? She scanned the length of the newly graveled driveway, past the lawn's reach to the point where the tidy white board fencing paralleled the road.

There he was. At least she figured it was him behind the wheel of a bright red SUV. She could barely make out an impression of a tall, dark-haired, wide-shouldered man behind the wheel, but with the glare on the windshield it could have been her imagination filling in the details.

So, why was he just parked in the middle of the road for no reason?

Then she saw the giant ungainly brown creature leap into the middle of the road, between the vehicle and the house. The bull moose lowered his massive four-point antlers, and he meant business. He bellowed an ugly, flat-noted call before he pawed the ground with his impressive front hooves.

Moose attack! Rachel dropped the phone and flew out the back door. She grabbed the first thing she passed by and ran full-out down the path, swinging what turned out to be the old kitchen broom.

"Get! Go on!" she waved the yellow bristles in the direction of the stubborn moose.

The creature didn't even bother to turn around. He kept his hind end to her, as if he already knew there was no way she was a threat.

Well, as if she'd let her brother's best friend and rescuer be bullied by a stubborn old moose! "You can't bully anyone you want. Get out of the road."

Nothing. The moose had dismissed her entirely.

Instead, his unblinking gaze remained on the shiny red vehicle that gleamed in the autumn sun. The animal swung his head as if in a challenge and pawed.

Disaster. All Rachel could see was the animal attacking that brand-new vehicle. That wasn't going to happen on her watch. She swung the broom closer to his hind end. "Hey!"

The moose didn't acknowledge her in any way. What he ought to be doing was bolting in fear of a human being with a weapon. Okay, it was a broom, but he was a wild animal. Weren't they afraid of people? "Go! Shoo!"

Nothing. How was she going to help Jake now?

The driver's-side window rasped down. That deliciously low male voice called out, "Need any help?"

"Oh, no. I can handle it."

"I see. You're doing an excellent job."

Was he mocking her? The moose shook his head menacingly, and bowed low, as if preparing to charge.

Okay, this wasn't going well. It would be a shame for the moose to bash up that new vehicle with his antlers, plus scare the city boy half to death. *Lord, a little help would be appreciated.*

The door of the Jeep whipped open and a lean hulk of a man dropped to the ground as if he'd fast-roped from a Black Hawk helicopter. "Shouldn't your pet be in the pasture or something?"

"Oh, he's not a pet. Are you kidding? Who keeps a moose for a pet? He's a wild animal."

And that's why he's not charging you? Jake didn't have a whole lot of experience with moose, but he did know they were dangerous. "Why don't you back off nice and slow?" He caught up a good-sized rock in his hand.

"You're going to hit him with a rock?" the woman with the broom huffed.

"Only to scare him off. Not hurt him." What kind of man did she take him for?

Jake didn't have time to find out because the moose charged. He was a huge creature. Bigger than the Jeep, the moose gained some serious speed with his awkward-looking legs. He could cause real damage if he hit the vehicle...and he'd probably scare little Sally.

Doing what it took to defend his small niece, Jake lobbed the grenade-sized rock. The hunk of granite bounced off the swoop of the moose's right antler, low enough to give him a slight bonk, but not enough to seriously hurt him. Was it enough to stop the beast?

The great animal shook his head, looking a little cross-eyed. That had to hurt.

For good measure, Jake chose a second rock, peering around the door frame to see if the animal was going to run off, regroup for a second attack or, more possibly, turn around and take his anger out on the woman with the pink furry slippers.

Ben's unmarried sister. Part of him couldn't help thinking, no wonder. But that wasn't fair, because she'd obviously not been expecting him so soon. Had she been lounging after a hard workday, maybe? She wore a big shapeless T-shirt with the faded logo of a local college and baggy shorts.

It was hard to get much of a good impression. Especially with her thick chestnut hair sticking in awkward directions and some of it nearly straight up. She wielded the old broom like a martial arts expert.

One thing he had to say about her was that she was no shrinking violet. She boldly marched toward the angry moose and swatted him on the flank with the bristle end of her broom. "Shoo! Go on! You stop being demanding and greedy. I'll feed you when it's time and not a moment sooner."

This animal *wasn't* a pet? Jake watched as the moose shook his head again, no longer threatening. The poor guy looked contrite before he ambled off in the direction of the lawn, as if he were going to wait there for his feed.

Thank the Lord no one was hurt—including the moose. Jake straightened, dropped the rock and considered his unlikely rescuer. Rachel was not what he expected. Ben talked about his sisters a lot, and it had been clear that he was closest to Rachel.

She looked like her picture. Ben had had family pictures in his dorm during their training years and later in his duplex in the years that followed. All of Ben's sisters were pretty. Rachel's picture had always given him the impression of a demure and introverted young woman, an innocent and a wallflower. Not someone who bossed moose around or had a sparkle to her soul that made him keep looking.

"Uncle Jake?" a small, candy-sweet voice asked from the back seat of the Jeep. "I wanna pet the deer."

"It's a moose, Sally baby," he answered without taking his gaze off of Rachel McKaslin as she held her broom like an M-4. "It's a wild animal. We'd be smart to stay back and give it room."

"Oh. All right." Her sigh was a wistful sound of disappointment.

He'd been hearing that sound a lot over the past few days since he'd come to take charge of Sally. He'd been pulled off active duty in Iraq, and he was still in shock.

One day he'd been rescuing a pair of captured marines and the next day he'd been on a cargo plane to the States with the news his sister had been in an accident, had died and been buried. And he was not only the executor of her estate, but the sole remaining family that his little niece had.

The trouble was, he'd been stateside four days, and it hadn't been time enough to settle his sister's estate, and already his colonel wanted to know when he could get back to active duty.

And Sally…how did he comfort a grieving child? He was a rough-and-tumble Special Forces soldier. As a para-rescue jumper, or PJ, he knew how to jump out of an airplane from twenty-five thousand feet, parachute in and set up a perimeter, execute a mission without a single mishap.

He had Sally, but what was he going to do? It had him stumped.

As if he didn't have enough on his mind, the moose was still glaring angrily at the Jeep from his field. Maybe it was the color that was making him so angry. While the animal had backed away, he hadn't backed down. He still swung his head from side to side and pawed the ground. The Jeep was definitely in danger.

But was Rachel?

"You stay belted in, Sally." He shut the door, leaving her safe and considered Rachel McKaslin, his best buddy's little sister. She was out in the open and unconcerned. Did she know the threat? He stalked the good five yards separating them, keeping a close watch on that moose.

Rachel lowered her broom. "I'm sorry. I should have anticipated this. Bullwinkle does this every evening."

"Bullwinkle?"

"It's just what I call him. I should have fed him and the horse earlier, and you wouldn't have been so rudely welcomed."

"I thought you said he wasn't your pet."

"Not a pet, no, more like a sometimes friendly, sometimes not, wild animal who's decided to take up residence around here and chase the horses away from his grain trough. He's a pushy moose."

"Pushy, huh?" Jake paced closer to protect Rachel, watching as the moose lowered his head and started to charge. Great. On a mission, Jake was prepared for every contingency. He just hadn't thought he'd have to be on alert on a simple trip down a gravel driveway. "Want to give me that broom? It looks like he's coming in for round two."

"I can take care of him."

Jake's hand shot out and he had the broom before she could blink.

"Hey! You took my broom."

"I did."

"But it's my moose. I can handle him."

"I'm trained to serve and protect, so I might as well make myself useful." The handle was solid hardwood. He'd excelled at hand-to-hand combat. "Rachel, stay behind me."

"You're a little bossy, too. It's a moose, not war."

"Everything's war, pretty lady." He timed the moose's gait, waited until the huge ungainly creature was coming head-on and then shot out and rapped him on the nose.

Big nostrils flared, the moose skidded to a stop and shook his head.

"That smarted, didn't it?" Jake kept the broom at the ready. "Do you need another smack?"

The moose's eyes rolled in anger.

Uh-oh. "Maybe that wasn't the best course of action. It works with sharks who get a little too aggressive."

"Smacking them in the nose?"

"Yep. It works every time."

"He's pushy, but mostly harmless. All I need to do is get him some grain. Wait here. With you at my back to cover me with a broom, I feel perfectly safe." She sauntered away, as if without a care in the world.

He was a soldier with fifteen years of experience spent in parts of this world few Americans saw. He'd seen evil, touched evil and battled it. Real evil. And he had the scars to prove it. Even remembering made his heart ache.

He was glad that Rachel McKaslin's biggest problem at the moment was her semi-pet moose. There was peace and goodness in this world. It didn't hurt that he got to see a rare glimpse of it before he headed back to guard this country's freedom.

It didn't hurt to see what he was fighting for.

Chapter Two

Could she see Jake from here? Rachel absently un-snapped the grain barrel's lid and stood on tiptoe. Her attention was elsewhere, straining to see across the aisle, through Nugget's box stall and past the open top of the half door.

Nope. No such luck. She saw plenty of sky and maple trees and the lawn in front of the house. But no Jake.

Pity, since he was such a sight. She had the right to look because he hadn't been wearing a wedding ring. He was pleasing to the eye, pleasing in the way God intended a man to be. But there was more to him, and that was the attractive part—Mr. Jake Hathaway, Special Forces hero, defending and protecting.

He sure had seemed to be in control. He had to be to participate in all kinds of secret missions in the military. Handling a moose was no challenge for him. He'd tossed that rock as easily as if he'd been skimming stones on a pond and expertly enough so that he'd winged the animal on his antler and hadn't caused any real harm.

And just what did he think of her? *Please, don't let him think I'm a nut bar.* She rolled her eyes as she removed the lid and reached for the scoop. She was still wearing her fuzzy bunny slippers!

She hadn't had a chance to run a brush through her hair or change out of her comfy after-work clothes. So she wasn't exactly looking her best; she was more like looking her worst.

Great way to make a first impression.

This was the reason she didn't have a boyfriend. She kept scaring them off. That was why she made sure, when she prayed for the right man to come along, that he have a sense of humor.

He would definitely need it.

She grabbed a pail from the shelf, dumped in three scoops of sweet-smelling grain and sealed the bin. Nugget was leaning over the side doorway, nickering in hopes of an early supper, poor guy. After leaving him with promises of grain to come, she hurried with the small bucket down the aisle and crawled through the paddock fence that faced the driveway.

Jake was still wielding the broom defensively, but the moose was a little farther off with his head down and snorting. Obviously there had been some action while she'd been in the barn. Before the big creature could charge again, she held the pail high and shook it.

The resulting ring of grain striking the side of the bucket brought the moose's head up. He studied the bright red Jeep gleaming like a big bull's-eye, and then turned to look at the bucket she held. To help him along with his decision to choose the grain over the vehicle, she shook the pail harder and hurried toward him.

"Give that to me and stay back." Jake seemed to take his self-assigned role of defender seriously.

Maybe it was because he thought a woman wearing big long-eared slippers might not be tough. Well, she wasn't afraid of a wild moose. She ignored Jake's advice, she was sure it was well meaning, but really, it wasn't as if she hadn't dealt with this situation before. She marched across the road and upended the bucket on the ground. The grain pellets tumbled and rushed into a molasses-scented pile in a bed of wild grasses, and the moose came running.

With her empty bucket banging against her knee, she hurried back onto the graveled lane as the moose attacked the pile as if he hadn't eaten in five weeks.

"A little theatrical for a moose, but he's mostly harmless," she told Jake, who'd rushed to her side looking pretty angry. "He didn't take a liking to your Jeep, though. I'd move it into the garage if I were you, while he's distracted."

"I can't believe you did that." He stood between

her and the moose. "You could have been killed. More people are killed every year in the Iditarod by moose than by all other predators combined, including wolves and mountain lions. You might treat him like a pet, but he's still dangerous and unpredictable."

She grabbed hold of her broom and was surprised at how worked up he was. She could sense how he'd been afraid for her safety, that was why he was all agitated. She didn't know why she could feel his emotions or his intent. Maybe she was reading a lot into his behavior, but it was hard to be upset with a man who only wanted to protect her. Even if it was unnecessary, it was well-intentioned.

And wasn't such goodness what she'd been praying for in a man? Not that he was The One, but still, a girl had to hope. "I'll run ahead and open the garage door for you, and I'll fix you a supper to remember. Is it a deal?"

"That's a pretty tall order, but I'd sure appreciate it." He didn't take his steely gaze from the gobbling moose. "I don't get home-cooked dinners very often."

"Then I'll see you at the house."

His attention remained on his adversary as he backed toward his vehicle. "Are you sure you don't want a ride? You'd be safer."

"I don't think so." How could it be safer to be in close quarters with the handsome, hunky, Special Forces soldier?

She glanced over her shoulder before she stepped

into the garage through the side door. She could barely see the driveway over the top of Mom's Climbing Blaze, the shower of red roses nearly hiding Jake's SUV as he guided it forward at a slow pace, as if expecting the worst.

She couldn't see through the glare on the windshield as the Jeep hugged the lazy curve of driveway along the edge of the lawn, but she imagined Jake was watching the road out of the corner of his eye and keeping a close watch on the moose.

All was well. The wild animal stayed crunching away at his diminishing pile of grain, his jowls working overtime. It looked as if the Jeep was out of danger for the time being, so she hit the button and the garage door groaned upward.

Jake's vehicle was right outside, waiting as the door lifted the last bit. The glare on the windshield had lessened and she could see his silhouette behind the wheel. He was tall. Now that she had a chance to think about it, she remembered looking at the upper span of his chest when she'd stood facing him.

He was really tall, she amended. At least six, six-one.

The vehicle rolled to a stop and she hit the button again. The garage door hid the moose from sight. It didn't hurt a girl to dream, Rachel decided as she backed through the threshold that led through the utility room and into the kitchen, sizing up the man.

He definitely looked like a beef-and-potatoes guy.

Maybe she'd take another pass through the freezer and find that roast she knew was in there—

The vehicle's door opened, but it wasn't Jake's door. It was the one directly behind it. What? That didn't make any sense. Jake was still clearly sitting behind the wheel. She could see him perfectly through the windshield with the dome light backlighting him. He sat soldier-straight and commando-powerful.

There was someone else with him? Her brother hadn't mentioned a second buddy coming in for the wedding that she'd have to feed, too. Not that she minded, but… Her thoughts stopped dead at the sight of a little girl climbing down from the back of the SUV.

Jake had a daughter? She was the cutest little thing, all spindly arms and legs and a cloud of chocolate-brown curls. She had to be about seven or eight and stylish in her matching pink-and-teal shirt and shorts set. Matching sandals with tassels decorated her feet, and a pair of pink barrettes were stuck into her thick, beautiful hair. Costume jewelry dangled from her wrist and her neck, and she held a tattered purple bunny that had seen much better days.

Oh, she was a sucker for kids. Suddenly it made sense that she'd found the Popsicles. It was as if one of God's angels was giving her a clue. Now there was a treat waiting for this adorable little girl. Determined to be friends, Rachel gave a little wave. "Hi there. I'm Rachel."

The little girl stared with big, wide, shy eyes and ducked back behind her open door for safety.

I know just how you feel. Rachel had been shy every day of her life. Her heart squeezed for the little girl, who had to be feeling out of her element.

Then Jake emerged, shrinking the cavernous size of the triple garage with his sheer magnetic presence. He held out one big hand, gentle despite his size. "C'mon, Sally baby. This is Ben's sister I told you about."

"'Kay." She took Jake's hand and let him lead her through the garage. The little girl looked resigned and not happy.

Determined to cheer her up, Rachel offered the child her friendliest smile, but the girl intentionally sent her gaze upward, looking around at the various shelves of tools, lawn stuff, Ben's old hunting gear and every imaginable outdoor activity stored overhead in the rafters—from the canoe to the cross-country skis.

Jake, however, did return her grin. He had a nice grin, one that softened the hard granite of his chiseled face and etched dimples into his lean cheeks. "I don't know if Ben mentioned I had Sally in tow with me. I had planned on picking her up after the wedding, but things didn't work out that way."

Oh, divorce, Rachel guessed. Shared custody. That

couldn't be easy for anyone involved. "No problem. Life rarely works out the way you think it will. I was just about to defrost a roast." *If I can find it.* "So that will be enough for all three of us. Sally, may I ask you something?"

The little girl nodded, her pretty emerald eyes wide and somber.

"Do you and your bunny want to help me pick out what kind of potatoes to make?"

Another shy nod.

"Excellent. Are you a mashed-potatoes kind of girl? Or do you like Tater Tots?"

"Tater Tots!" Some of her reserve diminished, and she hugged her bunny tight. "Uncle Jake don't know how to make 'em right."

Uncle Jake? Rachel shot a glance at the unlikely uncle closing his door and nudging the child along in front of him. "It takes talent to know how to get Tater Tots just right. Do you like 'em soft and crumbly or crisp?"

"A little crisp but still kinda all soft in the middle, but not so it's still cold."

"Me, too." Since it was hard not to like a man who took the time to spend with his niece, especially on his limited stateside visit, she'd ask his opinion, too. "Are you a Tater Tot man or a mashed?"

"Strictly French fry, but I can make an exception."

"Maybe I can rustle up a few fries for the man who

defended us from the dangerous wild moose. A man needs a reward."

Okay, he could tell when someone was amused at his expense. "You could have told me the thing was more of a pet than a wild dangerous animal. I did ask."

"He's not a pet. He's just…" She shrugged.

"Got your number." It wasn't too hard to see that Rachel was a genuinely nice person. "Okay, I went a little commando. I had Sally to protect. She's been through enough."

"I'm not blaming you, City Boy. I just wondered if you had fun playing with poor Bullwinkle."

"Not so much."

He liked her. He liked the twinkle of humor in her eye. That she was as friendly as could be without batting her eyes at him like a marriage-minded woman. He did not have a great neon sign pasted to his forehead that blinked, "Not married!" He liked that she was easygoing and that she was pretty up close. Very pretty.

And here he'd been dreading this. He'd originally planned to fly in tomorrow morning, bright and early, and do the wedding and fly home, but Sally had changed things. Here he was in town early, and Ben wasn't here to meet him.

He didn't blame his friend. Instead of a rehearsal dinner, the groom had reservations at one of the nicest restaurants in the area to spend a quiet pre-wedding evening with his bride-to-be, and there was no way Jake wanted him to cancel that. But when Ben had suggested this, Jake had felt obligated to accept this invitation. A home-cooked meal would be good for Sally.

Her hand in his felt so small and held on so tightly. There was a surprising strength in her fingers—or maybe it was need. The way she clung to him was an undeniable reminder of the promises he'd just finished making to her. From the day she'd been born, she'd had a sweet little spot in his heart and now that he was the only one left to look after her, he was only more committed. How he was going to keep those promises to her, he didn't know. Not when his job took him to dangerous corners of the world and kept him there.

Rachel had disappeared through a connecting door on the other side of a laundry room—it was a nice set-up. A closet lined one wall and a washer and dryer covered the wall on his right. Through the window he caught a glimpse of the backyard filled with lush green grass and blooming red roses and big yellow-faced flowers in tidy beds. Trees stood on the far side of the lawn, and that's all he saw before he tugged Sally into the kitchen after their hostess.

"Let me get you something," she said from across a spacious country kitchen.

Nice. He didn't know why he thought so, maybe it was because he'd been on Temporary Duty way too long. Home had become a desert base with a tent over his head and food served on a tray.

Everything smelled so good. The floor of fresh pine and the air like cookies. A chipped coffee mug sat on the granite counter stuffed with red roses from the vines outside. Their old-fashioned fragrance took him back to his grandma's house when he was a kid, where he ran wild during the summers on their San Fernando Valley farm. Maybe that was why he felt at ease with the pretty woman in the kitchen, who looked as if she were in her element as she yanked open the fridge door.

"We've got milk, soda, juice. What's your pleasure?" She looked to Sally first. "I have strawberry soda."

"Strawberry!" Sally gave a little leap, taking his hand with her. "Can I, Uncle Jake?" She beamed up at him with those big green eyes and he was helpless. They both knew it.

"Sure." He'd have to figure out how to say no to her eventually; being a parent was a whole world different than being an uncle.

Sorrow stabbed him, swift and unexpected. He couldn't get used to Jeanette being gone. He dealt with death a lot in the military; he'd lost close friends and team members and soldiers he'd admired. But to lose his sister crossing the street on the way to her office, it wasn't right. It wasn't fair to Sally.

"I've got two cartoon cups to pick from." Rachel

held the cupboard door open wide, displaying characters he didn't even recognize.

He hadn't watched cartoons since he was a kid. But Sally lit up and chose one with a big dinosaur on it while Rachel took the other one. She popped one can, filled it, foam and all, to the top of the plastic cup and set it on the round oak table to his right.

It was strange, this big kitchen and eating space, with kids' school pictures framed on the walls—the clothes and hairstyles from decades ago. Through the picture window next to the table he saw half of an old-fashioned metal swing set and slide, in good repair, as if someone had painted it not too long ago. "Ben didn't say. Do you live here alone?"

"Yep. It's way too big for me, but the memories here are good ones. What would you like to drink?"

"Ben said you were a waitress. I can see you're probably an excellent one."

"It's a hard job, tougher than people realize. But it's the family business, and I like it because I get to make all the chocolate milk shakes I want." She waited, hand on the refrigerator door, one slim brow lifted in a silent question. "What'll it take to wet your whistle, sir?"

"If you've got root beer in there, I'll be eternally in your debt."

"I'll hold you to that, soldier." With a wink, she reached inside the well-organized fridge and withdrew two more soda cans.

Before she could snag him one of those break-able glasses neatly organized in the cupboard on the shelf above the cartoon cups, he stole the can out of her hand. "I'm not used to being waited on. Put me to work."

"Work?" She looked him up and down, taking in the strong and capable look of him. "Don't tempt me, or I'll take you up on it."

He perused her big pink slippers and her comfy clothes and the fact that she hadn't had time to do up her hair into anything remotely involving hair spray and gels or whatever it was women put in their hair. That said everything. "Did you have other plans before Ben strong-armed you into doing this tonight?"

"Plans with the couch and an old movie. Nothing that can't wait until tomorrow night. Or the next night." She poured the contents of her can into the plastic mug, and the sweet-smelling pink liquid fizzed. "Wait!"

He had hold of the cup the instant she stopped pouring.

"Hey, what are you doing taking my strawberry soda?"

"What? Do you think I'm stealing it from you?"

"That's what it looks like. I call things like I see 'em."

"And what, that look of outrage is because you didn't know you were letting a strawberry soda bandit into your house?"

"That, and you're setting a very bad example for Sally."

"Is that true, Sal?" He sent a wink to his niece, who'd seated herself at the table and was sipping from the cup with both hands.

Her solemn gaze met his over the wide rim. Strawberry soda stained her mouth as she said the words of betrayal. "Stealing's wrong, Uncle Jake."

"Hey, I'm one of the good guys. Or at least that's what they tell me." And because he knew what it was like to put in a long hard workweek, he wasn't about to give up the glass of soda. "How about I wait on you? You said you had a date with the couch?"

"You've got to be joking."

"I never joke, ma'am. I'm an air force commando. Duty is my name."

"Yeah, yeah, you forget I have a brother who spouts that macho stuff all the time." She waved him off as if she knew better, as if she had his number.

Fine. The trouble was, now that he wasn't worrying about a rampaging moose, he could get a real good look at her. He liked what he saw. She was petite, there was no other word for her. Delicate, for lack of a better word. She had the clearest, creamiest skin he'd ever seen, and the gentlest manner.

A real nice woman. He wasn't about to impose on her like a deadbeat. No, he wasn't that kind of man, although he read her look of skepticism loud and clear. That was okay. He wasn't bothered by it.

"Follow me," he said, trusting that she would.

Chapter Three

She did follow him. Jake monitored the pad of her slippers against the carpet a good two to three paces behind him. "That's it. Keep coming."

"I want my strawberry soda back in the kitchen where it belongs." She didn't have a sharp voice or an angry edge. No, she was all softness and warm humor, as if he were amusing her to the nth degree.

He wasn't used to softness and humor, not in his life of duty and service. So, he thought he'd enjoy the chance to amuse her some more. "Is there a house rule about keeping all food and beverages in the kitchen?"

"There is, as a matter of fact."

"Funny. I didn't see a sign."

"It has to be a sign?"

"Sure. If it's not written down, it's not a law I have to follow."

"Yeah? Then for you I'll make an exception."

He liked the rumbling music of her chuckle. It

was an appealing sound, one a man could get used to. Nice.

And so was the house, he thought as he stepped inside the sizeable living room. Spacious. Comfortable. It was the kind of place a guy could get used to putting his feet up on that scuffed coffee table that sat in the middle of a big sink-into-me sectional. The TV was big and new, and in the winter this would sure be a great spot to sit and watch football with a fire in the gray rock fireplace.

He used an old television guide as a coaster and left the drink on the coffee table within easy reach. "Sit there. Put your feet up."

"That would be rude considering I'm supposed to be cooking you dinner."

He held out his hand, palm up and waited for her to take it. "C'mon. I'm the guest, right? So humor me."

"My mother taught me to be wary of men wanting to be humored."

"Sounds like your mama raised you right. And so did mine. It may be hard to believe to look at me, but I've got a few manners." He shifted closer to her with his hand still out, still waiting. "What's it going to be? Are you going to do what I ask? Or am I gonna have to make ya?"

"Men." Rachel sized up the commando in her living room, with his dazzling grin and his hand held out, palm up, waiting for her to place her fingers there. "Suddenly I remember why it is that I'm single."

"Those bunny slippers?"

He clearly thought he was a comedian, but he wasn't nearly as funny as he thought. "No, judging by my slippers you might be misled to think men have avoided me on purpose."

"I don't think that, believe me."

"But it's been my choice. Most men are bossy."

"We're made that way."

"Sadly." He didn't seem the least bit sorry about it. He was incorrigible, and she liked that in a man, too. He had nice eyes—kind ones—and she was a sucker for a good-hearted man. How was she going to ever say no to this one?

Willpower, she directed herself. "I'm supposed to be the hostess. You've flown all this way to be Ben's best man. The least I can do is talk you into sitting down and putting up your feet."

"Good luck. But let me warn you, I'm stubborn."

"I'm stubborn, too." There was no way she was going to give in to the temptation to place her fingertips on his big rough palm.

Oh yes, she wanted to. His palm was wide and relaxed, and calluses roughened the skin at the base of his fingers. He worked hard. She liked that in a man too.

His hands had scars—not big ones, just nicks that had long healed over, and those calluses. She imagined him fast-roping from a helicopter or carrying wounded on a litter. Essentially male, wholly masculine, everything a man ought to be.

And suddenly she felt it in the pit of her stomach. A little tingle of anxiety. Her shyness seemed to rear up and leave her speechless. It was one thing to have her brother's military buddy drop by. It was another to be alone with a smart, brave and warm-hearted soldier.

If only she could untie the knot her tongue had gotten itself into and say something wonderful to make him laugh some more. To show off the dimples in his hard, carved cheeks.

"I'm waiting." He arched one brow, but he wasn't intimidating in the least. He should be—he was a big man, and the slightest movement made muscles ripple beneath his sun-bronzed skin.

But he was a gentle giant down deep, Rachel was sure of it. "How about you and Sally sit down with me? We'll find something on the tube that all three of us can enjoy and after a while, I'll sneak into the kitchen and start supper."

"There'll be no sneaking on my watch. I've got a sharp eye." His hand hovered in a silent question.

And she answered just as quietly by placing her fingers in the center of his palm. *Wow.* It was all she could think the instant they touched. An energy jolted through her like a lightning strike—or heaven's touch.

She felt seared all the way to her soul. It was as if

her entire central nervous system short-circuited—
she couldn't seem to talk. She could barely manage
to be coordinated enough to sit down.

Wow, was all her poor fried brain could think.
Wow. Wow. Wow. Lord, he can't be the one. He can't
be. Look how he acted as if nothing had happened.
It probably hadn't on his end. She searched his clear
dark eyes and the calm steady way he moved away
from her with sheer athletic grace as he ambled out
of sight.

She'd read about moments like this, that instant
punch of something extra that said this man was special. Above the ordinary. Meant to last. Okay, she read
inspirational romances one after another. She always
had her nose in one, but she'd never believed, never
thought once that it could happen to her.

Not that it was a life-changing moment. It was just
a snap of something extra, making her more aware of
this man's goodness than others she'd come across.

Why? He couldn't be the one. He lived on the other
side of the country and he worked in faraway places
on other continents. Plus, he was leaving after the
wedding.

He's not the one. She was imagining all this, right?
She was tired, she hadn't eaten since she'd been able
to work in an early sandwich before the lunchtime
rush. She was feeling the weight of being a bridesmaid for the umpteenth time. Not that she minded,

no way. And especially because this was her brother's wedding.

But she wanted to be a bride. She wanted the real thing, a sweet storybook wedding with the man she would love for all time. That's why she was feeling this...wishful thinking. Pretty powerful, but wishful thinking all the same.

The pleasant rumble of his voice from the kitchen drew her attention. It was like a tingling warmth in her heart, and she'd never felt that before either. She could hear Sally's answer and then the faint scrape of the wood chair on tile.

That's why I feel so wowed by him. It all made sense now. She loved a man who was good with children. And his niece was a cutie, that was for sure. It was sweet he was spending time with her. And now that she knew why she was so taken with him, it would be easier to keep things in perspective.

"Hey, Rachel." Jake rounded the corner with Sally at his side, her small hand engulfed by his huge one. "Mind if she uses the facilities?"

"First door on the right." Rachel stood, but Jake waved her back and deftly disappeared beyond the edge of the fireplace. In a few seconds, a door closed down the hall.

What she really ought to do was to take another crack at finding that roast. The soda would keep—it was fizzing and bubbling merrily in the cartoon cup.

As for her aching feet, she could get a few more

hours out of them, she thought as she cut through the dining room and dashed down the basement steps. Her guests would be busy for a few moments, and if she could just find that roast—

"Running away from me?" Jake's baritone was filled with friendly, warm amusement.

Good thing she wasn't affected. "Not running any farther than the freezer. Why don't you help yourself to the remote? I don't mean to be a bad hostess, I'm just digging stuff out for supper."

"Suppose I help you with that?" His steps sounded behind her on the stairs.

"Oh, I can get things just fine." Actually, what she needed was someone who was tall enough to reach all the way to the bottom of the freezer. Was she going to admit that to him? No. "I'll be right up, okay?"

No answer was forthcoming, although the approaching rasp of sneakers on the cement floor trailed her to the freezer room. Rachel yanked on the light.

And there he was, he'd caught up to her, and let out a breath of awe. "Wow. Did you do all this canning?"

"My sisters lent a hand." She supposed the floor-to-ceiling shelving and all the jars sitting on them did look impressive. "We like to can."

"I'll say."

"It's something our mom used to do. She'd get all of us to help her, even Amy when she was just a preschooler. We'd all peel and cook and fill jars." She reached to open the freezer lid, but his hand was already there, lifting the lid and exposing the icy contents to the glare of the light.

That's how she felt, illuminated in the deep reaches of her self. How could talking about the preserving jars on the shelf do that? Simple, she realized. "It was everything good in our childhoods. Maybe that sounds corny, but the memories are good ones. The kind that really matter."

"That make you who you are?"

His comment surprised her, this tough commando who had lobbed a rock like a grenade in the driveway as if at war. He was understanding, and she decided she liked him even more. "When my sisters and I do our yearly frenzy of making jams and canning, it always brings us back, makes us part again of that time in our childhoods when Mom was alive and her warm laughter seemed to bounce around the kitchen like sunbeams."

Sometimes it hurt to remember, but it hurt even more to forget. And so she remembered. "When Dad would come home with packed meals from the diner because he knew Mom would have been so caught up she'd have forgotten the time. The whole house would smell like the strawberry jelly simmering on the stove, or the bushels of fresh peaches we'd have spent all day sitting around the table slicing."

"Ben said you lost your folks when you were young."

"It was like the sun going out one day." And that

was the part of remembering that hurt most, like a spear through the heart. "But Paige was just sixteen then and she took care of us."

"You were alone?"

"We didn't want to be split up, and no one could take on the four of us." Well, the spear remained lodged in her heart and the past was just going to keep hurting if she kept talking about it. She turned her attention—and the conversation—to the freezer. "You wouldn't want to reach down with those long arms of yours and dig around for a roast, would you?"

"A roast. Why, ma'am, I'd do nearly anything for a good roast. We don't get those much in the deserts where I've been spending my time." He leaned down as if to thrust his arm deep into the frosty mists, but stopped in mid-plunge. "I can't believe this. You have my absolute favorite fish sticks. I mean, these are the best."

"I love those, too. They're the best with the tartar we make at the diner. I've got a jar—"

"Forget the roast. Let's whip up a cookie sheet of these, bake up some Tater Tots and I'll be happy as a— Oh boy, you've got real apple pie in here."

"Homemade. If you want—"

"Yeah. Yeah, I do." He loaded up with the pie and the fish sticks before closing the lid. "You really don't mind?"

"Are you kidding? I've been on my feet all day.

Tell you what, how long are you staying in town to-morrow?"

"Uh… Don't know. We're on a standby flight back to L.A. I've got the last of the estate stuff to settle, it's a long process." The look on his face, one of grief, one of bewilderment kept her from turning off the light.

Estate stuff? Rachel's stomach twisted. Before she could ask, Jake reached up and snapped off the light, leaving them in shadows. "Sally's mom died—my sister. Hit by a bus on the way to work one morning."

No. That poor little girl. Rachel's heart wrung in sympathy. She knew just what that felt like for a child to lose a mother. "And her father?"

"Nonexistent. Ran off long ago and never wanted to be responsible. No one can even find him now. That's why I have her." He took off abruptly, speaking over his shoulder, sounding normal but his movements looked jerky and tense in the half-light drifting down the staircase. "That's why she's with me. If I hadn't taken her when I arrived home, then she would have had to stay in foster care while I came here. And she asked me not to leave her. So I didn't."

"I'm glad you brought her." Well, that was about the saddest thing she'd heard in a long time. "How long was she alone while you were in the desert?"

"Nearly seven weeks. That's a long time."

"Too long." Rachel's quiet agreement said every-thing.

I wish I could have gotten to her sooner. There was

no getting around that fact. Or the logistical problems of hunting him down in the middle of a covert deployment and getting him back to the States again.

Jake felt the weight of impossible guilt, dragging him downward. He'd done all he could, but it didn't change the fact that Sally had been left alone to grieve in a stranger's home, under a stranger's care, and she wasn't the same little girl he remembered. It was as if something essentially her had died too, of sorrow. How was he going to fix it for her? He didn't have a single answer.

Maybe the Lord would give him one, since he was all out of ideas. All out of everything.

"I'll do what I can to make sure she has some fun," Rachel said.

So much understanding lit her voice, and it struck Jake like a bullet to the heart. He hadn't registered his worries about bringing Sally—about everything. He didn't want to go there. He would handle it, things would work out. He was Special Forces trained to assess, adapt and overcome. He'd succeeded at every training exercise, every task and every mission. But a child was not a mission.

He headed up the stairs, box in hand, not sure if he could look Rachel in the eye. "I figured that since Ben had a nephew about Sally's age, she might not be too out of place."

"Oh, of course not. I happen to be in charge of the kids' activities. You know, receptions are so boring for the little people. All that sitting still and vows and kisses and then the manners at the sit-down meal. So we're going to have our own party outside. I'll take good care of Sally for you. I'm sure you and Ben will want to hang out for a while at the reception."

Jake nearly missed the last step up. "I hadn't thought about pawning her off on anyone. That wasn't what I meant—"

"I know. But I was simply informing you of our plans. If you want her to be with the other kids, we're going to have a lot of fun." Rachel shut the door and followed him to the counter where he'd dropped off the fish box. "We'll have games and races and our own cake. We're having hot dogs and burgers. It's going to be such a blast, I can't wait."

Ben was right. His sister Rachel was the nicest person ever. And she didn't seem to know it, didn't seem aware that she was as incredibly beautiful on the outside as she was on the inside. Her loveliness shone outward like sunlight through clouds, and it dazzled.

He had to turn away, blinking hard, affected and he didn't know why. He was used to keeping his feelings under lock and key. Why his emotions were staging a break-out, he didn't know, but he didn't like it. Not one bit.

Rachel clicked on the oven and there was a clatter as she dug a cookie sheet out of the bottom cabinets. Her "Oops!" was good-natured as she put away the other racks and cookie sheets that had tumbled out with the first one.

She had a patience about her, an inner harmony that he admired. It didn't take a rocket scientist to see that she was probably great with kids. "I'm sure Sally would like to hang out with you tomorrow. Thanks."

"Not a problem." She rose, a petite willow of a woman who moved like poetry, like grace, like all that was good in the world.

It was nice, it was normal. He wasn't used to nice and normal, he'd been away from a normal life for so long, he didn't feel as if he quite fit anymore. It was heartening to see, it gave a man pause, to watch a woman in a kitchen preparing supper and to know all was safe here, all was right in this tiny piece of the world.

Maybe he could lay down his responsibilities, the constant on-guard duty he carried, and rest for a short while. He hadn't realized how tired he was, but it washed over him like a warm rain.

"Jake, I'll whip you up some homemade fries," she said as she hauled real potatoes out of the pantry. "It'll only take a second. Sally is welcome to have her soda in the living room. Why don't I take that in to her before I start getting busy in here?"

His throat closed entirely. Unable to know what emotions were whirling around free inside him, and just as unable to speak, he held up his hand, stopping her with what he hoped wasn't too harsh a gesture and grabbed Sally's cup and his soda can.

He walked out of the kitchen and didn't look back, but he swore he left a part of himself standing there, awed by the woman and her kindness.

Chapter Four

It always made Rachel happy to be in the kitchen. With the hum of the TV drifting in through the dining room, she popped the tray of fish sticks and Tater Tots into the oven and plunked the small hill of hand-cut potatoes into the deep-fryer. Cooking was comforting, maybe because she associated it with her mom and dad.

Few things in a day made her happier than having someone to cook for, even temporarily. The fatigue that had built on her in layers throughout the day began to fade. As she set the timer, a new burst of energy lifted her up. The fryer's oil sizzled and snapped and the sound was a friendly accompaniment while she dug through the shelving inside the refrigerator's door and picked out the appropriate condiments.

After loading up a tray with napkins and flatware, she set out for the living room. The rise and fall of voices from the television grew louder, drawing her closer. On the couch in front of the colorful screen and washed in the glowing light, the big man and little girl sat side by side, intent on the old family movie.

Wow. It was awesome Sally had an uncle like Jake who would take her in without question. Otherwise, she'd hate to think of what the child might face. She'd been exposed to that fear as a kid. But probably Sally had it worse losing her home and having to move across the country to the house where Jake was stationed. While Sally battled her grief over her mom, at least she had Jake to love and protect her, to keep her safe from this world that often did not think of children.

Rachel set the tray in the center of the coffee table, leaning just right so she wouldn't block their view of the tube.

Jake stirred from his TV watching. "I ought to get off my duff and help you."

"There's nothing left to do."

Heaven save me from this man. It would be nothing at all to simply fall fast and hard in love with him. Well, not real love, that was something that deepened forever between a man and woman, but the initial tumble, *that* wouldn't take too much if she kept seeing more of his good heart.

Nope, she needed to handle things from here by herself. It was a matter of self-preservation. "You stay right there with Sally. She needs your company. I'll be back with supper."

"You eat in here?"

"Why not? It's Friday. It's the tradition in this house."

As she turned her back on the cheerful movie flashing across the screen, it was the past and its cherished memories that came with her. This was why she loved living in this house so much. The four of them together as kids, crowded onto the two couches that used to be in this room, pushing and shoving and laughing in good humor so that it was hard to listen to the movie.

Dad would be manning the grill outside if it was summer, and he'd pop his head through the slider door and shout at them to stop hitting one another. As she set up the TV trays, Mom would be laughing, reminding him that he was the one who wanted four kids, remember?

As often as not, one of them would jump off the couches to help her. Soon their favorite meal of cheeseburgers and Tater Tots would be served up on the trays, they'd all be eating and watching the TV. All through the show, Dad would make funny comments meant to make them all howl with laughter.

Yeah, she thought as she whipped the fries from the hot grease, this was the reason she hadn't settled down yet. Because she hadn't settled. How could she want anything less than the family life she'd had growing up? One day, the good Lord willing, she would know that brand of happiness again.

Until then, it was nice to dish up plates with everything just right for her guests. Tater Tots done just right—crispy on the outside and warm and chewy on the inside. Fresh fries still steaming, both heaped on half of the good stoneware she'd gotten for Christmas from her sisters, and plenty of golden crispy fish sticks. Small bowls of coleslaw, made fresh at the diner that morning, added the required vegetables to the meal.

The loaded tray made hardly a clatter as she carried it through the dark dining room and into the living room where the bold animation on the screen flashed enough color to light her way. Careful not to disturb the movie-viewing, she handed off Sally's plate, setting it right in front of her on the coffee table and adding the little bowl of coleslaw. She meant to circle around and slip Jake's plate onto the other side, but he held out his hand. "If that tastes as good as it smells, I'm gonna be the most grateful man in Montana."

"You really must be hungry. To be the most grateful man over a pile of fish sticks." She avoided his fingers as she gave him his plate heaped with steaming-hot food and then slid the bowl of slaw onto the coffee table before he could reach.

"Do you know how long it's been since I've had a home-cooked meal?"

"This isn't home cooked. It's straight from the freezer." It was funny he thought so, though.

"These fries look homemade."

"They are, but, well, the rest used to be frozen. But, hey, as long as you're happy."

"Happy? I've spent the last two years nearly straight in the desert. Eating MREs and mess-tent food, and let me tell you, this is the best. Just the best." He sounded as if she'd set an expensive, four-star meal in front of him.

"I'm glad you think so." That was what mattered. If Ben's best buddy was happy, then she was, too. "If your flight doesn't work out, I'll make you that roast dinner tomorrow."

"Deal. You want to say grace?"

"You're the guest." She unloaded her plate onto the corner of the coffee table and set the tray out of the way. "Please, you go right ahead." She was pretty interested in what he'd say. A tough guy, just like her brother, would probably be to the point. Her brother's favorite prayer, she guessed: "Good food, good God. Amen."

Jake's head bowed and his big hands steepled. Definitely not what she expected, but she liked what she saw—the sincere tilt of his profile as his eyes drifted shut.

"Dear Heavenly Father," he began in his steady baritone. "Thank you for the blessings we find at the end of this day. That Sally and I are together. We have had a safe journey from California and a peaceful solution to Bullwinkle's attack. And most of all, thank you, Lord, for bringing us a new friend in Rachel, and I'm especially grateful for the fish sticks."

His genuineness sounded somehow richer when mixed with his gentle humor, and as Rachel sat with her head bowed, she sneaked a glance at Jake through her eyelashes. He looked totally at ease and comfortable in prayer, and it was clear he had a solid relationship with the Lord.

If he hadn't been sitting next to her on the couch, all one-hundred-percent flesh-and-blood man, she would have figured him to be a daydream she'd woven of the perfect guy. A courageous warrior who served his country. An honest man of strong faith. Kind to children. Funny and handsome and...

Whoa, there, Rache. He's just visiting. As she managed to get out an "Amen" without sounding too distracted, she opened her eyes all the way, unfolded her hands and tried to remind herself that Jake wasn't looking for romance. He was leaving for good after the wedding and she'd never see him again.

Too bad. It was hard not to feel disappointment or a little bit wistful as Jake helped himself to generous spoonfuls of their secret-family-recipe tartar sauce, dragged four fries through it, and took a bite. He moaned even before he started chewing.

"I should have added the tartar to the list of blessings," he quipped, looking about as handsome as any man could with those dimples carved into his lean, sun-browned cheeks.

Her heart gave a little tumble. Of admiration, she firmly told herself, and not of interest. She fastened her gaze firmly on the TV screen and did her best not to look at Jake and his dimples.

Impossible. He leaned close so that their shoulders were almost touching. Only a scant hairbreadth of air stood between the curve of her shoulder and the hard line of his arm. "The tartar's even better on the fish sticks. I owe you, Rachel."

"Well, I didn't plan on charging for the meal," she joked.

And brought out the warm rumbling chuckle. "I'm doing the dishes and I don't want a single argument from you. Got that, ma'am?"

"Sorry. You're outranked."

"How can you outrank me? You're not a commanding officer. You're not even in the armed services."

"But I have the power to take away the tartar sauce." How she could banter so easily with this man, she didn't know.

She only knew that her chest and heart felt warm when Jake gave her a smile with those full-wattage dimples and leaned close to her ear, so close, his breath tickled hot against the curve of her ear. "Go ahead and try."

"Okay. I will. You watch out, soldier boy." She dunked a Tater Tot into the pile of tartar on her plate, surprised how she didn't feel shy at all. It was as if she'd been bantering with this man all of her life.

* * *

The brilliance of the September sunset came like peace to the evening. Rachel paused at the sliding door just to take in the awe of magenta streaks painting the sky and bold purple splashes staining the underbellies of the clouds. The colors glowed so brightly in the off-blue sky that the shadows streaking across the back lawn from the tall stand of trees at the property line were amethyst and an incredible rose light graced them.

Why this evening's sunset seemed particularly glorious, she couldn't rightly say. Especially when she'd been so beat after a long rough workweek and those last-minute, nerve-racking wedding preparations. Maybe it was the fish sticks and Tater Tots, which were one of those childhood favorites Mom used to make for them when Dad was working late at the diner. Good memories from her childhood always heartened her.

But having Jake and Sally here in this house had lifted her up, too. Having a child in this house, watching an animated movie and now swinging on the swing set in the big backyard stirred a longing inside her. Cooking for a man and child, even people she would never see again after tomorrow, made her wish for her own husband and child.

Maybe it was that over-thirty thing—the biological clock everyone talked about—but watching Jake give

Sally a hard push on the swing, sending the girl soaring up high, made her realize how lonely her life was.

Sure, she had a great family, she had a great job and she loved this life God had given her, but her heart was lonely for a man, someone strong and kind and good like Jake, and a little child to love and care for.

She knew if Jake and Sally hadn't come tonight, the sounds of laughter wouldn't be shimmering like the rosy light in the air. She would have come home, collapsed in front of the TV and eaten leftovers from the diner, then she would have done a few loads of laundry, caught up on the housework and probably started watering the yard. All the while the big house would have been echoing around her with the memories of family happiness in the past and none for the future.

She was beginning to think the Lord had forgotten about her deepest, most precious prayers. Or maybe He meant for her always to be alone. She hadn't minded it so much because she'd been so busy helping her sister Amy take care of her son Westin; having a nephew to dote on had filled her heart and her life enough that she didn't hurt for her own family so much.

And now, Amy had gone and gotten married, which was a great blessing to their family. She'd found a good man who cherished her and Westin, and was always eager to help with anything the family needed. Amy's new husband Heath spent a lot of time with Westin, and while Rachel was utterly thankful for that, she didn't see Westin as much.

Why tonight the loneliness felt so keen, like the crisp edge of light too brilliant to look at, she didn't know. Only she had tears burning behind her eyes and a pain like a blade slicing her heart, and there was no reason for it. Not when she had so much already in her life.

Jake gave Sally another push and paused to watch his niece shrieking with delight as she swept up toward the sky. "Rachel McKaslin. Have I told you why you're my most favorite person?"

"It wouldn't be because I'm holding grape Popsicles, would it?"

"Pretty much. You just know where to hit a guy."

"Oh, you're wrong there. I never hit. So, are you telling me that there's truth to the old saying? The way to a man's heart is through his stomach?"

"I don't know about the heart, but a grape Popsicle will put you at the top of my list." He stepped back in time with Sally's swing as she zoomed backward between them.

There was something awesome about a big tough man being tender with a child. Rachel waited tongue-tied as he gave Sally a big push.

The little girl squealed with joy. "Are those grape?" she shouted as she swept backward between them.

Rachel managed to nod, and the fact that she couldn't seem to speak didn't matter as Sally dug the heels of her little sandals into the grass to slow the swing.

"Is that for me?"

"Yep. I hope you like grape."

"It's only like my very most favorite!"

Rachel's heart melted at the sight of the little girl, an orphan and grieving the loss of her parent. Finding the Popsicles in the crowded freezer had seemed like a small thing at the time, and yet Rachel could see God working in her life as clearly as the tentative grin on the little girl's sweet face. "Grape is my favorite, too. Here you go. Be careful, because it's already melting."

Sally took the plastic bowl eagerly with one hand and grabbed hold of the wooden stick handles with the other. She'd been such a quiet little girl until now, more of a shadow than a child, and it was good to see the hint of the child Sally must have been before her mother's death.

And because she knew exactly how that felt, she added a silent prayer. *Dear Father, I know that you're watching over her. Please keep watching over her.*

When she opened her eyes, she realized Jake had stepped away from the swing and was sitting on the closest picnic table bench, watching her with serious eyes.

It was as if in that brief moment he could see right

through her to the places that mattered and held the greatest truths. Her heart skipped a beat and her soul brightened the way sunshine brightens the day after passing clouds.

In that moment it was as if the earth stilled and time halted and she saw the man he was; she saw beyond the warrior and her brother's friend and Sally's uncle. Jake was no longer a stranger. She couldn't say exactly why; it was only something she could feel. Like faith. Or like hope.

She could sense the heart of the man, his integrity and character and strength. And his goodness.

He folded his strong arms over his broad chest. "Come join me."

That sounded like the best idea ever. Her feet were moving her forward before she made the conscious decision. "Sally seems to be having a good time. I'm glad you brought her."

He took the bowl she offered him. "Being here seems to have done her a world of good. I haven't seen her smile since I came to pick her up. Now I owe you."

"For what?" She eased onto the far end of the bench. "I didn't do anything. Just made supper and apple pie and now I handed her a Popsicle."

"Ben told me you were humble, too. Not just nice and sweet and funny—"

"My brother is biased, plus he spends most of his time far away from here. You know that. Distance makes the heart grow fonder and dulls the memory of a person's faults."

"Sure, okay. I don't buy that." He bit off the end of his Popsicle. "You are funny."

"Me? I haven't said anything funny since you got here. I wish I were funny. You know, like a comedian."

"Well, you are the only woman I know who wears big pink rabbits on her feet."

"What?" She stared at her slippers. She was still wearing them? "I'd forgotten all about them."

"And you're nice. You could have let your pet moose attack me and Sal."

"It was tempting." She slurped the melting goodness off the top of her grape pop. "Like I said, I owed you for saving Ben when he was hurt."

"He seems to be doing better. They say he'll be back on base after his honeymoon."

"He's pretty psyched about being able to return to active duty."

"We're pretty psyched he's coming back. He might get back to work before I do." Jake nodded to where Sally sat twirling in the swing while licking the dripping goodness of the iced treat. There was a whole lot he didn't know how to say. His job wasn't just any job. He was a para-rescueman; he put his life on the line so that others might live. And he couldn't do that living near the base and being home every night to take care of Sally.

And yet if he didn't take her, then there was no one else but social services. He wouldn't do that to her. He couldn't. He loved her too much and he could never break the trust his sister had placed in him for Sally's sake.

Lord, I know this is all in Your plan. So please, show me the way to help Sally through this. Show me what I'm supposed to do with her and for her.

Jake had no idea how this was going to work out. He had orders to be back at Hurlburt by the end of the month. He fully expected to be deployed immediately. He'd rejoin his squad in the Middle East. Orders were orders, and how he was going to do his duty and be home to take care of Sally was a mystery. Was there a chance he could find someone trustworthy to take care of Sally while he was gone? A good nanny was his only option.

"I imagine having her in your life is going to change things a bit." Understanding shone in Rachel's lovely blue eyes, as if she could see his dilemma.

She was so friendly and kind, it was hard to remember he'd only just met her today. Maybe it was because he knew Ben so well and he'd seen the family pictures—with Rachel in them—that Ben had, as long ago as the tough seven weeks of PJ qualifications at Indoc that made boot camp look like a day at the beach. Whatever it was—probably God's hand in things—he felt as if he'd known Rachel far longer.

And that she was someone he could trust. That was something he hadn't had in a real long time.

"I'm lucky I have my own place off base. Ben lives in the same complex."

"Are you on the beach, too?"

"Oh, yeah. Not that I'm ever home to enjoy it. But at least I've got a roof and four walls and a bedroom to get fixed up for her." He bit into the sugary grape ice and savored the blast of flavor on his tongue. "First I've got to get her settled. Make her feel like she's got a home no matter what."

"That will mean a lot to her."

The gentle evening breeze gusted, catching wisps of Rachel's beautiful hair. The rich chestnut strands were shot with gold from the soft rosy evening's light and caressed the side of her face, emphasizing the creamy complexion of her skin and the delicate cut of her high cheekbones. Hers was a beautiful face, he realized. So lovely that he could not look away.

She seemed unaware of her beauty—both outward and inward—as she bit into her iced pop and watched Sally on the swing. She tilted her head to one side, her hair sweeping against the delicate arch of her neck. The breeze stirred between them, bringing him the scents of grape and a subtle sweet cinnamon scent.

"It's going to be a huge adjustment for Sally. She'll have to get used to living in a new place. She'll have a new school. She'll have to make new friends. And on top of that, she'll be grieving," Rachel said.

"You do understand." It was only proof the Lord had brought him here for a reason. He felt over-whelmed with his responsibilities toward Sally—not that he was about to let her down. He was all she had. "I want to do right by her. It's just gonna take a lot to help her through this."

"But she will get through it. She has you."

"I'm not going to be enough for her." Honesty. It popped off his tongue before he had a chance to think of a less-revealing answer. He felt exposed as Rachel turned on him her sympathetic gaze, as tender as a touch, and he reeled from it.

He wasn't comfortable being this close to anyone, and yet it was too late to take back the words. They could not be unspoken, and now he heard the silence between them. And he worried she would think the same thing. He didn't want this woman he liked—he really did—to think less of him.

"You're her uncle. You're a big strong warrior who has faced danger all over this world and put your life on the line for what was right. What better man to take care of a vulnerable child?"

He shook his head, as if he really thought she was wrong. "I know nothing about little girls. Not really. I hardly know Sally. I've been deployed most of her life. We're more strangers than family."

"I've seen you two together. I don't believe that."

"Then you're wrong." He didn't know how to ex-plain it. He'd kept contact with Sally and his sister over the years, they were the only family he had since his parents' deaths. He'd loved Jeanette and his niece, but his career was beyond demanding, and he had little time for more than a phone call every few weeks.

He loved Sally. But it had been from a great distance. He rescued soldiers who were in trouble wherever and whenever they needed him. He couldn't do that and be home to take care of Sally.

"If we're going to be friends, then there's one thing you'd better know about me right up front, Mr. Jake Hathaway."

"What's that?"

"I'm never wrong. Well, not about this. I know exactly what it's like to have your world shatter. But I was lucky. Paige was old enough to keep us together. To hang on to the diner and this house. She became the head of the family. Our uncle Pete kept a close watch on us, and he helped out always. But Paige kept us a family. She gave up her dreams of going to college to stay and raise us. To run the diner. To make the mortgage payments. To make sure we got through school and into college if we wanted."

"You went to college?"

"I'm a waitress with a bachelor in education and English. I wanted to teach."

"That's why you're so good with kids. You would have made a great teacher. Why didn't you?"

"That's tricky. It's about doing the right thing. I bet you know something about that."

Her gaze fastened on his. For all her softness she was a very direct woman. He could see the steel in her, too, a strength that made him sit up a little straighter and respect her. "Family," he guessed.

"Yes. Paige stayed to run the diner for us. And now that her son's a senior in high school, he'll be going away to college next year, Paige wants to get on with some of the goals she had to set aside. I've agreed to take over the diner for her. Which means I have to learn things like bookkeeping and purchasing and managing."

"When you'd rather be a teacher."

"I'd rather see my sister happy. She deserves it, after all she's done for me. For all of us."

Shame exploded in his chest. The Lord worked in mysterious ways, but He was always faithful. Always awesome.

Jake had been struggling with what to do—and the good Father had brought him here, to this woman of gentleness and goodness, to remind him of what really mattered in this life. Family. Keeping children safe. It was why he trained so hard and pushed himself so far every day he wore his uniform.

He believed in what he did—saving others, protecting others and defending this country so women like Rachel and children like Sally could live their lives in peace and safety.

Before he could turn to thank Rachel for her gentle reminders on this peaceful evening, the sliding door rasped open and there was Ben, walking with a slight limp, looking a ton better than he had the last time Jake had seen him in the field hospital. He chose to leave his thanks unspoken to Rachel and stood to greet his best friend.

Hours later in the hotel as he watched Sally sleep through the motel room's adjoining door, he remembered to give thanks for his time spent with Rachel. The thought of her stuck with him, like an imprint on his soul.

Chapter Five

There was something about weddings. A singular joy raced through Rachel's soul as she stood next to Cadence, her brother's soon-to-be wife, in the crowded little room in the church's basement. She would be gaining a sister today.

"Of course it would have to be the windiest day ever." Cadence rolled her eyes in good humor despite the tangle of her once-perfect curls. "At least I look more like myself this way. Ben isn't used to seeing me all dressed up, instead of with my wet hair tied back after a day working at the pool."

Cadence was a swimming instructor and diving coach at the county pool, and her hair was wet and tied back in a ponytail more often than not. As the first of the autumn leaves scoured the basement window, Rachel handed Paige one of the homemade pearl-and-ribboned barrettes that perfectly matched Cadence's homemade wedding dress. Paige wielded the curling iron with skill before plucking the barrette from Rachel's fingers.

Weddings were like fairy tales coming true. Rachel couldn't hold back the happiness she felt for Cadence and her brother. They had found true love, one of God's greatest blessings. *Please, Father,* she prayed, *protect them and guide them. Help them to make their love stronger with every passing day.*

Rachel caught Cadence's gaze in the mirror. "You have never looked more lovely."

The bride's chin wobbled. "I've never been more nervous in my entire life. I'm getting married, not competing in the Olympics. But look at me." She held up her hand, lovely with a new manicure. "Like a leaf."

"Nerves are perfectly normal," Amy commented from the doorway behind them, where she was gently shaking out the beautiful tulle and pearl veil. "When I married Heath, I was scared to death. And it didn't make any sense because I wanted to be his wife more than anything."

"That's exactly how I feel." Cadence lowered her trembling hands to the edge of the dressing table and took a steadying breath. "I love your brother more than my life. But I'm not sure if I can keep my knees steady enough to walk down the aisle to marry him."

"You'll be fine." Paige slid the final barrette into place in Cadence's thick, beautiful hair. "Once you see Ben, the nerves will slip away."

"Do you promise?"

"Absolutely."

"That isn't making me shake less." Cadence's chuckle was a nervous one.

Rachel took her trembling hands and squeezed. "It's an important moment and worthy of anxiety. You want it to go right. You want your life from this moment on to be full of love and happiness."

"I don't want to disappoint Ben. I love him so much."

Rachel melted, because this was the way love should be. The only kind of love she wanted for her friend Cadence and her brother, but also, one day, for herself.

"Oh! They're ready for us!" Amy exclaimed from the doorway. "Do you hear the organ upstairs?"

The first sweet strains of "Amazing Grace" sifted through the floorboards and the sound seemed to hearten Cadence. The beautiful bride managed a calm smile. "Ben is waiting for me?"

"He's at the top of the stairs," Amy answered as she carefully handed the veil to Paige.

Cadence's eyes teared. "This is it. I'm really going to get married."

"Really and truly." Rachel could feel the change as she helped Cadence to stand. "How are those wobbly knees?"

"Only a little shaky. I'm doing better. You're right. I just need to see Ben and I'll be fine." The bride gasped as Paige secured the veil, and the delicate fabric fluttered over her beautiful face. "Do I really look all right? Do you think he'll be pleased?"

"He's going to burst with pride when he sees you." Paige leaned close to hug Cadence, and then stepped aside so Amy could do the same. "Welcome to the family."

Rachel swiped at her tears. Her friend glowed with a radiance that only a bride in love could have. She passed out the bouquets. The gentle fragrance of roses and lavender seemed to bless them as they filed out of the room and up the stairs where organ music filled the sanctuary. Amy's strapping husband Heath offered his wife his arm and led the way down the aisle.

It was so beautiful. Rachel savored the moment, her heart full as she watched her younger sister and her husband progress arm-in-arm. Maybe it was the glint of jeweled light through the stained-glass windows that seemed to bless them with a caring touch. Or the sweet strains of Pachelbel's famous canon began, and the music seemed to draw the couple closer. Amy tilted her head back, her dark-blond locks tumbling over her shoulders, to smile up at her man.

Big, solemn Heath met her gaze and for an instant it was as if the world stopped moving, the music stood still and the sunlight beaming from above brightened. The abiding love between wife and husband seemed to have a shine of its own. A beauty that added to the beauty in the church. Although the pews were mostly

empty—Cadence and Ben wanted a small wedding—
a collective sigh of awe seemed to whisper through
the aisles.

Happiness wrapped around Rachel like a hug. The
loneliness of her own personal life hardly mattered.
Not when she saw how blessed Amy was. And how
happy Cadence and Ben could be. One day, she would
have joy like this. And until then, she gave thanks that
the people she loved most had found what her heart
yearned for. There was nothing more important on
this earth than love.

"They look committed to one another." A familiar
baritone rumbled next to her ear.

Rachel jumped. She hadn't heard anyone approach,
but there was a man right beside her, tall and handsome in a black tux. "Jake. You scared me to death."

"Sorry. I'm trained to be stealthy. Didn't mean to
sneak up on you."

"Well, you did. You're the dude I'm supposed to
let escort me down the aisle."

"Yes ma'am, if you're the maid of honor."

"Guilty."

She took one look at his strong arm. Even beneath
the black fabric she knew he would feel like tensed
steel. The aisle stretched out ahead of them, and the
idea of fitting her arm against his gave her a sudden
jolt of panic. She didn't know why, and she couldn't
explain it.

Before she'd met him, she knew she'd be walking

down the aisle with Ben's best friend. But now that she'd met him and actually liked him, and seen that in that tuxedo he was the single most handsome man she'd ever seen, her heart flip-flopped in her chest and gave a romantic tumble all the way to her toes.

It wasn't love, of course. Love took time, it took commitment and careful tending. But this was a serious case of like. As she threaded her arm through his, she had to fight to keep her feet firmly on the ground. The solid feel of him, his steady presence at her side, the way his gait seemed to match hers, there was something right about being so close to him, like a key in a lock. Her heart clicked.

The sun chose that moment to beam even more brightly through the rich panels of the stained-glass windows, and it felt like heaven's touch cradling them in light and color. The church was a blur—the candles, the flowers and the faces of the guests standing as the wedding march began. But none of that seemed to register, not next to the absolute calm that came into her soul.

Jake released her and she realized they were at the altar where their beloved pastor was smiling kindly, his Bible in hand. Dazed, she took her place beside Amy, her vision too bright to see anything but Jake settling into place beside Heath, putting his hands behind his back and turning to face the bride and groom.

She felt changed and she didn't know why. She

was still the same; she still felt the same, still thought the same. Everything around her was the same. But it was as if something had transformed; as if she'd taken a step in a fork in the road that she couldn't see, only feel.

"They are going to be so happy together," Amy leaned close to whisper. "Look at them."

The bride and groom glowed. Not in a flashy obvious way. But as they approached the altar, it was easy to see the deep steady light that filled them. The same light of an unshakable love that silenced everyone in the sanctuary.

I want a love like that, Rachel wished.

This time it didn't feel so far out of reach.

"Rachel."

The male voice coming from behind her in the diner didn't sound right, but she turned without thinking, Jake's name on the tip of her tongue. Even as she realized it wasn't the handsome best man who had approached her.

She took in the blond hair, the dark eyes and the familiar look to him. She didn't recognize him right off. "Wait. Derrick Whitley, right?"

"Yep, that's me." He strolled to a stop beneath the black and gold banner reading Congratulations! that swung over the aisle. He jammed his hands in his pockets. He'd matured, he'd put on a good thirty pounds, but he had a humble smile. "I don't know if you've heard, but I'm moving back to Montana."

"Your mom mentioned it to me the last time she was in the diner." Mrs. Whitley had also said that Derrick was an accountant who made a fine living and was single, since he'd divorced his unfaithful wife. It was hard not to feel sorry for Derrick. He still seemed as nice as ever. "Ben said you two have managed to stay friends."

"It's not easy keeping up with him. I hear he's going back to Florida after the honeymoon. And that Paige is leaving the diner to you."

"You know a lot for a man who's been out of town for the last decade or so."

"Mom keeps me updated." Derrick reached into his shirt pocket. "If you need help when you take over the diner, maybe you'll be looking for a new accountant. Give me a call. Or maybe I could just stop by and see you sometime. You know, during lunch."

"Sure." Not that she was so interested in Derrick, but this was more than a surprise. She couldn't shake the feeling that something had fundamentally changed in her life, in the path she was walking, and so she accepted the card with a nod and pointed Derrick in the direction of the buffet line.

Where had her nephew gone off to? She spun around, searching through the arriving guests for her favorite little boy. A little girl dressed in a pur-

ple sundress and matching lavender sandals gave a
little wave from the front door.

"Rachel!" Sally hung on to her uncle's hand, all
the trust in the world shining in her eyes as she clung
to him. "I gotta grape dress, too!"

"We match." Rachel gave her full skirt a swish.
"Do you want to come with me?"

"Um, okay." Sally tipped her head back, her full
curls cascading over her reed-thin shoulders. "You're
comin' too, huh, Uncle Jake?"

Rachel found it hard to keep her admiration volume on low as Jake gave a slow nod. She braced
herself against that high-wattage smile of his, but he
didn't smile. No dimples, nothing. Instead she saw the
iron curve of his jaw. The hard gleam of his stormy
eyes. And the military stance of a soldier at attention.

"Sure." Jake's lips barely moved. "Go ahead."

Was something wrong? The last time she'd seen
him, he'd looked happy congratulating Ben after the
ceremony. As Sally sidled up and reached for her
hand, Rachel decided Jake had a lot on his mind. He
carried serious responsibilities on those wide shoulders of his. She knew he was hoping to leave on a
late-afternoon plane. "Did you want to help yourself
to the buffet? I'll get Sally fed. Does that sound like
a good plan?"

"It does." He didn't look at her but pushed up the
sleeve of his jacket to study his watch. "We've got
plenty of time. I made a call to the airline on the way

over. As of five minutes ago, they have space available on their afternoon flight to L.A."

Okay, so he did have leaving on his mind. As she watched Sally press closer to her uncle, Rachel understood. The girl needed security. She was afraid of losing Jake, too. "Great, but I guess you won't be stopping by for that roast I promised you."

"That's too bad. Sal and I had a good time last night."

"Me, too." She didn't want to analyze that too much. He was leaving. Of course he was—she'd known that all along. It made no sense that she felt disappointed. "Hey, Sally. We've got a kids' party all set up on the patio. Do you want to come see?"

"Is Uncle Jake comin' too?" Endless hope rang in those words, and a child's honest need.

Jake let his sleeve slide back into place. "I'll come and see how you're doin'. You go have fun with Rachel."

"Oh. Okay." Sally swallowed hard. "Uh, when are you gonna come see?"

She thinks I'm mad at her, Jake realized and felt like a heel. "I'll come see you as soon as I get some grub. Deal?"

"Deal." Sally's eyes stayed wide and wary as she stuck to Rachel.

Rachel. Just looking at her made his temper want to erupt like a major volcano. He had to get a grip. He had to chill out. He was a highly trained soldier. He had discipline. Tons of discipline. So why couldn't he seem to calm down?

Good question. One he didn't have an answer for. He watched Rachel cast him an uncertain look, something between a grin and a look of relief, as she turned to lead Sally through the diner. The bridesmaid dress she wore was all soft-looking silk that flowed like a dream behind her. She was everything lovely and feminine and domestic, everything that was way out of his reach. He'd never felt turmoil about that before. He'd known long ago that his job and domestic tranquility weren't compatible. A settle-down kind of woman wasn't for him.

"Hey, Hathaway." Ben called above the crowd on the other side of the long buffet server. "Come meet Derrick. He jumps. We're talkin' about going up when I get back from our honeymoon. Are you still gonna be around?"

"What's that, three weeks?" Revved up at the thought of skydiving, Jake navigated around the small crowd at the end of the buffet. "I don't know how long my sister's estate is gonna take to wrap up, but maybe. Count me in, if I'm still on this side of the continent."

"Sweet. Jake, meet Derrick Whitley. We were in high school together. He used to have a crush on Rachel."

Derrick shook his head. "I did not. You don't have to go saying stuff like that."

Jake zeroed in on the civilian. He was lying. Flat-out lying. Jake didn't approve of dishonesty. Especially when he knew the man was just trying to save face. Yeah, he'd seen how this Derrick dude looked at Rachel. Like he was looking at a dream come true.

She's not your dream, buddy. The harsh bolt of jealously zinged through him like lightning. His entire being shook from the force of it. Why? He wasn't jealous. He didn't let those dark emotions into his heart. So where did that come from?

He certainly wasn't getting into a froth over some stranger's interest in a woman, no matter how good and how pretty she was. It made no sense to feel so possessive of Rachel. He'd probably never see her again…okay, maybe once, if he came back to take Ben up on his offer to jump. But other than that…no way. He wasn't a settling-down kind of man.

"U-uncle Jake?" Sally's small voice trembled with uncertainty.

He melted at her big eyes. He could feel her sadness as if it were her own. Okay, he was going to be a settling-down kind of man after all. "Hey, cute stuff. Aren't you supposed to be with Rachel?"

A solemn nod. "She's real nice, but you said you were gonna come."

So much need. She stared up at him with a quiet question, one she didn't ask, and it was as if she were afraid he'd say no. That he wouldn't keep even the small promise of coming back to check on her. "Tell you what. You hang with me while I load up my plate, and we'll eat together. How's that?"

She nodded hard, relief easing the fear from her pixie face.

"Ben, let me know about the jump. Derrick, good to meet ya. I'll see you around later, Ben." Jake had a lot to talk to his good buddy about, but Sally was leaning against his knee, a steady presence that reminded him of what she needed. That was what his life was going to be. Making sure she got what she needed to get past her grief and move on. To be a normal, happy little girl again.

How was he going to do that if he had to leave her with a stranger?

His chest ached with sympathy for her. And love. He splayed the palm of his hand on the top of her downy head. "Let's steer you to the end of the line, cutie. You can help me figure out what to get. Do you want some of this?"

"Nope. There's gonna be cake, too. And ice cream, but we gotta wait for that. There's candies and nuts, though."

"Gotcha. We'll make a loop past the goodie table on the way out."

That suggestion went over with success. Sally hung close as he waded through the slow-moving line. The food smelled great. There was everything from barbecue to fancy sandwiches to a lasagna that looked like the most delicious thing ever. He loaded up on that, and a few juicy pieces of barbecue chicken. Made sure he got plenty of fries—homemade just like Rachel had fried up for him last night—and tartar to go with it. He added buttermilk biscuits and that delicious coleslaw.

He wasn't the only one loading up. The wedding had been a small event because Cadence was on a limited budget, but Paige was hosting the reception and had invited the entire town. More people kept streaming in through the door carrying gifts and good wishes. Folk called out to one another by first name and stood around talking as if they were good friends.

So this is normal life, he thought as he managed to crowd three big pieces of garlic bread onto his plate. This is how most people spend their lives. Everyone surrounding him was talking and laughing with one another. These were friendships and family bonds and community ties that he'd never given much thought to before. He never had the leisure time to stand around and think about it. He'd been too busy lobbing grenades and trying not to get killed.

Sally tugged on his jacket hem. "The candy's over this way."

"Lead on, princess. Where you go, I'll follow."

"They're pretty." She halted in front of the cloth-covered table where various glass bowls of nuts, mints and chocolate and colorful candy crammed the surface. Sally helped herself to a small paper plate and began to pick through the pastel mints. "The pink ones taste best."

"Then you'd best get a lot of 'em." He waited patiently—and he wasn't the most patient of men—while she scored a half dozen pink mints. The crowd swirled around them, the conversations crescendoed as even more folks arrived. Rachel popped through the open side door, where a patio was visible behind her, looking for children in the crowd. She didn't look his way.

Good. The image of her standing and innocently talking with that Derrick dude still made him mad. It didn't make sense. Feelings weren't logical. He didn't like them, he didn't trust them, and he never made decisions based on them. Cool logic, that was the best way to make decisions. And the truth was, he was leaving town in about an hour's time. If he did step foot in this town again, it wouldn't be with the express goal of dating Rachel McKaslin.

Chapter Six

Except for the fact that Jake was avoiding her, he had to be the most perfect guy. Rachel did her best to stay focused, but her gaze kept sliding to the back corner of the enclosed patio where he sat at a patio table with Sally at his side. Uncle and niece stayed in companionable silence as he downed his heaping plate and she picked apart her hamburger.

Amy poked her head through the doorway. "How's it going out here? Do you need anything? More root beer? More fries? Oh, and I left the box of stuff for the games on the bench by the front door. It looks like the kids are starting to get restless."

Rachel glanced at her sister and replied, "Yep. We're almost done here. I figure we'll run off some of that energy at the park and come back for cake and ice cream. Thank heaven for our cousin Kelly. She's been great with the kids."

"I'm glad she could help out. You look tired."

"Oh, thanks. Next you'll be commenting on the bags under my eyes."

"They're not *too* bad." Amy winked, so light-hearted these days. "You've been here since six getting all of this ready. Why don't you let me take over? Take a load off. You can put up your feet. Maybe grab a bite under the umbrella. Talk to a cute guy."

Oh, she knew exactly what Amy was thinking. And there was no way she was up to dealing with any of her sister's well-meaning matchmaking. It was best to ignore the amazing Jake Hathaway in the corner and play innocent. "What cute guy?"

"The best man. Did you know that Ben thinks he's great?"

"Like that's a secret. They're best friends."

"He's hardworking. Brave. A fine soldier. *And* he's totally available."

"Available for what? Have you forgotten that he lives in Florida?"

"So does Ben. And Cadence will, too, as soon as the two of them get her moved. The Florida thing isn't a major obstacle."

"Then what would be? It's clear across the country."

"Sure, but you've heard of airplanes, right? You could get on one and go down and visit. That way you could get to know Jake a little better. Let him fall in love with you a little more?"

"What?" Had she been so transparent? Did every-

one know how she felt? Denial was always a reliable way to cope. "I don't know *what* you're talking about. I've got this diner. I have bookkeeping to learn. Paige is counting on me."

"You can study bookkeeping from a book. They have books in Florida. And what's one little visit? You work hard. You haven't had a vacation in forever."

"Vacation? That's the last thing I need." Rachel wasn't fooled one bit. Amy glowed with happiness; it was clear she loved being a wife and that Heath cherished her. That made all the difference in a woman's life. It made sense that Amy wanted that to happen for her.

But Jake wasn't for her. Couldn't everyone else see that? She wasn't going to open up her heart to the possibility. He was too good to be true, she was in serious like with him, and he kept avoiding her gaze. Probably because somewhere he'd overheard her sisters yakking on about how he was available and the poor man wasn't thrilled with the idea. "And it's the last thing Jake needs. He has his little niece to look after."

"And doesn't that just melt your heart? A big tough guy like him, he's so sweet with her. Don't you think?"

"Stop!" Laughing, Rachel held up her hands. "I give up. Just change the subject." She could never win when it came to her sisters. "I'm gonna set up a board game in case there are kids that don't feel like running around outside."

"So, you're taking me up on my offer?"

"Yep." Rachel spied a familiar little boy circling around the table to get to her. "How's my favorite astronaut today?"

"An astronomer, Aunt Rachel." Westin rolled his eyes in good humor, as if he'd given up trying to expect her to keep things straight. "Not an astronaut."

"Well, they both do space stuff. Are you ready to go run?"

"Yep." Fidgeting with boyish energy, Westin shot her a dimpled grin, designed to melt all of her resistance. "And then I can get a really big piece of cake? With lots of frosting?"

"No frosting for you. And only the smallest piece of cake. Go on, tell Kelly we're going across the street." Rachel grinned and ruffled the wild tufts of his cowlick.

She couldn't help the love filling her up for this little nephew of hers. She knew just how Jake felt. She could see Jake in her peripheral vision leaning over to swipe his last French fry through the plastic container of Sally's tartar sauce.

I'm gaping at him again. Embarrassed, she jumpstarted toward her cousin Kelly before Jake noticed she was sneaking peeks at him and got the wrong idea completely. The poor man. He probably got it all the time. Women probably fell at his feet in adoration. So she made sure to whisper as she sidled up to Kelly. "Tell me my sisters haven't been overheard trying to set me and Jake up."

"Okay, I won't." Kelly piled the last of the plates into the bus bin. "But they have."

"Great." No wonder Jake hadn't so much as looked her way! Her sisters were well-meaning, but they weren't helping. Ah, the joys of a close family. She rolled her eyes, unable to be really mad. "Go. I'll finish cleaning up. And don't forget to take Sally with you."

"Sure. I'll do you a favor and make sure her handsome uncle comes, too. I'll sacrifice myself just so you don't have to be around him if that'll help." Her eyes twinkled.

"Oh, that'll help. Thanks. Then my sisters can try to fix you and Jake up, and I'll be out of the loop." She liked that idea. "See how handsome he is?"

"But I thought you liked him."

"Like him, sure. Who wouldn't? But that's as far as it goes." Careful to keep her voice low, Rachel gathered the soda glasses from the table. The kids looked up at her with expectation. "I promised you milk shakes when you come back. Let me take your orders now. Allie, do you know what you want?"

"Strawberry!" Their little cousin sang with amazing cuteness.

"Okay, sweetie. You've got it. How about you, Anna?" she asked Allie's little sister and wasn't surprised when she wanted strawberry, too.

Rachel scribbled down orders as the kids started shouting out what they wanted. They were loud and funny and she loved that they made her laugh. Just what she needed. By the time the kids were shoving through the doorway and out of sight, she felt much better and ready to tackle the next problem.

Sally was the only child left on the patio. Streamers waved from the open table umbrellas. Bright balloons floated, tethered by their colorful ribbons. The wind breezed through the trees behind the patio wall, and the afternoon sun cast a solemn shade over the girl and her uncle.

This is an easy fix, she realized. She had nothing to do with her sisters' schemes, and Jake was leaving in less than an hour for the airport. Easy. All she had to do was smile. The Lord would take care of the rest, as He always did.

"What kind of milk shake can I get you, Sally?" Rachel kept her order pad handy.

But instead of belting out her preference, the little one simply shrugged her slim shoulders and stared hard at the table in front of her.

Rachel tried again. "You look like a girl who likes strawberry."

"'Kay." She didn't sound enthused.

Jake stirred. "Maybe we ought to get ready to go, Sal."

The little girl sighed. "I don't wanna go back to California. I don't wanna go home anymore. It's not my home now." Her voice rose with high emotion, and there was no mistaking her dark pain on this bright, beautiful day.

Nothing could be more unfair, poor sweetheart. Rachel knelt, wishing she could take the little girl into her arms and hold her until the pain eased up a bit. But Jake was there, swinging Sally into his sheltering arms and bringing her to rest against the wide expanse of his dependable chest. She pressed hard against him, her little body shaking with silent sobs.

An equal sorrow darkened Jake's eyes as he met Rachel's gaze over Sally's soft, downy head. "Thanks for everything, Rachel, but I'm gonna take her home."

"Is there anything I can do? Just ask."

But Jake was already striding toward the door, and he didn't look back as he shook his head in reply. The broad line of his powerful shoulders looked invincible, as if he could handle anything. He could take care of Sally, she had no doubts about that. Emotion wedged so tightly in her throat, and she couldn't rightly say how much was for Sally or how much was for Jake.

One thing was sure, she wouldn't be seeing them again. Sadness punched her square in the chest, and it was a sadness that lingered and did not fade.

"I found an extra blanket, sir."

"Thanks." Jake took the folded blue blanket from the flight attendant.

Sally lay snuggled in the window seat beside him, her head propped up by two pillows. He'd given her his, and she was already draped with one blanket. But her hand felt cold against his arm, where she clutched his sleeve, even in her sleep.

He shook the second blanket over her and tucked it beneath her chin, careful not to wake her. She didn't move, nestled with her head in the pillows, her other hand curled beneath her cheek.

Tenderness for her roared to life inside his chest. She was so small and vulnerable. The memory of her sobbing so hard as she clung to him haunted him like a mistake. Maybe he shouldn't be taking her back to California. Maybe it wasn't the best decision, but he had no one to leave her with. He knew this was going to be hard for her.

Rachel McKaslin's words came back to him. *She will get through it. She has you.* If only he had Rachel's faith in himself. He would do his best, his very best, to be what Sally needed. Whatever the cost. But his best would be hard to give her when he was far away in Iraq.

Tragedies happened. He'd seen his share overseas, and here, too. He remembered what Rachel had said about her family's loss and her older sister's sacrifice.

Rachel McKaslin. He couldn't remember the last time a woman had disarmed him. From trying to rescue him from the moose with a broom to the absolute empathy on her face when he'd carried a sobbing child in his arms. There was no way Rachel could have known that Jeanette always made milk shakes or that the board game that had been sitting out in the corner, probably for the kids to play later at the reception, was Candy Land, a favorite game Sally used to play with her mom.

Sally sighed in her sleep and curled up more tightly into a ball. He watched her for a moment, making sure she wasn't about to start a nightmare—she'd been having them ever since he'd come to pick her up in foster care. She was so little. It was killing him. How could he find a nanny good enough for her? No matter what, he'd find the best one. *I'm going to make sure you're well taken care of, princess.*

A woman across the aisle caught his eye. "She's awful cute. I don't see a wedding ring, so are you a single father?"

She said that last part with a hopeful lift, and the bachelor in him balked. She was pretty enough and somewhere in her twenties. And definitely looking for a husband, for she had that certain intensity to her.

Too bad he wasn't interested, he thought, as he shook his head. Maybe he *ought* to be looking for a wife, for someone who could mother Sally. Help him raise her. Well, too bad he wasn't interested in marriage either, because it would be the perfect solution. "No," he told the woman. "I'm her uncle."

"Oh. You must be great with kids."

"Not really. Sally tolerates my incompetence," he quipped, looking away.

He wasn't interested. He didn't want this woman to think he was. He didn't want to be thinking about nannies or finding a quick, convenient wife. He wanted Sally to have her mom back. He wanted to be with his squad leading them through the desert on a search-and-rescue mission. He wanted to be back in Rachel's yard eating another Popsicle and watching her smile.

And where did that come from? It was out of the blue, that's what. And probably what he got from being so jet-lagged. He was starting to lose it. Just like back in the diner when he'd gotten bent out of shape because an old high-school friend of Ben's had been talking with Rachel.

And why did she keep popping into his thoughts? He was short on Z's, that's why, had been traveling too much. He needed some downtime, some sleep and to get back to his normal routine. He'd best keep up on his running. If he got out of shape, he'd be in a whole world of hurting when he got back to base. That's where his energy ought to be, on returning to duty and finding someone to care for Sally. That's it. No more thinking of Rachel and her slippers and her Popsicles and her sweet, endearing smile.

Tomorrow morning, he would have this all in perspective. And he'd have all thoughts of Rachel McKaslin out of his system.

It wasn't like he was going to be seeing her again anyway. He leaned back in his seat and closed his eyes. That thought should have given him comfort. So why did he feel more restless than before?

He didn't want to think about that too much. The plane lurched in a pocket of turbulence and the fasten seat belts light popped on. As the plane nosed earthward, climbing down from cruising altitude with the sprawl of Los Angeles in sight, he had enough to put all thoughts of Rachel out of his mind.

Three weeks and two days later, Rachel buried her face in her hands and made a long sound of frustration that echoed in the diner's small office. "Paige, I'm never gonna get this."

"Sure you will. You just have to concentrate."

"My gray matter is under way too much pressure. If I concentrate anymore, my brains are going to start spewing out of my ears."

"Well, I have a mop handy."

"Ha ha." What Rachel wanted to do was to run outside and keep going until she reached a land where there were no computers, no bookkeeping programs and no general ledgers she didn't understand anyway. "Derrick is back in town. He's a CPA. I could pay him to do this."

"With the little profit the diner makes, you can't afford to pay him."

"Maybe I can pay a bookkeeper then. They have

bookkeeping services. They're listed in the Yellow Pages. I really think I should call or something. The good Lord clearly did not mean for me to handle accounting responsibilities or He would have given me even a smidgen of ability or something."

"It's not you, Rachel. Everyone feels this way about keeping their books. You just get used to it."

"I don't think I want to get used to this." Rachel didn't think Paige understood. How could she? Paige was smart and capable and she could do anything. "I've been trying to learn this stuff for the last six months. It's not sticking. I'm totally lost."

She smacked the endless and meaningless reams of printouts with the flat of her hand. It didn't help that she couldn't properly concentrate because her thoughts kept straying to a certain someone who was long gone and whom she wouldn't be able to see again. "None of this balances. None of it makes sense. You know you could still leave me the business, but you could teach Amy how to do this."

"But it will be your business. And what happens when Amy decides to stay home? Maybe she'll want to have another baby? Or go back to school. She has more options now that Heath is getting his state medical license."

"You're right. You're always right." Rachel loved Paige. She just wished she was more like her wonderful big sister. "I'm a failure. We have to admit it. There's no point in being nice about it. I'm doomed."

"I don't allow doom in my diner." Paige tried to lighten the mood.

But the alarm on Rachel's wristwatch gave a musical jingle saving her from more bookkeeping woes. "Oops, we'll have to continue this drama later. I've got to race over and pick up Westin from school. I promised Amy."

"And where is our illustrious sister? Isn't she supposed to be prepping in the kitchen?"

"Oh, I did most of that for her already. She got a call from the Realtor and she had to race over to look at this house that just came on the market. I'm so sorry, I have to go." Rachel decided to leave the papers where they were and grabbed her purse off the back of the tiny desk wedged into the hallway next to the diner's kitchen. "And my keys...?"

She spotted them on the counter and ran off before Paige could stop her. "I'll be back!"

"You'd better be. I'm not done torturing you!"

"Are you sure you want me to take over? When Alex graduates, you never know, you might be overcome with nostalgia and never leave this place. And then I'll have suffered the torture of computer work for nothing."

"Wishful thinking, little sister." Paige seemed to drift off into a daydream.

It was so uncharacteristic of her that Rachel couldn't move. Paige had worked so hard over the years. Harder than any of them had in return. They hadn't needed to, because Paige was always there, carrying the load, shouldering all of the responsibilities without complaint. She solved every trouble before anyone even knew there was a problem.

Paige seemed to shake herself out of her thoughts, and wherever she'd gone in her mind, she looked happier. Younger.

Wow, she's really counting on leaving the diner.

Rachel breezed through the kitchen, where Dave, the evening cook, was prepping for supper, and banged through the back door and out into the chill of the early-winter afternoon. She shivered and realized she'd forgotten her jacket. She wasn't used to thinking summer was over, even when her sneakers crunched over the last of the amber and brown leaves carpeting the ground. Soon snow would be falling and the holidays would be here. Life went on, she knew, but she still found herself thinking of Jake.

Maybe she ought finally to accept Derrick's polite but persistent requests for a date. But the second she thought it, her stomach twisted with the simple truth. As nice as the accountant was, there wasn't that certain something. That special "wow" she so wanted.

Maybe she was too romantic. Maybe she had her hopes set too high? But if she didn't, then she would settle for less than true love. And that seemed sad, she thought as she opened her car door and dropped behind the wheel. The instant she sat down, a digital tune chimed from inside her purse. It was Paige, no doubt about it. Classic Paige.

Rachel unzipped her purse and fished around as the tune grew louder and the shaking continued. Where did it go? Oh, there, beneath her wallet and a roll of wild cherry candies. "Hey, what did I forget?"

It wasn't Paige's voice that answered, but her brother's. "Nothing that I know about. How are ya doin'?"

"You sound happy. Being married must suit you."

"What's not to like?" She'd never heard him sound so relaxed or so at peace. He was back from his honeymoon and a very happily married man. "Do you know where I can find Amy? I'm tryin' to track her down."

"Uh...you could try her cell." Rachel slammed the door and reached for her belt with one hand. "Or is she out of range?"

"That's why I'm calling you."

"What do you need?" She sorted through her keys and jammed the wrong one into the ignition. Of course it didn't fit, and so she had to shake through the key ring again until she found the right one.

"Jake's in town."

Jake's in town. "Nobody told me that."

"He's on his way back to Florida, but he's swinging by to help me load the moving van tomorrow, but I'm taking him jumping in about fifteen minutes."

"Jumping. As in out of a plane. Into thin air?"

"Sure. Piece of cake. Trouble is, if Amy's MIA,

then we're staying grounded. Amy said she'd keep Sally for Jake."

Suddenly Amy's disappearance made sense. So, Amy knew all about Jake being in town and yet she hadn't said a thing cooking breakfast this morning. Now, wasn't it a coincidence that the moment Jake needed help, Amy had disappeared?

She loved her sisters, boy, did she, but she didn't need to give Jake any more reasons to run the other way. Her face was already hot.

Ben sounded mad. "Well, we were supposed to meet her here."

"Oh, are you at her house?" Rachel jammed the phone against her shoulder and maneuvered the gearshift into Reverse. With the clutch going out, it was kind of tricky and she had to listen hard to hear Ben's answer over the grinding gears. She gave it some gas.

"No, cutie. I'm parked right behind you. Could you *stop?*"

What? She hit the brakes. She'd only backed up about two feet, but there was Paige's extra truck— Ben used it while he was in town, glinting in her rearview mirror behind her. She had a good two yards between her bumper and his, but still. Yikes! Did thinking about seeing Jake again have her rattled or what? "Sorry about that. What are you doing creeping up on a girl like that? You know I've been banging my head against the wall trying to learn Paige's accounting system. I'm not right in the head."

"Sure, like that's news," he kidded fondly. "I have pity for you, really I do, but if Amy's gone, then who's picking up Westin?"

"Where do you think I'm going in such a hurry?"

"Oh, to get him from school. Cool. So, let me get this straight." She could just make out Ben's face through the glare of the truck's windshield but he was there alone. "You're going to be looking after Westin."

"Yep." Where was Jake? Maybe Ben was meeting him at the airport. That made sense. He wasn't actually going to be in town.

Ben kept talking, but a strange sound buzzed in her ears, making it impossible to hear more than distant gibberish as he began to explain something. Her attention had zeroed in on a movement in the passenger's-side mirror—there was a blur of color and that color became a man with amazing shoulders and a lean, athletic build. A man with dark, military-short hair and an awesome presence that made her heart roll over and fall and keep falling.

Jake Hathaway was striding toward her passenger door like a soldier on a mission. Panic set in, but it was too late. He was already yanking open her door, already filling the space between them with a half frown and that intensity that made her stammer instead of speak like a normal person.

"Uh, well, h-hi." *Smooth, Rache, real smooth.* She gave a weak grin.

He didn't smile back.

Chapter Seven

"H-hi back," Jake stuttered, for his tongue seemed to be paralyzed. He couldn't believe that seeing Rachel again would be such a shock. Like jumping at twenty-five thousand feet where there was only icy atmosphere and empty vast air.

She seemed just as surprised to see him, as her lovely mouth was gaping like a fish out of water.

Yep, I know just how you feel. And that troubled him too because whatever this was, it affected both of them. That can't be good, he thought as he cleared his throat and tried to sound like a normal person. "Aren't you gonna come skydiving, too?"

"I'll keep my feet planted firmly on God's good soil, thank you very much. I'm not about to jump out of a perfectly good plane."

"Well, I just thought I'd offer. I appreciate you watching Sally for me."

"Go ahead and bring her in. I've got to run. School

is over this exact minute. But Ben has my cell number, and I'll be out at the house. You can find me when you're done." There was only friendliness in her manner, and he wondered about that dude who'd been talking to her in the diner.

It wasn't his business if she was seeing someone and he wasn't about to lower his pride and ask Ben about it. Why would he? He wasn't interested in getting married. He was an independent sort and always would be, right? This deep awareness he felt for Rachel McKaslin would go away, right?

Sally nudged against his side. She'd climbed out of Ben's truck and was stalking him like a navy SEAL. "Uncle Jake, you won't make me stay with her, right?"

Okay, well, he wouldn't have to worry about this awareness he felt for Rachel because Sally was going to scare her away anyway. The girl had been getting steadily more clingy over the last few weeks. "Sweetie, I won't leave you for too long. I can't take you jumping with me."

"Oh." She couldn't hide her enormous disappointment.

Rachel came to the rescue. Somehow that didn't surprise him a bit. She flashed a winning smile their way. "Sally, you and I are going to have the most awesome time. I promise. Hop in."

"I guess." Sally's head sank forward in defeat.

Jake's chest gave a hard bump. The girl seemed like nothing but shadow. He'd done his best by her, but he couldn't blame her. Going back to California and facing memories of her old life had refreshed her grief. Maybe Sally needed Rachel's empathy today.

And he was grateful. "I can't thank you enough, Rachel."

"No thanks needed. I'm always happy to spend time with a good friend. Right, Sally?"

Sally didn't look as if she agreed but she climbed into the car and grabbed the buckle. Worry darkened her pretty eyes. "You'll be back for supper, right?"

"You won't have time to miss me much, I promise you that, darlin'." She'd been keeping close track of him, as if she were afraid of losing him, too.

Sally looked up at if she didn't believe him at all.

I'm not ever gonna abandon you, little girl. He couldn't help running his hand over the top of her head or the love that kept getting stronger for this child.

"Hey," Rachel broke through his thoughts. "I gotta scoot! Have jun fumping! I mean, fun jumping." She put the car in gear—forward this time— and he slammed the door shut.

The sedan cut through the long slant of sunshine and the stir of golden autumn leaves. His heart stirred, too, a strange mix of emotions he didn't want to acknowledge or name.

Jun fumping? Could she have bumbled that any worse? Rachel still wanted to wither up and die an hour later as she pulled into the garage with both kids tucked in the backseat.

It was too much to hope that Jake hadn't noticed. With any luck, she'd never have to see him again.

And hadn't she been in serious like with the man? Well, she might as well give up those thoughts now. What he must think of her, she couldn't guess, but chances were one hundred percent that he wanted to run in the opposite direction the next time he saw her.

Liking a man was a tricky thing—it was the first step on a path that made a girl way too vulnerable. As much as she wanted love and romance, a lovely wedding and a good marriage, she wanted it to be with the right man. That man wasn't Jake.

Rachel took a deep breath and tried to imagine the perfect man, if there could be one better than Jake. A man who would love her truly and cherish her forever, the same way she wanted to love him. The truth was, she wanted to love Jake. Her soul seemed to calm in his presence. This was simply another lost opportunity for true love.

She put the car in Park and turned off the engine. Westin's reflection in the rearview mirror caught her attention. He was already free from his buckles and clambering out of his seat. His hair was tousled and windblown from a busy day at school, but his energy not a bit dimmed. He bolted out of the backseat and gave the door a good slam, all before she had time to do more than pull her keys from the ignition and open her door. "Are you gonna be a gentleman and wait for us girls?"

"Well then, you gotta hurry." He grinned at her through the rolled-down window. "Cuz I'm hungry. What do ya got for me? Cupcakes?"

"Nope. Nothing but cold ashes for you."

"You can't eat ashes!" Westin laughed. "C'mon, Sally. Aunt Rachel probably's got cupcakes on the counter. You can have the first pick."

"Good boy." Rachel poked him in the stomach, just to hear him laugh again. Then she rummaged around for her purse, wherever it had gone to. "Sally, go ahead with Westin. I know I put it in here somewhere. Have you seen my purse?"

"Nope." Sally released her seat belt and dropped to her knees in the small space between the seat and the glove box. She looked under the seat. "It's not here."

"Thanks, I know it's here somewhere. I hope." This was what happened when she had tried to learn the modern torture known as bookkeeping. "I'll find it later. What I need more than my purse is chocolate. How about you?"

"'Kay." Sally managed a small smile. "Uncle Jake likes chocolate, too."

"Then we'll wrap up a few for you to take with you. Deal?"

"Deal!"

"Then let's go. Westin looks like he's gonna pop like a balloon if he has to wait another second for us."

Rachel climbed out of the car, then ducked back in to grab her keys. Her nephew was holding the garage door, but was hopping up and down in place. "Why, thank you, sir. You're such a gentleman."

"My new dad says a man treats ladies real nice. Holdin' doors and stuff."

"A good man, your new dad, and you, too." Rachel waited for Sally and laid a hand on her shoulder to guide her through the doorway.

The girl was such a small thing, more shadow than substance, that Rachel's heart gave a hard wrench. She was clearly worried about something happening to Jake and being left alone again. *Well, maybe I can make the next few hours a little easier for the child to get through.*

"How about some chocolate milk to go with those cupcakes?" Rachel tossed her keys on the counter. Sunlight streaming through the windows made the kitchen cheerful and toasty and welcomed them over to the table. "Sally—" she gestured toward the chairs, "Go ahead and sit. Westin, grab the napkin holder for me, would you?"

"Can I have two cupcakes, no, three?"

The phone rang, saving her from answering. Westin already knew her answer—could she ever say no?—and she ruffled his head as she skirted past him to grab the receiver. "You guys decide if you wanna play a board game or go outside when you're done. Hello?"

"Hey, it's me." Her brother's voice warmed the line. "Got a question for you."

"First I've got one for you. Are you going to make sure your parachute is packed right before you jump?"

"Here, I'll let Jake answer that, since he's listening in."

There was the sound of male voices, a crackling sound as the phone was handed over, and Rachel didn't have time to swallow her panic before Jake's confident voice rang in her ear.

"I'm as safe as can be. We're about to go up, but I wanted to give you time to think about this." Jake's words dipped low and serious.

Rachel felt the impact deep in her soul. See how he affected her? No man had ever done this to her. How was she going to act normally, now? "What exactly are you going to ask?"

"Ben said he could use help moving on Wednesday, and since that's two days away, I can switch our flights, no problem, and stick around to help. But seeing as I don't make the big bucks, Ben suggested Sal and I could stay in the apartment. I wanted to make sure that was okay with you first. Say no if you're uncomfortable with a single old bachelor like me hanging around your house."

"The apartment's over the diner. Did Ben tell you that?"

"Ah, no, he didn't. Then I guess I ought to be calling your oldest sister. Isn't she in charge of the diner?'

"I'm taking over, and trust me, she won't mind if you stay. Ben could use the help, I know, it'll make this easier on him. And this way I get to spend more time with Sally."

Jake didn't miss the genuine affection in Rachel's words. He could just imagine her in that house of hers meant for a family, she was probably in the kitchen. Yep, he could hear the clink of dishes. The refrigerator door opened and his mind flashed back to the evening spent in her home in her company, and his world stopped spinning. Everything within him stilled. The back of his neck tingling like it did right before things got hot on a mission.

Except there was no danger, no enemies, no imminent ambush, no unseen threat. Just the pulse of his heartbeat and a strange stillness in the deepest part of him. It was as if God was letting him know that this woman was significant.

It was probably because Sally needed so much right now. Rachel, who'd known the same loss, maybe had the kindness to help Sally a little. Sure, his conscience scolded him, but Sally would be the only reason, right?

Right, he *wanted* to say. But he knew that was wrong. Sally wasn't the only reason. Jake didn't want to think about what that meant as Ben called out to him. The pilot and plane were ready and waiting. He said goodbye, hung up and took off down the tarmac, determined to keep nothing but blue skies on his mind.

Rachel heard the kitchen door open. The sound of boots hitting the floor told her two people were coming her way. She slid the dice across the coffee table to Westin as she rose from the floor. Ignoring the snap in her knee and the creak in her lower back, she ambled around the sectional, expecting to see Jake.

It wasn't Jake who strode into sight, but Amy and her handsome new husband. Heath did not look happy, and Amy appeared flushed either from upset or from a disagreement, Rachel couldn't tell which. But it couldn't bode well.

"What's up, guys?" Rachel left the excitement of the board game behind, knowing the kids were well occupied, and headed for the cupboards. "You look like you need chocolate."

"Chocolate's a start." Amy collapsed on the nearest chair. "No, please tell me these aren't your secret-recipe cupcakes because I can't eat just one. Heath, world wars could start over these, they're so good."

"The secret's in the filling." Rachel handed down two dessert plates. "Go ahead. Take as many as you want. They're only good when they're fresh. Want soda or chocolate milk to go with?"

"You shouldn't be waiting on us." Amy had

dropped her purse, shrugged out of her coat and was unwrapping the paper from a cupcake. Chocolate crumbs tumbled everywhere. "But I love ya for it. We just looked at another house we couldn't afford."

"It wasn't affording the actual house," Heath added as he took a cake. "It was figuring out how to pay for the repairs it needed just to make it halfway livable."

"It's a tight market." Amy bit into her cupcake with a moan. She slumped against the chair back as she chewed. The chocolate seemed to be doing the trick. Amy already looked five times more relaxed.

"This is great, Rachel." Heath said around a bite of the crumbly goodness. "I feel better already."

Rachel poured two cups of cold milk and grabbed the chocolate syrup. With a few long squirts and a brief stint in the microwave, she had two cups of steaming goodness that made her sister smile. As she served the drinks, she thought she heard a car in the driveway, but it was the wind knocking the lilac bushes against the siding.

She had to stop thinking about Jake while she could. What she ought to be concentrating on was her sister, who had a real problem. Three people living in a single-wide trailer was do-able, sure, but it was a small trailer. Rachel knew that they needed something bigger, especially since they were hoping to add to their family. Not that Amy had said anything, but Rachel knew from the looks Heath and

Amy had been sending to one another. They were so in love, so joyful, just so everything.

"I know of a house that would be perfect for you." She couldn't help grabbing one of the cupcakes for herself, not that her hips needed more padding than they already had. "This house I'm thinking of has four big bedrooms on the main floor, a roomy living room and this great country kitchen."

"No way. We're not arguing about this again."

"Not unless these cupcakes are included in the deal," Heath quipped before he took another healthy bite and said to Amy, "What? What's wrong with that?"

"That's an offer I'm gonna accept." Rachel ignored her sister, who was giving her new husband the narrow glare that all men learned to fear. "It's too late to back out. Your word is binding, Heath."

"Wow. And I was kidding about the cupcakes. We don't want your house, Rachel."

"Yeah, Rache, you've lived here nearly all your life." Amy abandoned her cupcake and caught Rachel's free hand with hers. "You deserve this place. I know what you're going to say, that this is where I grew up, too, but I left home, remember? I ran off and left you and Paige with the diner and when I came back, I didn't have the right to oust you. I still don't."

"This isn't about your feelings." Rachel couldn't believe she sounded so irritated—and she *was* irritated. Because even as she tossed the cupcake wrapper in the garbage, she wanted to whack it upside her sister's head—not hard, of course—to make her see. "This place is too big for me."

"But you're happy here. You love the memories that are here. I'm not taking that from you. The right house for us will turn up."

"This *is* the right house." Couldn't anyone else see it? "This is a house for a family, and I don't have one of those."

"One day you will."

"Good, I would love nothing more, but one day isn't today. And today your family needs a larger place—this place. Look." She gestured to the window where a movement caught her eyes. Westin and Sally were leaping from the deck. "He's happy here. Look at him. Plus, there's already a swing set and the roof is good for another fifteen years."

One of these days, Amy was going to see reason. Until then, Rachel wasn't giving up her cause. She took a big bite and savored the rich fudge frosting and moist chocolate cake crumbling across her tongue. The secret whipped-cream filling was so sweet that it ought to make her forget her upset over the house and the fact that Jake was going to come breezing through that door anytime—

"Hey, do I rate enough to get one of those?"

His voice. Jake's voice. The pleasant rumble of it wrapped around her soul and squeezed. Unfortunately her mouth was full of cupcake, and the instant she locked her gaze on the fine sight of him, she automatically gasped. She felt a few crumbs being sucked down the wrong way and she fought hard not to start coughing. Too late. She covered her mouth and luckily the cough wasn't a big one. Tears filled her eyes and blurred her vision as she struggled to clear her throat.

Ben came to her rescue, amazing as always, as he strode straight to the table and stole two cupcakes. "Now this is what dessert tastes like in paradise. C'mon, take a bite." He tossed one to Jake who caught it with one hand. "Hey, Rachel."

She mumbled hello as she watched Jake catch the cupcake with one hand. Was it her imagination, or did he look more awesome than usual? His short dark hair was seriously windblown, and it seemed impossible that a man could look even better every time she saw him. And kinder, she added, when their gazes locked. "Did you guys have a good jump?"

"Yep, went up a couple a times. Good weather. Great views. I could see all the way to Yellowstone."

It took no effort at all to imagine him falling fearlessly with a packed chute on his back, the airplane above and the earth below. His cheeks were windburned and his inner spirit glowed from the exhilaration. It was as if the layers had been peeled away and she could see the true soul of this man—fearless and stalwart and unfailing.

Her heart gave a little tumble. Not that she was

falling for him or anything, but it was hard not to like him more and more. And how could she help it? She took another bite of her cupcake, just to keep her jaw from sagging.

One brow hooked upward, as dashing as any silver-screen star's, Jake asked, "Did you bake these?"

Her mouth was full again, so she nodded, chewing fast and swallowing. "I've been known to dabble in the kitchen."

"Pretty fancy."

"Just the outside. Wait 'til you taste it."

He rose to her challenge and took a huge bite. He rolled his eyes as a sign of ecstasy.

"My own secret recipe." She couldn't help smiling wide. "I made two whole dozen, so have as many as you'd like. How about a plate to go with that?"

When he shook his head, she asked, "A napkin? A glass of chocolate milk?"

"I'm a fan of chocolate milk. Count me in," he said around a mouthful.

"One tall glass, coming up." She tossed him another smile before she made a U-turn toward the refrigerator. "How about you, Ben?"

He nodded as he took a big bite, his attention focused on dragging out a chair next to Amy. "Gonna sit, Jake?"

While Jake's pleasant baritone answered, and another chair scraped along the linoleum, Rachel plopped her half-eaten cupcake on a napkin and got to work. Glasses, plenty of chocolate syrup and cold milk. While she stirred each glass, she enjoyed the sounds of conversation: Ben and Heath talking about the real estate market, and Amy asking Jake if Sally knew how to swim and could she come along with her and Westin on their planned jaunt to one of the county pools.

That would be good for Sally, Rachel thought as she gave the milk a final stir. But what about the uncle? What did Jake have planned for tomorrow? *None of your business, Rache. Just serve the milk.*

A firm hand settled on her shoulder, and it didn't startle her. Although she hadn't heard him approach, she felt the zing of his presence, and her pulse thudded loudly in her ears.

"That sure does look good. You are amazing, Rachel."

"Me? Really? That seems like a pretty big compliment over chocolate milk." Rachel tried to resist falling in like with him a little more. "Oh, you could charm the moon to the earth. I've heard chocolate milk is the cure for false flattery. You're in luck." She handed him the closest glass. "Do you think you need two?"

"No, thanks. That wasn't false flattery." His dimples flashed and made her knees weak. "I meant every word. You are amazing."

He walked away, leaving her smiling. He thought she was amazing? Jake Hathaway, Mr. Perfect and

Wonderful, liked her? She couldn't believe it. It was all she could do not to shout joyfully and that's when she noticed her reflection in the side of the toaster. She had chocolate smeared on her teeth.

Yeah, she was awesome all right. If she didn't stop embarrassing herself in front of Jake, they really might have a chance.

Chapter Eight

Concentrate on your work, Rache. Before you drop the potatoes. In the diner's warm kitchen, Rachel made sure Mr. Brisbane's Southwestern Special had plenty of extra hashed browns, just the way he liked it. Work was tough this morning because she could not get Jake out of her thoughts. And when she wasn't thinking about Jake, she was fighting off the icky feel of embarrassment.

How could a guy as cool as Jake think of her as anything more than his friend's little sister? She certainly didn't act the part of the sophisticated classy woman. If only she could be more like Paige.

"Hear that man of yours is back in town again," Mr. Winkler commented as he made his way from the front door down the aisle.

"Uh, he's not my man."

"Oh, pardon. My mistake."

Mine, too. Rachel looked around at the diner. This

wasn't how she pictured her life turning out, but she was content enough. Soon this place would be hers to run, and that was all right. Her dad had worked in this diner as a teenager and bought it on a risk when the owners were facing bankruptcy. There wasn't a lot of money to be made in a small-town diner, but her parents had done okay with good food, friendly service and hard work.

As she spotted Mr. Corey, another of their morning regulars, through the hand-off window and cracked two eggs—whites only due to his recent heart attack—on the grill, she could feel the memories of her dad standing right here, merrily calling out to the customers as he cooked. It was as if she could feel a little of that happiness, and it heartened her.

One day, she might find a man who could make her laugh, someone like her dad, someone strong and good and big enough to fill her world.

Mr. Winkler's sausages were perfect, browned and juicy, and she piled the links onto the plate, added toast and hit the bell. Leaving the plate beneath the warmer, she took a moment to slurp down another bracing swallow of coffee and, taking advantage of the lull, measured up pancake batter.

Jodi swept by to pin up an order on the wheel and grab Mr. Winkler's meal. "Hey, I got a request from a customer."

What customer? She hadn't noticed anyone else coming in, but then she didn't have her eyes glued to the front door either. "You know I'm here to please. What do I need to cook up special?"

"You'll have to take that up with the customer. Can she come back?"

"Sure thing." It had been a long time since she'd had someone talk to her in person. Probably someone on a special diet, which would be no problem at all. The door swung open and a little girl ambled in, squeezing her worn stuffed bunny in both arms. Sally. Did that mean Jake was here? But before she could think to look for him, she noticed the dark circles under the child's red, swollen eyes. Had she had a real tough night? "Sally, come on over here and give me a hug. Would that be okay?"

Sally nodded her head solemnly. She was stiff with hurt and fear—Rachel could feel it as she gave the girl a gentle hug, bunny and all. She added a deep prayer from her heart.

Help her, Father. She ached to smooth some of the stray wisps that had already escaped her turquoise barrettes. "What can I get special for you, sweet girl?"

"P-pancakes with smiles on them. They t-taste better that way."

"They sure do. I'll get to work on that right away." She stirred Mr. Corey's eggs, then drew a chair over from the corner. "Come stand here and coach me, okay?"

A single nod was Sally's only answer. She still

clutched her stuffed rabbit and didn't let go as she climbed up to stand on the chair.

Rachel remembered standing in the same spot, at her dad's elbow while he cooked and whistled show tunes. It was a dear tug she felt on her heart as she plated Mr. Corey's meal and got a good look at what had to be Jake and Sally's order ticket on the wheel, although she couldn't see Jake seated at any of the booths along the front window. Thank goodness.

He was probably in back at one of the tables, she figured, safely out of sight. Which was a real good thing, since she had a certain effect on her, and her embarrassment over last night—and her teeth—remained. She sure knew how to make a great impression on this man—not!

"Do you want a smiley sunshine pancake too?" Rachel snatched the tongs and added a half dozen sausage links onto the grill. As they sizzled, she gestured toward the jumbo-sized cookie cutter. "Go ahead and grab that for me."

"'Kay." Timidly, Sally freed the cutter from the nearby hook and held it by one of its rays. "I used to help my mommy all the time."

"Then you're a seasoned cook's helper. Just what I need." Rachel grabbed the pitcher of fresh buttermilk batter. "Go ahead and put a couple of 'em down. How many pancakes do you want?"

Sally bit her lip as she debated. "Three."

"Then can you get two more cutters?"

Rachel kept an eye on Sally to make sure she didn't slip and scorch a fingertip while she poured out rounds of pancakes to fill Jake's Plentiful Pancake Combo and Sally's perfectly aligned sunshine smiles. "Can you tell me when those start to bubble?"

A tentative nod.

Well, at least she was doing better. Her rabbit had been sat on the edge of the counter, as if to keep a watch on the grill, too. The bell over the door jingled cheerily to announce more customers. The oven timer binged. After reminding Sally not to touch the grill, Rachel donned an oven mitt, stopped to turn the sausages and rescued the muffins, golden-topped and glazed with sugar. She popped the two dozen muffins onto the cooling rack.

"Um, bubbles."

Rachel grabbed the spatula. Perfect timing. "Let's get those turned, okay? Want to hold the plate for me?"

Another nod. Sally held steady the white plate Rachel handed her and in a moment she'd flipped the pancakes, let them sizzle and slid an egg onto the hot grill. While the whites bubbled, she stacked the pancakes for Jake and spread them across the plate for Sally.

It was pleasant being here like this with a little girl. Maybe one day she'd have her children here, the way she and her brother and sisters had stayed here in the mornings before school started. Wistful, Rachel tried not to pin so much on a future that hadn't happened yet, but it was hard.

"Hop down and come over here with me." There were the ghosts of memories again, good and dear ones, following her along the counter where it took only a few seconds to add juicy blue huckleberries for eyes and a sweep of strawberry jam for a wide smile on each sunshine. "Do you like strawberries?"

"Yep."

"Good, then we'll put them here, so each ray from the sun is a strawberry slice."

"My mommy used the white stuff."

"Whipped cream?"

"In the spray can."

"Well, I've got some right here."

There's a beautiful sight. Jake froze in the doorway, staring at the woman and child who were side by side. With their heads bent together, they didn't hear the swinging door sweep open, nor did Rachel notice that he was there. He didn't move a muscle as everything within him stilled.

Sunlight filtered through the open slat blinds and graced them with a soft golden haze that seemed like a sign from heaven. He'd have to be blind not to see the way Sally leaned close to Rachel, her little shoulders almost relaxed. Her grief seemed several shades less as she watched Rachel spray whipped cream on a bunch of pancakes.

"How about a nice big mustache on this one?"

"A big curly one," the girl encouraged, leaning in closer and planting her hands on the counter. As Rachel swirled the spray can, Sally watched, enchanted.

Jake was enchanted, too, but for entirely different reasons. That strange calm seeped through him, deeper than his heart and into his soul. *She's the one,* he thought, seeing God's plan for his life as clearly as the sunshine through the window. Rachel's voice reassured him like a soft summer wind moving over him. A feeling he'd never known before.

"Let's make this one a girl. We'll give her curls. Okay?"

Sally nodded, more animated than he'd seen her since her mom's death. There was hope. He could feel it taking root within him. He'd asked God for a solution, for things to work out for Sally's sake, and He had led them here, to Rachel, who had a loving heart and a kind enough nature to nurture a hurting child back to life. To Rachel, who'd experienced the same loss herself as a kid.

I know what I need to do. Goose bumps shivered down Jake's spine as he knew with certainty what he was to do. Sally needed this woman, and marriage was the answer.

The bell above the door chimed, drawing Rachel's attention. "Oh! Goodness. I've got to get back to the grill. Hold on, just a sec, Sally." Rachel set down the whipped cream can and leaped to save the food sizzling to a crisp. She was still so wrapped up she didn't see him.

Was she humming? He couldn't quite get the tune, but her smile was dazzling as she called out a greeting to whoever had entered, one of the regulars, as she deftly filled his order.

"I'll get your usual right on, Jim!" she called as she hit the bell. "Jodi, I'll take Sally back to her ta—"

She'd spotted him, and he felt the effects of her beautiful smile. "—table. Hi, Jake. I'll get his order, Jodi."

"No, I'll get it," he insisted and held out his hand. "C'mon, Sal. Let's let Rachel get back to work because we don't want the cook mad at us. Especially one so lovely."

She blushed prettily. "It's always good to compliment the cook. Now, go, out of my kitchen before I burn Jim's sausages." She reached for a mixing bowl and started stirring.

He took the image of her standing there, haloed in light, with him.

So far so good, Rachel thought as she plated the morning's special and added a side of hashed browns. Her hand kept shaking as she shoved the plate next to the other ready orders on the window ledge. Jake's words still affected her. He thought she was lovely?

The back door blew open and Paige charged in, briefcase slung over her shoulder, her arms full of ledgers. "I'm sorry I'm so late. It's been one disaster after another."

"That's not fair. It's only seven in the morning."

"Exactly. I fear what the rest of the day is gonna bring." Paige marched through and disappeared down the short hallway. There was a thud as all the books she carried landed on the desk.

Knowing Paige hadn't had a chance to eat yet, Rachel plated her last order, a number seven for the town deputy, Frank, and carried it out to him. He was sitting near the door, the sports section of the morning paper on the table in front of him. As she slid his plate on the table, she glanced down the aisle, but no sign of Jake and Sally. They had to be seated around the corner. "How are you this morning, Frank?"

"No real complaints. As long as I can get another refill."

"You've got it." She bounded to the beverage station, where a fresh pot of coffee had just finished brewing. She grabbed the carafe and topped off Frank's cup. Taking advantage of the lull, she went in search of Paige in the office by going the long way around. Sure enough, she spied Jake and Sally in the back, next to the last window that looked out over the patio.

"Heard you're the next one in your family that's lookin' to marry." Mr. Winkler called out down the aisle. "Is that true?"

Did he have to say it so loudly? She felt bad the

instant she thought that. Mr. Winkler wore hearing aids, so it wasn't his fault. But still. All the customers turned with interest. She felt Jake's piercing stare above all the others. Did she really want Mr. Amazing to know about her going-nowhere romantic life?

No way. She spun on her heel and backtracked to Mr. Winkler's table. "You should know better than to listen to rumors."

The kindly man brushed back his silver hair, as if to straighten himself up a bit. "Rumors? Why, missy, we've got a pool goin' as to how long it'll be before you got a second date with that fella."

Was it her imagination or could she feel everyone straining to hear her answer? She glanced around and Frank gave her a thumbs-up—apparently he was interested in her answer. Her cousin Kendra, across the aisle with her husband, Cameron, didn't even bother to pretend she wasn't listening, and, worst of all, Jake was watching her over the rim of his coffee cup.

Her chest tightened as if an enormous boa constrictor had wrapped around her when she wasn't looking and was crushing her ribs. "No comment."

Embarrassed again, she thought as she took a fortifying deep breath and headed up to his table. Best to pretend nothing had happened, she thought. It was the only way she could face Jake.

He was smirking when she approached and set down his cup for her to refill it. "How's it going?"

"The usual torture and embarrassment, nothing

new." She concentrated on pouring the coffee without disaster. "How were the pancakes, Sally?"

Sally looked up from a coloring book she must have brought down from the upstairs apartment. "I liked the blue eyes."

"Those were huckleberries. A local wild blueberry," she explained when Jake quirked his brow. "And that was our homemade strawberry jelly, by the way. Can I get you two anything else? Paige just came from the bakery. We've got fresh cinnamon rolls."

"I can't believe I'm gonna say this, but I want one of those."

"Coming right up. How did you two sleep last night?"

"It's a nice set-up you have up there." Jake tried to swallow the panic bubbling up from his guts. He'd faced ambushes, doomed rescue missions and prisoner-of-war camps and never had he felt this sudden urge to run. He was a man who faced live fire regularly and he would not flee from this. "Sally and I owe you dinner for a change. How about tonight?"

"Sorry, I'm working the dinner shift."

"Then we'll figure something out." He watched her walk away, an average woman in jeans and a blue T-shirt, with a ruffled apron tied at her waist, but somehow there wasn't anything average about Rachel McKaslin. Her rich chestnut hair was tied back at her nape, and her leggy gait was easy and relaxed.

As she pushed through the swinging door, he heard the low notes of a song. She was humming.

A second date, huh? Well, maybe he'd give her one to remember. He checked his watch. *After* he helped Ben move their stuff out of their apartment.

Marriage. It wasn't something Jake had given a lot of thought to before this. Now it was all he could think about.

The image of Sally and Rachel side by side in the diner's kitchen, cradled in gentle sunlight, remained in his mind's eye like a sign from above that would not fade. As did the desperate look on Sally's sweet face when he'd left her with Ben's sister Amy and the feel of undisguised need as she'd clung to his hand as if to a life preserver. Yeah, he was giving the idea of marriage some serious thought.

"What's with you?" Ben asked from the downside of a huge bedroom-cabinet thingy. "Staring off in space, that's not normal. What are you doing, thinking of some pretty woman?"

How did a tough, fearless soldier admit to that? "Just wondering how you did it, man."

"Did what?"

"Tie the knot."

"That was the easiest part. Okay, I'm ready. Let's lift on three." Ben counted off and they heaved the heavy armoire around the corner of the bedroom door. "Hold it. We're gonna take out the wallboard."

Jake froze, holding his share of the load. "This isn't as heavy as that log we had to pack around during Indoc."

"What did that thing weigh, a thousand pounds? That doesn't mean it isn't still heavy, though. Okay, let's shimmy a little to the left."

"You got it." Jake gritted his teeth, maneuvering around the tight corner and into the relatively open area of the living room. "How's that injured leg holding up? Want me to take the lead?"

"My leg's sore, but a few more weeks and I'll be back in fighting shape." Ben blew out a breath as they lurched through the threshold, slowing down to clear the door frame, and then they were in the clear. The moving truck, with the lift down, was waiting.

"Being a married man must agree with you since that bullet wound's healed up just fine."

"I'm determined to get back to the front with you and the rest of our squad." There was a clatter as Ben backed onto the metal floor. The lift groaned beneath them.

"Ready?" Jake asked. His back complained, his knees smarted, but they let the enormous cabinet down without any smashed fingers or toes. "What does your new wife think about your heading right back overseas?"

"She understands that I'm TDY most of the time. It's just the job."

Jake knew some women started out feeling that

way. They liked the idea of being supportive of their Special Forces husbands, but the reality was often different than they imagined. It was one thing to take care of all the demands of a home and family, another to deal with car problems and military paperwork that inevitably came up, not to mention the long stretches of lonely evenings and weekends. "She'll be all right handling everything on her own?"

"Are you kidding? Cadence won Olympic gold. If she can't handle it, then it can't be done. Not that I want to leave her for so long, but I know she'll be fine."

"You have a lot of belief in her."

"I married her, didn't I?" With a grin, Ben blushed, turning away to hop off the lift.

Love. It seemed like a risky state of being, more dangerous than tiptoeing through land-mined territory or fast-roping from a helicopter under fire. Those things he'd done and still did without pause. But love and feelings and opening his heart—well, it was a lot to consider.

Jake waited until the lift was done beeping and in place before he gave the armoire a shove. "I got this. You want to make sure there isn't anything else Cadence wants to fit inside this truck?"

"That would be an impossible mission, bud." Ben laughed. "I'll go check with my wife."

There was no mistaking the dip of emotion on that final word, *wife,* and Jake figured that was a fine thing. He put some shoulder into the cabinet and shoved.

"Hey," Ben called from the sidewalk. "Why are you on the subject all of the sudden? Have you met someone?"

"You could say that." Jake gave a final Herculean push and the armoire skidded into place. Keeping his back turned, so his buddy wouldn't guess, he reached for a cord to tie down the furniture.

"Someone you met in the desert? Or back on base? In L.A?"

"Nope." He tightened the cord and gave it a good yank. Yep, it would hold firm.

"You haven't been in one place long enough to meet anyone else. Hold on—" He paused, as if either gearing up his anger or his disbelief. "It isn't anyone here, is it?"

And how did he answer that one? Rachel was his best friend's sister, and that was treading on dangerous ground, too. "Let's just say no other woman has affected me the way Rachel has." It was the truth, at least.

"Not Rachel."

"Rachel." The tying-down was done, so he turned and jammed his fists on his hips. "You got a problem with that?"

"As long as you're good to her, not a bit."

"Then there's no problem." He might not be a domesticated, settled-down type of man, but he believed in treating women right. How could anyone not be good to Rachel? She was so kind, sweet and endearingly funny. She was like coming home. It wouldn't be hard at all to be married to her.

"Hey, handsome." Ben's wife appeared with a medium-sized box in her arms. "This is the very last of it. Except for the cleaning stuff and the vacuum."

Jake watched, a little envious and a little awed, as Ben took the box handily and stopped to kiss his wife. There was no missing the bond between them; it was like an unalterable light shining from her eyes and into his. What they had was obviously real. It humbled even a man as cynical as him.

Happiness. Maybe it did exist. Maybe he could have something like that. He was grateful to the Lord for nudging him down this new path.

Chapter Nine

Rachel ignored the burning ache in her feet and the dull bite of pain in the small of her back. Another twelve-hour day so far and it wasn't over yet. She'd gone from cook to bookkeeper to waitress to hostess and back again and, unless her teenaged twin cousins held up their end of the duties, she'd be handling more of the hostessing.

"Here's your chicken fried steak, Nora." Rachel handed down the first plate, positioning it just so. "I had Dave add extra butter to the whipped potatoes, I know how you like that, and here's an extra basket of dinner rolls."

"You're a dear. The best rolls in town."

"Thank you, since I made them. And for you, Harold, our blue cheese New York steak with baked potato and homemade slow-cooked beans." She gave the plate a little twist as she set it down. "And extra glaze. I know you like it. Now, do you two need anything else?"

"You've thought of everything." Nora's face curved into a smile. "Is your brother's send-off party tomorrow morning?"

"Yep, bright and early. Enjoy your meal. I'll be back to check on you." Rachel checked the aisle—she'd have to make a pass with a few soda pitchers.

A movement outside the windows caught her attention. More customers, she figured, since the SUV was parked right near the door. The long rays of the setting sun sliced across the man, simply dressed in a navy sweatshirt and jeans, silhouetting him as he opened the passenger's-side door.

Jake. He must have finished helping Ben and Cadence pack for their move south. Ben had to report to duty next week.

Which reminded her. Jake was Florida bound, too. He'd be heading back to his base, back to his life, back to protecting and defending. Her heart gave an impossible wish—just a little one—but it was more of a dream than anything else. Those shoulders of his looked strong enough to carry any burden. And his chest. What would it be like to have the privilege of laying her cheek there? She knew that no place in this world would feel safer.

"Rachel!" Brandilyn darted down the aisle. "You've got a bunch of orders up. I'll grab some and help you catch up."

"Ooh, me too," chimed in her identical twin. "You're gonna, like, turn into me, Rache. Daydreamin', like, every second."

"I don't have time to daydream." A lot of responsibility was going to land square on her own shoulders soon and she had to be ready for it. This diner was her future, that was where her wishing energy ought to be instead of directed at a man who was impossible for so many reasons. Mostly because guys that great, that handsome, that cool, that awesome, looked right past a quiet girl like her. Maybe she was too simple in this world of technology and fancy degrees and exciting careers. She didn't know.

God knew what was best for her, she believed that with all her being. But sometimes…just sometimes… it would be something to have her most secret wish come true. Her secret dream man was too good to be true—sure, she knew that. But still, the image of him would always live in the deepest places of her heart and had taken root in her soul.

It's time to get back to reality, Rache. There were so many people who needed her for more coffee, to grab another ketchup bottle, to refill their sodas. This was her life and it was enough.

"I'll grab the pitchers and be right back," she promised Mr. Corey on her way by the table, hurrying to help the teenaged twins, who meant well but often brought disaster right along with them.

They were juggling the orders for the party of

twelve in the back. Clearly a nightmare. One of them—Brianna—was about to lose an order of teriyaki chicken, and Brandilyn was going to drop all four plates she was struggling to keep level.

"Let me grab these!" Rachel rescued the teriyaki chicken and tucked it along her forearm, swiped a steaming plate of lasagna from Brandilyn and checked the orders—Krista Greenley's meal was short her substituted baked potato—and hollered through the window to Dave and juggled two more plates. "Let's get these served, ladies."

She led the way to the back, and as she passed the long row of windows, Jake filled her thoughts again. She'd managed to go a whole minute without thinking of him. The front bell chimed, and the cool evening breeze wafted down the aisle. It was probably him and Sally, come for their supper. As soon as she and the twins reached the table, she'd send Brandilyn back to seat them. The less she had to deal with Jake the better.

A dark color caught the corner of her vision—the navy of Jake's shirt. He was still outside. As she turned her head to see him more clearly, he disappeared behind the open passenger door, but only for a second. When he emerged, he held a sleeping Sally tenderly in his arms. The soft evening light bathed them in a gentle rosy light as Jake pressed a kiss to his little niece's forehead. She stirred, snuggling more deeply against him.

Rachel lost a little more of her heart. Just like that. At this rate, she wouldn't have any left.

"Uh, Rache." Brianna brushed by, as if heaven was reminding her what was important. "Do you know where these go?"

With some relief, she got back to concentrating on work, serving the meals and checking out the newcomers up front. "Krista, I'm sorry, your baked potato is on its way. I'll bring it with the rest of the orders. Jenna, here's your chicken teriyaki. And—" she whipped out a small bottle with her now-free hand "—a soy sauce."

She moved her way around the table so she could check the front of the restaurant, but Jake wasn't one of the customers waiting to be seated. He must have carried Sally up to bed. With promises to bring steak sauce and Krista's potato, she hurried through the swinging doors and thanked Dave for having Mrs. Edison's order boxed and sacked. After grabbing more condiment bottles, she set the ticket beside Brianna, who was now at the cash register and talking to herself as she rang it up.

"I put in an extra container of tartar," Rachel told her former teacher as she handed the boxed meal to the older lady. "Have a good evening, Mrs. Edison."

"Thank you, dear."

Jake charged into her thoughts again. As she bustled down the aisle, avoiding the party Brandilyn was currently seating, she wondered if he and Sally had

had a chance to eat. She caught herself just in time. *It's not your business, Rache.* She wanted to tell herself that she'd show the same amount of concern for anyone who was staying in the upstairs apartment, but she knew that wasn't the truth.

"Your baked potato with extra sour cream." She presented the plate to a smiling Krista and then handed out the Cheeseburger Deluxe and Mom's Super Meat loaf. She produced a few different bottles of steak sauces and everyone was happy.

She handed off the fresh container of ketchup, grabbed a pitcher of soda and one of decaf and made the rounds. Made another to distribute more butter and a complimentary second order of fries for the deputy who was not only a loyal customer, but who always went beyond the call of duty for her sisters and their diner. Rachel then sent Brandilyn away from the cash register—she looked too befuddled while ringing up a family of four.

"Bus for me, would you?" she asked the teenager, who agreed cheerfully and hurried off, cracking her gum.

"Busy night?"

That familiar baritone had her toes curling. She handed over the Coreys' change, thanked them for coming and as they moved away from the counter, she saw Jake. His short hair was tousled, his sweatshirt rumpled, and yet he'd never looked more handsome. Maybe it was the remembered image of him holding the sleeping child so tenderly. Or the depth of affection in the parental kiss to her forehead. His strength and manliness was warrior-honed, and he had a heart like her father had had, that of a loving and good man.

"It's a home football-game night. It always keeps us on our toes." Rachel handed Brianna seven menus, and as the Sheridan family followed the teenager, she realized that was the end to the first rush. Everyone was seated, Paige must have come in the back because she was serving table four's meal. "We'll have a big push out the door in about twenty-five minutes, and then things will quiet down. How's Sally?"

"Exhausted. She hasn't been sleeping well, and I think spending the day with Amy's son, playing and swimming and whatever else they did, tired her out enough. She's out like a light."

"I saw you carrying her." Great, now she sounded like a stalker. "Through the windows." She gestured at the long row of glass reflecting the parked cars outside and the impending twilight.

He didn't seem to respond. "I don't want to leave her for long. Do you do takeout here?"

"Sure. Here's a menu." No more social blunders around this man, Rachel. "There isn't a phone upstairs, but did you want to take my cell? You can call the order in, and when it's ready, I'll send one of the twins up with your meal. That way you don't have to leave Sally alone."

"You'd do that?"

"For you. Sure." She realized what she'd said a second too late, and embarrassment burned her face. She did sound like a stalker or something, because now he was staring at her. The openness was gone. He stood like a granite statue, and did not look up from the menu he was studying. Not even when she took her cell from her pocket and set it on the edge of the counter.

It's just not meant to be. She knew it; she'd always known it. She stepped back, determined to keep her distance and what, if anything, was left of her dignity. "The number's on the front of the menu. Just give us a call."

"Thanks." His hand shot out and covered hers. She felt the warm comfort of his skin, the way his wide palm engulfed her hand. And in that moment, when his dark gaze found hers, she told herself it wasn't her future she saw. So why, when he left, did it feel as if he'd taken her destiny with him?

Jake hesitated at the bedroom door, looking back at his little niece. Sally was still fast asleep. Curled up on her side, bunched in a fetal position, so small and helpless.

He eased the bedroom door shut. The fierce need to protect her roared up in him, and he fisted his hands in frustration. What good was all his military training and all the specialized skills he'd learned to defend this country, when they couldn't do a single thing to rescue Sally from what was hurting her?

Grief wasn't something he could ambush or capture, fight off or beat down. He'd never felt so inadequate or lost, but he trusted the Lord to guide him through this, for Sally's sake. Because he couldn't do this alone.

He heard what he thought were footsteps on the outside stairs. When he'd called down his order, Rachel hadn't been the one to answer the phone. He knew she was busy—he'd seen how hard she was working and how crowded the restaurant was, so he didn't expect her to be on the other side of the door. But when she was, peace settled in his soul.

Definitely nice.

"Surprise." She spoke low, as if she expected Sally to be still napping and gestured with the huge sack she carried in both arms. "I told you there would be a lull. I hope you don't mind that I came. The twins are on break and I couldn't talk them into coming."

"It's okay."

"I brought the makings for hot chocolate. Enough for two, uh, in case you want some."

He could only stare because she blew him away. He'd never known anyone this thoughtful. She just kept wowing him. He stepped back, holding open the screen door for her. "Come in. Can I take that?"

"Oh, no."

"Then what do I owe you?"

"Nice try, but I don't want your money." She moved past him like poetry of beauty and grace.

His chest tugged hard in a painful, inexplicable way.

"I don't want a free meal." He pulled the door closed against the crisp evening winds. "That's not why I ordered from your place."

"So? You helped Ben, we help you." She moved through the half-lit room, circling the couch and disappearing through the kitchen door, and her gait tapped to a stop. The refrigerator door opened. "I'll just put the milk in here. And I wrapped up Sally's dinner, so all you need to do is take this out and pop it in the oven, preheated to three-fifty, for fifteen minutes, and it will be just right for her."

Jake watched as she set a foil packet in the refrigerator. Her cheese pizza from the kid's menu, he presumed, and it looked like a little more than a pizza. Rachel added a large container, the milk he guessed, and another covered plate.

"For dessert," she explained as she closed the door and folded the big sack she'd carried everything up in. "Did you want to eat in here or the living room? I could put this on a plate."

Okay, so maybe he wasn't in love with this woman, but he didn't really believe in love. And if the hard pang that settled dead center in his chest and throbbed like a bullet wound wasn't deep, serious-like, then he didn't know what was.

He *did* feel something for this woman, he could admit it. He admired her. God was right. She would be great for Sally. She was perfect, she was wonderful, she was a dream, and he couldn't speak like a normal, sane man when he was near her. So he managed to grunt and nod. Maybe he felt more than like for Rachel. He wasn't sure if he felt comfortable with that. He was a lone-wolf kind of guy.

She moved around the small, rather dusty kitchen as if she were at home. She brought down the plate and found silverware, and he just watched her work, humming a little.

"You really enjoy this, don't you?"

"Enjoy what? I noticed you had the TV on. I take it you want to eat in there?"

He nodded. There were some reruns of a family sitcom that had just come on. He got all of two channels with the rabbit ears on top of the decades-old set, and neither was as interesting as Rachel. "You wouldn't be able to stay for a few minutes, would you?"

"Oh, I wish. You have no idea." She blushed, as if she realized what she'd said. How much she revealed.

So, he wasn't alone in this attraction, or whatever it was he felt. The weight in his chest began to hurt and hope at the same time. It was hard to breathe. "You said there was a lull. And I'd like nothing more than to spend more time with you."

"It's a football night, and the game is about ready

to start. You can see the stadium lights from here. In about five minutes the band is going to be warming up, and everyone is going to be leaving me. Paige's son is playing, so she's gotta be there. And the twins are that age where they don't want to miss anything. I'll be off until the game is over, and we'll get slammed again. I'll need to help out."

He felt her apology, it hung in the air like the faint dust; it seemed this apartment wasn't used very often. But the place wasn't as neglected as his courting skills. Courting was different than dating. The decision to court, well, now, he'd never exactly been in this position before. So, he was at a loss. "Maybe you'd want to come to the game with me and Sally?"

"Isn't she napping?"

"Uh, yeah, but we can eat here. Have you had dinner yet? No? Well, Sally's bound to wake up sometime. When you on break and we can go on over. I haven't been to a football game for a couple of years. And besides, we'll be leaving for the base. I'd like to spend as much of the time I have left here with you."

What? Rachel *couldn't* have heard him right. Had he really said it, or was her mind just playing tricks on her? He wanted to spend his time here with her? A chunk of meteorite could hurtle down through the heavens, punch through the roof and strike her in the forehead and she wouldn't be more surprised.

Jake inched closer. "Would that be something you'd be interested in?"

"Uh…" She knew her mouth was hanging open. *Brilliant, Rache.* She knew the capacity for speech had flown right out of her repertoire of social skills. The worst part of it was that she'd gone utterly paralyzed, in the middle of bending down to leave both his plate and his boxed meal on the coffee table, and she couldn't seem to make herself straighten up and act like a normal, sane person.

Jake didn't seem to notice as he bounded across the room, closing the distance in easy, powerful strides like the latent power of a panther stalking his prey.

He appeared taller from her bent-over position. He towered over her, his chuckle easy as he took the plate from her grip and set it on the table. "Does 'uh' mean yes or no?"

"Uh…" There she went again, in command of her verbal ability. "Yes. I'll just run down and, uh, finish up a few things."

"Bring up a meal. I'll wait."

"Uh, no. Don't wait. Your burger will get cold. I, uh, I'll be just a few minutes." Or had she said that already?

See, this is why you don't date a lot, Rachel. She was no dating genius, that was for sure. Was there such a thing as being date-impaired?

"Sounds great. I'll look forward to it."

"I'll, uh, look forward to it, too." His baritone dipped low and charming.

Were her toes curling? Sure enough, in the cramped

quarters of her sneakers, her toes seemed to curl of their own volition. Somehow her feet carried her forward, but she didn't feel the floor because she was floating through the room.

Floating. As if that made any sense! She felt even more lost as she fumbled with the doorknob. She might as well be groping in the dark. Surely, Jake Hathaway wasn't The One. If he was, then why did he live across the country? Why would he be gone from her life before she even had the chance to get to know him?

She let the screen click shut behind her, careful not to let it slam shut and wake Sally. Twilight had lengthened until the shadows were dark and thick, and she welcomed the privacy of that darkness and the wintry wind that battered her hot face.

Why do I want him so much, Lord? It would be nothing at all to fall absolutely in love with him. To see herself in his kitchen, fixing his meals, picking up after Sally, keeping house and sharing his life.

You're just setting yourself up for heartbreak, you know that. She wasn't sophisticated and dazzling, cool and coy, flirty or confident. Men hardly noticed her. There was no way a rugged, man's man like Jake would see past her mousy appearance to the real woman she was—or was there?

The high-school band blared into life. Cheers rose up from the stadium. All those families huddled in the bleachers, bundled well against the cold night. All those people living lives that she could only dream of.

Jake was only being kind to her. She was his best buddy's sister, of course he'd be nice to her. That's all it is, Rache. Don't go seeing something that isn't there, she told herself firmly, protecting her heart well used to disappointment.

Jake needed a friend, that was all. And if there was one thing she was used to, it was that. She took a deep breath and hurried down the steps to the diner.

Chapter Ten

"This way." Jake's lips brushed her cheekbone, his breath warm and pleasant against her. "I see a couple of seats."

Rachel's soul shivered at his nearness. It was like a dream to feel the singular intimacy of being at his side. This big, strapping man who moved with agile caution—he was always scanning his surroundings, watching the people around them, and she could see the soldier in the man. Steely discipline and skill; he was a strong enough man to be gentle as he protected Sally from the bump of the milling crowd below the bleachers. Her heart fluttered more watching him lift Sally onto the top step, swinging her until a small grin cracked her solemn face.

"Where?" Rachel stood on tiptoe to try to look up into the stands, but she was short, always one of the banes of her existence, and she couldn't see over the heads of the people going up the steps in front of her.

"Up toward the middle," Jake answered, leaning close to be heard above the roar of the crowd as the home team apparently made a down. "See?"

She followed the line of his muscled arm, bulky with his winter coat, and saw the spot he meant. There was a patch of bench visible through the throng of families crammed together, cheering along with the cheerleaders or shouting out on their own. Okay, it would do, considering they were such latecomers. But it was a little spot, she and Jake would be pressed shoulder to shoulder, side to side, thigh to thigh.

She gulped. Maybe they should put Sally between them. Good idea. She took another step and the faces of the people on that bench came into clearer focus. Her blood iced. Her shoe missed the step. She recognized a face in the crowd—boy, did she. "Do you think we could sit somewhere else?" Anywhere else.

His hand settled on her back, between her shoulder blades, and his touch was a steady, amazing connection and ached as much as it soothed. The warmth of his hand, the outline of it, even through her heavy winter coat seemed to zing straight to her soul and settle. "We can sit anywhere you want, beautiful."

Did he know what he was doing to her? she wondered, as she tried to find the stair with her foot and succeeded. No, there was no way he could. She drew in a breath and hoped her voice would sound normal when she spoke, but it came out all strangled as if she was in the greatest agony. "Anywhere but next to my old boyfriend and his wife."

"Old boyfriend?" Surprise lit his voice, and Rachel turned in time to see his left brow arch upward. Sympathy flashed on his hard-chiseled face. "Now, how could any man be so dumb as not to want you?"

If only he didn't sound so sincere. If only her heart didn't warm in response. Her whole world shifted. The next step she took wouldn't have felt so monumental—something had changed, everything felt as if it changed, and yet nothing had. Like the moment in the church, she felt an odd calm seep into her soul.

It was this man. This man and the right things he said and the good things he did and how he made her feel deep inside. He was going to render her helpless. She was going to fall so hard in love with him there would be no recovery. No saving face, no shred of dignity she would have left when he took off for Florida and his exciting life as a para-rescueman. She would never be able to hide the strong, strident emotion blazing to life in her chest like a Fourth of July fireworks display.

"We can go somewhere else." His words, his breath, his lips grazed her cheek and made everything worse. And everything more clear.

The crowd blurred. The cheers and clash of the game faded. Even the brisk cold wind ebbed away until there was only the light in the center of her heart, coming to life and then flaming higher until it seemed to take over her entire being. She did not want to fall in love—one-sided again.

Jake's gloved hand caught hers and held on. "This way."

He's leaving for Florida, Rachel. She vowed to chant that over and over until she got it through her head that she was only doomed for disappointment again.

She was hardly aware of climbing through the stands, only of the dread of sitting close to him. And the thrill. Of settling onto the bench and the feel of his hand at her elbow, helping. Of the dependable strength of him as she sat squished against his side. This close, she could see the day's growth shadowing his granite jaw, but she had no right to lay her fingertips there, against the side of his jawbone and discover the texture of his day's whiskers.

"Rachel!" a voice called through the crowd.

She recognized her friend a few rows down, sitting with her family. "Margaret. How did Kaylie's teacher's conference go?"

"It was a disaster. She's in so much trouble." Margaret's kind eyes said otherwise. "Wait until motherhood happens to you, and you'll—oh." She gave Jake a second look. "Isn't that Ben's best man? His buddy from the army?"

"Air force," Jake started to correct her, but bit his tongue. Not his conversation. Rachel was already doing it for him, explaining that he and Ben served together.

Margaret, a pleasant-faced woman with really frizzy hair, gave him an approving look. "So, how long have you two been together?"

"Oh, we're not together." Rachel blushed, and it was a pretty sight. She dipped her chin, and the crowd began to roar as a huddle on the field broke up. The woman turned to family talk, Margaret had a couple of kids that Rachel was asking after.

He listened with half an ear; he didn't want to eavesdrop, but there was no way he could ignore their conversation entirely because he was pressed so close to Rachel. Which wasn't a bad thing. Her cinnamon scent kept tickling his nose and he had to fight the need to put his arm around her and draw her close, just to see what it felt like; just to see if it felt *right*.

"I'll see you at choir practice, okay?" Rachel finished her conversation, exchanged parting smiles with her friend, and then turned to him. "Margaret and I are both sopranos in the church choir, if you can believe they let me sing. We've been friends since we were in preschool."

She was pure sweetness when she smiled, and he could picture her singing in church. He already knew she was a faithful woman; and faith was important to him. "The church I go to when I'm at home has a great choir."

"Really? Is it a big church?"

"It's probably bigger than yours here." He'd seen the town church, prominent on a quieter corner past the park, and its high steeple and white siding spoke of traditional values. "It's a more modern place, but that has a lot of advantages." He waited.

"It sounds wonderful. I lived in Seattle for a while, when I went to the University of Washington, and I attended this great church with a fantastic choir. I love music. Of course, our little town has nothing like that, but it makes up for it in a thousand other ways. It's the people in my life who matter most."

"That's how I feel." It blew him away like a bullet to the chest. "That's why I do what I do."

"You have a very demanding job. A man has to be very motivated to do it."

One thing he was good at was motivation, and at setting a goal and sticking with it until it was achieved. If he'd had any doubts about God's plan, it would be at this moment. Anyone could see Rachel was happy here. The crowd roared, Sally's hand crept into his, and he turned to her. "What is it, cutie?"

"I gotta go to the bathroom." She looked so pale in the bright light from the dozen floodlights blazing across the field, that he could see every freckle blanketing her nose and cheekbones.

His iron-hard heart wrenched; he hated seeing her so unhappy. At that moment he felt the incredible warmth of Rachel leaning against him to speak with Sally, and it was such a range of emotion he felt. He wasn't used to this; he was overwhelmed. It was as if he went deaf, for he couldn't even hear the crowd's wild cheers at an interception. That stillness washed over him like the ocean when he was on a night dive. The rush of water rising up over him as he plummeted downward from his jump. The blades of the chopper silenced, the view of his buddies gone, and he was alone and sinking.

"C'mon, Sally," he heard Rachel say, holding out her gloved hand across his chest. "I'll take you. And on the way back, let's get a good look at the concession stand, okay? That way we know what to make your uncle buy you."

"'Kay." Sally seemed to like the idea as she bolted up and grasped Rachel's hand like a lifeline. "Bye, Uncle Jake."

Rachel McKaslin laughed down at him as she took a side step to make her way through the packed bleacher row to the aisle. She held Sally's hand and guided her over the obstacles of feet and purses and stadium blankets like a natural. Of course, she had a nephew she spent time with, so she was used to taking care of a kid. She was perfect. So, why wasn't she married? Was it because she didn't want to be?

She paused midway to the aisle to speak with a woman who looked to be about her same age in the next row back. Jake lived for football, he wouldn't mind watching the game, but so far he hadn't watched a single play. Rachel drew his attention and held it, and he couldn't explain why.

As the women exchanged pleasantries, he noticed how Rachel lit up, subtle as a twilight star, as she spoke with another friend. Here he sat in the freezing cold with his heart feeling like it was on the outside instead of safely tucked in his chest. He didn't like feeling vulnerable. For all he knew, Rachel wanted nothing more than a life here, with her family and friends, working in the diner alongside her sisters.

But You wouldn't steer me wrong, right, God? He thought of what was at stake. Sally, who clung to Rachel's hand and began to fidget. Rachel noticed right away, laughingly said goodbye to her friend, and then she and Sally made it to the aisle, where they descended the steps. Like a good mother would, Rachel kept a steady hold of Sally's hand and helped her down the wide, steep stairs.

He straightened, trying to keep Rachel in his sight, and it wasn't because she looked adorable and attractive and amazing even in a bulky blue parka and wash-worn jeans. Her lustrous chestnut-colored hair bounced around her face and shoulders. His heart seemed to drag after her, and that made no sense at all.

He was a tough soldier. He could handle being ambushed and cornered, facing it with the steel he'd been given from the Lord.

But he didn't do love, and he didn't know how to

draw back the tenderness that made it feel as if she had taken possession of some vital place in his heart. He only knew he had to be careful.

What happened next was in God's hands, he knew, as everything was; but he also knew that the Lord helped those who helped themselves and he wanted to help Sally. He didn't need anyone—not really.

Sally did.

"Another licorice whip?"

Rachel accepted the offered red rope with thanks. "I have a sweet tooth."

"I noticed." He didn't seem to think her weakness for candy was a fault. "I've never known a woman who liked licorice so much."

"It's a sign of great character. Just like a man who can eat a hot dog after having a huge deluxe burger and an extra order of fries."

"I indulge when I can. A month from now, I'll probably be scarfing down an MRE and falling to sleep with my M-4."

"I gave up my machine gun for a cup of cocoa and an electric blanket. They kept me warmer." She liked that she made him laugh. The warmth of his chuckle filled her. "No electric blankets where you go?"

"No, and the desert can get chilly at night."

"And lonely, I bet." She sighed. She knew something about that. She focused on the field glimmering beneath the floodlights like a giant rectangular emerald. The suited-up high-school kids were grim during the last four minutes left on the clock. They were ahead by a field goal, but they'd lost the down. One slip and they could lose the game.

On the field, her nephew Alex, so tall and grown-up, gave his face mask a yank, concentrating, as the players lined up, ready to scrimmage. Cheers rose, the band sent a musical challenge, which the crowd picked up on, and the excitement in the stands rose to a crescendo.

All around her were friends and acquaintances, people she'd known all her life. People with families of their own, her friends married with their own children. They were happy and seated beside their husbands. It was wrong to be envious, because she wasn't truly. But she so wanted a life like theirs.

And this man, who saw her as a friend, was on the edge of capturing her heart. And she couldn't let him. She had to be strong. She had to fight against it as hard as she could.

Wasn't it just her luck that when she'd found the right man she could love, he wasn't in love with her? It was her usual pattern. Nothing surprising about that. Not one thing.

It's almost over, she thought as the visiting team's center hiked the ball, and the quarterback stepped back to pass. The clock was counting down, the home team charged and the quarterback went down before he could throw. Sacked! The game was won, although a full minute stood on the big scoreboard.

Cheers exploded full volume. People leaped to their feet, the band screeched to life, and the cheerleaders hurled their pompoms. The game was as good as over. For her, it was.

"This is where I leave you." She leaned close so he could hear her over the fray and couldn't help noticing how pleasant he smelled, of spice and man and the night. "I have to get to the diner before these people do."

"Then we're coming with you."

"But—"

"No buts. We're not going to let you go off alone." He plucked Sally from the bench beside him and swung her into his arms. "Right, Sal?"

The girl nodded on cue, sleepy-eyed, the last five inches of a thick red licorice rope dangling from her fist. She yawned and laid her cheek against Jake's sturdy shoulder.

Jake smiled, always a dazzling experience. "This is a date. I'm not about to bail on you because you have responsibilities."

This is a date? Her mind skidded to a halt. She could only gape up at him in her best fish-out-of-water imitation. *This can't be a date. I'm in my work clothes. My hair's a mess.*

Jake's free hand lit on the back of her neck. Even through the thick parka, she could feel the warmth of his hand like a brand. A slow trickle of joy flowed into her; it was all that she would allow. Okay, if this was a date, then it was a casual one. An impromptu one. Last-minute. It didn't mean anything. She'd do best not to read too much into it, even if she wanted to. Getting her hopes up scared her. They were bound to come crashing down.

As she excused her way down the row, Jake stayed right behind her. His hand remained on her nape and didn't leave, as if he were determined to maintain some sort of tie between them. When she reached the bottom of the stands, Jake moved to protect her from the shuffle and bump of the crowd, striding easily and predatorily and in control. It was easy to see the soldier in him, strong and tough, and she couldn't help thinking, *Wow*.

Finally they were through the gate and out into the open street behind the school grounds. The street curbs were jammed on either side with overflow parking from the school, but the two of them were alone. It felt like a special night, Rachel thought as she watched the tall leafless maples reach their black, frosty limbs high toward the black sky, so silent and still. The tidy residential street was quiet, too, as they passed Craftsman-style homes with their curtains closed and windows glowing from the lights within.

So, this was a date. She'd never quite had one like this before, especially a first date. But as they walked companionably along the street toward the park, she thought it might be the best first date she'd ever been on. There was something right about walking at his side. Something real about the silence that lingered gently between them. She felt comfortable. She felt complete. *Is he the one, Lord? Please, send me a sign, so I don't mess this up.*

"She's asleep." He spoke low, hardly louder than the night, leaning closer still.

Sally was slumped, carefully cradled, against his chest and shoulder, her weight easily secured in his strong arms. She was as relaxed as a rag doll. What a safe place to be, Rachel thought. "Maybe tonight she'll sleep better."

"I sure hope so."

They were at the street corner, and the unlit expanse of road showed there wasn't any reason to check for traffic. They stepped off the curb together, in synch. Their breaths rose in misty clouds at the same time and place as if they were made to be together.

"So, tell me," Jake broke the silence. "Why don't you have a husband and a family to fill that big house of yours?"

She tripped on her own feet. *Real graceful, Rache.* She caught herself before she could do more than stumble, but her mind couldn't stop tumbling over his words. Was he making pleasant conversation, or was there more to his question? "Because I'm waiting for God to send me the very best man."

"You're beautiful and smart and funny—"

"Because I trip over my own feet, you mean? Or wear those huge fuzzy slippers?"

"Yeah, and chase a spoiled wild moose with a broom. You're a great cook, you help run a business, everyone who knows you thinks you're the sweetest woman ever. Including me."

"Really? Wow, I'm glad I've deceived you so much. I'm not all that sweet. I can be feisty and difficult. Just ask Paige."

He knew what he saw. He spent his life fighting evil men who would harm the innocent in other people's countries to defend his own. He knew goodness when he saw it, and he loved her for it. For the humbling way she waved off the truth like a shrug of her slender shoulders. For the kindness she'd shown Sally. For the peace just being with her brought to his war-battered soul.

He needed her. He could see now why Ben had married. Being a lone wolf had its benefits. He worked most of the year in dangerous places, it was his call of duty. But when he was home, it would be something to have a real home, to have her at his side just to talk to, to walk beside, to share a quiet evening with. Those were the real things in life, the moments that mattered, and how he felt had nothing to do with needing someone for Sally or any single influence outside of his heart. Rachel made him feel taller and stronger, more vulnerable and afraid at the same exact moment. "So, you'd like to be married like your friends I saw at the game. You just haven't been asked by the very best man yet."

"Well, yes, if you want to put it that way. That's implying the best man is out there somewhere."

"Maybe he's closer than you think."

What did that mean? What was he saying? Rachel gave thanks that she still had the wherewithal to remember to lift her feet high enough to step over the railroad ties that marked the edge of the city park. Maybe he wasn't talking about himself being the best man. Maybe he was trying to be encouraging. "I can hope so. So, now it's your turn. Why aren't you married?"

"It's hard to find the right person. You know how it is."

"I do." She sighed, disappointment sifting through her like the cold air through her parka. She'd been right—he was making conversation, not trying to tell her that he was her best man. She took a slow breath, finding her dignity. There was no reason he needed to know that she was hurting. "It feels impossible to find that one person that lights you up inside and shares your values and your faith and wants the same things from life."

"Yep. Aside from being compatible and loyal and good."

"Exactly. That's why I'm still solo."

"So, you'd like to get married one day. Maybe have a couple of kids."

"Definitely." Rachel felt something brush her cheekbone. It was featherlight and cold. A snowflake. She tipped her head to stare up at the sky and dots of white tumbled toward her, falling as if sent from heaven. "I suppose it's not very modern of me, but I'm an old-fashioned girl. I've always wanted to have a good marriage and a happy family. Maybe because I lost my folks when I was young. It's been elusive. But maybe it won't always be that way." God willing.

"Good. I'm glad I'm not wasting time." Jake stopped in the middle of the grassy park and cupped her chin with his free hand. His gaze was unreadable; his face was set as if in stone.

Wasting time? What did that mean? Her mind began to swirl like the snowflakes as a light wind hit them. She realized as he leaned ever closer that he was speaking about her. About him. Incredibly, his lips slanted over hers in a tender brush. Their first kiss. Quiet, sweet joy filled her heart unbroken, until he lifted his mouth from hers.

Her future shone in his eyes as he gazed down at her, solemnly, for she knew that he felt this, too.

She didn't know how long they stood together, with Sally asleep on Jake's shoulder, gazing into one another's eyes. The distant blare of car horns and the shrill shrieks and cheers of teenagers rejoicing came distantly, and hardly important at all.

"Guess the game's over." Jake spoke first. "We'd better get you to the diner. Judging by the sounds of things, it's gonna be busy."

Like a dream, he took her hand.

It's a sign, she thought as she twined her fingers with his. Snow was falling everywhere, frosting the world as if making it new. She remembered to thank the Lord as she let Jake lead her through the storm and the dark.

Chapter Eleven

Jake sipped his second cup of decaf and watched Rachel over the rim. He'd chosen this booth and this seat on purpose because he could see her through the order window. And every time he saw her, he remembered the gentleness of her kiss. The scent of her perfume clung to him, cinnamon and wholesome. He couldn't stop the tenderness building within him; and it was that tenderness that scared him. It would make him vulnerable if he let it. He wasn't a man to give up control.

"Aw, she's such a cutie."

Jake hadn't noticed one of the teenage girls approach the table, but there she was with a carafe and chomping her gum. She topped off his cup. "Hey, if you, like, ever need someone to babysit, you should call me."

"Or me," chimed her twin who bustled down the aisle with a plate of French fries. "So you could, like, go out with Rachel again. I mean, if you wanna date her."

"Which you should totally do, because there's no one nicer than Rachel. She's, like, way cool."

"Do you like her?"

Jake looked up at the girls and tried to remember being a teenager. It was too long ago, and he felt his age as he reached for the sugar canister. "If you're serious about babysitting, I'll take you up on it."

"Great," they said in unison, with identical grins, before breaking up and going separate ways.

"What do you think, Sal? Is it about time to take you upstairs?"

His niece gave a big yawn. "Do I hafta see Rachel first?"

"She looks pretty busy in the kitchen. You like her, don't you?"

"I guess." She didn't sound too enthusiastic. "Oh, she's coming."

How did he miss that? Sure enough, when he looked up, there she was breezing toward him. The tender ache in his chest, the one he'd better figure out how to control, sharpened as she drew near.

"I brought you another cup." She slipped a big mug onto the table in front of Sally, blushing as if she were remembering their kiss.

Sal took one look at the mug frothing with whipped cream and drizzled with chocolate syrup. "Thanks. I guess."

"Good. I aim to please." Rachel's unguarded spirit shone for one brief moment as she gazed on the child.

He would love her forever, just for that. For caring so much for Sally.

"Is there anything else I can get you two?"

"You're always doing for us. What about you?"

"Me? I work here. I'm supposed to cook and wait on people."

"That's not what I meant." Jake, being a man of action, knew exactly what he had to do. "It's nearly eleven. Isn't that when you close?"

"Lock the doors, yes. But there's work enough to keep me here for another hour at least. Why? You're welcome to stay here as long as you want, but Sally, you're looking droopy."

Was it his imagination or was Rachel avoiding his gaze? He patted the seat next to him. "Sit down here for a second."

"I, uh—" Her eyes sparkling with humor, she glanced down the aisles at the half dozen full tables where groups of teenagers munched on fries and slurped down milk shakes. "Why should I sit down? Maybe you have a complaint for the manager?"

"Yeah. I do, so you'd best sit on down here and listen up."

Oh, he looked like trouble itself as he laid his arm along the back of the booth, waiting for her to slip in beside him. How could she refuse? She still tingled as if filled with the gentlest light, and all from his single kiss. She obliged him and it felt wonderful as his arm hooked over her shoulders. She felt whole, as if she were made to be at his side. "Was there something wrong with your order?"

"*You* didn't serve it to us."

"That's because I was in the kitchen."

"Come closer." He pulled her so they were practically hugging. It was wonderful to lay her head on his shoulder and just to be.

So this is what it's like to truly come home, she thought with a contented sigh. The silence in her deepened as his arms came around her and his chin pressed against the top of her head. She was right. No place could feel safer than being in Jake's arms.

"How much more do you have left to do?" His question vibrated pleasantly through her.

She pressed more tightly against his iron chest. "I've got the kitchen mostly cleaned up. The twins are off in a few minutes, so they won't be around to help with the mopping. I still have to do the deposit and deal with the twins' over-rings. That could take hours. Although sometimes I take that work home with me."

"Those are some pretty long hours you put in."

"The life of a businesswoman. When Paige hands over complete responsibilities, I don't want to think about how many more hours, but then..." She shrugged, not finishing. She'd almost said, "I don't mind because what else do I have?"

Tonight, things had changed. But her responsibilities had not. The phone at the front counter rang. "Oops, I need to get that."

Jake pressed a kiss to the crown of her head before she slid away from him. "Are those twins good babysitters?"

"They're very reliable, believe it or not, except with the cash register." Her grin sparkled and then she bounded down the aisle.

One of the twins looked up from refilling cola glasses with a big pitcher and laughed. "Hey, I heard that!"

Then Jake understood. This diner was important to Rachel because it was about her family. Family was everything to her. He respected that because it was important to him, too, and now he had one of his own. Across the table, Sally was drooping again. It was way past her bedtime. "Hey, princess. Are you done with that cocoa?"

She nodded, her eyes drifting closed again.

That was the final sign. She needed to be put to bed, and he'd have to wrench himself away from Rachel's presence. He didn't want to. It was a nice feeling, strange for a man who lived his rugged life, but not unwelcome. Funny how a few months ago he'd been happy with the challenge of being in the Middle East, with the missions he'd been assigned, and couldn't have imagined this. Being here, in this peaceful hometown diner with a kid needing to be tucked into bed. He would never have guessed he'd be wishing to hold sweet Rachel in his arms a little longer.

God sure moved in mysterious ways, but always for the best. Jake believed that. Rachel wanted her own family. Sally needed a new mother. And he needed...well, he didn't need anyone. It was hard to need anyone when he had a heart of iron.

The twin who'd laughed at Rachel's comment skidded to a halt at his table. "Oh, were you asking about tonight? I could watch her and stuff. You're just staying upstairs, right? You like Rachel, don't you?"

He could see Rachel out of his peripheral vision, chatting to someone on the phone, and the sight of her made the affection inside him flare dangerously. It was hard to admit, but he could understand the girl's question. Of course Rachel's family would be protective of her. "I like her very much."

"I thought so." Brianna—it said on her name badge—cracked her gum. "She's, like, the nicest person ever. You could marry her. Oh! Then she could move to Florida with you and, like, Ben lives there too, so she'd know people there. Rachel loves pale-pink roses. Just in case you want to give her some. Oh, want me to take Sally up for you?"

To be a teenager again and have that much energy. He fished the door key out of his pocket. "Her nighttime storybook is on the nightstand by the bed. Sal, is it okay if you go with Brianna?"

But Sally was gazing up at the teenager in awe. She nodded and silently gave her hand when the twin reached for her.

"C'mon, sweetie. I'm a great reader. I do voices and everything. Okay?"

Sally clambered to her feet. She cast a worried look across the table.

"I won't be long, princess."

"'Kay." She trotted off alongside her newest heroine.

Rachel hung up the phone and knelt to say goodbye to Sally.

Bingo, he thought, watching how Rachel seemed to melt as she smoothed back the girl's stray curls with an affectionate hand. This path his life had taken was a good one, he decided. Rachel was the sort of woman a soldier like him needed, someone strong and independent, but so wonderful he couldn't wait to come home to her. Think of how great she'd be for Sally, and Sally for her.

Thank you, Father, he remembered to pray as Rachel released the girl, waved her through the door, and then disappeared into the office.

"Hey, I need to talk to you." Paige was no-nonsense as she slid into the booth across from him, her voice low but firm. "I know you're Ben's best friend and we are grateful for you hauling him to safety when he was shot, but you listen up. I don't want you using Rachel."

"That's not my intention, ma'am."

"What is your intention?"

"I'm going to marry her." He waited while Paige's eyes narrowed, as if she were trying to peer into him to see if he was worthy.

She frowned, as if she thought he came up short. "This isn't some kind of quick solution to your situation, with that little niece of yours, is it?"

"Still not convinced, huh?" Avoidance was better than admitting that on one level, Paige was right. But only because God had led him here and it was as if by heaven's grace that he realized how good Rachel could be for Sally.

And maybe Sally for Rachel. "Your sister would be a great wife. Why hasn't anyone swept her off her feet before this?"

"Rachel is shy and she's a homebody and a lot of men overlook her."

"Well, I'm not a lot of men."

"That remains to be seen." There was no mistaking the warning she sent him as she stood. "You'd better not hurt her."

"I would never hurt her."

Footsteps padded in their direction as a party of teenagers headed for the door. "Thanks, Miss McKaslin," one of them said. "The sundaes were real good."

"Good game, boys. See you next time." Paige grabbed a tall blond boy from the crowd and gave him a squeeze. "I know, not in front of your friends, but I'm proud of you, running the winning touchdown. Are you going straight home?"

"Yes, Mom." He rolled his eyes, but he was clearly a good kid, and shook his head, apparently used to public humiliation as he wiggled away from her. "Bye."

"Boys." Paige glared right down at Jake. "I give the team free sundaes if they win, although it's probably a bad decision. Never give a male an inch, he'll take ten miles."

Someone has an attitude, Jake thought, as she marched away.

"Rache?" The remaining twin called out at the front door. "Do you want me to stay and mop?"

"No," came the answer from down the hallway. "Escape while you can."

"Bye!"

The last customers in the place, a clean-cut teenage boy and his girlfriend, crawled out from their booth, their voices low and tender as they ambled down the aisle hand-in-hand. Jake felt alone, not solitary as he always had, but lonely. See what caring for Rachel had done to him? He had to fight the urge to head into the kitchen just to see her. Just to be near her.

A bell rang at the front counter, calling Rachel from the back. "Are you ready to go?" she asked the young couple.

"Yes, and you promised to give me your hot chocolate recipe," the teenage girl answered.

"Jot down your email address and I'll send it to you." Rachel gestured to the cup of pens on the counter as she took the order ticket and the boy's ten-dollar bill. The register chimed as she rang in the sale. "William, if you're still interested in the busboy job, give Paige a call sometime this weekend."

"Gee, thanks. I will." He took his change, grabbed a toothpick and held the door for his girlfriend.

Jake watched, not the boy, but Rachel. She gazed at the two with a wistful sigh. She was a romantic at heart, he realized. Pale-pink roses. Snowflakes and kisses. He knew next to nothing about romance, since his interests tended to be geared toward skydiving, motorcycle-riding and guns, but hey, he could figure it out as he went. He wanted to make her happy. He wanted to take care of her.

He didn't do true love, but he did responsibility just fine. And he cared deeply for her. How could anyone not?

"You're still here." She studied him over the top of the register while she pulled out the cash drawer. "It's going to be a long while until I'm done."

"You would be worth the wait."

His reward was her smile. She looked beautiful, fresh and bright in her simple worn jeans and a white long-sleeve T-shirt. There wasn't a thing fancy or sophisticated about her, not that he could see, and yet she rendered him speechless. "I have a slice of chocolate pie left in the case. Interested?"

"Tempted, yeah. But I'll pass. I don't think I've ever eaten this well."

"Then my work is done." Small dimples pinched into her cheeks, and his heart rolled over.

He hadn't lied to Paige. He cared for this woman more than was wise. He wanted to take care of her. He wanted to care for her. As she bounded away, he wanted to protect her from every heartache. Defend her from any trouble. Put more happiness into her life than she'd ever known before.

I've always wanted to have a good marriage and a happy family. Maybe because I lost my folks when I was young. He remembered what she'd said on their walk. He could give her what she wanted and more.

There was no time to waste. He slid out from the booth, bussed his cup and Sally's. He was ready to move this to the next level.

She had to be dreaming, that's what this was. A big wonderful dream where a fantastic man of integrity and honor was falling in love with her. Rachel squirted toilet cleaner around the bowl and beneath the rim. As she grabbed the toilet brush, she had to reconsider. She'd never been cleaning a bathroom in any of the dreams she'd had about the man she would marry. Which meant this night was real and no dream.

"I'm going to take this mess home with me so you don't have to deal with it." Paige poked her head in the ladies' restroom. "One day the twins are going to master the cash register. I suppose we have to be patient until then. If it doesn't drive us crazy first."

Rachel recognized the smile in her sister's voice. "I owe you big-time. I'd never get the deposit together. Those girls ran the till most of the night."

"I know. Are you going to be okay here alone? Should I take that man out with me when I go?"

"You don't like Jake?" Rachel knelt and gave the bowl a good scrub.

"I don't dislike him. Just thought I'd ask you what you wanted. I'm headed home, then. I've checked all the doors and windows. Everything's locked up. All you need to do is set the alarm."

"Thanks for your help tonight. Drive safely, okay? It's slick out there. Call me when you get home so I don't worry."

"That's my line, sweetie. I'll see you tomorrow early. Good night." The door swung closed, cutting out the tap of Paige's shoes on the tile.

Rachel gave the toilet a flush and scrubbed some more. As the water swirled, realization struck. She'd been so determined to keep from letting anyone know how much she liked Jake, and then so surprised that he felt the same way, she hadn't thought about the ramifications. Of course she knew Jake lived in Florida. He was stationed there. He was rarely stateside.

But she'd made a promise to Paige. What if this relationship progressed? He'd sounded as if he wanted it to, and heaven knew she was hoping. Then she would be forced to choose between a promise she'd made her sister and the encouragement she'd given to the man she was falling in love with.

Don't put the cart before the horse, she thought as she hauled the cleaner and brush to the next stall and gave the toilet a flush. *We've had one date. Just one.* And how on earth could they manage a relationship if he was stationed on secret bases throughout the Middle East?

Maybe she was getting her hopes up with this man for nothing. When she thought about it, there were too many obstacles. He had Sally as a priority. Then his duty. And she was stuck here in Montana, duty-bound to her family diner.

Disappointment trickled into her until she was cold. Until the happiness she'd felt after their kiss had completely faded. She scrubbed until the porcelain was clean and carried her cleaning supplies to the hall closet. She'd check on the dishwasher, see if a cycle was done before tackling the sinks and the counter. And then all that would be left was the floor.

Jake would be waiting, so she wanted to hurry, but her heart weighed her down. A true loving relationship took time and work and closeness, and even if he'd hinted he was interested in marriage, it was a long way from first date to wedding day. How could this ever work?

Maybe it was better to save her heart from falling any further while she still could.

The mop was gone from its hook in the closet. That was weird. Maybe it was in the kitchen and she hadn't noticed. Sometimes the evening cook gave the kitchen a swab when things were slow. Maybe he'd already cleaned up. Wouldn't that be nice? She grabbed her bottle of bleach mix and bopped down the short hallway to the kitchen. What she saw made her skid to a halt and blink. Was she dreaming again?

Jake was in the middle of the kitchen with his broad back to her, swabbing the mop across the floor. And not in a careless way either, but with sharp, effective strokes. He bent to douse the mop and wring the water from it and then went back to work, nudging the water bucket along with him with his foot, back and forth over and over, leaving spotless, gleaming tile in his wake.

He'd taken off his sweatshirt, and wore a long-sleeved navy T-shirt beneath, and she couldn't help noticing the way his hard muscles bunched and rippled beneath the knit fabric. In that moment, with only half the kitchen lights on, the partial shadows cast a powerful image of him, illuminating more than his physical self, but his essence as well. It was his spirit she saw, a core of honorable character, a warrior at heart, even here in a peaceful small-town diner in the middle of rural Montana.

He would never belong here, and she would never ask him to give up who he was, who the Lord had made him to be.

He spoke without looking up from his work; he must have heard her footsteps. "Thought I'd pitch in. I've swabbed a few floors in my day, especially in boot camp."

She couldn't swallow past the lump of emotion wedged in her throat. "Pitch in, huh?"

"Yep. You may as well get used to it. I'm not a man to sit on my, uh, laurels." He grinned at her over his shoulder as he dunked the mop into the bucket and dowsed it. "I just want to help you."

"N-not many men wouldn't mind mopping a floor." She walked woodenly to the counter.

"I'm not just any man. I meant what I said tonight, Rachel. I don't waste my time, and I always know what I want. I'm here because I'd rather be cleaning your kitchen with you than anywhere else without you."

She set the bottle of cleaner down with a thunk. She couldn't believe him, could she? Men didn't just walk into a woman's life and change it, did they? Did he know what this meant to her? Maybe it was just a little mopping to him, but to her, it was so much more.

She'd never known a man she'd dated to treat her like this. To pitch in, to help out or to say the things he did.

Her heart gave another tumble. It wasn't wise or prudent, no rational woman would let it happen, but this felt beyond her control. Love, sweet and true, rushed through her, filling her with brightness.

How strange. She'd always figured she would fall in love irrevocably and forever surrounded by roses and sunshine or on some momentous occasion, like Valentine's Day. She would have never thought love would happen to her like this, in a quiet calm glow, in the middle of the kitchen.

Emptiness echoed around her, or maybe it was the shadows, and the faint swish and clink of Jake's mopping in the dining room.

Maybe it *was* fitting, she realized, with the echoed memories of her life surrounding her. Her parents' happiness as they worked in this kitchen. Her childhood with her sisters and brother helping out or playing board games around the prep table. The ties of her family, of the past and the present both heartened her and tore at her.

The good experiences growing up in her family and in this diner had made her who she was. And the obligations that came from it felt smothering because she could not turn her back on this place or on her promise to Paige, just as she could not deny loving this man who pitched in to help her.

Torn, she went in search of clean rags, knowing this—as her life always was—in the Lord's care.

The snow fell like a blessing. Rachel brushed the softness from her cheek and turned the key in the dead bolt. The parking lot behind the diner was empty except for her trusty sedan and the twins' decades-old VW. "How do I properly thank you?"

"How about a kiss good-night?"

"That I can do."

It was a blessing to step into his arms. To have the privilege of his kiss. His lips brushed hers. The space between one breath and the next became infinity. She wrapped her arms around his neck and savored the secure feel of his arms wrapping around her.

What luxury, to be held by this wonderful man. She would not think about the future. She would not think at all. She wanted to savor the warm velvet of his kiss. The tender brush of his lips. The love like a light flaring to life within her in this one perfect moment.

He broke their kiss, and she could feel his love. He held her gently, and even in the half shadows of the night she could see the regret in his eyes. "I hate that I have so little time with you."

This is it, she thought. *Where he says goodbye. Where he says it was nice, but he's moving on. And why wouldn't he say that,* she reasoned as she laid her hand against his rugged jawline. They had entirely different lives, and very demanding and full lives. This love affair had to end. The pain of it gathered like a sharp blade at the base of her throat, slicing until she felt too raw to speak.

His fingers, so thick and powerful, caressed the curve of her face, making her heart ache. She pressed against his touch, and as he kissed her again, her heart opened. She couldn't deny that she loved him, and every time she was with him, she loved him a little more.

"It's not fair I have to leave." He pressed his forehead to hers. "Not when I've just found you. No woman has ever made me feel this way."

See, he was leaving. She knew he would be. There was no other choice for him to make. "I will never forget you."

"I'm going to make sure you won't." He brushed snowflakes from her face with her bare fingers.

She let her eyes drift shut at the rasp of his calloused fingertips against her skin. For all his strength, his touch was gentle. Did he know how much of her heart already belonged to him? She didn't think so, or why would he be talking like this? "Does that mean you want to stay in touch? Like friends?"

"No. I do not want to be friends with you."

"You don't?" The faintest hope fluttered in her soul.

"No. I want more." His head dipped to catch her lips with his. "I want everything."

"Everything?"

"I'm going to ask you to marry me."

"You are?"

"I've never met anyone like you, Rachel. And the way you make me feel—" Jake couldn't complete the sentence. He couldn't say the words that would render him vulnerable.

He could love her beyond logic and good sense, and trust her with everything he was, heart and soul. Which was why he had to hold on to his sense and his heart. Hiring a nanny for Sally would be easier. Finding a woman to marry who didn't affect him would be smarter. But the Lord had brought him here; He'd brought him to Rachel. Funny, beautiful, gentle Rachel.

He'd have to be strong and firm; he could do this for all their sakes. "You are perfect."

"Me? Oh, I don't think so. That just proves you don't know me. I lose my keys all the time, and I can't learn bookkeeping, and I have a thousand flaws. You have to have noticed that."

Her luscious hair was trying to escape the confines of her wool hat and silken strands were hanging out in random tangles. He smoothed the wisps and the act of touching her made the tenderness he felt for her flare like a launched missile. "You are perfect for me."

He watched her melt. She was amazing, this woman God had chosen for him and Sally. And the truth be told, even if heaven hadn't put him on this path to her, he would have fallen for her. He would have wanted her more than any woman in the entire world. "Here it is, almost midnight and snowing like we're in Alaska and I don't want to let you go."

"I know just how you feel."

"Then you don't mind if I spend as much time with you as I can while I'm here?"

"No. It would be a wish come true." Rachel bit her bottom lip, amazed at the honest words that just seemed to spill out of her.

She'd never felt this close to a man. She'd never had a man feel this way about her, and it was frightening and thrilling all at once. This was true love. "I'll see you in the morning. At Ben's sending-off party?"

His kiss was his answer, a gentle brush of lips, yes, but more. So much more. When his lips touched her, she felt the brush of his heart to hers. Of his soul moving with hers, and she held him tight, hope lifting her up. She would have floated home through the snowflakes dancing in the air except for Jake's rock-solid hands that held her firmly to the ground.

She'd been praying so long and earnestly for the right man; the very best man. She'd nearly given up hope. But some prayers were answered, and the answer was all the sweeter for the wait.

Chapter Twelve

"It's not the best weather for Ben and Cadence to start their move," Paige observed as she shouldered through the back door. "Now I wish they had left last night."

"The snow wasn't forecast." Rachel, who was waitressing this morning, slid a bottle of hot sauce into her apron pocket and grabbed two plates of giant cinnamon rolls from the warmer. "Now we're going to be worrying about them every moment from when they leave until they are safely through the entire state."

"I think the storm hit Wyoming, too. I heard it on the radio on the way in." Paige shrugged off her snow-dappled parka. "I dragged Alex here, not just for the party, but because we're short a bus person. If you see him lolling around, order him back to work. Got it?"

"Yes, ma'am." Rachel shouldered through the swinging door and into the dining room. The banners she and Amy had come early to hang were glittering from the ceiling and stretched the width of the eating area. Good Luck! flapped overhead in black and gold as she hurried down the aisle.

Cousin Kelly looked up from her college textbook as Rachel eased the plate onto the table. "Are they here yet?"

"Ought to be any minute. I bet the roads are slow going. Would you like a refill?"

"Looks like that handsome dude of yours is here. When you get done seating him—" Kelly grinned "—then worry about my coffee cup."

Jake was here! Rachel whipped around and there he was, standing in the open door with snow tumbling in all around him. Sally clung to his side, and in his arms was a glass vase of pale-pink rosebuds. They were long-stemmed and gorgeous, and there had to be two dozen of the stunning flowers.

The sight of the roses wasn't what glued her feet to the floor. His gaze fastened on hers over the top of the delicate petals and she felt the brightness only he could bring to her soul. It was as if he saw the real Rachel McKaslin and beyond, deeper, to the dreams she held so close.

When he smiled, she fell in love a little more.

Vaguely she heard someone call, "They're here!" and the murmur of the customers, many of whom had come to send Ben and Cadence off, but it all seemed so far away.

Jake came to her, and she wondered if he felt this

tug of awareness down deep within, and if he had the same sweet wish. *I'm going to ask you to marry me.* His words of last night lingered with her. *You are perfect for me.*

She'd come to fear she would never hear such beautiful and sincere words. And she stood in the diner she was duty-bound to take over and the conflict hit her like a blast of arctic wind. *You would have been perfect for me, too.* She laid her hand over her heart for the pain building there.

"Good morning, beautiful."

Longing filled her—chaste and sweet—as he came closer, and it was a longing that strengthened and expanded. She was blinded by joy as he set the exquisite flowers on the counter and leaned close. His mouth hovered over hers for a brief moment. She felt a click of connection as their hearts joined. Her soul stilled as he brushed his lips against hers in a brief, meaningful kiss.

"I had a hard time convincing a florist to open early, but Ben mentioned that Cadence had a friend who was a florist, so I did a little sweet-talking and you have two dozen roses. Do you like 'em?"

"I love them. They're gorgeous. And my very favorite. How did you know?"

"I'm good at reconnaissance."

"That's what I get for falling in love with a soldier." The flowers were perfect and she was floating with happiness again.

"This is only the beginning of the good things I'm going to do for you." His hand cupped her jaw, loving and sure of his promise.

She was sure of his promise, too. He was a man who kept his word. She knew it; she could feel it in her heart, for it was inexplicably linked to his. Certainty filled her. This was the right man, sent from God above.

The bell above the door jangled cheerfully, and the sound cut into the bubble that seemed to have formed around them. The morning was the same as any other—the scent of fresh coffee, the sound of Paige's voice, and the chill of the winter wind slicing through the warm diner.

But it was no average, ordinary day. It felt like the first day of her life. It felt as though all the years up to this point had only been to bring her here, to this man who towered over her. His hand found her shoulder and rested there. Together they turned to face the door. The pleasant masculine scent of him, the shampoo in his hair and the detergent on his clothes made her dizzy, and she couldn't help letting her forehead lie against his chest.

With greater understanding, she watched her brother release the door he'd been holding for his new wife and lay his arm across her shoulder. The love between them was unmistakable as they exchanged intimate smiles, as if they knew what the other was thinking without the need for words.

The diner around them exploded with cheers. Family and friends packed the place, and congratulations and good luck wishes rang in the air, drowning out every other sound. Only then did Rachel realize she was still holding a plate with a cinnamon roll she'd promised the deputy. How could she move away from Jake?

"I'll take that." Paige whipped the plate out of her hand on her way by. She said nothing else, not even to send a look of disapproval Rachel's way.

But guilt stung, anyway. Rachel yanked herself away from Jake's wonderful chest, feeling cold and bereft as if she'd been shoved out in the snow. People were pushing by in the aisle wanting to greet the newlyweds and offer good-luck prayers for a safe journey. After slipping the cinnamon roll on Frank's table, Paige wrapped her arms around Cadence first and then Ben. Amy came rushing from the kitchen, where Heath had been helping with the extra cooking, and her diamond wedding set caught the light and shimmered as she joined in the hugging.

Everything is changing. Rachel didn't look back at Jake or the little girl clinging to his other side. She dutifully tugged the hot sauce bottle from her apron pocket and nudged it onto the edge of the deputy's table.

"For your eggs, Frank."

"First your sister and now your brother," Frank commented. "Looks like you might be next."

Heat flamed across her face. How did she answer that? Paige had overheard as she'd pulled back from the group. The hard set to her face said everything. Her older sister didn't look at her again as she hurried past, intent on seeing to something in the kitchen.

What am I going to do? Rachel felt as low as the snow melting on the rubber mat at her feet.

Ben's arms closed around her and his voice was a comfort as he spoke low in her ear, so only she could hear. "Jake's a decent guy. I trust my life to him every day. I think he's good enough for you, little sister."

Ben would understand. She swiped at the wetness on her cheeks. "What about Paige?"

"Have you talked with her about this?"

"No, you know how it is. I promised her. She stayed here all this time for us. And now with Alex graduating…" More people were pushing up to give their good-luck wishes and say their goodbyes. This was not the time. Rachel kissed her brother's cheek. "You two have a safe trip. Be so happy, okay?"

"I already am."

Bob Brisbane prodded in to shake hands with Ben, and as she sidestepped out of the way, someone grabbed her around the wrist and pulled. Amy hauled her close. "I was just telling Cadence all about you and Jake."

"What? First Ben and now you two. It's just—" She glanced over her shoulder where the flowers were being admired by her cousins Kelly and Michelle at the front counter. Jake and Sally had disappeared in the crowd, and she felt keenly alone without him near.

"Yep, it's what we thought." Amy sounded triumphant. "I've been praying for this, Rachel. For you to finally have the good man you deserve."

"He lives in Florida. He's away from home most of the year, just like Ben. And wait." She held up her hand, tucking away her pain because she didn't want Amy to know what this was costing her. "Before you go on about how Cadence is moving to Florida and how I could do the same, consider this. Jake and I are hardly even dating."

"Only a man who's serious brings you roses like that."

She blocked out Jake's words of last night. How he wasn't a man to waste his time. How he was serious about her, so serious he was looking into the future and seeing a marriage between them. "Florida is a long way away, and Jake and I haven't known each other that long. Love takes time."

"No," Cadence corrected gently. "Love takes heart."

"That's right." Amy's hold tightened as she tugged Rachel down the aisle in Jake's direction. "If this is something God means for you, then it will work out between Jake and you, and between Paige and you. It's in the Lord's hands, not yours."

"Right now, I'm in yours. You're taking me to him."

"Guilty, but then you know that about me. I want what's best for my big sister. This is your chance, Rachel. Don't mess it up. Just believe." She gave her a small shove.

Rachel stumbled forward and there, around the corner where the window booths stopped and the table arrangements began, she saw him. Jake, who was coloring with a green crayon on the children's menu, right along with his niece. The sight of the strapping man next to the fragile little girl simply caught her heart all over again with love so pure she ached from its power.

"I'm going to work your shift today," Amy whispered. "And Heath and I will babysit tonight. Love, no matter what, is always a great blessing. Don't waste a minute of his time here."

Jake spotted her, put down his crayon and stood. He held out his hand for her to come join him. Everything faded, except for the love she felt for him. She floated forward to place her palm on his. They would have this day together. She couldn't wait to show him her world.

Rachel ignored the bite of frigid wind blowing hard against her face and driving the snow directly in her mouth as she tried to nudge Nugget out of the bitter wind. "Are you having fun yet?"

Jake was nothing more than a silhouette in the thick snowfall behind her, the image of Western masculinity with his head bowed to the wind, his Stetson shielding his face from the precipitation, his broad shoulders set as he rode the equally impressive gelding he'd borrowed from Paige's son. "I don't call this fun."

"You're a city boy, that's why. Now, this is what I call living." She pulled her horse to a halt at the crest of the rise. The valley below spread out before them, misted by the thick veil of snow, and it was breathtaking and ethereal all at once. The gray light, the twilightlike shadows, the impressive rolling land so silent made the cold ride worth it. "This probably isn't exciting enough for you."

"You know the mountains behind us?"

"The Rockies?" The great mountains speared up and disappeared in the snow clouds, caught in a most severe part of the storm. "It wouldn't be safe to go up there right now."

"Well, give me an ice axe, crampons and a climbing buddy, and find me a glacier to climb. *Then* I'll be having fun." He halted Bandit and knocked the snow off his hat.

He could have been a hero in an old Western movie, and Rachel couldn't help a little sigh of appreciation. This man was hers. Somehow this would work out however the Lord saw fit, she would simply have to let go and let God handle it. Easy to say, not so easy to do. But up here, in the crisp, clean moun-

tain air, she felt closer to the Lord and hoped understanding would come to her a little more easily, too.

"You can't get much ice-climbing at home in Florida."

"No, but there's sailing, jet skiing, waterskiing,
diving, parasailing and hang gliding. That keeps me
busy when I'm not training or on TDY."

"TDY. That means you're overseas, right?"

"Something like that. Temporary duty or tour of
duty. Usually it means I'm in a chopper with mud
on my face and a gun in my hand." He leaned close.
"Have I told you how glad I am to be with you? I am,
you know. I think this is the happiest I've ever been."

"Me, too." It was as if every shielded part of her
opened, the places she kept safely hidden away. More
vulnerable than she'd ever been with anyone ever,
she dared to kiss him. And what a kiss it was. The
moment his lips slanted over hers, more love for him
lifted through her. She never knew that true love was
like this, maturing more with every moment, every
touch, every loving act. And this is only the beginning, she thought. *Please, Lord, I want to be with
him so much.*

How she wanted to start each day with him. To
come home to him after her work was done. To share
the ordinary and average moments of grocery shopping and choosing a movie at the video store and
paying bills and settling down to a quiet evening at

his side. To have the right to kiss him like this, and more, for eternity.

When their kiss ended, neither pulled away. Their breaths rose in a single cloud as he kissed her forehead and her cheeks and the tip of her nose. How was it possible to love so much? She felt as if she'd come alive for the very first time—all over again.

"I've been afraid to ask when you have to go back."

"I have to report on Monday. They're going to keep me close to home for a little while until I get Sally settled. And then I'm back in the Middle East." He sidled his horse closer to hers and towered above her, blocking the wind and some of the cold. Leaning close to thumb the snowfall from her cheeks and eyelashes, he said, "There's nothing I can do about that. Orders are orders. You know that, because of your brother."

"Yep. We haven't seen him much at all since he graduated from PJ school."

"It takes more dedication to make a marriage work when a soldier is gone so much. My hat's off to him and Cadence. They seem to have a strong enough bond to make it."

"Of course they do. It's true love."

Jake's chest clutched. It was just what he thought. This peaches-and-cream, pale-pink-rose-loving lady was a pure romantic at heart. In the harsh realities he often faced as a warrior, he valued that about her. That she was as sweet and as good as could be.

Rachel's touch to his arm drew his attention. She pointed, and whispered, "A moose."

Sure enough like a ghost in the mist, a figure emerged, antlers held high. The animal's head was up and studying them with great suspicion. The musical tap, tap of snow was the only noise.

"Bullwinkle?" he whispered.

"No, I don't think so. He's not getting ready to come boss me into giving him some grain." She laughed, a quiet chime that sent the moose leaping into the underbrush. In the next instant the animal was gone, but it didn't feel as if they were alone.

Never more had Jake felt the steady calm of the Lord's presence, and he could feel the whisper in his heart. *Ask her.*

He'd planned on proposing after dinner on bended knee, with more roses he'd had delivered in collusion with Amy who'd agreed to have someone at the house to let in the florist. But with the fog of snow seeming to cocoon them from the strife and busyness of the world and the regal silence of the mountains surrounding them, he could think of no better place.

He dismounted and sank past his hiking boots into the snow. He ignored the sting of cold penetrating his jeans and wetting his socks.

"What are you doing? Don't tell me you're going to go find a glacier to climb."

"No, I'm going to do something much riskier."

"What on earth could that be?" Below the cuff of

her knit cap, her jeweled eyes were sparkling as if he amused her greatly.

He held out his hand. "Come down and I'll show you."

"Okay." She easily swung down before him. "But you've gone completely pale. Are you all right?"

"No. Don't you know that a man always is pale when he's going down on one knee." He watched her eyes widen as he sank into the freezing snow, but his discomfort didn't matter. The surprise spreading across her lovely face did.

"What are you doing? I—" Her eyes widened and then she smiled all the way as if to her soul. *"Oh."*

"I need to ask you something."

Rachel shivered, but not from the cold. Could he tell she was trembling? That she was excited and scared all at once? The sight of the big man kneeling before her made her eyes blur. She couldn't believe it. And yet, when he took her hands in his, he was solid and real.

"Almost from the moment I saw you, I knew you were the one. The woman I would want to honor and cherish for the rest of my life. Will you marry me?"

Pure joy seeped into her soul, slow and steady, like a winter's sun rising.

"Marry you?" Her brain wasn't working, but her heart was. She tumbled to her knees and wrapped her arms around him, her cheek pressing against his wide chest. Snow flecked her face and caught on her lashes and she was laughing and crying all at once.

Jake was laughing, too. "Is that a yes? Or did I just make a huge fool of myself?"

"It's a yes. And you could never be a fool, not to me." She met his kiss with one of her own. Held him tenderly as the snow fell like grace over them. Her eyes drifted shut and he tucked her against him, where she rested, despite the cold and the rising wind. Happiness warmed her as she held on tightly to this man who was her love, her heart and all of her future.

She was getting married!

I know You know what You're doing, Lord, but this marriage stuff is hard on a man. Behind the wheel of his rented SUV, Jake checked his watch, trying to act as if everything was fine. Beside him, Rachel was on her cell with Amy, asking how Sally was doing without her uncle.

"I've kept her so busy she's hardly noticed he's gone." Jake could hear Amy's cheerful answer in the quiet of the vehicle's compartment, but after a few more words, Rachel ended the call.

"You didn't tell her your news?"

"I wanted it to be our secret for a little while longer although I think she suspects." She blushed prettily. She was even more lovely when she was happy, for it radiated from her like light from the sun. As she slipped her hand on top of his, where it rested on the console, it struck him again how incredibly lucky he was.

His throat tightened. He'd been alone for so long, he'd never noticed how lonesome life was. In truth, maybe that's why he loved his work so much. It kept him from noticing what was missing. But not anymore. For better or worse, he was marrying Rachel, the sweetest, loveliest woman ever. She steadied him, and he felt as if he were making the smartest move of his life.

The traffic inched forward and he had enough room to turn into a plowed parking lot. Ice shone as he eased to a stop. "Looks like we're here. Are you ready for this?"

She didn't answer. She was staring at the jewelry store's elegant lit sign. "I—uh." She flushed again. "I didn't expect this."

"I wanted you to pick out the ring you want. Any one you want." He turned off the engine and pulled the emergency brake. "Are you ready?"

She sparkled with a quiet joy and made him feel ten feet tall. He wanted nothing more than to make her happy as much as he could. Any way he could. When he helped her from the vehicle, he'd never felt so important. The way she looked at him with such pure affection weakened the titanium shield he'd secured around his heart.

"Hello, Mr. Hathaway?" A pleasant woman in a business suit met them at the door. "I'm Carol. We spoke on the phone. And you must be Rachel. Congratulations on your engagement. Please, come with me. I have a room all ready for you, along with quite a selection of our loveliest diamonds."

Even hours later, after an incredible dinner at the area's finest restaurant, he could not forget how great it felt to know he was giving Rachel her dream. He'd sat at her side and offered his opinion on the array of fine rings he'd asked the store to set out for her. His bride-to-be was far more elegant and classy than any of the exquisite stones. When he slipped the diamond she finally chose on her finger, he could not hold back the adoration for her beating in his heart.

Chapter Thirteen

What a beautiful night. It seemed to be a promise from above, Rachel thought, as the last snowflakes danced lazily against the windshield. The defroster was on high to drive away the gathering chill of the night that penetrated the passenger compartment. It looked like it was going to be an early and long Montana winter. But would she be here to see it?

She gazed down at her left hand and the marquis-cut diamond set between two smaller stones gleamed in the glow from the dash lights. The ring, as beautiful as it was, felt foreign on her finger.

She still couldn't believe it. She was getting married to Jake. As he shifted into four-wheel drive for the last stretch of driveway, she realized this was where they'd first met. She tried to imagine what he'd thought of a woman racing down the road waving a broom and wearing her big fluffy slippers.

Who would have thought that evening, when she'd

been so exhausted and not expecting her one perfect man, that her life would change the very moment they met?

Jake pulled into the carport, where drifted snow pulled at the tires and they skidded to a slow sideways stop. "How's that ring feel?"

"Perfect because it's from you."

"It's your hand that looks so beautiful." He leaned across the gearshift to kiss her, this woman who tied him up in so many confusing knots. When her lips met his, those knots pulled a little tighter. What he felt for her was a powerful thing. How was he going to keep it under control? When he pulled away, he didn't miss the dreamy cast to her face. Moonlight filtered through the icy window to burnish her with a rare, platinum light. He felt too much.

He welcomed the bite of the frigid temperatures that assaulted him the instant he stepped foot into the night. He helped Rachel from the vehicle with care. She might be a capable woman, but she was also going to be his wife. He remembered the way his dad had always held the doors for Mom. They had been happy together. His father's words of advice back then meant little, but came back as great wisdom now. *Treat her right, son. You aren't here for yourself, but for her.*

Good advice. Because of Rachel, he'd be able to get back to work. Sally would have a kind woman to raise her. And in return, he was giving her what mattered most. A marriage. A family. His respect and his honor. That was a good marriage in his book. And he thanked the Lord for this fine woman. Maybe he wasn't thankful for the knots in his guts, but he could survive the discomfort. For Rachel, he felt ready to do anything.

"I need to talk to Paige first thing in the morning." She leaned into him.

He put his arm around her and drew her close, protecting her from the wind and making sure she didn't slip on the ice. It was his job now to care for her, and it meant a lot to him. Filled him with a purpose he'd never known. "Is there anything I can do to help you?"

"No, thank you." She snuggled against him a little closer. "This is something between Paige and me. All I can do is explain what's happened and see what comes from it. Thank you, though. It's nice to know that you're here for me."

"Baby, that's something I plan on being as much as I can. We're a team now. I care about what matters to you."

"No wonder I love you so much." On the top step, she went up on tiptoe to kiss his cheek, the sweetest gesture.

His chest filled with a welcome sense of wonder. It was going to be really nice to belong with her.

She unlocked the front door and disappeared into the unlit foyer. He stomped the snow from his boots before following her, and he sensed something was wrong. Someone was in the house. He could smell a faint perfume, and there was that awareness that made his neck prickle. Someone was watching him in the dark—

"Surprise!" The lights flashed on at the same moment he saw shadows move in the darkened archway.

Years of training had already kicked in and he was standing in front of Rachel, between her and the danger which was her family rushing toward her with arms outstretched.

"Did he propose?" one of her cousins asked.

"Let's see the ring!" Amy demanded.

As the women gathered close around Rachel to ooh and aah, Jake wished he could shrug off the charge of adrenaline pumping through him as easily as he slipped out of his coat. He caught Paige's hard, measuring gaze and didn't fault her for it. She'd been in charge of the family and watching over Rachel for a long while.

He had the gist of what that would be like, because the thought of watching over Rachel battered at his defensive shields. He couldn't deny she made him feel a mess of weak and vulnerable things that couldn't be good for a man—things that were never wise for a soldier. He'd seen too much war, too many wounded, too much heartbreak, and the only way he could deal was to keep those shields up. It was all he knew to do.

"Uncle Jake?" Sally wandered down the hall-way, scrubbing her eyes. She was still dressed, but she'd obviously fallen asleep in one of the bedrooms. Maybe Amy had carried her back there. Unmistakable relief flashed across her pixie face and she flung her arms wide.

He went down on both knees to draw this dear child against him where he hoped she felt secure as her arms wrapped right around his neck. "I didn't mean to be gone so long, cutie pie. Rachel and I just went out to a nice dinner, but we're back now."

Instead of comforting her, his words seemed to make everything worse. Her little body drew as tight as a tensed bowstring and her arms squeezed him until she cut off his air supply. So he rose, cradling her weight against him, murmuring low as he carried her back down the hall.

A faint golden glow led him through the shadows where it became a night-light in the shape of a crescent moon and five-pointed star next to a canopy bed. Gauzy pink drifted from the frame overhead, matching the flowers on the bedspread. Rachel's room, of course. A knit blanket was rumpled, as if tossed aside.

He sat on the edge of the comfortable mattress, holding his niece in his arms. He might be helpless to stop the pain that had a hold on her heart, but the solution to her problem was in sight. It was only a matter of a wedding. "I've left you longer than this before. Why the tears, sweet girl?"

She sniffled against his shirt. "Cuz I don't wanna go back."

"Go back where?"

"To Mrs. Thompson's. Sh-she was n-nice, but I wanna stay w-with you." She sobbed and burrowed into his shoulder.

"Who said anything about you going back into foster care? I told you, we're together now. I promised you, didn't I? No one's going to take you away from me. You come live with me. It's a done deal. You can't change your mind now."

"I c-can c-come with you and R-Rachel?" A sob shook her little body.

So that was it. The lightbulb went on in his head. Of course, why hadn't he realized she would have worries of being left alone at this important change in his life? He pressed a fatherly kiss to her brow, because that's what he was, not just an uncle, but her father figure too. "That's why I'm marrying her. For you, princess."

"Oh." She gave a last sniff and smiled through her tears. "Okay."

At that moment, Rachel padded through the door, her face shrouded in the room's shadows. With the light to his back, he couldn't see the expression on her face, but she froze, her slender form tensed.

Then he realized what he'd said. And how that might have sounded, as if the only reason he'd proposed was for Sally. While that was true, it wasn't the whole truth. Not judging by the sinking feeling in his chest and the gathering fear like clouds before an impending tornado. Had she overheard him? Did she think he didn't want her? He'd give his life before he'd want to hurt her in any way. It was as if his blood stalled in his veins and his lungs had forgotten how to draw in air while he waited for her reaction. While he dreaded her reaction.

"Oh, Jake." Her voice sounded hollow.

He braced himself for the worst. Groped for the right words to try to fix this. *Please, Lord, let me be able to make this right.*

Then she kept talking. "I never thought this might be too much for Sally. Sweetie, do you want me to make you some cocoa?"

He couldn't believe it. Relief left him dazed. *Thank You, Lord.* How could he not adore this woman who tried to make every hurt better with hot chocolate? Sally nodded against his chest, but she still didn't look at Rachel. He held her tight. He had to wrestle down the weak emotions threatening to overtake him.

"I'm so sorry, Jake. I guess my sister figured out what we were up to." Rachel's ring shimmered in the shadows as her hands flew to cover her heart. "I didn't want Sally to find out this way. My sisters meant well with this little get-together."

"I know." He studied the ring on her finger. His ring. "I want to marry you now. I don't want to leave for Florida without you."

"You're leaving tomorrow."

He swallowed. "I know. I have to report Monday morning, but after that I'll know my schedule. I'll be training some of the new students while I'm stateside. I'm putting in a request to stay at least through the end of the year. If we get married right away, we'll have most of December together before I go away for, well, probably six to nine."

Six to nine months. So much for the dream of marriage. She was jumping into the reality with both feet. "I won't have time to plan much of a wedding. I'd always wanted—" She stopped the image forming in her mind, the one she'd envisioned more times than it was possible to count. The picture of the town church, where her parents were married and she was baptized, soft with candlelight and scented with roses.

Her sisters and cousins would be draped in pale-pink bridesmaid's dresses and lined up at her side, and her family and friends would be gathered as witnesses. Pastor Bill would be standing before her, and she would be wearing her mother's wedding dress.

But everything she'd ever wanted for her wedding was not as important as the man who would be at her side. It wasn't the wedding but the vows, not the setting but the marriage that mattered.

"What's best for you?" she asked. Those dreams of a wedding began to float away, but she didn't mind, for the greatest dream of all was right in front of her. "Would it be better for you if I came down to Florida to get married? Don't get me wrong, I would love to have you come here, but we could have more time together."

"You choose. You tell me when and I'll show up to marry you."

"That's a promise?"

Was that a note of worry he heard? Jake wondered. Somehow it made it easier to open up a little. To see that they both had so much riding on this. So much to lose. He fought down the wave of emotion trying to hook him like a riptide. "Not only is it a promise, but I'll give you my credit card. Plan a wedding for here, or fly down there and we'll have a quick ceremony. You decide. I just want you to be happy. From here on out, that's what I live to do."

"That's what I plan to do, too. To make you and Sally so happy. I—" She swiped at her eyes before her emotions gave her away. She was so in love with this man. More than she'd ever thought anyone could be. The thought of spending the rest of her days with him filled her with such gratitude. How could she ever ask for more?

"Come here, gorgeous." Jake held out his hand and pulled her close. Sally yawned against his chest, her eyes barely open.

Everything seemed to click into place. Tomorrow, she would have to say goodbye to these two people who were now the most important people in her life. She would start packing up her life, talk Amy into taking this house, and book a ticket to Florida. She was ready for this beautiful new start the Lord had given her.

As if Jake felt the same way, he leaned to press a kiss to her cheek. Sweet as could be, infinitely tender, there was no mistaking the love between them. And a great love it would be, she vowed. She couldn't wait to stand before God and say the blessed vows that would make her Jake's wife.

It was decided. "Then we're going to have a Florida wedding. Sally, are you going to be my maid of honor?"

"With flowers 'n stuff?" The little girl perked up, rubbing her still-wet eyes.

"Any kind of flowers you want. Is that a deal?"

Sally nodded, her curls bobbing.

I want to hug you, little girl, until all your hurt is gone. Rachel knew it wasn't her right yet, but she laid a hand on the child's tiny shoulder, so fragile to the touch, and willed all the comfort she could from her heart to Sally's.

"Thanks, Rachel." Jake's baritone warmed when he said her name. As if he loved her as greatly as she loved him.

The Lord had given her a great blessing, two for the price of one. A sacred gift she would cherish for all the days of her life. She would never be able to thank God enough for these two people or this beautiful day. A bright, loving future stretched out before her, one spent taking care of them, and maybe a baby or two to come. Joy bloomed through her as she promised to be back with two cups of cocoa. She couldn't help glancing back as Jake settled onto the bed and reached for a child's book left on the nightstand.

Now, to face Paige. This wasn't the way she wanted Paige to find out about this either. She owed her older sister so much. If Paige wasn't happy, then Rachel didn't know what she would do. How could she turn her back on her sister? How could she give up this bright new future?

Paige was in the kitchen at the stove, stirring the contents of a saucepan. So tall and lovely and looking so like their mother, Rachel did a double-take. The past felt close enough to touch on this night when she could see her future so clearly. *Help me to say the right things, Lord. Never would I want to hurt my sister.*

But Paige was as happy-looking as she'd been earlier when Rachel had walked through the door with Jake. "I should leave, so you and Jake can have some time alone, but I have something to say to you. I don't think it can wait."

"This just happened so fast, Paige. I didn't mean for it to be like this. I wanted to talk to you first, because if you aren't okay with this—"

"—I've been giving it a lot of thought—"

"—then you need to tell me the truth. Because I can't leave here if it's not all right—"

"It's all right." Paige wrapped her in a brief hug. "No one expected this to happen. You and Jake fell in love. This is your turn to live your dream, Rachel. To really grab hold of what matters in life. So don't waste this chance. Forget about the diner."

"But what about your plans?"

"I'll figure something out. Maybe one of the cousins would be interested in taking over. Do you want some hot chocolate?" Paige returned to the saucepan to give it a few more stirs.

Mom's secret cocoa recipe was the cure for all heartaches, and the memory of being young in this kitchen with Mom at the stove and warming chocolate scenting the air made her throat burn with tears. "I always thought I'd be raising my own kids in this house."

"Jake lives in Florida. Sounds like you'll be raising them there."

"Yeah." The thought made her sad and blissful at the same moment. How could so many polar emotions be inside her at once? "I'm really leaving."

"Don't say that out loud because you're breaking my heart." Paige kept her back firmly turned as she reached down a set of mugs. Her voice sounded thick with unshed tears. "If that man doesn't make you happy, all you have to do is tell me and I'll put some sense into him. Okay?"

"Okay." Rachel grabbed the marshmallow fluff

from the refrigerator door and twisted off the lid. "You can stop being my big sister now."

"I'm never going to stop being that. What are we going to do without you?"

Rachel couldn't speak. She spooned fluff onto the cups of steaming cocoa that Paige poured. Amy had taken off for the West Coast instead of graduating from high school and had been gone for several years. Ben had joined the air force, never to return for more than a brief stay. And although Rachel had gone to college, she'd come back.

But not Paige. She'd stayed to do the tough work of holding the family together, making a small-town diner do a good enough business to support all of them, all while raising her own wonderful son. "I'm going to be gone for a long time."

"This is just occurring to you?"

She nodded. "The reality is starting to sink in. I'm getting married. Finally. He's such a wonderful man. I know he'll be good to me."

"Of course he will be." Amy burst into the room. "Or we'll kick some sense into him. I don't want you to leave, Rache. What are we gonna do without you?"

"I—I don't know what I'm going to do without both of you. This is supposed to be happy, getting engaged. I always thought of getting married as adding to my life. Not changing it."

"Marriage is like nothing else. It changes everything." Amy grabbed the chocolate syrup from the fridge and popped the cap. She joined Paige, who'd returned to the counter. "Then again, marriage is one of God's great blessings."

"Well, so are sisters." Paige's eyes were filling with tears, but she was always so strong, Rachel had never actually seen a single tear fall. Never. "Here. Take these to that man of yours and that sweet little girl. You belong with them now, but know this. Your home will always be here, too."

Love and hot chocolate, the family cure-all. Rachel couldn't speak as she took the cups in her hands, trying hard not to spill them. This is a beginning, not an end, she told herself firmly as she disappeared down the dark hall. Everything she knew and loved was here.

No, not everything. She paused in the doorway, mesmerized by the low murmur of Jake's voice. How was it she could love this man even more than her life? He was her family now, and little Sally her daughter. Already she had them to love. And it made the pain of knowing she would leave this place vanish. Her own husband and a child to care for.

Contentment spread through her, sweet like the warm rich cocoa she carried until nothing remained but gratitude. Jake grinned at her over the top of the book he was reading out loud. Her soul sighed, and she was fulfilled.

She was truly loved, at long last.

Chapter Fourteen

Florida was hot, even in the winter. Rachel squinted into the foggy mirror in the hallway off the base's chapel, afraid sweat was beading on her forehead and her veil would be in danger of becoming plastered to her face.

She so wanted this short ceremony to be perfect, although nothing so far had gone to plan and she felt weary from struggling to right it. The last week she'd spent in Montana, after Jake and Sally had left, had been a whirlwind of packing and making arrangements and saying goodbyes. She'd given up her whole life to be here with Jake.

If Jake hadn't sent her roses every day they were apart, she wouldn't have made it this far, because the obstacles had continued to mount. Her plane had been diverted due to a thunderstorm and she'd spent hours circling over Tampa, gazing down at the incredible scenery and feeling so out of place. She'd left four feet of snow behind and near-blizzard conditions that had almost kept the plane from taking off in the first place.

Add lost luggage, traffic jams, Jake being called at the last minute into the field for training and she'd seen him only at the courthouse to get the marriage license.

"Don't worry, you look lovely." Cadence, who had stepped in as a true sister over the last few tough days, smoothed the back of the veil. "Jake is going to take one look at you and he won't believe how lucky he is."

"I'm the lucky one." The Lord knew it was true. She pinned on her mother's cameo, the one Paige had given her as a goodbye gift. Once the delicate clasp was secure, she took a steadying breath.

Jake was waiting to marry her. This moment was everything she'd ever wanted and prayed for. It seemed as if heaven were smiling, or maybe that was just the joy bubbling within her soul, as she took her first step on the plain brown carpet that would lead her down the aisle and to her groom, to the man God had found for her.

The ivory silk of her mother's wedding gown whirled and whispered as she took another step following Cadence. Jake was there, looking like a promise made and kept in his dress blues. He stood solemnly before the simple altar with Sally leaning against his side, her eyes wide with uncertainty. All eyes turned to Rachel, but it was Jake she saw. Jake she *felt* deep in her soul.

I never realized how deeply sacred a wedding was. As she stood there, poised at the aisle where simple wooden pews marched the length of the small chamber, Rachel felt it. More than the dreams of a little girl wondering and wishing for this day. More than the committed, emotional ties of a woman to her man. It was as if heaven waited, too, watching to celebrate the blessed gift of true love, a victory in a wide world that included heartache and cruelty.

The opening notes of the bridal march filled the chapel as sweetly as grace.

Ben offered his arm. "Are you ready for this, little sister?"

"Without a doubt." She slipped her arm in his and they moved forward together. Every step brought her closer to Jake. She was not nervous. She was certain.

As the minister asked, "Who gives this woman?" and Ben answered, "I do," she accepted her brother's kiss on her cheek and his good wishes, knowing she would not need them. The blessing of Jake's love was enough. Their love would be strong enough. Jake held out his hand, and there was no need for words. She knew he felt the same.

"Dearly beloved," the minister began those time-honored words, the ones she knew by heart.

The words she'd been waiting to hear like this, at Jake's side.

Then the sound of the minister's voice faded away and it was like being underwater in a warm and clear ocean. There were the two of them—her and Jake—his hand steady and sure, and his gaze fastened on hers. It was as if an unseen current flowed between them, beyond the physical, to their spirits within.

She realized true love was greater than two people. More powerful than both man and wife combined. It was a force that also connected them to a greater love, a greater purpose. And she felt awed by the calm that filled her. She repeated those sacred vows to love and honor and cherish.

The surge of love that overtook her was unconditional and infinite and there was nothing that would ever diminish it. Not sickness. Not hardship. Not even death.

As Jake slipped the ring on her finger, a diamond band to match the solitaire, she saw the emotion gathering in his dark eyes. He might stand warrior-tough, but he had a good loving heart. There was no mistake about that. When he lifted her veil and his kiss sealed their vows, happiness like no other filled her. Now they were two hearts and one soul.

It was surreal carrying Rachel through the doorway of his modest town house. After a celebration supper with Ben and Cadence and Sally at a fancy seafood restaurant not far off base, he left Sal with his good friends, promising to pick her up bright and early in the morning. Here he was, carrying a silk-clad bride into his very beige living room.

No visions of grandeur and luxury, just a comfortable couch he'd bought secondhand from a squad member who'd gotten out, and battered-looking end tables. He hadn't realized just how shabby his things were.

Please don't be disappointed, he thought. She'd spent last night with Ben and Cadence to save the cost of a hotel room, and training had run late, so there had been no time to show her what she was getting into.

"Oh. You have a view." Her eyes were shining. "And there's the beach. I could get used to this."

"Yeah?" That was good, because he'd be stuck in Florida for some time to come. "I've got three more years left. I know this isn't what you're used to, but I sure hope I can make you happy here."

"I'll be happy anywhere as long as I'm with you. You are my everything now." She blushed rosily and she'd never looked more amazing. This woman was his wife now, this incredible lady, and he couldn't stop the rush of affection that would take him over if he let it.

It's gratitude, he told himself as he set her on her slippered feet, not love. He was deeply grateful for a woman he respected and who was so kind. She was exactly the kind of lady he'd hoped to find some day.

The Lord sure worked in awesome ways, he thought, as he nudged the door shut with his foot. Awesome because He'd brought the exact right wife into his life when he was at a loss as to what to do with Sally. The timing was God's he knew. Sally wasn't the only reason Rachel was wearing his wedding ring. No, he'd been at a loss for a long time, he could see that now that she was standing in his living room.

This house he lived in was suddenly a home. The life he'd filled only with the challenge of work now had a deeper purpose: to take care of Rachel with all of his might. He never wanted to fail this woman entrusted to him.

"How about a walk on the beach?" he suggested, smoothing back the thick bounce of curls that had tumbled against her face.

She pressed against his hand, her eyes drifting shut, as if valuing his touch.

"I would love to. But I've got to change. I'm not sure how easy it would be to walk in the surf like this." She gave her skirt a twirl and the full hem flared out to reveal her white ballet slippers. "Where are my things?"

"Ben brought them over this morning. I put them

in the main bedroom. Up the stairs. It's the first door on your left."

"Okay. I'll be right back. I'm psyched. Wow! We live on the beach." They were a team now, and she was a wife!

Her life kept getting better and better, Rachel thought as she blew her husband a kiss, gathered up her skirt and dashed up the stairs. The gentler light of early evening was thinning, and she so wanted to have the daylight left to go on a long walk with her husband. They would be just another married couple, out for an evening stroll, hands linked, hearts content.

She half expected Jake to be coming up behind her, so she left the door ajar, spotted her suitcase under the wide picture window that gazed through the spears of palm leaves at the endless stretch of turquoise water. Pale sunshine poured through the slatted blinds and she turned the wand to close it. The light dimmed, and she gazed around the room she would be sharing with Jake.

The bed looked wide enough to be a queen-size. It was neatly made with a pale-blue bedspread covering it, and four plumped pillows in matching blue shams. Two mismatched nightstands sat at either side of the bed, holding matching lamps and a phone, an alarm clock and a thick, tattered military suspense paperback were crowded on the nightstand to the right side. That must be where Jake slept. And that meant she would be on the left side.

It gave her an odd, thrilling joy to think about the night to come. What a blessing to be held and loved by her husband, she thought, and, feeling bashful, decided not to think anymore about it.

The phone rang, echoing in the quiet house, then died in mid ring. Jake must have grabbed it downstairs. She waited. Sure enough she could hear the mumble of his voice. Maybe it was Sally calling. She hadn't been sure about staying with Cadence, who'd been spending a lot of time watching her over the past few weeks. As Cadence had said, now Sally was her niece to watch over and spoil as much as possible.

I hope Sally's not having a hard time away from Jake, Rachel thought as she managed to loosen the hooks-and-eyes at the back of her dress. The poor girl had been through enough. If she was afraid, then they would swing by and take her on their evening walk, too.

She knelt and popped open her largest suitcase. In a half a second she'd grabbed her favorite pair of walking shorts and a light T-shirt and headed for the attached bathroom. She wasn't surprised by how clean and tidy everything was. Jake had clearly picked up and cleaned to make a good impression for her.

The small room had a high window that let in light as she pulled her hair into a ponytail and changed into her comfy clothes. Carefully, she gathered up the treasured dress and laid it out on the bed. No sign of Jake, so he must still be on the phone. She slipped her feet into her old sneakers and trotted down the steps.

He *was* on the phone, talking earnestly and low to whoever was on the other end of the line. He looked serious so maybe it was military stuff. She wandered into the kitchen and admired the cozy room. The appliances were a good decade old, but in good repair and very handy. She could imagine whipping up dinner while she waited for bread dough to rise and talking to Jake over the breakfast bar all the while.

Could anything be more perfect? This cute little duplex, full of good views and cozy places and a husband and child to care for. This was her home. This was her life. She was infinitely grateful.

She spotted a small bottle of water on the top shelf of the fridge and not much else, and thought how exciting this would be. To discover new favorite spots like grocery stores and coffee places and used bookstores. Things she could do with Jake and Sally. What an adventure it would be.

Brimming with happiness, she let herself outside, leaving Jake to finish his call in privacy. She sat down on the concrete top step and let the breeze off the ocean brush against her face. It was like a whole new world the Lord had given her, full of promise and good things. She could *feel* it. She thought of Paige and Amy, who would be handling the Friday-night supper rush about now. Tonight was the last high-school football game of the season and more snow had been expected, she knew. And she was staring at the Gulf of Mexico, wearing shorts!

The door behind her rasped open and Jake bounded down next to her, all business and tight energy. One look at his hard face told her something was wrong.

"Is it Sally?" Her heart jumped. "Is she okay? She was so quiet today, she's not sick—"

"No. I've got field training tonight. It's a drill. There's not a single thing I can do about it. I've tried to get out, but I can't. You get the call, and you go. It's a mock emergency scenario and I've got to grab my gear and get rolling."

Rachel studied the naked apology so stark on his handsome features and she knew with a sinking feeling that she had to let him go. It was as if the sun dimmed. "This definitely makes me feel like a military wife. You're sure you have to go, huh? No, don't answer that. I know you do. I just don't want you to go."

"Neither do I. Baby, I'll make it up to you. I swear. I've got to run."

"I know." She trusted him, she knew he would make sure they'd have another evening that would be special together. Although this, their first night as husband and wife was not what she'd expected. She tapped down the rising disappointment.

"Thanks, baby. I'll be back." He kissed her quickly and bolted away. The door clicked shut. Less than a minute later she heard a pickup roar to life. His red truck sped down the driveway between the units, honked and disappeared around the corner.

Now what? Rachel still couldn't believe she was sitting alone on her wedding night. The sun sank lower, casting a rosy glow directly into her eyes. She squinted and tried to remember where she'd put her sunglasses. The phone rang inside. Maybe that was Jake. Maybe his field emergency thing was cancelled. A girl could hope!

She snatched it up on the third ring. "Hello?"

"Rachel." Cadence sounded unruffled, and Rachel remembered that Ben was on Jake's team. Maybe he would have gotten the same call. "I bet you've suddenly found yourself without plans for the evening. How about coming over and watching a movie with Sally and me? We've got some good family favorites to pick from."

"I'll be over." See, God never closed a door without opening a window. She'd spend the evening with her new niece and her sister-in-law. And maybe Jake would be back before bedtime. She left a note, just in case.

* * *

Jake sat in the belly of the chopper with his pockets heavy with extra ammo and protectively holding his M-4. He couldn't get Rachel out of his thoughts. Not good for a soldier when lives depended on his absolute mastery of his emotions and iron self-control.

He'd had to leave her on their wedding night. That couldn't be a good sign. Not at all. What if she doubted his commitment? The knots in his chest that thinking of her always brought him stretched so tight, he couldn't breathe.

What defense did a man have against the power a woman could have on him, and against the strength of love that he could feel for her?

"Hathaway. Focus, man."

He looked up to see his squad leader snapping his fingers at him.

Not good. They were at the mock LZ, and his team members were standing, preparing to fast-rope down under simulated hostile fire. He brought his mind to the task ahead, but his heart was heavy. Something was going to go wrong, he could feel it. Very wrong.

With Sally's cold hand tucked safely in hers, Rachel held the screen door and helped the girl find her way into the dark house. She hadn't thought to leave a light on, mostly because she'd been so disappointed she hadn't thought too far ahead. She fumbled along the wall for a light switch and didn't find one.

Sally let go in a hurry and her footsteps sounded impatient as she crossed the living room. Faint shadows crept between the blinds to give the furniture shape, enough to navigate around. There was a click and a lamp turned on, illuminating the wariness on Sally's usually cute face. Rachel had the feeling Sally wasn't going to be cute tonight.

She's lost a mother and had to move away from everything she knew, Rachel reminded herself. Her heart softened for this child who was hers now to nurture. She trusted the Lord to guide her through this, because she was going to need some big-time help. Jake getting married must be a scary change for a little girl who'd already lost her stability. It made sense she would be worried. "Tell you what, you run up and change into your jammies and I'll whip up some cocoa and be up to read to you."

"It's too hot for cocoa."

"Okay, how about some chocolate milk? I noticed a carton in the fridge. I'll—"

"No." Sally glared at her and crossed her hands over her chest, as if preparing for a fight. "I want Uncle Jake to get it for me."

Uh-oh, this is going to be harder than I thought. Rachel headed to the kitchen anyway. "I'm going to make some for myself."

Sally's answer was to storm upstairs. Rachel found two blue glasses in a pretty bare cupboard, wondering how to help Sally the most. She was afraid, and Rachel knew something about that. *Me, too, kiddo.* Love was an act of faith, that was for sure. She poured a cup of milk and sipped it. The comforting chocolate and blessed cold did wonders for her. It was still warm at nine-thirty at night. Florida weather was nice, but it would take some getting used to.

The empty kitchen echoed around her with promises of tomorrow. Things would be better in the morning. Jake would be back, she felt sure, and she'd be frying up breakfast. If there was food to prepare.

A quick inventory of the pantry told her there was a half-used bag of pancake mix, and the prerequisite syrup and jam to go with it. She found half a carton of eggs in the door of the fridge and a half-pound of bacon in the freezer. She set that on a refrigerator shelf to thaw and, satisfied, locked up, turned off the lights and snatched Sally's overnight bag on the way to the stairs.

No light shone down the short and narrow hallway. She knocked on the first door on her right—no answer. "Sally?" She cracked the door a little and saw the faint dusting of moonlight sifting through half-slatted blinds.

The silver glow fell on a mattress on the floor, made up with fresh sheets and a blanket and a plump pillow. A man's clothes hung in the open closet and fatigues were neatly folded on the floor. Jake's things? No, that didn't make any sense. Maybe the mattress was for guests. It would be handy if one of her sisters could come down to stay. And those were extra clothes of Jake's. That's all.

"Sally?" She went in search of the girl's room and stopped outside the next room. A faint glow that crept beneath the door told her a television was on. She knocked and turned the knob. "Sally? I've brought your bag."

The only answer was friendly electronic music beeping and bopping from the TV. Rachel pushed the door open enough to see a child's video game flashing on the screen. Sally sat crossed-legged on her bed, still in her cute turquoise shorts set, not at all ready for bed. And with the way she stared intently at her game, working the controls with concentration, she wasn't interested in bedtime just yet.

Okay, she's testing me. This was normal, typical kid behavior. After all, the two of them didn't really know one another. Sally didn't know that it was okay to trust her, and that already Rachel loved her so much. With patience, she'd figure it out. "Bedtime. Let's get out your pajamas."

"I'm not tired." Sally didn't move her eyes from the screen. She spoke more like a robot than the sweet kid she was in Jake's care.

Rachel unzipped the bag and tossed the pink jammies onto the bed. "Suit up, and we'll settle down to read."

"No." Sally gave the pretty garments a shove off the bed and then went right back to her game. "I don't have to do what you say. You're not my mom. You're not even my real aunt. Uncle Jake just made you come here to take care of me."

"I'm not trying to replace your mother, sweetie."

"Don't call me sweetie." Sally tossed down the hand control to her game and turned her back.

Rachel ached for the little girl. She wished she knew how to take away her pain. What if by coming here, she'd caused Sally even more pain? Troubled, she made her way down the dark hall, praying for the Lord to heal the child's broken heart.

Intending to give Sally a little space before trying again, Rachel shouldered open the master bedroom door. Seeing the wide bed all made up and waiting steadied her. Sally's words hadn't rattled, her, had they? No. The wedding dress shimmered like rich ivory, bringing back the memories of the day.

Rachel studied her new wedding band, glittering as pure and true as the vows she and Jake shared today. She remembered the affection in Jake's gaze, the comfort of his touch, the steady promise in his voice as he'd sworn to cherish her through this life.

I'm just feeling sad because he's not here, she realized, reaching for the dress. While she'd hoped for a much different night, she'd married a soldier and as a soldier's wife she realized there would be a lot of ways she would need to be extra supportive of him. Being okay about his call tonight was one of those ways.

She nudged the closet door open and searched for a hanger, which wasn't difficult considering the entire closet was empty. There wasn't a shirt or a hanger in sight on the bare rod.

Sally's words rolled back into her mind as she hustled across the hallway to the room where Jake's clothes hung. *Uncle Jake just made you come here to take care of me.*

That's not true. Rachel knew in her heart that it wasn't. So why then, had Jake planned for separate rooms for their wedding night?

Chapter Fifteen

Jake hauled his duffel out of the truck, slung the bag's thick strap over one shoulder and squinted against the rising sun. Exhausted, sweaty and limping, he hobbled up the steps to the back door. The first thing that greeted him was the scent of freshly brewing coffee and the greasy, meaty smell of cooked bacon. The second was fresh-faced, lovely Rachel in the kitchen.

His wife. That was hard to believe. The impossible knots tangled inside him yanked even more tightly—a warning sign. Danger ahead. He'd better get his emotions under control.

She was turned away from him, flipping pancakes. Her thick chestnut hair was swept back in a bouncy ponytail that swooped past her shoulder blades. She wore a pink tank top that showed off the graceful lines of her arms and her back, and wash-worn cutoffs hugged her slender hips. Her feet—toenails painted a pearled pink—were in a pair of pink flip-flops.

He'd never seen her like this. Relaxed, moving easily as she plated the pancakes and slipped them into the oven to keep warm. His heart turned over like an adoring dog and lay there, belly up and exposed.

Definitely danger ahead. He would not be weak. He would not be vulnerable. Panic set in because he didn't want to feel this way. Not in combat, not in life and never in love. Combat he was trained for but this—Lord, he didn't know how to leave the most vulnerable part of him exposed.

"You're back." He could tell that he'd startled her again, for her hand was over her heart and she sagged against the counter. "You're very good at being a stealthy Special Forces guy. I'm going to have to get used to that. You look exhausted. How about some coffee?"

Her hand was shaking as she poured a cup. Shaking. That's when he noticed she wasn't smiling. He didn't think he'd ever seen Rachel like this. Dimmed, as if she were holding back that light that always shone within her. She slipped the cup on the breakfast counter, pulling away before their fingers could meet. Turning away before he could do more than notice how sad she looked. *Sad.*

Then it was gone so fast, he wondered if he'd seen it at all. She looked tired, he realized. The stress of moving and leaving the responsibilities of her old life behind. And picking up those of a new one. He wanted to make this as easy on her as he could. "Coffee would be good. Figure you and I can take Sally to school, I'll show you around Fort Walton Beach. Show you where the grocery store is. The post office. That kind of thing. Maybe we can get in the walk I promised you last night."

"That sounds fine. Do you want breakfast?" She returned to the stove, where she poured more batter on the griddle.

She didn't seem fine; she didn't seem angry either. What did that mean? He didn't know. He was too tired to think. Every muscle he owned was killing him, he'd gotten out of shape since he'd been gone. It didn't take much. The ten-click run in full gear last night had taken a toll. "Is Sally up yet?"

"She's still sleeping. I think. She's refusing to talk to me."

"*What?* I thought she was looking forward to you being here."

"This is going to take some adjustment, Jake. I'm not her mother, and yet I'm telling her what to do and taking care of her. It's going to be hard."

"She wasn't rude to you, was she? She was so glad on the nanny's last day. I'll talk to her."

Rachel realized Jake didn't understand. Because he'd never been in Sally's position? Or because he saw his new wife as just another nanny with housekeeper skills? He couldn't be that cruel, right?

She flipped the pancakes, considering this man she'd thought was so wonderful. He *was* wonderful.

Strong and decent and tender. His kisses were tender. A bad man didn't kiss like that, at least, she didn't think one could. His kisses felt like a perfect sunrise on a cold morning, chasing away the night shadows and giving light where there was none. They made her spirit lift like those quiet sweep of clouds at dawn, washed in a heavenly gold.

"Do I have a few minutes before breakfast is ready?"

She nodded as she checked the pancakes with the edge of the spatula. It was easier to concentrate on her cooking. Strange, this felt more like working in the diner than cooking for her family.

He set down his cup. Maybe he was going to kiss her now and hold her tight. Tell her how much he'd missed her. "Then I'm gonna grab a fast shower. Do I have ten minutes?"

She forced a nod, unable to believe her eyes as her new husband pivoted on his boot heel and bounded up the stairs, all soldier. But not a newlywed.

She already knew where he was going. As she sipped her coffee, she listened as his heavy step on the stairs without hesitation turned right and sounded directly overhead. He was not in the master bedroom, but the one where his clothes were. His room.

His room. She didn't understand. The diamonds on her left hand sparkled as if in celebration, tearing at her even more. He didn't use the shower in the main bathroom upstairs. She could hear the boards overhead squeaking slightly beneath his weight as he came and went. She heard the door to his room close, and she didn't understand. Married people shared a room. They were together. They were loving. If he didn't want to be with her, then what did that mean?

It means you may have made a mistake, Rachel. The sick feeling she'd been fighting all night returned. She flipped the last batch of pancakes, plated them and turned off the burner. She was hardly aware of anything but the footsteps overhead as Jake dressed and then ambled down the hallway. Coming closer.

She set out the last of the butter, moving woodenly, feeling cold inside because she knew what was coming. Whether they talked about it now or later tonight, it didn't matter. Nothing mattered but the truth.

The ring glittered, mockingly this time, taunting her as shame gathered in her stomach. She was married. That was a final, done deal. She'd vowed to honor this man before God, and so she would. The question was, what kind of marriage would this be? She'd been so eager to fulfill her dream that she'd accepted Jake's proposal without asking questions that now seemed vital.

He emerged from the shadows in the stairwell, looking heart-stoppingly handsome, striding easily toward her like a well-honed athlete. His cropped hair was jet-black, still wet from his shower, and his jaw was smooth-shaven. Even in jogging shorts and a tank, he looked fierce and capable, as though there wasn't anything he couldn't handle.

He did not look like the man who'd rescued her from Bullwinkle. Or who'd cradled a little grieving girl against his wide chest. Or a man who'd romanced her with roses and kindness and charm. That man was gone, she realized. A warrior was in his place, and she did not know this man. Was her Jake in there somewhere, she wondered, deep inside the toughness and steel?

"You are awesome, Rachel." He grabbed the syrup bottle she'd placed on the breakfast bar and upended it over his plate. One hard squeeze of his mighty hand was enough to make the maple sweetness shoot out like water. "I can't tell you how great this is. I'm starving. I am so glad I married you."

She felt the cup slip out of her clumsy fingers, but she didn't hear it hit the floor. Blood rushed through her ears, and like an ocean's tidal wave surging up to wash her away, it drowned out every sound. Jake looked startled, but she waved him away, emotion wedged in her throat so she couldn't speak. She grabbed at the roll of paper towels but tugged too hard and the roll jumped across the counter, unrolling as it went.

Her vision blurred as hot tears filled her eyes. A voice inside her was saying, "He didn't mean that the way it sounded. This isn't as bad as you think." But it was.

She hadn't been married twenty-four hours and it was so different from what she'd thought. It fell so far short of what she'd imagined. There was no companionable happiness, no affection and conversation and togetherness, and the dream of it shattered at her feet and lay in pieces, right along with the cup.

"Baby, let me get that—"

"I've got it," she croaked, her voice sounding raw and broken as her dreams. Blinding hot tears scalded her eyes as she gave the paper towels another yank and this time the paper tore away. She had way too many lengths, but she didn't care. She wadded them up quite as if she saw them, as if everything were perfectly fine, and knelt at Jake's feet to swipe up the mess. Ceramic edges clanked together as she swiped. "Go on and finish your meal."

"No, you aren't fine." He knelt and she could feel the tender wave of his concern. He was so close, she could lean forward a few inches and she'd be able to lay her cheek on the chest she knew felt as solid as steel. But she would not lay her troubles there. She could not find the words to tell him her fears. Or how foolish she'd been.

"This is about me leaving last night. It was unfortunate timing."

"Trust me, that is not an issue. I told you I understood. I knew about your commitment to this country when I agreed to marry you." But what about his commitment to her? This was a man who'd swept her off her feet, told her how wonderful she was, told her everything she'd wanted to hear. It was a man who'd stood before God and vowed to honor and cherish her, to love her and care for her. Surely he'd meant that. Surely he had.

She blinked back every tear. Swiped up every piece of ceramic and coffee spill, feeling as if she were mopping up what was left of her lost dreams, too.

"Tell me. Please." Jake took the sodden paper towels and broken shards from her and set them on the counter. He towered over her, so strong and distant and remote. Then held out his hand to help her up.

Oh, it felt right when her palm met his. The twist of her heart. The sigh of her soul. It was a new day, this would be their first full day as man and wife. Surely, she could trust him. She came into his arms, he folded her close, and she was home. "I guess I need reassuring."

"Then I'm you're man. What do you need, baby?"

Oh, she liked it when he talked like that, with his voice a low rumble in his throat. "I noticed how your things were in the extra bedroom and then Sally had said you'd married me just to take care of her."

She felt him stiffen. She heard his heartbeat flutter. He wasn't saying anything.

This can't be right. She pushed away from him and kept going. A cold chill swept through her, and she shivered as hard as if she'd stepped out into a Montana blizzard without a coat on. "You didn't marry me to be a nanny, right? This is a real marriage. You'll be with me, tonight, forever, right?"

"Rachel, I thought we would both need our space. That's all. I can move my stuff back."

"That's not what I want. Not like this. You're acting as if this is a convenient arrangement, something practical and sensible because you're leaving in two weeks and you'll be gone for the next six months. Tell me that's not true." She watched his eyes harden. Felt the answer in his silence.

The tiniest hope within her faded. Despair shrouded her like a cocoon. Everything around her seemed distant and dim and muffled. Everything within her turned to ice until there was no pain, only a void where no wishes live, and no dreams prosper.

"It's not exactly true." His words sounded choked, as if he were in great pain, too. "I can't lie to you, Rachel. I value you too much."

"Value me? You married me to watch your niece and cook your meals. You sent me roses. You romanced me. You made me fall in love with you and believe that I was special to you. That I was your one true love."

He broke at the sight of her tears. What had happened? He would never want to hurt her. He hadn't hurt her, not really, and yet tears pooled in her eyes and he could feel her heartbreak as mightily as if he'd taken a bullet in the chest for her. He would take a bullet for her, he would protect her with his life. But he could not make her understand. "There is no such thing as true love. I've been all around the globe, and I haven't seen it."

She recoiled as if he'd slapped her in the face, and he couldn't say why but he could feel the shock of it in her battered heart—her heart that he was hurting.

That wasn't what he wanted. He wanted to keep her safe and protect her. To shelter her and make her happy. He'd married her, he would give her all he could.

Except your heart, a tiny voice inside him whispered. And it was the truth. A truth he could not deny. He'd shielded up his heart so well, that not war or evil or the horrors he'd witnessed could touch it. Only this woman and her gentle kindness had come close. He'd protected his heart so long, he didn't know if he could do anything else.

All he knew for sure was that he could feel Rachel's hurt as surely as the ocean breeze on his face and hear her heartbreak in the brittle sound of the palm leaves overhead. The bright blue Gulf shimmered like jewels in the first sunlight and he swiped the pain from his eyes. He had to fix this. He took a step toward her, sure that all he needed to do was to comfort her in his arms.

She took two steps back, looking up at him as if he was a stranger she didn't know.

He definitely had to fix that. "You are special to

me. More than I know how to say. Don't you know that I'd do anything for you, anything you need?"

"Then tell me that you love me. Really love me. Tell me the truth."

He could not say the words. He was afraid that they would diminish him, tear down the core of steel he had to have to be a good soldier. But he wanted to. He wished he could surrender. "I've loved you more than I've ever loved anyone."

"That's not the same."

"I'll do my best to be a good husband to you, but you know that it's not roses and horse rides and starlight, right? Any marriage is a practical arrangement."

"A practical arrangement?" She said the words with a look of horror twisting across her beautiful face. A face that did not stop gazing up at him with all the light draining from her loving eyes, and taking that affection with it.

Failure shattered him. He was failing at this, the most significant thing that had ever happened to him. This woman was his wife, the woman who meant more than anything, and he was failing her. Failure was not an option in his world. Nor was softness. *Help me, Lord. I'm drowning here.*

Her eyes were liquid sadness. She turned away from him and his silence and all the words he could not say and things he could not be and stared down the beach. Two units down, the neighbor was noisily putting up a six-foot ladder. The aluminum clang echoed like a gunshot over the hush of the tide on the shore. The guy was putting Christmas lights on a palm tree in his yard. His wife came outside, holding two cups of coffee, and told him in a soft voice to be quiet. His answer was good-hearted, but the breeze carried his words away.

Jake felt his world fracture even more as he watched his neighbor hop down from the ladder to join his pretty wife at their small patio table. *That's* what he wanted, that kind of closeness, that connection, and he was afraid of it. He could admit that now. Afraid to place so much stock in something that could not be seen or conquered, only felt. Afraid to take down the shield that had kept him safe through over a decade in his career and leave his heart and soul completely unprotected.

He took a few steps after her out of the open doorway and onto the cement patio. How did he do it? How did he start? The titanium he'd closed around his heart began to buckle. "I didn't want to rush you."

"What?" She turned to study him over her shoulder, confusion on her face and tears on her cheeks.

I made her cry. Nothing could seem more horrible. He didn't want to hurt Rachel ever. He would never do so again. He took a step toward her, the warrior in him unable to figure out how to attack and win this fight.

He'd need his heart for that. His whole heart, unshielded and vulnerable. "The separate bedrooms. I rushed you into marriage. I wasn't sure if you would be ready for a real wedding night."

"That you even have to ask that is so wrong." She only seemed more upset. "Do you understand? I thought you married me to love me. I thought you saw in me—" Her face twisted in sheer agony and she turned her back on him. Her hands went to her face and her shoulders shook. *That you saw in me someone to truly love.*

How could she tell him that? He didn't understand, she'd seen that clearly on his face. He thought she'd be grateful for a practical arrangement. It made sense, she realized. It all made sense. How he overlooked her faults and asked the right questions to find out how desperately she just wanted to be married.

What she did not tell him was how sacred she believed marriage to be. She meant her vows, heart and soul, those vows that were the strongest on earth. To love and cherish through hardship and trial, to find love in your heart without fail.

And he wanted a nanny and a cook. The sunrise splashed stunning bright colors across the waiting sky, and the pure golden light that followed dawn seemed to mock her, for she felt as if there could be no more sunshine in her world, no more beautiful days and bright clear skies. How could she have made such a monumental mistake?

"Rachel?" He was behind her, his hand on her shoulder, his touch more calming than anything on this earth. He leaned close and she shivered with longing for what could not be.

His lips brushed her cheek as he spoke quietly, as if they were in church, as if they were the only two people on a beach in paradise. "I love you."

"But you said—" She choked on a sob. She couldn't believe him, not anymore. He'd tricked her, or so it seemed. But maybe she'd tricked herself in believing in fairy tales to begin with.

"I want my happily-ever-after to be with you, Rachel Hathaway." His voice sounded strangled, and his strong hands caught her around the waist and turned her in his arms. "I married you for Sally, it's true, but I married you for me even more. I n-need you."

"N-no," she sputtered on a heart-wrenching sob. "You want a p-practical m-marriage."

"Only because I'm dumb and I thought it would be safer. But I'm starting to get this marriage thing." Jake shook all over. He'd never done anything so terrifying in his life. But for Rachel's happiness, he would do anything, even tell her the truth that terrified him.

He would show her the part of him that he trusted to no one. The shields fell, all defenses were abandoned. He could not protect his heart at the cost of hers. "I love you more than my pride or my life or my very being, and it scares me. More than anything ever has. Can you understand that?"

The sadness ebbed from her beautiful eyes.

"Nothing in my life—no one—could ever mean as

much to me as you. I love you. I'll say that as many times as it takes for you to believe it. I intend to honor and cherish you, above myself, above all my fears and my stubborn pride. I am trusting you with my heart. Can we make this marriage of ours all you've dreamed of?"

"I think it already is. Now." The warm ocean lapped at her toes as the hush of the morning seemed to reassure her. She saw her future being loved by this strong, tender man. His kiss was like paradise; his embrace like eternity. She thanked the Lord for this beautiful dream of love come true.

Jake took her hand and led her through the sand toward the open sliding door, where Sally would need to be woken up and breakfast eaten. The demands of the day remained but for them, there were only blue skies ahead.

* * * * *

Dear Reader,

The McKaslin Clan continues when Rachel meets her brother's best friend. Jake is on temporary leave from active duty in the Middle East so that he can take guardianship of his orphaned niece. Rachel falls in love with both the man and the little girl, and forsakes the life she knows in Montana to move across the country to where Jake is stationed. Always a romantic, Rachel marries her knight in shining armor and means her wedding vows with every bit of her heart and soul.

Love, like faith, takes great belief and trust. But will her love be strong enough to open Jake's battle-weary heart?

Thank you for choosing *Blessed Vows*. I hope you enjoy Rachel's story as much as I've enjoyed writing it.

I wish you joy and the sweetest of blessings,

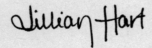

REQUEST YOUR FREE BOOKS!

2 FREE INSPIRATIONAL NOVELS

PLUS 2
FREE
MYSTERY GIFTS

Love Inspired®

YES! Please send me 2 FREE Love Inspired® novels and my 2 FREE mystery gifts (gifts are worth about $10). After receiving them, if I don't wish to receive any more books, I can return the shipping statement marked "cancel." If I don't cancel, I will receive 6 brand-new novels every month and be billed just $4.49 per book in the U.S. or $4.99 per book in Canada. That's a saving of at least 22% off the cover price. It's quite a bargain! Shipping and handling is just 50¢ per book in the U.S. and 75¢ per book in Canada.* I understand that accepting the 2 free books and gifts places me under no obligation to buy anything. I can always return a shipment and cancel at any time. Even if I never buy another book, the two free books and gifts are mine to keep forever.   105/305 IDN FEGR

Name _____ (PLEASE PRINT) _____

Address _____ Apt. # _____

City _____ State/Prov. _____ Zip/Postal Code _____

Signature (if under 18, a parent or guardian must sign)

Mail to the **Reader Service:**
IN U.S.A.: P.O. Box 1867, Buffalo, NY 14240-1867
IN CANADA: P.O. Box 609, Fort Erie, Ontario L2A 5X3

Not valid for current subscribers to Love Inspired books.

**Are you a subscriber to Love Inspired books
and want to receive the larger-print edition?
Call 1-800-873-8635 or visit www.ReaderService.com.**

* Terms and prices subject to change without notice. Prices do not include applicable taxes. Sales tax applicable in N.Y. Canadian residents will be charged applicable taxes. Offer not valid in Quebec. This offer is limited to one order per household. All orders subject to credit approval. Credit or debit balances in a customer's account(s) may be offset by any other outstanding balance owed by or to the customer. Please allow 4 to 6 weeks for delivery. Offer available while quantities last.

Your Privacy—The Reader Service is committed to protecting your privacy. Our Privacy Policy is available online at www.ReaderService.com or upon request from the Reader Service.

We make a portion of our mailing list available to reputable third parties that offer products we believe may interest you. If you prefer that we not exchange your name with third parties, or if you wish to clarify or modify your communication preferences, please visit us at www.ReaderService.com/consumerchoice or write to us at Reader Service Preference Service, P.O. Box 9062, Buffalo, NY 14269. Include your complete name and address.

LIREG11B

*When a baby is left on the doorstep of an Amish house,
Sheriff Nick Bradley comes face-to-face with his past.*

*Read on for a preview of A HOME FOR HANNAH
by Patricia Davids.*

The farmhouse door swung open before Sheriff Nick Bradley
could knock. A woman with fiery auburn hair and green eyes
stood glaring at him. "There has been a mistake. We don't
need you here."

The shock of seeing Miriam Kauffman standing in front
of him took him aback. He struggled to hide his surprise.
It had been eight years since he'd laid eyes on her. A life-
time ago.

"Good morning to you, too, Miriam."

After all this time, she wasn't any better at hiding her
opinion of him. She looked ready to spit nails. Proof that
she hadn't forgiven him.

"Miriam, don't be rude," her mother chided. Miriam
reluctantly stepped aside. He entered the house.

His cousin Amber sat at the table. "Hi, Nick. Thanks for
coming. We do need your help."

Ada Kauffman sat across from her. The room was bathed
in soft light from two kerosene lanterns hanging from hooks
on the ceiling.

He glanced at the three women facing him. Ada Kauffman
was Amish, from the top of her white prayer bonnet to the
tips of her bare toes poking out from beneath her plain
dress. Her daughter, Miriam, had never joined the church,
choosing to leave before she was baptized. Her arms were
crossed over her chest.

Amber served the Amish and non-Amish people of Hope Springs, Ohio, as a nurse midwife. Exactly what was she doing here?

He said, "Okay, I'm here. What's so sensitive that I had to come instead of sending one of my perfectly competent deputies?"

"This is why we called you." Amber gestured toward the basket. He took a step closer and saw a baby swaddled in the folds of a quilt.

"You called me here to see a new baby? Congratulations to whomever."

"Exactly," Miriam said.

He looked at her closely. "What am I missing?"

Amber said, "It's more about what we are missing."

"And that is?" he demanded.

Ada said, "A mother to go with this baby."

He shook his head. "You've lost me."

Miriam rolled her eyes. "I'm not surprised."

Her mother scowled at her, but said, "Someone left this baby on my porch."

Will Nick and Miriam get past their differences to help little Hannah?

Pick up A HOME FOR HANNAH by Patricia Davids, available August 2012 from Love Inspired Books.

SHLIEXP0812R

Patricia Davids

brings you a tale about unexpected surprises
and new beginnings

Yearning to find a meaningful life in the outside world, nurse
Miriam Kaufman strayed far from her Amish community.
She also needed distance from Nick Bradley, the cop who
had caused her so much pain. But when her mother falls ill
and a baby is mysteriously abandoned on her doorstep
she turns to Nick for help. Can two wounded hearts
overcome their history to do what's best?

A Home for Hannah

BRIDES OF
Amish Country

Love Inspired

← TEXAS TWINS →

Follow the adventures of two sets of twins who are torn apart by family secrets and learn to find their way home.

Her Surprise Sister by Marta Perry
July 2012

Mirror Image Bride by Barbara McMahon
August 2012

Carbon Copy Cowboy by Arlene James
September 2012

Look-Alike Lawman by Glynna Kaye
October 2012

The Soldier's Newfound Family
by Kathryn Springer
November 2012

Reunited for the Holidays
by Jillian Hart
December 2012

Available wherever books are sold.

www.LoveInspiredBooks.com

LICONT0812